THE SUSPECT

Also by John Lescroart

The Hunt Club
The Motive
The Second Chair
The First Law
The Oath
The Hearing
Nothing but the Truth
The Mercy Rule
Guilt
A Certain Justice
The 13th Juror
Hard Evidence
The Vig
Dead Irish
Rasputin's Revenge
Son of Holmes
Sunburn

THE
SUSPECT

JOHN LESCROART

DUTTON

DUTTON
Published by Penguin Group (USA) Inc.
375 Hudson Street, New York, New York 10014, U.S.A.
Penguin Group (Canada), 90 Eglinton Avenue East, Suite 700, Toronto,
Ontario M4P 2Y3, Canada (a division of Pearson Penguin Canada Inc.);
Penguin Books Ltd, 80 Strand, London WC2R 0RL, England;
Penguin Ireland, 25 St Stephen's Green, Dublin 2, Ireland
(a division of Penguin Books Ltd);
Penguin Group (Australia), 250 Camberwell Road, Camberwell,
Victoria 3124, Australia
(a division of Pearson Australia Group Pty Ltd);
Penguin Books India Pvt Ltd, 11 Community Centre, Panchsheel Park,
New Delhi – 110 017, India;
Penguin Group (NZ), cnr Airborne and Rosedale Roads, Albany,
Auckland 1310, New Zealand
(a division of Pearson New Zealand Ltd);
Penguin Books (South Africa) (Pty) Ltd, 24 Sturdee Avenue,
Rosebank, Johannesburg 2196, South Africa

Penguin Books Ltd, Registered Offices:
80 Strand, London WC2R 0RL, England

Published by Dutton, a member of Penguin Group (USA) Inc.

First printing, January 2007
1   3   5   7   9   10   8   6   4   2

 REGISTERED TRADEMARK—MARCA REGISTRADA

Library of Congress Cataloging-in-Publication Data
Lescroart, John T.
The suspect / by John Lescroart.
    p.   cm.
ISBN-13: 978-0-525-94998-5
1. San Francisco (Calif.)—Fiction.   I. Title.
PS3562.E78S87 2007
813'.54—dc22
2006026704

Printed in the United States of America
Set in Adobe Garamond
Designed by Spring Hoteling

PUBLISHER'S NOTE

Back to basics, this book is to Lisa Marie Sawyer

THE SUSPECT

"Truth is the cry of all, but the game of few."

—George Berkeley

ONE

———

ON A CLEAR, STILL AND SILENT Sunday at the end of the second week in September, a fifty-year-old outdoor writer named Stuart Gorman sat on a flat-topped rock at the edge of a crystalline lake set in a bowl of granite near the California Desolation Wilderness Area a few miles southwest of Lake Tahoe. The lake's mirrored surface, unsullied by even the trace of a breeze, perfectly reflected the opposite shoreline—more granite, studded with pine and a purple sky above.

Stuart could barely be seen to breathe. In the warm afternoon, he'd removed his T-shirt and placed it beside him. Now he wore only his hiking boots and a pair of brown shorts. Though he had a good head of medium-length dark brown hair, the gray in his two-day stubble and on his chest betrayed the bare fact of his age. Without the gray, the developed torso, perhaps dangerously tan, could have been that of a man half Stuart's years. His solid barrel chest spoke of hours spent outdoors in vigorous exercise; there was a hollow of tight skin under his rib cage where most men his chronological age carried their fat.

There was age, though, in the face. Lines scored the skin around the deeply set blue eyes and at the corners of his mouth. The stubble wasn't long enough to camouflage the strong jaw nor the nearly surgical cleft in his chin; neither did the lines mar the clear expanse of his forehead. The only obvious flaw in his face, although some might not call it that, was a silver-dollar-size port wine stain high on his right cheek.

Stuart held a fly rod across his lap. He wasn't fishing yet. The evening hatch wasn't due for at least another half hour, until the sun ducked out of sight behind the foothills to the west. Then a few feeding trout would ripple Tamarack Lake's smooth and calm surface, and on a typical evening Stuart would find his spot, play out line, place his dry fly in the center of one of the few ripples and hope for a strike. The trail ran along Tamarack's shore, and so there was a great deal of pressure on the lake's fishery. The few trout that remained tended to be larger and wily, and Stuart relished the challenge. Normally, in the last moments before the beginning of the true gathering of dusk, while he waited for the first mosquitoes to hit the water, he felt closest to peace. In moments such as this one, and in the poetry, solitude, and even athleticism of the fly-fishing that would follow, he'd come to define who he was, what he was made of.

The sun kissed the top of Mt. Ralston, and Stuart caught a glimpse of the first ripple—actually a rare splash—as a fish broke through the surface of the water somewhere across the lake. Normally, this would have been his signal to stir himself, but this evening he remained where he sat, unmoving.

And very far from in a state of peace.

Two days before, he'd driven up from his beautiful home on San Francisco's Russian Hill to his family's rustic cabin at Upper Echo Lake. His mood, dark enough as he'd left the city, faded to deep black when he got pulled over for speeding a few miles east of Sacramento. At that moment, his rage with the world in general and at his wife in particular had boiled over and had so nearly overtaken him that he'd lost his temper at the highway patrol officer who was writing him up. Even if he was "barely" exceeding the speed limit, every other car on the road was passing him, so Stuart wanted to know why was *he* the one getting a goddamn ticket? In response, the officer then had him get out of his car and take a field sobriety test, followed by a warning that he was "this close" to getting himself arrested. In the middle of this, Stuart lucked out when the officer suddenly recognized his name—the man was a fisherman who'd read two of Stuart's books and loved them.

Apologizing, and somewhat mollified, Stuart explained that he was still reacting to a terrible fight that he'd had with his wife, that he was coming up to his mountain retreat to get his head straight. The cop still gave him a speeding ticket, but then he'd gotten his autograph and let him go.

But now he'd been up here for two days and his head didn't feel any straighter. In fact, if anything, he had grown more angry, frustrated and depressed at the realization that his twenty-two-year-old marriage to his charismatic, brilliant, difficult, headstrong and still-pretty orthopedic surgeon wife, Caryn, seemed to be over. In almost every imaginable way, they had grown apart. Her thriving practice, her investments, and the new medical office she was starting with her business partners had taken almost every spare minute of her life for the past couple of years.

Now, with a purple dusk gathering around him, Stuart looked out over the water and saw a few more promising signs of trout feeding, but he couldn't even bring himself to move from where he sat to throw his line. His mind refused to leave the familiar rut it had been plumbing since he'd come up here.

How could his life with Caryn have come to this?

They'd met when he'd been a guide on a Snake River rafting trip her parents had given her for a graduation present. He had been twenty-eight to her twenty-two, and they were soul mates from the minute they'd laid eyes on each other. She was going to med school at

Stanford in the fall, but nothing was going to stand in the way of their being together. Stuart moved from Wyoming out to California, and they were married in the second week of November.

In those early days, their lives complemented one another. Caryn studied round the clock. Stuart submitted his writings everywhere he could think of and augmented his meager writer's income by working as a word processor in the law offices of Jedd Conley, one of his friends from college.

At home, Stuart kept the apartment clean, made their dinners, did the dishes, quizzed Caryn on her classes. She read and helped him edit his articles and early manuscripts and took every chance to get into the wilderness with him—the Bay Area was good for that. They jogged together three or four times a week, talking the whole while. They liked the same music, the same books; they laughed at the same jokes. Busy lives notwithstanding, they found time to make love often. They would often brag to each other that in the history of the world, nobody had ever been as happy as they were.

If that had been true then, Stuart thought, now there were few if any couples as miserable.

On Friday, the fight had erupted when Caryn came home for lunch after her hip-replacement patient had caught a cold and canceled on her at the last minute. So her entire afternoon loomed open and free, and when she got home, she was in a foul humor. Stuart, who'd been planning to drive up to Echo Lake anyway and get some writing done, suggested that she take advantage of the unexpected opportunity and accompany him.

She had no interest. No, she didn't have other plans, but why would she want to come up to *his* cabin for an entire weekend? What did he think they would do that she would remotely enjoy? Another *hike*? She'd done her share of Stuart's hikes. Eight or ten or fifteen miles up and down steep and difficult terrain. Two or three or even six thousand vertical feet in one day? Wow, what a good time that was! And all to accomplish what? To get some outdoor exercise or a variation of a nice view that they'd both already seen a thousand times?

She'd pass, thanks. She'd outgrown all of that.

He had offered to stay down in the city, then. Maybe they could go out to dinner, or even eat at home, get some overdue and richly deserved quality time together, maybe reconnect.

"You mean sex?" she'd asked.

"That wouldn't be the worst idea in the world. But I wasn't just thinking of sex . . ."

"No surprise there."

"What does that mean?" The thing heating up between them.

"You haven't thought of sex at all in a couple of months, Stuart."

"I've thought of it all right, Caryn. It's just never been at a good time for you."

"Oh, so it's all my fault?"

After which it had gotten ugly fast, Caryn finally admitting that she was sick of the sham marriage between them. Kymberly, their incredibly high-maintenance daughter whose birth had forever altered the dynamic of their life together, was gone off to college now. There was no reason to stay together.

She wanted a divorce.

Stuart had slammed out of the house. Yesterday he'd walked for miles in the grip of an incoherent rage that seemed to grow with each passing minute. Last night, he drank off most of a quart bottle of vodka that had lain untouched in the cabin's freezer for five years. This morning he found that he'd trashed his cabin, thrown dishes around, broken two chairs and smashed the framed family photos. He woke up still mostly drunk and with little memory of what he'd done. But today, monstrously hungover, feeling ashamed and sorry for himself, he'd hiked for a grueling six-hour loop before taking a long afternoon nap and then walking up here to Tamarack, hoping the evening peace would soothe him.

He wasn't really interested in tracing all the roots of his anger, though the strength and depth of it left him in a kind of shock, and exhausted. God knows there had been reasons enough. The last few years Caryn had all but abandoned him emotionally and physically, but he'd stayed on because he believed you should fight to save your marriage, even when it looked impossible. He'd stayed on, too, in order to carry the vast amount of the load of raising Kymberly because his wife didn't have the time. He'd stayed on in all of his own good faith, trying to get to compatibility with Caryn, from which he hoped they might again approach affection. Until Friday—just two days ago!—he'd repeatedly told her that he loved her, he loved her, he loved her. In these admissions, he realized that he was probably culpable of dishonesty, but he thought it might help, might bring her back. And if he said it enough and she came around, it might even become true.

Now, after all that sacrifice and despair, all the hope and commitment, all the pain and constant work, she wanted to end it anyway. He had been such a fool, and he hated himself for that almost as much as he hated her.

Tamarack Lake had grown dark and still again. The hatch and the bite were over, and the only sound off the lake was a whisper where the water met the shoreline.

Stuart forced his stiff body to its feet. He could get back to his cabin by the moonlight, to his car and back to the city by midnight— have it out with her one last time on his schedule for a change, and not hers. It would be great to wake her up, which would make her miss a day of her precious work. It would do her good to see him in the full flower of his outrage at how she'd used and abused him, his naïve belief, his basic good nature.

He broke into a jog, in a hurry now to get on the road and finally give her the real piece of his mind he'd been holding in for too long while trying to be fair, to be patient, to give her and their marriage yet one more chance. To be a good guy.

What an idiot he was. What a loser. What a goddamn pansy.

Well, all that was over, he thought. Now and forever. If she was done with him, he was done with her, too. And good riddance.

As he ran, his footsteps crunched on the granite. Riding the wave of his anger, he wasn't consciously aware that he was saying anything, but to the rhythm of every footfall, he fell into the mantra and let it escape into the night on every exhale: *Fuck her, fuck her, fuck her.*

The fish that Stuart heard breaking water at the first sign of the hatch was very large for a Sierra Nevada alpine lake—a fourteen-inch rainbow trout. It rose to the sight of a mosquito larva shimmering off the surface of the lake, slurped at the insect in the gentle way of all trout, then exploded in sudden fury out of the water as it felt the set of the tiny barbless hook.

Gina Roake, a forty-seven-year-old attorney, fought the fish on very light 6x line for about five minutes—a really nice fight with at least four good runs—before she netted it. She stood in her moss-green hiking shorts on a shallow, submerged ledge that reached out about fifteen feet into the lake. When she saw the size of the fish, she whistled in satisfaction, then turned and, dipping the trout and her net into the water, walked back to the shore. There, grabbing the fish through the netting, with a humane efficiency she slapped its head hard once into the side of a large granite boulder.

Besides her shorts, she wore a long-sleeved buttoned shirt of some space-age fabric that wicked out perspiration and then dried almost immediately. The clothes were functional in the extreme. Over her bare feet her legs were well-muscled and tan, her ankles slim. She had stopped dyeing her hair a couple of years before, and now the wisps that showed from beneath the red handkerchief around her head were a shining, silvery gray.

Laying the now-still fish in a small concavity at the top of the boulder, her movements bespoke a temperament of brisk competence. Removing a six-inch Buck knife from its sheath on her belt, she picked up the fish by its gills and turned back to the water, where she paused

for a moment to appreciate the setting. In the dying sun she saw another person, small in the distance, sitting on a rock across the water.

Returning to the task at hand, she inserted the tip of the Buck's
blade into the trout and slit up its belly to the gills. Pulling out its guts,
she threw them out beyond the reach of the ledge, where they sank into
the lake's depth and disappeared from view. After she'd scraped the dark
line of gunk along the backbone, she pulled off and threw away the
gills, then dipped the trout in the water and rinsed it clean.

She'd pitched her tent on a level spot back a ways into the trees.
Campfires weren't allowed here, but previous campers had left a clearing surrounded by large rocks for seating. As the far eastern end of
the lake grew into shadow, she touched a flame to her small gas stove.

For longer backpacking trips, Gina tried to keep her pack to under thirty-five pounds. Besides her portable stove, she'd carry a Girl
Scout–style mess kit and a bear canister filled mostly with dehydrated
fruits and ready-to-cook meals. But she'd planned this trip to be day
hikes out of this base camp. She'd come up on Friday and would go
home tomorrow morning. Beyond that, the camp was only a couple
of relatively level miles from the Echo Lakes trailhead. She didn't
need to worry about her pack's weight for this type of trip, and she'd
loaded up her canister with GORP—good ol' raisins and peanuts
(and added M&Ms)—for quick energy, then for her lunches a couple
of small loaves of San Francisco sourdough, a block of cheddar
cheese, a chub of Italian dry salami.

Heaven.

For dinner tonight, she had even thought to carry a half-bottle of
decent white wine. Using the mess kit's covered pot, she'd boil her
fresh green beans in a little lake water, finishing them with fresh
minced garlic, pepper and salt, and olive oil. The trout was far too big
for the mess kit frying pan, too long in fact for the ten-inch Cal-
phalon from her own kitchen, so though the concept offended her,
she was forced to cut the trout in half. A squeeze of olive oil from its
little plastic container, salt and pepper, mixed Italian herbs, a few
drops of Tabasco sauce.

Beat that, Farallon, she thought as she laid the halves of trout into the oil and spices. Eat your heart out, Boulevard—Farallon and Boulevard being two of San Francisco's finest restaurants.

When she finished eating, she took some boiling water and the dishes she'd used down to the lake to wash them. Back at the camp, she settled against her rock and sipped at the last of her wine from her Sierra Cup. The moon was up, and so was Venus, in a wine-dark sky.

The diamond in the ring on her left hand caught a glint from the bright moon and for a second she looked at the thing as though its presence there surprised her. There was no rational explanation for this reaction—she'd worn the ring now for almost three years, but in truth she didn't often think of it because it was too painful.

Now she stared at it for a long moment. Putting her wine down, she reached over, twisted it off her finger, and held it up in front of her. The facets in the diamond caught more moonlight as she turned it around and around, as though she were trying to find some secret magic within it.

But she knew there was no secret. There was no more magic in her life anymore, not as there had been when David Freeman had stunned her by proposing marriage and then placed the ring on her finger. Freeman, much older than she was, and a legend in the law world of San Francisco, was a slovenly dressed, big-living, profane, cigar-smoking genius in an ancient gnome's body whom, much to Gina's initial surprise, she'd come to love.

She often felt that he'd literally cast some spell on her. She would look at his ill-fitting brown suits, his scuffed shoes, the rheumy eyes under unruly and wiry eyebrows, the rosacea-scarred nose—Freeman didn't appear to be joking when he said that he liked to think of himself as mythically ugly—and during the six months she had lived with him, she couldn't think of a more attractive man of any age. Objectively, he was a frog, but she could see only the prince. It had to be sorcery. But whatever it was, it had worked and she had fallen under his spell, satisfied and happily in love at forty-four, for the first time in her life.

And Freeman, for his part, a seventy-something lifelong bachelor and notorious womanizer, apparently felt the same way about her. When he'd proposed, nervous as a schoolboy, this man who could be eloquent in front of the Supreme Court could barely get the words out. They were already living together most of the time in David's apartment, although Gina had kept her own place as well, and they decided to have a small, no-frills civil ceremony within the week.

But then David, who considered himself "bulletproof," had decided to walk home from work one night that week after he'd finished at the office. At the time, he'd been embroiled in some highly contentious litigation with a local mobster, and the gang leader's men had set upon the old barrister and beaten him into a coma from which he never recovered. When he died three days later, Gina felt a part of herself die with him.

But unbeknownst to her, in those last months of his life, David had changed his will, and Gina found herself the owner of the Freeman Building, downtown on Sutter Street. The large, gracious, recently renovated, three-story structure, complete with underground parking, housed the forty-odd employees of David's firm, Freeman & Associates, as well as one rogue "of counsel" tenant named Dismas Hardy. In the months following David's death, Gina, Dismas, and another colleague named Wes Farrell had reconsolidated the firm as Freeman, Farrell, Hardy & Roake, and it had become somewhat of a power player in the city.

But although Gina had been a practicing defense attorney for her entire career, and was a name partner in FFH&R, as time passed she took on less and less of the firm's law work. Her heart had gone out of it. She preferred to spend her time with physical exercise, with hikes and solitude, with the slowly accumulating pages of a novel—a legal thriller—that she was struggling without much passion to finish.

"Oh, David," she whispered, sighing. A tear hung in the corner of her eye. "Help me out here, would you?"

And suddenly, as she stared through the prisms of her engagement ring, she felt her shoulders relax as though relieved of a great load. She felt David's hovering ghost as an actual physical presence and realized that he was letting her go, telling her that she had mourned him enough.

He was gone, never coming back, and it was time to move on. The writing, the constant exercise, the long, lonely hikes, even the beautiful moments such as this one—she all at once came to see what David would have had to say about all of them: "That's not you, Roake. That's avoidance. That's not what you do. You always attack life. You engage. Something's beating you up, you take it on and wrestle that motherfucker to the ground. Why are you still wearing that ring, anyway? So guys won't hit on you? You want to get old and live alone? I don't think so. You've got good years to live, so don't wimp out now by not living them."

She *was* young, she told herself, or at least not yet old. Perhaps she was even desirable.

She brought the ring up to her lips and pressed it against them. Then she put it on her third finger, but of her right hand this time, and stood up. Walking to her tent in the moonlight, she let herself in, crawled into her sleeping bag and almost immediately was asleep.

Two

———

IN HIS CITY-ISSUE TAURUS, INSPECTOR Sergeant Devin Juhle pulled up and parked where the front walk of a house on Greenwich Street on San Francisco's Russian Hill met the sidewalk. He was responding to a dispatch he'd received just as he was leaving his home on Noriega. In the past eighteen months, Juhle's previous two partners had been killed. Now, in a compelling demonstration of the superstitious nature of his colleagues in Homicide, he worked solo.

Two black-and-white squad cars were already at the scene, at the curb across the street. A Fire Department vehicle sat in the driveway. A knot of bystanders—three women, one man, four kids—had gathered at the corner, a hundred feet away. They all stared at the house as a unit, curious and intent, waiting for some official person to come over and tell them what had happened. Thus far, no media had arrived, but Juhle knew that this aberration in the natural order of things would soon correct itself.

Juhle waited behind the wheel and let his mind switch to what he called his "detail gear." From here on out, he wanted to register everything he saw, heard, thought, or felt. He'd trained himself to pay attention from his first moments at any crime scene. Now, satisfied that he had taken in all he needed from the street, he looked at the house. A pair of uniformed patrol officers stood at its open door. The occupants of the second squad car, Juhle presumed, were inside.

He checked his watch. It was just shy of 7:30 on Monday, September 12. Juhle exited his car and took one last look around. The morning was glorious, the sky blue and cloudless, the sun casting its long shadows down the street in front of him.

He turned and walked toward the house.

Stuart Gorman's hollow eyes stared into the distance over Devin Juhle's shoulder. "I'm sorry, what?"

"You said you got home just before six. I asked you where you had been."

Gorman brought his eyes back. "We've got a place at Echo Lake, up by South Tahoe. I was there for the weekend."

"So you must have left there early."

"A little before two. I couldn't sleep, so I figured I might as well come on home."

"And you were up there alone?"

"Yeah." Gorman raised his chin, thick with stubble. His face was drawn, the skin with a pronounced pallor even under the sunburn. The whites of his eyes were shot with capillaries. "I'm a writer. I went up there to do some work."

They sat across from each other at a round, wooden table in a kitchen that was considerably more well-equipped than Juhle's own. A bank of windows in the eastern wall admitted a bright line of sunlight up where it met the ceiling and reflected off the surfaces of the bright copper pans that hung from the opposite wall. Juhle had faced Gorman so that he wouldn't have to watch the crime-scene techs and assistants to the medical examiner as they passed through the living room and out to the back porch, where Caryn Dryden's naked body still lay on the wooden slats of the deck next to the hot tub.

They were just getting started. Juhle had his small tape recorder concealed and running in his pocket. To any homicide cop, the death of a spouse always entails initial suspicion of the surviving partner. When husbands got killed, you looked first to the wife, and vice versa. And even though the death of Caryn Dryden might, from what he now knew, be ruled a suicide, the possibility of murder lurked somewhere in the back of Juhle's mind.

But the last thing Juhle wanted was to raise a flag with the husband at this point. He kept his questions innocuous. "Did you get any writing done?"

"No." Gorman ran a workingman's hand down a ravaged cheek. "I might as well tell you. The last time I saw Caryn was here at the house on Friday afternoon. She told me she wanted a divorce. That's all I could think about while I was up there."

"How'd you feel about that, getting a divorce?"

Gorman's gaze went off again, then came back. "You married, Inspector?"

"I am."

"You love your wife?"

Juhle nodded. "Most of the time."

"Me too. Except when I hated her."

"That happen a lot?"

"Most of this weekend, to be honest with you."

"So you didn't want to divorce her?"

Gorman said, "The word—we called it the D-word—it wasn't something I allowed myself to entertain. I figured once you're saying it out loud to yourself, it starts having its own reality. Caryn and I were together and committed and that was that, I thought, for better or worse. So I never wanted to give myself that option."

Juhle nodded. "Okay. But she wanted out?"

"And got herself out, didn't she?"

Juhle leaned back in his chair. "You think she killed herself?"

"That's what it looks like to me."

"By drowning? That's a reasonably difficult trick to pull off by yourself."

If Gorman's shrug struck Juhle as chillingly nonchalant, his actual words were perhaps colder. "She was a doctor. You check, I wouldn't be surprised if it wasn't a drowning after all. She kept a stash of Vicodin upstairs. Take some pills, have a few drinks, go sit in the hot tub turned up to one-oh-five. Adios."

Absorbing this intelligence, Juhle felt all of his senses sharpen. Stuart Gorman had just supplied him with chapter and verse on a perfectly plausible scenario for Caryn's death—one that, if adopted by the medical examiner and the police, would remove him, the husband, from any suspicion. If he'd been involved in his wife's death, this was a slick, high-stakes gamble—smart and dangerous.

"Can we go back," Juhle said, "to how you found her?"

Gorman indicated the room behind him. "I already told those guys. What's it matter?"

Because now I've got you on tape, Juhle thought to himself. And in fact, it probably wouldn't really matter, but Juhle's aim was to keep him talking. "Just making sure we get the record straight. You've said you got here a little after six and parked in your garage under the house . . . ?"

"All right." He sighed. "I expected her to be up by then. She usually is on Monday. But the house was quiet, so I figured she was sleeping in and I thought I'd let her. Maybe she'd had the kind of weekend I'd just had. So I make a pot of coffee and go out to get the paper. I finish them both and it's still quiet. I don't hear the shower yet, so I go upstairs and she's not in bed. It's still made. So I figure maybe she took off someplace for the weekend herself."

"Where would she have gone?"

"I don't know. Her sister's, maybe. Or up to visit . . ." The first real sign of distress. Gorman brought a hand to his forehead. "Oh,

Christ. Kym. Our daughter. She's up at college in Portland. She just started a couple of weeks ago. Oh, Jesus. This is going to destroy her. I've got to call her."

Juhle didn't want to stop in the middle of his interview. He said, "Are you sure you don't want to let us do that for you? I can call the Portland police and have somebody with her."

Juhle watched Gorman pull himself heavily to his feet and cross to the phone on the kitchen counter. "No." There he paused again, his hands flat on the counter, all of his weight on them. His head flopped forward and Juhle heard the deep exhale of a sigh. "Oh, Jesus," he said again. He picked up the receiver, brought it to his ear, then placed it back down on the counter. "I've got to do this myself."

Juhle left him like that, working up the strength to make the call.

Leaving the kitchen, the inspector looked left through the large, high-ceilinged living room. Beyond the cop stationed at the front door, he could see that, sure enough, a couple of Minicams and their news crews had arrived. He wasn't about to talk to them, not at this stage anyway. Instead he turned to his right and walked through a leather-couch kind of book-lined den and out onto the enclosed deck.

The body lay covered now with a sheet that still clung in wet places. A police photographer was snapping pictures of the hot tub and deck. Behind him, some ME assistants were wheeling a collapsible gurney through the house. Two other officers in uniform were down the steps in the backyard, conversing on the tiny fenced lawn.

In shirtsleeves, Lennard Faro, lean and dark with a well-trimmed black goatee, was a lab specialist with the Crime Scene Investigation unit. Seeing Juhle at the back door, he closed his cell phone and walked over.

"He break yet? The husband?" Faro asked.

"He wasn't here. He was up in the mountains. You're saying this is a homicide?"

A shrug. Faro wasn't going to commit until the medical examiner had drawn his conclusions and he himself had spent some time in the lab. Still, he said, "She's got an impressive, and I'd guess recent, bump over her right ear."

"Enough to kill her?"

"We won't know until the autopsy, but I'd say it's not impossible."

"How long has she been dead?"

Faro frowned. "The hot tub's going to screw that calculation up for a while. Nobody's going to know until we get cutting on her. Body temp's way up, but that's what you'd expect when the water's still at one-oh-five."

The number struck a chord. "Exactly one-oh-five?"

"Pretty close. The thermometer's still . . . why? That a magic number?"

"No. It's nothing." Juhle didn't want to start a rumor. He'd get what he could, then see where it led him. "Any sign of what caused the bump?"

"Maybe. We found some broken glass, plus one big piece, up against the bottom of the tub. Some still have a whiff of wine on 'em. Another empty glass was in the sink. The rest of the broken glass and an empty bottle was in the compactor in the kitchen."

"So she was drinking?"

"Maybe. Blood alcohol will tell."

"The husband said she's got Vicodin upstairs in their bedroom. He thinks it's a suicide."

Faro pulled at his goatee. "She hit herself on the head?"

"Maybe she fell first. Slipped on the wet wood."

Faro was still scratching at his beard, without comment, as the two uniforms came up the four steps and onto the deck. The older one—thirty pounds on the wrong side of healthy, with jowls and a walrus mustache—introduced himself as Captain Allen Marsten from Central Station on Vallejo. The other man was Jerry Jarrett. Marsten told Juhle that they had been the first ones to arrive after the 911 call. He was just getting off his graveyard shift when the call had come in.

Did Juhle need anything else from him? If not, since now the scene was secure, he wouldn't mind going home and getting some shut-eye, and he didn't think Sergeant Jarrett would mind it either.

"Anything either of you feel like I ought to know?" Juhle asked.

Marsten looked at his partner, got a shrug, then worked his lips for a moment under his hanging mustache. "Nothing jumps out at me. He—the husband—left the front door open for us and we made it here in I'd say two, three minutes after the call came in. We come inside and he's got her out of the tub and on the deck where she's lying now, still trying to do CPR on her, although you could see a mile away it was too late for that."

"So he must have thought she'd only recently gone under?"

"I don't know about that. We took a pulse and called him off."

"And what'd he do?"

"He just stopped, no fight in him. Breathing hard, you know. Then he stood up and tried to cover her up with that towel over there."

"What do you mean, 'tried'?"

"Well, it was too small for all of her. And, you can see, she's a little bent up. He started low, then moved it up, then over her face, then back down. It was kind of pathetic, tell the truth. Then finally Jerry here walked him off and sat him down inside."

Sitting on the counter, still on the telephone, Stuart Gorman was crying silently, making no attempt to stem the flow of tears. His shoulders were hunched, one arm tucked under the other one. He barely whispered, saying, "I know" and "Yeah, baby, I don't know," and Juhle could watch no more. Instead he went back outside to the deck and stood in silence as they bagged the body and began to lift it and load it onto the gurney.

Juhle didn't want to watch that, either. Reflecting that there weren't that many fun things to do at homicide scenes, he went back to the kitchen. He pulled around a chair and sat on it.

The phone conversation continued a few more minutes before

Gorman said, "Do you need me to come up there? You're not. Where are you? You've only been up there two weeks and . . . ? Okay, okay, you're right, it doesn't matter. Call me when you get close, and I'll come get you."

He clicked the phone off and, as though it were a high explosive, placed it next to him on the counter. He closed his eyes and, for a long moment, didn't move.

Finally, Juhle spoke. "She going to be all right?"

Gorman tried and largely failed to arrange his face into a controlled expression. "I don't know," he said. "I don't have any idea." He exhaled heavily. "I don't believe this. This can't be happening."

Juhle resisted his urge to leave the man to his miseries. If he had in fact killed his wife—and his obvious pain and possible remorse now did not in the slightest degree rule out that possibility—then this was the time to exploit his vulnerability. Juhle needed to get him talking again, so he asked, "What school does she go to?"

"Reed. My alma mater. Although it turns out she's down in Santa Cruz now. Don't ask me why. But she's enrolled at Reed." He paused. "She's smart and weird, like her dad, and the place worked pretty well for me."

"How were you weird?"

A dry chuckle caught in Gorman's throat. "How was I *not* weird? I just never fit in as a kid. I was big, gangly, ugly." He pointed to the birthmark on his face. "This thing. I liked solitude. I wanted to write. That by itself is weird enough. When I think about it, that was probably half the problem with me and Caryn. She wanted someone normal, and I wasn't him."

"Normal in what way?"

"Motivated by money, for example. Guys my age, we're supposed to be driven by money. It's how we gauge our success in the world, right?" He shrugged. "I don't really think too much about money and never have."

"And this bothered your wife?"

Gorman smiled, but there wasn't any humor in it. "Are you kidding me? What greater failing can a man have than not to be the primary wage earner in his family?"

"You weren't that?"

Another shrug. "I make more than decent enough money, I think. Eighty or a hundred grand a year, give or take. I'm a writer, so there's good years and bad years. But eighty grand to me is a fortune. It's not like I don't publish, like I'm not putting out good work. It just doesn't pay enough to suit Caryn."

"She wanted you to make more?"

He shook his head impatiently. "It wasn't so much that. With her income, we certainly didn't *need* any more money. She made enough for most third-world countries."

Juhle cast a quick glance around—the eight-burner stove, the Sub-Zero refrigerators, the shining copper pots and pans, all the gadgets on display on the counters, the other creature comforts he'd noticed everywhere. To say nothing of the size and location of the house itself—probably four to six million dollars in real estate and furnishings alone. "So she felt she was carrying you financially, was that it? Did she resent that?"

Gorman paused. "I don't know what she felt anymore, Inspector. I didn't think she was anywhere near asking me for a divorce until Friday, but then she did. I mean, after Kym left for school, we both knew there'd be . . . adjustments. But here it's only been a couple of weeks and that's it. It's all over, like we never had anything together, like everything we'd ever done was just a fucking stupid charade." He stopped abruptly, then started again more calmly. "She was just waiting for Kym to go. After that, there wasn't any reason for us to stay together."

"No discussion?"

"More like an announcement. 'My life with you is over. Do whatever you want. You're nothing to me.' "

"That bother you?"

"No. I fucking loved it. What do you think? Did it bother me? Give me a break, Inspector."

"Taking that as a yes, then."

Gorman's eyes narrowed. He visibly reined himself in. "You don't know how hard I tried to keep it together. And she wasn't easy, let me tell you. She was *never* easy the last few years. You know what that's been like? And then hearing that you're a nonentity, that her world is just so much more important than yours, more *financially rewarding*, more everything. How's that make me feel? Like a piece of shit. Like a worthless piece of shit."

Something was going on behind Juhle in the living room, and suddenly Gorman straightened all the way up. *"Hey! Wait a minute! What are you doing?"* Boosting himself up from the counter, he was across the kitchen before Juhle could even stand. In the middle of the living room, the medical examiner's assistants with the gurney and its body bag had stopped at the interruption. "What are you doing?" Gorman demanded again.

Juhle stepped in front of him. "They're taking the body downtown, sir. The medical examiner is going to need to do an autopsy, then . . ."

"You mean he's going to cut her up?"

"To determine the exact cause of death, yes."

"But . . ." Gorman turned from Juhle to the men pushing the gurney, then back to the inspector, a low-wattage panic now evident in his eyes. "Why do you have to do that? I told you she had pills upstairs. If she'd been drinking and then got in the hot tub . . ."

"That's one way it might have happened," Juhle said, "yes."

"Well, what else?"

"She might have slipped getting into the tub. There's a good-sized bump on her head."

This news seemed to confuse Gorman, but he shook his reaction off. "That doesn't matter. What matters is she's dead! If she killed herself or it was an accident, what difference does it make?" He brought a hand back to his face, rubbed at the birthmark. "Jesus Christ, this is unbelievable. She's just now dead. It's only been a few hours. Don't you understand that? You don't have to cut her up. It won't make any difference."

Juhle wondered if Gorman could in fact be so clueless, or if this was some kind of an act. Every schoolchild knew that homicide victims got autopsied. Juhle had been playing his role as understanding cop comforting a victim's relative up until now, but this was the time to bring some reality into the discussion. "Mr. Gorman," he said, "surely you realize it makes a difference if somebody killed her."

Gorman opened his mouth and started to say something, then decided not to. His shoulders sagged, he shook his head from side to side. "God help us," he said.

THREE

———

AFTER GETTING UP AT DAWN AND hiking out from Tamarack Lake, Gina Roake drove to her Pleasant Street condominium on Nob Hill in under four hours. By noon, she had unpacked and stowed her gear, showered, and changed into her work clothes—a light mauve business suit and black low heels.

As she came out the doors onto the sidewalk in front of her building, Gina discovered that, somewhat to her surprise, she wasn't inclined to go straight to her office. True, that had been her intention since last night, but now that the moment had arrived, something about it didn't feel quite right. She knew that she could go in and report to her partners that she was ready to get back in harness. At that announcement, right away they would probably be able to throw her some work on cases they were handling, get her back up to speed, give her some billable hours.

But Gina knew that those hours rightly belonged to the nineteen long-suffering and hardworking associates within the firm, each one of whom was expected to amass twenty-two hundred billable hours in the course of a year, a daunting and unending struggle for young attorneys that demanded fifty weeks of eight-billable-hour days. Lunches didn't count; administrative hours didn't count; prep time and research often didn't count; and certainly schmoozing by the water cooler didn't count. Hours were limited and finite, and it wasn't uncommon for an associate to put in twelve hours on the clock in order to bill eight of them. As a partner, Gina was under no illusion that her legitimate role was to garner clients for the firm, and they in turn would provide the billable hours of work that she would then dole out to her associates.

She was ready to go back to work all right, but damned if she was going to be a drain on the firm's resources. She needed to reestablish her contacts in the city and attract her own clients to the firm—to do otherwise would not only be unfair to her associates, it would put her in a subservient position vis-à-vis her partners, and she wasn't going to let that happen.

By the time she got to the corner, she'd made up her mind and when the cab pulled over to pick her up, she slid into the backseat and said, "Hall of Justice, please. Seventh and Bryant."

In terms of longevity in the city, Lou the Greek's wasn't exactly Tadich's or Fior d'Italia, or even Original Joe's or the Swan Oyster Depot. Nevertheless, with forty-plus years in its same location across the street from the Hall of Justice, it had its full complement of tradition, albeit in a slightly less savory vein than those other famous eateries.

The whole "eatery" designation was something of a misnomer. Certainly, anyone drawing up a business plan for the place in today's world would be hard-pressed to attract investors with a menu that included only one item per day—the Special—and very few appetizers besides the occasional edamame or dried wasabi-coated peas.

Forget about lunch standards everywhere else, such as chicken wings or hamburgers or fried calamari or garlic fries or, God forbid, salads or other raw green stuff—the regulars at Lou's referred to martini olives as the vegetable course. Instead, Lou's wife, Chui, sought on a daily basis to meld the disparate culinary cultures of her own China and her husband's Greece with original and, it must be admitted, creative dishes such as Sweet and Sour Dolmas, or Pita Stuffed Kung Pao Chicken, or mysteries such as the famous Yeanling Clay Bowl. Whatever a yeanling was.

Often edible, but just as often not, the food was not why people gathered at Lou's. Like so many other restaurants, Lou's location was the key to its success. If you had business with the criminal justice system in San Francisco, Lou's was where you ate. It didn't matter that it was stuck down in the basement of a bail-bond building, that it always smelled a little funky, was darkly lit and ill-ventilated. It wasn't fifty yards from the front door of the Hall of Justice, so juries on their lunch breaks, cops, reporters, lawyers and their clients, witnesses, snitches, families of victims, and visitors to the jail—a vast, often unwashed and unruly, certainly boisterous clientele—filled the place from the first legal drink at 6:00 a.m. until last call at 1:30 a.m.

Now Gina Roake, fresh from her cab ride, walked down the six steps from the street and waded into the surging tide of humanity on the other side of Lou's black-painted glass double-doors. The crowd did not intimidate her. This was her milieu. Smiling, jostling, pushing her way inside, she cleared the immediate crush and across the room saw her firm's chief investigator, Wyatt Hunt, sharing a four-person booth with another man. In ten seconds, she was standing over them. "If I joined you, would I be interrupting important business?" she asked.

"Not at all," Hunt said. "We haven't even ordered yet."

"You're sure you wouldn't mind sharing half your bench with an old woman?"

Hunt leaned forward and back, looking around behind her. "No problem," he said. "Where is she?" But, grinning up at her, he slid in to give her room, then pointed across the table. "You know Devin Juhle, I believe. Homicide."

"Sure. How are you, Inspector?"

"Better now that it's not just me and Wyatt. He's decent company for about fifteen minutes, then usually starts to babble."

"It's when I start using longer words," Hunt explained. "Devin gets confused."

"He uses them in the wrong context. He needs to take a course or something. I tell him it's no good using big words if you don't know what they mean."

"Teleological," Hunt said.

"A perfect example." Juhle turned to Gina. "As you can see," he said, "you're not interrupting." Then to Hunt. "And no way is that a real word."

"Teleological." Hunt held out a hand across the table. "How much?"

"Lunch."

"You're on."

"Spell it for the record."

Hunt strung out the letters, then said, "Gina? Word or no word?"

She made a reluctant grimace across at Juhle. "I think it's a word, Inspector. Sorry."

"It is a word," Hunt said. "It means 'relating to design in nature.' Like a teleological argument. Man started to walk upright because he got out of the trees and started hanging out in tall grass, where he had to stand to see over it. Which got him—us, I mean, the human race—to walking."

"Imagine that," Juhle said. "I never would have guessed." Across the table, Juhle sotto voce'd to Gina: "We're getting into the babble phase I told you about."

Fifteen minutes later, they were all having the Special—pot stickers stuffed with taramosalata—which was not particularly, by unanimous opinion, Chui's greatest triumph. But by now they weren't paying any attention to the food anyway.

". . . just a feeling in my gut," Juhle was saying, "but anytime you've got a murdered spouse and a mega-million-dollar estate, you've got to think maybe the husband, huh?"

Gina said, "Do you have anything on him?"

Juhle shook his head. "It's too soon. We don't even know time of death yet. But if there was foul play, and the bump on the head looks an awful lot like there was, then it was either him or somebody else she knew pretty damn well."

"Why do you say that?" Hunt asked.

"She was naked," Juhle said. "She's not having wine and getting naked with whoever he might have hired to get rid of her, I don't care how cute he was."

"Does this guy have a lawyer?" Gina asked.

Juhle started to pop a pot sticker, then thought better of it and put it back on his plate. He shook his head. "Again, too early."

"It's never too early."

"We don't even have a murder yet, much less charged him with it."

"But you talked to him this morning? And you let him tell you all this stuff?"

"I didn't twist his arm."

"And about money, and being resentful of his wife, and spending all last weekend just thinking about how much he hated her? Somehow I think that if a lawyer had been with him, he would have toned things down a notch or two."

Juhle pulled down the sides of his mouth, erasing the smile that had started there. "He might have, at that. But fortunately, no offense, he didn't think to call one."

Hunt spoke up. "In his heart, Devin already thinks he's guilty."

"I'm getting that impression," Gina said.

"Not true," Devin said. "I'm in wait mode, that's all."

"Are you going to talk to him again?" Gina asked.

"Probably later today, if he's where he should be."

"As opposed to . . . ?"

"His house." Juhle was matter-of-fact. "Hey, I went upstairs with him so he could get some fresh clothes. But no way he spends any more time at his house until we're through with the place."

"So where's he staying?"

"The Travelodge down on Lombard. It's close enough."

"And you're going down to see him there?"

"That's my plan."

"And he still won't have a lawyer?"

This time, Juhle's smile stayed. "If my luck holds," he said.

Gina hated it when cops played these silly territorial games. For Juhle's benefit, and mostly just for the fun of it, she decided to put a little of the needle in. She turned to Hunt. "Just as good citizens, Wyatt, we ought to get in touch with this guy and give him a heads up."

"Hey, come on!" Juhle put some humor in it, but not all that much. "Give a poor cop a break. Besides, he gets lawyered up, I'm *really* going to think he's guilty."

"Having a lawyer means he's guilty?" Gina asked.

"No. Of course not. How silly of me." Juhle remained genial. "You're absolutely correct. Perish the thought."

"Don't be fooled," Hunt said. "He doesn't agree with you."

"I'm picking that up, Wyatt."

Juhle stabbed one of the awful pot stickers with his fork and picked it up. Staring at it for a second, he again put it back down on his plate. Gina's casual dig at him had obviously struck a nerve. "Let's put it this way. He hasn't been charged with anything yet. If the autopsy comes back looking like someone murdered his wife, I would hope that he'd want to cooperate in every way he could to help us find the killer. If he's got a lawyer there with him, running a screen every time I ask him a question, I'm going to wonder about what's going on with him a lot more than I would if he just sat and talked to me."

"But you admit you're trying to get him to implicate himself."

"No." Then patiently, "I'm trying to get at the truth. If he's innocent, the truth—pardon the phrase—the truth will set him free."

"Only in a perfect world, Inspector. You know that."

"Okay, granted," Juhle said. "But an innocent guy doesn't call a lawyer before he's even charged with anything."

Gina thought this was turning into a ridiculous discussion for two old pros to be having. She'd started out totally goofing with Juhle, and now she was enjoying the rise she was getting out of him, so she went on. "He does if he's going to talk to cops and say things that could get misconstrued. That's all I'm saying."

"And all I'm saying," Juhle responded, "is that to us cop types, that happens and we're going to think the guy's got something to hide."

"Well, to quote the Beatles," Hunt said, trying to lighten everybody up, " 'everybody's got something to hide 'cept for me and my monkey.' "

"Thanks, Wyatt," Gina said. "That was helpful."

Self-effacing, Hunt said, "I try to contribute."

"I think I got your friend mad at me."

"Naw. That's just Devin. He's a cop, so he thinks like a cop. It's a whole mind-set they test you on at the Academy. First question is whether you think if a guy's got a lawyer, is he guilty? If you say, 'Not necessarily,' you flunk out."

"How heartening."

They were crossing Bryant Street at the light. "So," Hunt asked, "what brings you down here? I haven't seen you near the Hall in forever."

"At least. Maybe longer. I don't even remember the last time I was down here."

Reaching the opposite curb, they turned right together and started up the block. In front of them, unmarked as well as black-and-white police cars and taxicabs were double-parked in the street all the way up to the front steps of the Hall. Someone had chained a large Doberman to one of the handrails in the middle of the wide and shallow stairs, and his barking competed with the Jamaican in dreads who was exhorting all and sundry to embrace Rasta as their salvation and Haile Selassie as the one true God. A homeless man wrapped in newspaper slept just beyond the hedge that bounded the steps. A full dozen attorney types stood talking with clients or cops in the bright sunshine while regular citizens kept up a stream in and out of the glass doors. "Can you believe? I think I've actually missed the place," Roake said.

"You get inside, I predict you'll get over that pretty quick. You meeting a client?"

"No. I'm hoping to latch on to a conflicts case." These cases were very common; the Public Defender's Office would in the normal course of events be assigned to an indigent client who had been accused of a crime. If that suspect committed the crime with a partner, the PD could not also defend the accomplice—it was a conflict of interest. So the court would assign a private defense attorney such as Gina, whose fees the city would pay, to represent the accomplice.

They reached the steps. Gina stopped, hesitated, gestured to the door. "You going inside?"

"No. I was just doing some computer searches at home and Devin called to have lunch and I took pity on him. I live just around the corner."

Again, Gina showed a slight hesitation.

"What?" Hunt asked.

She lay a hand on his arm. "I was just wondering if Inspector Juhle happened to mention the name of the husband we were talking about back in there."

"Sure. It's Stuart Gorman. The writer?"

She shook her head. "I'm afraid I don't know the name. What does he write?"

"Outdoors books. Fishing, mostly. I've read a couple of 'em. He's pretty good."

"A couple of them?"

"Maybe three by now."

"I hate him already," Gina said. "I've been trying to finish my one damn book for almost four years, and he's already finished three?"

"Maybe he started earlier than you."

"Maybe he's just better at it."

"Could be that, I suppose. Though you're probably a better lawyer than he'd be."

"If he were a lawyer."

"Which, based on Devin's talk with him, he's not," Hunt said. "And that in turn leaves you wondering if he's got himself legal representation yet, doesn't it?"

Now Roake smiled. "No flies on you, Wyatt. The thought did occur to me."

"You want me to call him and find out for sure?"

Gina shook her head. "Thanks. I can chase my own ambulances. The man's just lost his wife. Let's go wildly out on a limb and presume for a minute that he had nothing to do with killing her, in which case he's probably—no, undoubtedly—devastated. But I kind of think he'd be better off if he gets somebody before your Devin gets another shot at him."

"Well," Hunt said. "If I know Dev like I think I do, he'd better hurry."

FOUR

AT A FEW MINUTES AFTER ONE o'clock, a haggard Stuart Gorman, collapsed in a wing chair next to the television in his hotel room, hung up the telephone. "I can't believe these people."

Sitting across from him on the front two inches of his bed, his longtime friend and ex-college roommate, Jedd Conley, raised his head. Conley was the first call Stuart made after the police had chased him out of his own house that morning. In spite of being the State Assemblyman representing San Francisco, Conley had cleared his entire calendar for the day and met Stuart at the Travelodge within twenty minutes of checking in.

Conley had a good face, closely shaved. Both his nose and his six-foot bearing were strong, straight, aristocratic. The broad, unlined forehead under his dark hair could have belonged to a man twenty years his junior, but the youthful look was somewhat mitigated by the lines around a mouth that had perhaps been forced to smile more than it wanted to. Today Conley was wearing a tan business suit with a white shirt and light gold tie. "Who was that?" he asked.

"Some guy capping for a lawyer, wanting to know if I'd retained legal representation yet. The distinguished citizen had somebody he wanted to recommend. What a sleazeball. I got rid of him."

"I heard you."

"Fucking shysters. How'd they find me here so fast?"

Conley shrugged. "Word gets out. It's already been on TV. They probably called the cops and asked. It's just business."

"Just business." Stuart Gorman blew some of his anger into the dim room. "It sucks."

"I don't know." Conley stood up and crossed to the window, where he pulled a cord on the blinds and let in more light. Turning, he said, "You're going to need a lawyer, after all. You can't blame them."

"I wasn't *here*, Jedd. I wasn't physically present when she died," Stuart said evenly, his mouth tightening up. "How am I going to be a suspect?"

"I didn't say you were a suspect. I said you're going to need a lawyer. The cops, the press, the estate. It's an automatic."

"As you know, I've already done that, talked to the cops. It was no sweat. Besides, I don't know why we're talking about me needing another lawyer. I've already got one, if I'm not mistaken."

Conley pulled at his forelock, sighed, shook his head. He chose his words with care. "Listen, my man," he said, hand over heart, "you're my best friend and my heart is breaking here for what's happened to Caryn. To you and her and Kymberly. But I haven't done one lick of actual law in ten years, so I'd be lousy at representing you, besides which maybe you've noticed, I've got another full-time job. It just can't be me. But you're going to need somebody."

Stuart stared coldly at his old pal for a few seconds, and then the anger passed and he settled back into his chair. "We don't need to argue about it."

A pause, and then Conley said, "When you're ready, there's somebody I'd recommend." Conley was back on the edge of the bed, and now he came forward. "Don't be an idiot, Stu. You have no idea how all this stuff works. Even if Caryn took some pills and drowned . . ."

"Hey. Read my lips: I was up at Echo Lake. Whatever happened last night, I wasn't any part of it."

"Can you prove that?"

"What do you mean?"

"I mean, did anybody see you up there? Did you have company last night? Did you talk on the phone?" When Stuart didn't respond, Conley continued, "I'm taking your silence as a no. And this in turn means that your alibi sucks and you're going to be on your cop's list."

"Okay. Maybe. *If* Caryn was murdered . . ."

Conley shrugged. "Maybe even if she wasn't. You remember that guy a couple of years ago? He was like a telemarketer or something, and she owned about half the real estate in the Western Addition? Anyway, the two of them went camping and the story was that she went out for a midnight swim all alone while he was sleeping, and didn't come back. Turns out she drowned and the husband stood to inherit like fifty million dollars. *Did* in fact inherit fifty million bucks. You don't think the cops considered him a suspect? You think the fact that she drowned was a defense against them thinking he killed her? You want to know the truth, you want to kill somebody, drowning them's probably the best way to do it, evidence-wise."

"Okay, but did they charge him? Did they have any evidence?"

This brought Conley up short. "Do me a favor, Stu. Don't ask your friendly inspector that kind of question."

"What kind of question?"

"Evidence questions. Whether or not crimes got charged. Legal questions."

"Why not?"

"Because they demonstrate what they call a degree of criminal so- phistication. How about that? It could sound, to a trained investiga- tor, like you had premeditated your actions and possibly even studied the rules of evidence."

"I was just asking you if they brought to trial the guy you were talking about."

Conley said, "In the end, no. But I was around at the DA's for a few of the discussions about whether they had enough to bring charges or not. The cops' position was that they had fifty million good enough reasons. And they came *this* close to taking it to the grand jury, even without a shred of evidence. And the grand jury would have indicted."

"So why didn't they charge it?"

"Because they would have lost at trial, and the DA knew it. And hell, nobody doubted even for a minute that the husband had done it. He was there where she drowned, he was going to inherit, they'd been having troubles in their marriage, which I know you and Caryn . . ." Spreading his palms out, Conley continued. "Anyway, you see what I'm getting at. How much was Caryn worth on her own? Six, seven million? Plus your life insurance . . . ?"

"Jesus, Jedd!"

"Get used to it, Stu. You're going to hear it from the police, and you're going to have to know how to answer them. Or even whether or not *to* answer them. And you don't have a clue. Which can hurt you. A lot. Kymberly, too. That's all I'm saying. Friend to friend."

Finally, Stuart seemed to get the message. He settled back into his chair, chin down on his chest, his arms hanging over the sides. "So who do you know?" he asked.

"Oh, God! It's true, then, isn't it? It's really true."

Debra Dryden—Caryn's younger sister—stood just inside the room's doorway in front of Stuart, her face washed in anguish. Then she stepped into his embrace. Pressing herself up against him, holding him tightly, she began to shake. Stuart held her and let her go on, his hands locked around her back, over the silk of her blouse. "I know," he whispered. "It's all right." At last he extricated himself and stepped back.

"When I got your message, I didn't want to call you back," Debra said. "I didn't want it to be true."

Stuart nodded. "I know." He half-turned. "I don't know if you've met Jedd Conley."

Debra lifted a hand perfunctorily. "Thanks for being here for Stuart."

"I couldn't not be," Conley said.

The woman's obvious pain and suffering did nothing to camouflage, and perhaps even served to enhance, her physical beauty. Shoulder-length, white-blond hair surrounded a captivating face— turquoise eyes, finely pored light tan skin. Debra wore a short white skirt and teal silk blouse, a gold necklace and diamond earrings. She brought both hands up to her eyes and dabbed under them. She said to Stuart, "But what are you doing here? Why aren't you home?"

"They're not letting me go back there until they're finished with their investigation."

"But why? You said she drowned. In the hot tub. Is that possible?"

"She may have been drinking and then taken some pills . . ."

"You're saying she might have killed herself?"

Stuart shook his head. "If she did, I don't think it was on purpose."

"Of course it wasn't," Conley said. "She wasn't suicidal."

Debra turned to him, a cold eye, at the interruption. "How do you know that?"

"I just talked to her Friday afternoon . . ."

Stuart spoke with some surprise. "You did?"

"Sure." Conley went on. "You know that, Stu. She was all in a tizzy about her invention. Remember she'd asked me to have my office look into some questions with her VC"—venture capital—"people. I'd been reporting back to her pretty regularly."

Debra asked, "What does your office have to do with that?"

"Nothing specific," Conley said. "But I'm with the State Assembly, and Caryn thought I could find out some stuff that wasn't public yet. And she may not have been all wrong about that."

"What was the news Friday?" Stuart asked.

"It wasn't anything that was going to make her want to kill herself. We'd found some evidence that PII"—this was Polymed Innovations, Inc., the manufacturer of the Dryden Socket, which Caryn had invented—"hadn't reported some negative results in the clinical trials—post-op leg clots—that apparently they'd known about. Caryn was furious about it. And furious is pretty much the opposite of suicidal."

"Maybe she started out furious," Debra said, "but over the weekend it turned into depression."

"If she had gotten herself depressed by last night, it wasn't about business," Stuart said. He drew a breath. "Both of you might as well hear it from me, since it's going to come out eventually. She wanted a divorce."

Debra said, "That's not wanting to kill yourself either. That's wanting to move on. Ask me how I know. I'm three years free and haven't regretted a day of it."

"I don't want to believe it was a done deal," Stuart said. "But it is what she told me."

"She couldn't have wanted to leave you," Debra said. "I mean, you're . . ." She came at the thought again: "In what way exactly have you not been the perfect husband?"

Stuart said, "A lot of ways, Debra. Too many, believe me."

Conley touched his friend's arm. "You're getting whacked every which way but loose here, aren't you, Stu? Why'd she want to leave you? Did she say? Maybe a boyfriend?"

A quick shake of the head. "I don't think it was that. When would she have had the time? But I don't know for sure. It could have been anything. Or everything. She just wasn't happy with us together."

Debra's eyes had gone glassy again. She reached out to touch Stuart's arm, then moved a step closer to him. "Let's not think about that right now, okay? Let's all just try to get through what we need to do here and now."

"Good idea," Conley said. "Maybe you could help talk Stuart into getting himself a lawyer. I've got someone in mind. And with this divorce in the mix, he's going to need one."

Her hand still on his arm, Debra nodded. "Stuart," she said softly, "I think you ought to listen to your friend."

FIVE

IN THE NORMAL COURSE OF EVENTS, Devin Juhle would not have heard word one about the autopsy of Caryn Dryden for at least a few days. But in the great yin and yang of the city's population, this turned out to be a slow weekend for death. San Francisco's homicide rate—with about two killings every week—was not comparable, say, to Oakland's, eleven miles across the bay, with its two hundred and twenty murders a year, but since autopsies were mandated not just for violent deaths, but for deaths of the homeless, deaths anywhere with an element of suspicion to them, usually the medical examiner's office had an autopsy backlog of at least a couple of days after the body arrived at the morgue.

But today, still hungry from his lack of lunch at Lou's, Juhle wasn't ten seconds back inside the door to the homicide detail on the fourth floor in the Hall of Justice when his lieutenant, Marcel Lanier, saw him and called out his name.

The door to Lanier's small office, built into the corner of the cluttered room that served as headquarters for the city's fifteen homicide inspectors, was open. Behind it, at his outsized desk, the lieutenant was having his lunch—an enormous construction of marbled rye bread stuffed with three or four inches' worth of what looked like pastrami or corned beef with cheese and pickles. Lanier finished chewing, took a sip from his can of Diet Coke, swallowed, and said, "This is impossible if it's true, so it's probably a hoax. But Strout"—this was John Strout, San Francisco's septuagenarian medical examiner—"called and said they're done with the preliminary cutting on your girl and maybe you'll want to go down and see where they're at."

Juhle would normally have attended the autopsy if he'd known it was going to happen, but he'd never expected it so soon. "They've got something?"

"That's what it sounded like. I can't see him calling us up if he didn't have something to talk about."

"Yeah. That wouldn't make any sense."

"Okay, then." Lanier sunk his teeth again into the sandwich.

"You going to eat all of that, Marcel? I'd pay you five dollars for a bite."

Lanier chewed another few seconds, drank, swallowed, smiled. "Why am I thinking you had lunch at the Greek's?"

"If you want to call it that. Lunch, I mean."

"What's the Special today?"

"I don't know what it was. Some kind of fish eggs and this rubbery, doughy stuff. I couldn't eat two of 'em. I don't know how the guy stays in business."

"Clucks like yourself."

"Okay, then, ten bucks. One bite. Come on."

Juhle wanted to get to Strout's office, but the sandwich was going to come first, dammit. Lanier took pity on him and, since very few mortals could eat an entire pastrami and swiss on rye from David's Deli at one sitting anyway, he gave him half of it. For free! Said if his legendary generosity went toward motivating his troops, that was enough thanks for him.

So feeling motivated at least in spirit, Juhle left Lanier's office and poured himself a cup of coffee, then went to his desk to eat. Juhle couldn't *believe* how good the sandwich tasted. The pastrami was still warm, the Swiss cheese nearly melted, the mustard pungent enough to get his eyes watering. It somehow made even the stale coffee more than palatable. For a second, he idly wondered if maybe Lou or his wife hadn't yet heard of the concept of "sandwich" as a possible lunch item. Maybe Juhle could swing by David's and buy a few pounds of lunch meats and cheeses, a selection of condiments and some loaves of rye bread, deliver it all across the street, and leave Chui written assembly instructions. Fresh sandwiches on the menu at Lou the Greek's might improve the dining experience for the city's entire criminal law community for generations to come. As the source of the bounty, Juhle could become a cultural hero.

Meanwhile, though, he thought as he ate the last delectable bite, he was a cop on a case that, if his gut was right, looked like it was about to become a righteous, high-profile homicide. Suddenly energized, he pushed back from his desk and went out the door, where he turned left and began to jog down the hallway toward the elevators.

The ambient temperature in the medical examiner's lab was fifty-five degrees. Since this was very close to the average San Francisco temperature regardless of season or time of day or night, most of the time visitors to the morgue were dressed in enough layers of clothing that they didn't notice the chill. Today though, the city basked in its sixth consecutive day of an unusually warm Indian summer and Juhle was in shirtsleeves. In his hurry to get downstairs after dawdling in his sandwich reveries, the jog had worked up a light sweat. Now, standing with Strout over the table where Caryn Dryden's body lay, he found he was having to fight himself to keep his teeth from chattering.

Oblivious to his visitor's discomfort, lost in his work as he always was, the medical examiner had paused in his perusal of the internal organs, most of which—Juhle was happy to see—were thankfully still inside the body cavity. Now Strout probed at a spot in the skull at the temple in front of the right ear, the surrounding area of which he'd shaved bare. "I went ahead and measured the diameter of the depressed skull fracture, which here you can see. I've concluded this was probably caused by an object with a rounded cylindrical surface like, say, a baseball bat."

"Why do you say that?"

"No cut. Nothing with an edge, anyway. This looks like somethin' round hit her."

"You got a round indentation in the skull?"

Strout nodded. "I'd say enough to knock her out, which might have been the point of it."

Juhle persisted. "But something round?"

"Looks like that from the fracture."

"A wine bottle?"

"Coulda been."

Juhle folded his arms over his chest for warmth. "There was a wine bottle in the trash compactor."

Strout nodded, then spoke in his trademark Southern drawl. "You want to go get it from evidence and bring it on down, I could tell you if that's probably what hit her. They ought to check that sucker for prints and blood and hair, which you're probably already doin', right? Although, the guy had any brains, he washed it before . . ." Suddenly the ME frowned. "The trash compactor?"

"Yep. In the kitchen."

Strout wagged his head. "Most folks here in the city, don't you think, if we get glass, we recycle it?"

Strout was right. Most San Franciscans of a certain economic level—and the Gorman/Drydens fit within it—recycled glass and paper as a matter of course. The city even provided separate receptacles for regular pickup. The people he was talking about simply did not normally throw an empty wine bottle into a trash compactor. "So what does that say to you, John?" Juhle asked.

"Well, two things. One, whoever threw it away wasn't thinking straight, maybe in a panic over what he'd just done. Two, maybe he didn't know where they normally threw away the recycling."

"I don't like that one so much," Juhle said.

"Why not?"

"It would tend to eliminate the husband."

"Yes, I s'pose it would. You thinkin' it was him?"

Juhle played it close. "He called it in. It would help if I knew what time she died, since he says he didn't get into town until six this morning."

"Well, if that's true, it wasn't him. Although due to the hot tub immersion, the exact timin's goin' to be squishy, I'm afraid."

"I don't want to hear that."

An amused flicker crossed Strout's face. "Somehow I didn't think you did, Inspector, but even so there might be enough to hang your man."

"I'm listening."

"Well, the plain fact is that by the time we got my people there this morning, she was in full rigor, meaning she'd been dead at least an hour."

"One hour? I thought—"

"I know what you thought—that rigor kicks in at about two hours. But the heat speeds it up and it can be well advanced in an hour."

"Which would have given the husband plenty of time."

"Maybe it would have. 'Cept for one thing."

"What's that?"

For an answer, Strout reached out and grabbed Caryn's arm by the wrist, lifting it to bend at the elbow. When he let it go, it fell back down to the table. "The rigor's pretty well passed, as you can see. Time we got her in here and on the table, which was eight forty-three exactly, it had already got to where you could move her joints if you exerted some pressure. So full rigor, which is from about hour three to hour eight, was over. And that makes the latest time of death at twelve forty-three, or sometime the hour before."

"What about her body temperature?"

Strout shook his head. "Useless here, I'm afraid. She cooked up to right around one-oh-five. Her core temp when my staff arrived at her house was a hundred and three. When she got here it was still over a hundred. You want, you can put on some gloves and get a feel for where she's at right now. Go ahead."

"I'll pass, John, thanks."

"Well, suit yourself." He put his own rubber-gloved hand into the cavity he'd cut below her chest, and nodded as though verifying something to himself. "Damn close to what you and me are right now," he said. "My guess is she was in the tub most of the night, and that agrees with the time of death we're talking about."

Juhle folded his arms and tried to rub some life into them. "So she didn't drown?"

"You cold, Inspector? We could get you a lab coat. No?"

"I'm fine, thanks."

"Can't let it get too warm in here. You know what I'm sayin'? But to answer your question. Yes, she did drown. Probably got knocked out first, then held under the water. But definitely drowned."

"The blow to the head? Would it have killed her if she didn't drown first?"

"No. My guess is somebody pushed her down and held her. Probably didn't take thirty seconds. And, of course, she probably couldn't put up much of a fight. But it's going to be a hell of a thing to prove."

Juhle frowned. "Why's that?"

Strout lovingly ran his rubber-gloved thumb over the shaved contusion. "Well, this area around the fracture we're looking at. You can see it's got some swelling, which means blood flowed to it after she got it. Any good defense attorney is going to say that she just banged her head sometime before she hopped in the tub, and there's no real solid way anybody's gonna prove she didn't. And by the way, her blood alcohol was point one one, so she was legally drunk, plus she had what looks on the first scan like she had some opiate on board . . ."

44   JOHN LESCROART

"Vicodin," Juhle said.

Strout shrugged. "Don't know yet, but could be. The point is, she could have just passed out from the wine and drugs and heat and slipped under the water and drowned. No way to prove she didn't."

"So you're not going to call it a homicide?"

Strout knew the game intimately, and his enjoyment of it played on the features of his face. "Well, it's a homicide, you know, until I rule otherwise. And from what I'm seeing here, with this bump, I'm not going to call it suicide. So the door's still open for you anyway."

"But you're not ready to call it a homicide?" Juhle broke an easy grin. "I'd buy you a nice lunch at Lou's."

"Can't. Sorry. Not there yet. If it was a murder, and just between us I'm thinkin' it probably was, you got yourself a tough row to hoe. Guy did a hell of a good job, just speakin' from a professional point of view. Gonna be damn hard to prove a righteous murder since I can't swear on the stand that it even was one. They'll ask me if it could have been an accident or even a suicide, and I'm gonna have to tell them yes. And that's not what you want to hear, is it?"

"Okay, but here's the other image I can't seem to get out of my mind."

After he left Strout, Juhle had stopped upstairs on the third floor where the DAs worked, and in particular the cramped office of an assistant district attorney named Gerry Abrams. Juhle was seated in the uncomfortable wooden chair behind the desk of Gerry's office mate, who was in court for the afternoon. "Stuart Gorman gets home at the ungodly morning hour of what? Six o'clock, six thirty, some-where in there, right? You ever start a drive at two a.m.? Me? Never. Anyway, he putzes around for a while, goes upstairs and sees the bed is empty, then goes down and out to the hot tub and finds his wife. You with me?"

Abrams, feet up on his desk, hands templed at his mouth, opened his eyes and inclined his head about an inch. He was paying

close attention. He made a circle in the air with his index finger, indicating that Juhle should keep talking.

"Okay, so he pulls her out of the tub and when the first cops arrive, he's doing CPR on her." Juhle stopped. "Get it?" he asked.

Abrams opened his eyes again. "What's the problem with that? If
he knows CPR, he's going to try . . ."

But Juhle held out his palm. "Not so fast, Tonto. The problem,
according to what I just heard from Strout, is that this would have
been while she was still in absolutely full rigor. She was stiff as a
board. And I don't care how much experience somebody has with seeing dead people. Even if it's your first time, you're not going to mistake a body that's already stiffened up with somebody who's got a
chance to get resuscitated."

"Probably true." Abrams' eyes flicked the corners of the room.
"And the point is?"

"The point," Juhle said, "is that Gorman obviously had to know
his wife was dead. How could she not be? He was putting on a show
for when the guys from Central Station answered the emergency call
and showed up. They come in and see him doing CPR . . . you see
what I'm saying? He looks like he's trying to help, not like he killed
her."

"Maybe he just panicked and was really trying to save her."

"Gerry, she'd been dead underwater for six hours. This isn't like a
close call."

"In real life, maybe not. But it's colorable, as they say, to a jury. If
I'm defending him, I can hear myself: 'Ladies and gentlemen of the
jury, in the intense emotion of finding his beloved wife of twenty
years dead in the hot tub, Mr. Gorman couldn't think of any other response than to try and breathe some life back into her, even if it
seemed impossible. He loved her so much, maybe that love could
produce a miracle. There was literally nothing else he could do.' "
Abrams spread his hands. "This flies on gilded wings, Dev. Two or
three out of your twelve are going to completely accept it, no problem."

"I can't."

"Well, of course not. It's ridiculous on the face of it. So since when has that been a reason not to make an argument to a jury?" Abrams finally brought his feet to the floor and pulled himself up in his chair, elbows on his desk. "How's his alibi?"

"He says he was on the road, driving down from Echo Lake, a little southwest of Tahoe. Leaving, as I believe I've mentioned, at two o'clock because he couldn't sleep."

"So he could have left at say, eight the night before, and who would know?"

"Right. Nobody."

"So you think it's him?"

While he'd been talking, Juhle had straightened out a paper clip and now he was bending it around his finger. "I'll tell you what I got in some kind of order and then you tell me. First, she'd told him just Friday that she wanted a divorce. Second, she made a ton of money— I mean, evidently a large ton—and now it's all his, although he's never really cared much about money."

"No," Abrams said. "Me neither."

"Few are so shallow," Juhle agreed. "Then the CPR thing. Except really for truly, it doesn't strike me that he's in any kind of mourning. Their daughter being hurt by all this, okay, that got to him. But the wife? They were over anyway."

"You got all that from him? From Gorman?"

"Most of it. Not the CPR. But everything else, horse's mouth. Finally, he plants this scenario with Vicodin and alcohol and a hot tub with a temperature of exactly a hundred and five degrees, which he just happens to mention to me in case I needed to have a theory for how she died. And which, p.s., fits the facts perfectly."

Abrams, his eyes with a faraway look they got when he was concentrating, scratched at a blemish in the wood of his desk. "Too perfectly, you're thinking."

Juhle nodded. "Strout even said it was a damn professional-looking job."

Finally, Abrams met Juhle's eye. "Well, you've got your work cut out. Especially if his alibi holds. I wouldn't go near a grand jury yet with what you've got." Abrams paused, shook his head disconsolately. "Strout's sure, huh? Cause of death was drowning?"

Juhle nodded.

"'Cause drowning is a bitch to prove murder. Any sign of struggle?"

"Just the bump."

Abrams was staring at the wall behind Juhle's head. Suddenly he snapped back into focus, flashed a quick smile. "Well," he said, "it's early innings. Meanwhile, you hear about the woman's body they found this morning out in the flats in the bay?"

"No. What about her?"

"She was so ugly even the tide wouldn't take her out."

"Wow." Juhle shook his head in admiration. "A joke, right? And people say lawyers don't have a sense of humor."

SIX

———

WES FARRELL RARELY WORE A COAT and tie except when he was in court, and almost never when, as now, he was in his third-floor suite at the Sutter Street offices of Freeman, Farrell, Hardy & Roake. When Gina walked in on him after returning from her frustrating time in Department 21, one of the courtrooms in the Hall of Justice, the near-legendary schlumpiness that was Wes's trademark was even more pronounced than usual. He wore only a T-shirt, red running shorts that read STANFORD across the back, a pair of black knee-length socks, and Birkenstock sandals. His long gray-brown hair was partially tied up in his usual ponytail and he was down on one knee over by what passed for a work desk by the window. Wes liked to think that he had the world's greatest collection of epigrammatic T-shirts, and perhaps he was right. The one he wore today read I'M OUT OF MY MIND . . . PLEASE LEAVE A MESSAGE.

"Am I interrupting something?" Gina asked, mostly in jest. "What are you doing?"

"Training Gert, or trying to." He looked vaguely over to the other side of the large room. His office was haphazardly decorated, to say the least: a couch with some floral touches, a battered coffee table, two leather upholstered chairs, a television set on an old library table, a sagging Barcalounger over by the wet bar, which was in turn piled with drafts of legal briefs and old newspapers. "C'mere, girl, come *on*, now! Bring the ball. Good girl."

Gina stepped farther into the room, closing the door behind her, and only then saw Wes's new Labrador puppy chewing a yellow Nerf basketball. As soon as she saw Gina, the dog forgot the ball entirely and bounded across to her, tail wagging, turning in little circles, jumping up. Wes hopped up to his feet, scolding. "No, Gertie. No, no, no. Bad girl."

Gina reached down to pet the dog, who was now on her back in apparent dog glee. "It's all right, Wes. She's a good girl." Gina scratched her belly. "Aren't you, sweetheart? Good girl." Then, to Wes, "Have you been bringing her in here a lot?"

"Nothing on my calendar this afternoon. I thought I'd work on her fetching. I'm starting to think she's got a learning disorder or something."

"ADHD," Gina said. "All dogs have it."

"Bart didn't." For nearly fifteen years, Bart had been Wes's pet, a good-size boxer that he'd had to put down a few months before. The experience had nearly broken his heart until his girlfriend, Sam, had come home with Gert about three weeks ago. "You threw a ball for Bart, he knew what to do with it. Gertie doesn't have a clue. Maybe it's a guy thing."

"A guy thing?"

"You know, Bart was a guy. Gertie's a girl. Maybe girl dogs don't like ball games."

"Maybe you haven't trained her yet, Wes. Could that be it?"

"I'm trying. We've been at it half an hour now and look at her." Gert was still enjoying the tummy rub Gina was administering. "Hopeless."

Gina straightened up and brushed some dog hair off her skirt.

"Well, keep at it. I'm sure she'll get it someday." Suddenly, she seemed to notice her partner for the first time. "Nice outfit, by the way. Very professional. I'd like to have seen Phyllis's face when you passed her."

Phyllis, the firm's elderly, opinionated and dictatorial reception- ist, manned the phone banks from an oval station in the center of the lobby one floor down with all the warmth and personality of a gla- cier. Wes looked down at himself and shrugged. "She has yet to see me this afternoon. I came up by elevator directly from the garage." A pause. "Hey, I told you I wasn't expecting clients," he said. "Or company."

"Well, I'm afraid you've got it." She boosted a haunch onto the back of the couch and swung her leg back and forth. "I've just come from the Hall. You know how many lawyers they have on the list waiting to pull conflicts cases? It used to be twenty-five. You'd get a day about once a month. Now it's a hundred and ten. You're lucky to get three days a year."

Walking across the room, Farrell picked up the Nerf ball, cleared a space on his library table, and sat on it. "Three's not a big number. I guess the word's out. You bill the city and you get paid. It's a good gig. Gertie." He wagged the Nerf ball, threw it back across the room, and came back to Gina. "And you never know what you get. Last time I went down, all I got was a deuce"—a drunk driving case— "and had to plead it out. The guy was doing fine, almost passed the field sobriety test, but when the cop asked him when he started drinking, his answer was 'Panama, 1989.' "

"Wonderful," Gina said.

"Why were you there, though? Last I looked, we had a pretty good caseload downstairs. Besides which, I thought you'd more or less retired from, as we say, the active practice of the law." He pointed. "Get it, girl. Get it."

"Yeah, well, I thought about it a lot over the weekend and decided it was time I jumped back in. I'm a lawyer; I ought to do some law."

"What about the book?"

"The book isn't going anywhere. It'll be there if I decide to go back to it. It also isn't going anywhere in the literal sense. It's just something to hide behind." Gina glanced over to where Gertie was circling the ball, sniffing at it. "Anyway, I didn't want to steal away billing hours from the kids. I've always kept my name on the conflicts list, and I decided I'd take my turn this time instead of passing."

On the library table, the intercom on the phone buzzed and Wes picked it up. "Yes, Phyllis? How intuitive of you, dear. Yes, she is. Hold on a second, I'll put her on. Can I tell her who it is?" His eyebrows went up. "Really? In person?" Holding the mouthpiece out to her, he whispered, "Jedd Conley. Not in person, but on the phone."

For any number of reasons, Gina didn't want to talk to Jedd Conley in a room with anybody else in it, so she had Phyllis ask the assemblyman to wait for a minute while she said good-bye to Wes, then swiftly descended the stairs from his office down to the main lobby. There, she gave Phyllis the signal that she'd take the call in her own corner office and she half-ran the length of the hall, picking up on the second ring. "Hello. This is Gina."

"Gina. It's Jedd Conley."

"That's what I heard, but I wasn't sure I believed it. It's been a long time."

"Yes, it has. We've both been busy, haven't we?"

"You a little more than me. How are you?"

"I'm good. Basically good. And yourself?" He lowered his voice. "I was so sorry to hear about David. The man was a giant."

She stifled a sigh. "Yes, well . . . thank you. Are you calling from Sacramento?"

"No. I'm in town, down at the Travelodge on Lombard. You know it?"

"Sure. But to be honest, I've never really thought of you as a Travelodge kind of guy. You're staying there?"

"Actually, I'm with a friend of mine who is in the way of needing a lawyer right away."

"If memory serves, Jedd, wouldn't that be you?"

"Not anymore. I haven't been in a courtroom in years. Since not long after you and I had a few of our last . . . tussles, actually."

Gina felt a flush rise in her face. She and Jedd had never been seriously involved on an emotional level, but long before Conley had gotten married, they'd indeed had some tussles in each other's bedrooms as well as in the courtroom. "Well, I'm flattered you called, but I must say I'm a little surprised that you thought of me."

"Well, you're an excellent attorney, that's why."

"Who never once beat you in court, if I recall, and I do."

"That's because all of your clients were guilty."

"I guess that's true," she admitted ruefully. "So what about your friend? Is he guilty?"

"Stuart Gorman," Conley said. "And no. He's not guilty. But he does need a lawyer making sure he doesn't screw things up and to walk him through the process." After a small hesitation, he said, "I know this is short notice, but that's the way these things go."

"It's not that," Gina said. "Actually, the timing couldn't be better. You're talking about Stuart Gorman the writer?"

"Yep. You've heard of him?"

"Not until a couple of hours ago. But in the small-world department, I just had lunch with the cop who talked to him at his house this morning."

"You're kidding."

"Not. Devin Juhle. Who, by the way, isn't as sure as you that your friend just needs to walk through it."

"He say that?"

"I read between the lines. But he's a cop. They always think that."

"Well, he hid his suspicions pretty well. Stuart thought he was a good guy."

"Maybe he is. He just thinks that if he's got a dead spouse on his hands, the other spouse probably has something to do with it."

"Not this time. Do you think you could come on down?"

"When?"

"More or less now."

A silence, then Gina said, "I'm thinking. You know that I've never defended anyone in a murder case?"

"It won't come to that," Conley said.

"I'm not sure Inspector Juhle would agree with you."

"All right. But even if it does, haven't your partners both done murder trials?"

"Yes, but they wouldn't . . . I mean . . ." Suddenly Gina shook herself. "Oh, what am I saying? Of course I'm interested. I just don't want to misrepresent myself to your client."

"He's not my client. He's my friend. He'd be your client."

"Okay," she said. "But make sure you tell him what I told you. He's got to know who he'll be dealing with."

"So you're coming down?"

"Give me a half hour."

"Gina. Thanks for coming." Jedd reached out to shake her hand. His eyes took in all of her with one approving glance. He covered their grip with his other hand and held it. "I thought under the rules we were supposed to look older as time went by."

She shook her head, smiling up at him. "Don't start. You haven't held up all that badly yourself." She tightened her grip briefly, then withdrew her hand. "Am I on time?"

"Neither the police nor the press have reappeared yet, if that's what you mean."

"That's what I mean."

"Then you're on time. Come on in."

He turned to reveal the two people who'd just gotten up off the couch behind him. "Gina Roake, Stuart Gorman. And this is Debra . . ." He stopped on a questioning note.

The beautiful young woman stepped forward. "Dryden," she said, shaking Gina's hand with a cool, firm grip. "Debra Dryden. I'm

Stuart's sister-in-law. Caryn's sister." She half-turned and rested her hand protectively on Stuart's arm, bringing him up into the introduction, her body language trumpeting at the very least a strong attraction for her dead sister's husband. "We're so glad you could come."

"I just hope I can be of some help." Gina reached around Debra and extended her hand. "Mr. Gorman, nice to meet you."

"Stuart," he said, "not Mr. Gorman." He took her hand. "Everybody seems to agree that I need a lawyer, so thanks for coming."

Gina cocked her head. "So I gather you don't agree."

He shrugged. "As I've mentioned to all and sundry, I wasn't here when my wife died, so I think it might be a stretch to conclude that I killed her."

"It might be at that," Gina said. "But you want to be careful what you say when you talk to the police. Did Jedd tell you that just coincidentally I had lunch with Inspector Juhle today? I didn't get the impression that he thought your wife's death was a suicide. Or that you couldn't have been involved."

Stuart lifted his shoulders, then dropped them. "Well, he'll find out. I wasn't around."

"Where were you?"

"Up at my cabin. We've got a place up on Echo Lake."

Gina took a beat. "You were at Echo Lake this last weekend?"

"Yeah. Why's that such a surprise?"

"Because so was I. Tamarack Lake, actually, right beyond Echo."

"Hey, I was there too. I mean, at Tamarack. God, could that have been just last night? It seems like a year ago. You really were at Tamarack?"

She nodded. "Camping. On the western shore."

Stuart was warming to the conversation, his face showing signs of animation now through the fatigue. "I was on my favorite rock on the east side just at sundown."

"Oh my God." Gina was caught up in it herself. "I think I might have even seen you."

But Debra cut in. "Well, all this is really special, but whether or

not anybody saw Stuart up there isn't really the point, is it? Unless"—
she spoke to Gina—"unless you saw him leave his cabin early this
morning."

Debra's tone brought Gina up short. There was more, it seemed
to her, than mere protectiveness here. It struck her as jealousy, which
might mean something going on between Debra and Stuart.

Debra again put her hand on Stuart's arm, and this time he covered it with his own and left it there for a moment. "It doesn't matter
where you were last night at sundown, Stuart. It matters that you
didn't leave your cabin until sometime early this morning."

Gina realized that everybody else in the room knew more about
the particulars of the case than she did. "What time, Stuart?" she
asked.

"Two," he said.

Gina's face showed her dissatisfaction with that answer. "Two in
the morning?"

"Maybe we all ought to sit down?" Jedd said. "Catch up on our
facts."

Two chairs bracketed the small couch. Gina and Jedd took them
as Stuart and Debra went around the coffee table and sat next to each
other on the couch.

As soon as everyone was settled, Gina came forward in her chair
and repeated her earlier question. "Stuart, you're telling me you left
your cabin at two this morning?"

He nodded. "I couldn't sleep, so I decided to drive on down and
beat the traffic."

"Did you stop anywhere for gas or anything like that?"

Another nod. "I pulled off and got gas just outside Sacramento.
Used the bathroom." He suddenly shifted and brought his arm off
the back of the couch, reaching into his back pocket, coming out
with his wallet. "Here you go," he said after a quick search. "ARCO
All-Nite in Rancho Cordova. Four fifteen a.m., this morning." He
held the receipt out to Gina.

But striking quickly, Debra took it first and gave it a glance.

When she was done, she passed it over to Conley, who looked at Stuart and said, "Well, there's your alibi." Finally, he gave it to Gina.

"I told you," Stuart said. "I wasn't here."

"If they've got a security video there," Gina said, "it's even better."

Jedd Conley nodded. "There you go."

"Well," Gina added, "it's not a lock, but it's a help."

Finally, the pressure and weariness seemed to weigh in on Stuart. He came forward on the couch, frustration etched in his features. For the first time, he raised his voice. "I don't understand how I keep hearing things like 'It's not a lock.' *What's* not a lock? I didn't kill my wife. What's so hard to understand about that?"

Debra put a restraining hand on his knee and left it there. Depleted, Stuart sank back into the seat of the couch.

Gina, noting the physical connection, drew a breath to give herself a minute. If Stuart and Debra were lovers, it complicated matters considerably. She forced a conversational tone. "Stuart, she had a large bump on her head."

"I know that," he said.

"Possibly enough to have knocked her out."

"Possibly," he said, "but even Juhle said not definitely. Maybe she fell down. That happens too."

"Yes, it does." Gina wasn't going to argue. "You told Inspector Juhle that she told you Friday she was filing for divorce. Yes?" She didn't wait for a reply. "How much insurance did your wife carry?"

"I think the policy was for three million on each of us."

Gina's eyebrows went up a fraction of an inch. "Three million," she said flatly. "And besides that, how much money are you worth today?"

"I don't really know. I haven't thought about that."

"All right. But in any event, your own personal net worth is many millions more than it was on Friday, isn't it?"

"I suppose so."

"You suppose so. And Inspector Juhle knows that too, doesn't he? Because you told him, am I right?"

"Maybe not all the details, but yeah. All right. Generally."

"And you also told him about how resentful you felt toward your wife? And in fact, that you'd spent all of this past weekend just thinking about how much you hated her?"

Jedd spoke up. "You didn't say that, did you, Stu?"

A shrug. "I might have. 'Hate' sounds a little strong. I don't remember saying I exactly hated her."

"I don't think Juhle was making stuff up when he was telling me about it at lunch, to say nothing of the fact that he'll have your exact words on tape anyway," Gina said.

Clearly, the fact that Juhle had secretly taped him began to sink in and shake him.

She softened her voice still further. "All I'm saying, Stuart, is that you are a big blip on Juhle's radar, and you shouldn't let the bare fact of your innocence, and even an apparently strong alibi, lull you into thinking that you couldn't find yourself in a world of hurt and charged with your wife's murder. That bump on her head is bad news. So is your newfound wealth, like it or not. And let's not even talk about the fact that you have something of a public face, which the media will eat up before you know what hit you. Even innocent, even with your alibi, you could turn into the next O.J. Simpson in a heartbeat." She sat back, nearly finished. "That's why it's better to err on the side of caution here, and not let you talk to the cops alone anymore."

"But unlike me, O.J. actually did it," Stuart said.

"No." Gina shook her head. "According to the law, which did not prove him guilty, he was innocent, even if in fact he was not. And— listen up, Stuart—just as easily, the law could find that you did kill your wife, even if in fact you didn't. You've got to understand that and take it very, very seriously. The law is not about the fact of guilt or innocence. It's about the settlement of disputes. So basically what we're trying to avoid here is having you become any part of the dispute about who killed your wife. And you're already damned close to being smack in the middle of it, which is where you don't want to be. Is that clear enough?"

Stuart said, "I think it stinks."

"I couldn't agree more. But it's reality. Now, if you don't mind, I'm going to place a call to Inspector Juhle and tell him that you've retained me and that of course we're anxious to cooperate with his investigation in any way we can, but that I've instructed you not to talk to him outside of my presence from now on. You think you can live with that?"

Stuart still didn't like it, but he gradually started to nod. "It sounds like I have to."

"That's the right answer." No nonsense now. Gina got her cell phone out of her briefcase and started punching numbers.

"And now, if both of you don't mind," Gina said, "I wonder if Stuart and I could have a private discussion."

Debra's back straightened, an electric shock through her. Her eyes suddenly blazed as she whirled around on the couch. "What for?"

Gina, annoyed, threw her a quizzical look. "I'd think that would be obvious enough. We need to talk about strategy and then he can catch me up on everything I've missed."

"You haven't missed anything. Haven't we just established here between us that he didn't do anything wrong? He got home this morning and called emergency, then had the talk with your inspector, which you already seem . . ."

Stuart butted in. "Deb. It's okay. That's why she's here."

"But you need . . . I mean . . ." She couldn't express exactly what she meant, and tried it again. "I don't think we should have to go. We can be here to help you if you need anything."

"It's the attorney-client privilege," Jedd said. "If you talk to your lawyer and you let somebody else listen in, the privilege doesn't apply."

"But," Debra said, "this isn't a good time for him to be alone."

"He won't be alone," Gina told her. Matter-of-factly, putting on a tight smile, she added, "I'm afraid that this isn't really a request." She spoke to Stuart. "It's a condition."

Stuart nodded. "Don't worry, Deb. I'll be fine. She's on our side."

Jedd was already on his feet. "Stuart's right, Debra. The best thing we can do is let them go to work."

Worrying her lower lip, Debra seemed to be fighting it for another second, but finally she shrugged, huffed an "Okay, then," and stood up. Stuart got up with her. She put a hand on his arm one more time and told him she'd be on her cell phone if he needed her. "Have you had anything to eat? I could bring you dinner when you're done here. Or we could go out."

"Maybe," he said, "but I've got to be picking up Kym sometime. She's taking the bus up from Santa Cruz."

"Oh God, that's right. Kym. We could go down to Greyhound and get her together. Just let me know."

"I will."

Jedd Conley was standing by the open door, holding it. "Gina, if you need anything else from me, you've got all my numbers. And again, thanks for coming." He cast an expectant glance at Debra, motioned to the doorway.

Debra turned and clipped a cold "Yes, thank you" in Gina's direction.

When they'd gone, Gina sat down in her chair and let Stuart get comfortable on the couch. Meeting his eyes, she smiled. Sitting back, adopting a casual air, she crossed her legs. "So," she said, gently now, "how are you holding up?"

The question caught him off guard. He rubbed a palm along his unshaved cheek. Finally, he drew in a lungful of air and let it out. "Not too well. I keep thinking this can't be real, that I'm going to wake up and it won't have happened."

"I know. That's how it feels at first." Gina took in her own deep breath. "My fiancé was killed a few years ago. Sometimes it still doesn't feel real."

"I'm sorry," he said.

Gina shrugged. "You go on." Regrouping, not having meant to reveal even so little about herself, she said, "But you've already told Inspector Juhle that you and your wife were having troubles."

"Having troubles doesn't mean I wanted her to die."

"No, of course not. But how you felt about her may become an issue. It is an issue."

"Is that a question?"

"This is one: Did you love her?"

He hesitated, scratched at the birthmark near his eye. "Once upon a time I did."

"But not anymore?"

"We just weren't very compatible anymore. We didn't like to do the same kinds of things. But until last Friday . . . I don't know, I had more or less considered it another phase that we'd probably get through like we'd gotten through other ones. Our daughter just started college a couple of weeks ago, and the house felt different without her, but I figured it would settle back to normal sometime. Until then, I'd just wait it out."

"So you didn't want the divorce? On your own?"

"I wasn't actively thinking about it before she mentioned it, if that's what you mean."

Gina nodded. "Close enough. So you weren't fighting?"

"No. She worked all the time and I mostly tried to keep out of her way when she was home. But we hardly talked enough to fight."

Gina took a beat, then came out with it. "What about her sister?"

Stuart's face went dark. "What about her?"

"You and her."

"What are you talking about? There's no me and her. Deb and I are friends."

"Yes, I could see that. Your wife wasn't jealous of her?"

"No. Or, at least she had no reason to be."

"That's not the same thing. I'm just telling you that if you have been having an affair with your wife's sister, and it gets out, which it will if you were, it's going to cause problems."

Stuart's voice went up a notch. "It wouldn't mean I killed Caryn, for Christ's sake!"

But Gina needed to nail down this fact. She uncrossed her legs and leaned toward him. "So for the record, Stuart, your relationship with Debra is not now and never has been intimate?"

"No. Yes. Correct, is what I'm trying to say."

Sufficiently ambiguous, Gina thought, and nicely camouflaged. But she simply said, "Okay. Because if you were involved with her, it would be a very strong motive."

"I just said I'm not."

"I know you did." She stared at him and waited.

He returned her steady gaze for several long seconds, unbending. Finally, he came forward on the couch himself. "Besides which," he said, "I was at Echo Lake when Caryn was killed, or died, or killed herself. I believe I've said this once or twice. So who cares what motive I might or might not have? I couldn't have done it."

"Yes," Gina said. "I know that." Again she waited.

"What?" he asked.

"You're not going to like what I'm going to ask you next, and I want you to know that I'm not being accusatory. I'm trying to get my arms around where you are."

This almost brought him to a resigned grin. "I think I can take it."

"All right. If you still loved Caryn enough to say that you were committed to your marriage before she mentioned divorce on Friday, I'm just wondering about where you're putting any sign of grief. Are you sorry, or even sad, that your wife of twenty-some years is suddenly gone? Because if you are, I'm not getting much of a sense of it."

"I told you. It hasn't sunk in yet. I'm probably in shock. I don't know how I'm feeling, to tell you the truth. Conflicted, I guess. Confused. If there's a book or something on proper feelings you're supposed to have when your wife dies, I haven't read it. I loved her once.

We used to be great. Lately we haven't gotten along very well. Last weekend I finally let myself get pretty pissed off at her, and this morning I come home and she's dead." His shoulders sank as he sat back, rubbed at his cheek again. "You mentioned sad. I don't know if I'm sad. I don't know how much I'm going to miss her. I'm sorry if that's the wrong answer."

"There isn't a wrong answer," Gina said. "And even if there were, that was a pretty good one. So what was it that made you stop getting along?"

He barked a one-note, bitter laugh. "Everything. Money, issues with Kymberly, money, me, her, time. Did I mention money?"

"What about money?"

"She became obsessed with it. I didn't."

"Obsessed how?"

"The way people get obsessed with anything. It's all she thought about, cared about, worked on, you name it. If it wasn't going to make her money, she wasn't interested."

"And you didn't feel the same way?"

"Not even close." He held up a hand. "It's a flaw in my character, I know. And if you didn't know, she'd tell you."

"Are you saying she complained about you to other people? In public?"

"I imagine so. She complained about me to me enough."

"But you weren't fighting? Were you ever tempted to hit her?"

"Tempted? Sure. Did I ever? No. Let me ask you one: Juhle really thinks somebody killed her? He thinks this was a murder?"

Gina nodded. "I got the very strong impression he's leaning that way."

This gave Stuart a moment of pause. His eyes scanned the corners of the ceiling, then came back to Gina. "I'm starting to be pretty glad they talked me into you," he said.

SEVEN

Juhle got Gina Roake's message that she was representing Stuart Gorman, but couldn't do anything about it in the near term. He was only a few blocks away from the Travelodge, but he was on his way to Russian Hill to try to talk with some of the neighbors.

He got lucky on his first try. Juhle was sitting in a breakfast nook, talking to Stuart's next-door neighbor, Leesa Moore. Their conversation was competing with the low drone of a television set that sat on the kitchen counter next to the microwave, tuned to some talk show with a male host. Juhle had no idea who the host was or why anyone would want to listen to him talk to his similarly unfamiliar female guest about the details of the two months she'd apparently spent, from what Juhle could gather by half-listening, confined in a basement as a sex slave for three teenage boys in upstate New York.

Leesa Moore was a well-preserved sixty-three-year-old who had lived in this house for twenty-six years, the last five of them alone after her husband had died. She was a retired schoolteacher who volunteered five mornings a week at a library branch in the Marina.

"Especially this past summer," she was saying, "it seemed the fighting was just about constant."

"Between Stuart and Caryn?"

"Oh, yes."

"Did you hear anything like a threat?"

"Like what, exactly?"

"Like, 'I'm going to kill you.' Anything like that?"

"Well, no. Not specifically that. But swearing, a lot of swearing. It surprised me, coming from a doctor like she was. And such a respected writer. You'd think he'd have a better vocabulary. But it was a lot of 'F-this,' and 'F-that," and 'F-you.' I'm sure you can imagine."

"Yes, ma'am." Juhle had used a few F-thises in his life and thought there were worse crimes, but he had his witness talking and wanted to keep her in the mood. "Do you know if the argument had ever led to anything else?"

"Not to my knowledge." Eyes on her television, suddenly Leesa Moore came alive. "Oh my God," she said. "I don't believe it. Do you mind, Inspector, for a minute?" She pointed over to the TV, then reached and turned up the volume. "Look at this. They've got the boys on the show too."

And it was true. The host was explaining that they'd all been released from jail by now and were in their twenties. The poor woman, to whom this turn of events was evidently a surprise, was stuck to her chair, mouth agape, between tears and hysteria. The television audience was going wild.

"That's got to be staged," Juhle said.

"No, no. He does this kind of thing all the time. It's a great show."

Juhle and his witness followed the action together on the screen. After the woman had finally left her chair, got her language beeped as she swore at the host, and ran off the stage in tears, Leesa Moore turned the volume down again to a conversational level and brought her attention back to the inspector. "I'm sorry. Where were we?"

"We were talking about if Stuart and Caryn's yelling at one another had ever led to anything else. Something physical, I mean. And you said you didn't know about it if it had."

"That's right." She squinted in concentration, finally reaching over again and turning the TV sound off entirely. "Except, oh wait, maybe there was one time in the middle of last summer. I don't know if it was because they'd had a fight or something, but I got home from work and there was a police car parked in front of the house."

"Stuart and Caryn's house? Next door?"

"Yes. I stopped and stood by it for a minute, wondering if I should knock and see what had happened and if there was anything I could do to help. But in the end I just came home. When I looked out later—not too much later—it was gone."

"You're sure it had come to their house?"

"Well, no, I wasn't at first, although it was parked right in front of their place. But after it was gone, I called over there and asked Stuart if everything was all right, that I'd seen the police car and all. And he said everything was fine. That it had just been a misunderstanding."

"A misunderstanding?"

"That's what he said."

"About what? Did you ask him?"

"No. He didn't seem anxious to talk very much about it."

"Did you ever notice any kind of marks on Caryn? A black eye? Anything like that?"

She shook her head. "But I didn't see as much of her anyway."

"So you never found out why the police car was there?"

"Well, not from them." The answer seemed to embarrass her. She went on. "Have you talked to the Sutcliffs yet? The neighbors on the other side?"

"Not yet."

"Well, Harriet—Mrs. Sutcliff—she was the one who had called the police. She thought somebody was going to get killed over there."

* * *

Q: Three, two, one. Case number 07-232918. This is Inspector Devin Juhle, badge 1667. The time is quarter after fifteen hundred hours on Monday, September 12th. I am at a residence at 1322 Greenwich Street and speaking with a sixty-four-year-old Caucasian woman who identifies herself as Harriet Sutcliff, the owner of the residence. Mrs. Sutcliff, I appreciate your agreeing to talk with me. How long have you been neighbors with Stuart and Caryn Gorman?

A: Since they moved in here. That was, I guess, fifteen or so years ago.

Q: Did you find them to be good neighbors?

A: Yes. At first. We liked them very much. Especially Art—my husband?—when he found out that Stuart wrote those fly-fishing books. Art's a fisherman himself. So it was really exciting for him getting to know a celebrity like that. But the last couple of years, we haven't seen too much of them.

Q: And why is that?

A: It just seemed that they changed. First they seemed to stop doing social things together. And certainly with us. Stuart would still come by sometimes and talk to Art, but we almost never saw them together anymore. And then, by the summer, they seemed to just be fighting all the time.

Q: You heard them fighting?

A: Yes.

Q: Just words, or more than that?

A: More, I'd say.

Q: Like what?

A: Well, I definitely heard some things breaking over there. As though they were thrown. It was hard not to hear when that happened. And then one day last summer, I didn't want to but I felt I had to call the police. I thought somebody was going to get hurt.

Q: And so you did, in fact, call the police?

A: Yes. And a car came. It stayed a short while, but I don't think anything ever came of that. And since then I haven't talked to either Stuart or Caryn very much. I think they must have figured out that I'd been the one that called and they were mad at me.

Q: Did there continue to be fights after that one?

A: A couple, I think. But none so bad.

Q: Did you hear anything like a fight last night over there?

A: No. We—Art and I—we went to a movie and got back about ten thirty, and it was all quiet over there. Dark. And we were asleep by the time Stuart got home.

Q: By the time Stuart got home?

A: Right.

Q: And what time was that?

A: I don't know exactly. I gather pretty late.

Q: You mean this morning?

A: No, I don't think so. I believe he got home last night.

Q: Why do you believe that? If you were asleep and didn't hear him?

A: Well, I didn't see it myself, but because that's what Bethany said. There was a bunch of us from the block that gathered at the corner this morning. We didn't know what else to do, so we were all standing there waiting for someone to tell us what had happened, although we knew it was probably bad, with all the police and everything.

Q: I'm sorry, Mrs. Sutcliff. Can we go back to Bethany for a minute. Bethany is who?

A: Bethany Robley. She lives across the street, that stucco place right there two houses up. She and Kymberly know each other.

Q: And Bethany told you that Stuart came home last night?

A: That's what she said. She said it was around eleven thirty.

Q: Why did she think that?

A: I got the impression that she saw him. Her bedroom's right in that upstairs front window. You can see it from here, see? I can't believe he actually killed her, though I guess somebody must have. He really seems like such a nice man.

Q: Well, that's still kind of an open question.

*   *   *

The door at the stucco house across the street opened to a heavyset, gray-haired African American woman in a brown jogging outfit. "Yes? Can I help you?"

Introducing himself, Juhle had his badge out, and held it up in his wallet. "Is this the home of Bethany Robley?"

"It is."

"I'd like to ask her a few questions, if you don't mind."

"Maybe I do. I'm her mother. What's this about? What's she done?"

"She's done nothing, ma'am. It's about your neighbors across the street there. The Gormans. You may have heard that Mrs. Gorman died this morning."

"There wasn't any Mrs. Gorman. There was Dr. Dryden, Caryn, married to Stuart, if that's who you mean." Mrs. Robley had her arms crossed, and stepping forward, she completely blocked the door. "And that's got nothing to do with my daughter. She had nothing to do with them."

"I understand she was a friend of Kymberly's, their daughter."

"Okay, that. They know each other, all right, but Kym's gone up to school and she hasn't been over there since . . ."

Behind Mrs. Robley, Juhle heard a younger voice. "It's okay, Mom. I can talk to him."

"Not unless I say so, you can't." The mother came back at Juhle, holding her daughter back with an extended palm. "Are we going to be wanting a lawyer here, Inspector? You think my little girl had anything at all to do with Caryn's dying?"

"I've got no reason to think that, ma'am. I'd just like to ask her a couple of questions about what, if anything, she might have seen last night. From her window."

"And that's all?"

"That's all. Promise."

The mother half turned and Juhle caught a glimpse of a young woman of about his own height. She was wearing a Galileo High sweatshirt, a short black skirt, white tennis shoes.

"I'm gonna be with you the whole time," Mrs. Robley said.

"Fine with me."

A few seconds passed, and then the large woman sighed and moved to the side to let her daughter come forward. Bethany stepped up into the doorway—a clear, wide forehead and a solemn expression on her face. A keen intelligence seemed to emanate from a penetrating gaze out of deeply set eyes. To Juhle, she looked far too serious for a young woman of her age; she could easily have passed for twenty-five.

And Juhle immediately recognized a key truth: If Bethany was going to be one of his witnesses—and he thought that was a reasonable likelihood at this stage—he couldn't have asked for a better one. "I won't take up much of your time," he began. He looked behind Bethany to her mother, held up his tiny tape recorder. "I'd like to record what we say here." He shrugged apologetically. "It's just that I don't take really good notes, and I want to make sure I've got it exactly right. Is that all right with you, Mrs. Robley?"

"Ask my daughter."

Bethany shrugged with a slight awkwardness. "That's okay, I guess."

"Thank you." Juhle quickly dictated his standard intro into the device, then came back to his subject. "Well, Bethany, I was just over at Mrs. Sutcliff's house talking to her, and she told me that you were one of the people with her standing on the corner this morning when I pulled up. Do you remember that?"

"Sure."

"Well, she—Mrs. Sutcliff, I mean—she told me that you said you saw Mr. Gorman get home last night. Is that true?"

"Yes."

"Do you happen to remember roughly what time that was?"

"Actually, I remember exactly. He got home at eleven thirty. That's my lights-out time on a school night, and I was just finishing at my desk when I saw him turn into the driveway."

"And where's your desk?"

"Just under the window there that looks down on the street."

Juhle paused to consider his next question. "And you're sure it was Mr. Gorman? Did you see him get out of the car?"

"No. But it must have been him. He opened the garage automatically and went inside. Then closed it behind him. So I never saw him. But it was his car."

"You know his car on sight?"

Her lip curled downward, the question apparently striking her as insulting. "Sure. I've gone skiing in it with Kym maybe ten times. So yes, I know the car."

"I didn't mean any offense," Juhle said. "I guess I'm just asking how sure you are."

"What? That it was Stuart? I don't know. I told you I didn't see him. But if he was driving his car, it was him. Because that was his car."

"And how did you know that?"

"I don't know. I just knew."

Mrs. Robley decided to put in her two cents. "She knows what she knows, Inspector. She's not lying to you."

"Of course not. There's no question of that." Juhle spoke matter-of-factly to Bethany. "I'm sorry if I sound critical. That's not my intention. I'm just trying to make sure of what you're saying. So now, getting back to Stuart, you watched him pull his car into his garage across the street and then close the garage door behind him?"

"No." Again, the question seemed to frustrate her. "Look, I'm sure. No. I just saw him pull up and I'm like, 'Oh, Stuart's getting home,' and then went over and got in bed. I didn't think anything about it, except that I noticed it. The end. And I didn't sit at the window and watch until he closed the garage door behind him. Why would I do that? It wasn't all that interesting, dull though the rest of my life might be."

Juhle hesitated, a fragment of a barely remembered something nagging at him. "But I believe you said . . . can you give me just a second?"

"Sure. More, if you need."

He thanked her, then walked a few steps down to the sidewalk and rewound the tape recorder. In a minute, he was back up at the door with Bethany. "Here," he said, "listen to this."

When he pushed the recorder's play button, they heard her voice saying, *"No. He opened the garage automatically and went inside. Then closed it behind him. So I never saw him. But it was his car."*

"See?" he said. "You hear it?"

"What?"

"You say, 'Then closed it behind him.' Which you just said you didn't see him do."

"I didn't. See him close it, I mean."

"Well, which is it?"

"It was closed."

"Okay." Juhle rubbed away the crease in his forehead. He killed another few seconds fast-forwarding his tape recorder to the end again, and turned it back to record. Then he said, "Excuse me, Bethany, for being so dumb. But then how did you know it was closed behind him if you didn't see him close it?"

For a brief moment, the question seemed to stump her. Her normally grave expression turned to a look of near-despair before she suddenly broke into a surprisingly quite lovely smile. "Because I saw him *open* it later," she said. "So it had to be closed."

"You saw him open it? When was this?"

"Twelve forty-five. Pretty much exactly again." She brought her shoulders up in a shrug. "I had insomnia. I always have insomnia. I hate it. But then I had to get up and go to the bathroom and

I noticed it had been an hour and fifteen minutes already that I'd been awake, which made me start freaking out about how tired I'd be for school today." She let out a heavy sigh. "And which I am. Was. God."

"So what happened? You looked out the window and . . ."

"And Stuart was backing out again . . ."

"Backing out? At quarter to one in the morning?"

"I know. I thought that was a little weird too. But really, I wasn't thinking too much about him or anything else except getting some sleep." Stifling a sudden yawn, she smiled again. "Sorry. Just talking about it, sometimes, you know . . ."

"I hear you. But I noticed you called Mr. Gorman Stuart. Do you know him well?"

"Not well, no. But he's Kym's dad. I know him okay. He doesn't like to be called Mr. Gorman."

"And you and Kym are friends?"

"Well, kind of. She's a little up and down, you know. Hyper up and then kind of a drag down. And lately not so much. Actual friends, I mean, except we ski together sometimes. Anyway, we've known each other since fourth grade." She brought a finger to her mouth and chewed the end of it. "This is going to kill her."

"Were she and her mom close?"

"No. I mean her dad."

"What about her dad?"

"Well, you just said. What you were investigating. I mean, if he killed her."

"I didn't say that, Bethany. We don't have any one suspect right now. But you're saying Kymberly and her mom didn't get along?"

The girl shrugged. "Her mom was pretty busy most of the time." Reaching back, she touched her own mother's hand briefly, then came back to Juhle. "Caryn wasn't really that bad."

"Did people say she was?"

Bethany shrugged. "Sometimes the two of them—Stuart and Kym—they'd be a little sarcastic. But they both loved her, I think.

You don't think Stuart killed her, do you? I can't believe he'd do anything like that."

Juhle kept it matter-of-fact. "I'm just talking to people, Bethany. Trying to get to what happened. I might have to talk to you again. Would that be all right?"

"Sure. I guess."

Juhle peeked around behind her. "Mrs. Robley?"

"If it's okay with her."

"All right, then. Thank you both for your time."

EIGHT

STUART WAS STANDING BY THE COUCH, stretching. He and Gina had been going over issues for the past couple of hours when suddenly he'd become aware of the time and jumped up. "Well," he was saying, "whether or not we hit most of it, I've got to get going if I want to be on time for Kym, and I do. If Juhle calls you, maybe you can just set up a time we can all talk. But not tonight, okay, please. My girl's going to need me. That's the most important thing right now."

"Sure. Of course." Gina had pulled her heavy satchel over in front of her and dropped her well-used legal pad into one of its sections. "We'll just stay in wait-and-see mode until we hear from Juhle. If he calls me tonight, I'll tell him you need time with your daughter and ask if we can set up a time tomorrow or the next day."

"You think he will? Call you tonight?"

"Maybe not, unless there's been some break in the case we don't know about. Either way, I'll try to check in with him again, get some sense of things." She looked up at him. "Are you sure you're all right?"

He shook his head, weariness now all over him. "Just thinking about Kym." Staring into empty space across the room, he blinked rapidly a few times. "And Caryn. She's really gone, isn't she?"

"I'm afraid so."

Squeezing at his temples, he sighed deeply, then looked across at her. "Jesus, what a waste. What an unbelievable, colossal fucking waste."

The Travelodge was barely a mile from Gina's condominium. Most of it was uphill, true, but to Gina's mind, that just made it a better exercise opportunity. So after she told Stuart that he should go on ahead, that she'd let herself out and get the door, she waited until he'd gone, then took off her black pumps, dropped them into the satchel and replaced them with the pair of tennis shoes that she always carried in her bag.

Outside, the evening was still warm, although the ocean breeze had increased enough to stir up the occasional wisp of dust or debris in the gutters. Gina walked with an athletic ease, her satchel converted to a backpack. Ahead of her, across Van Ness Avenue, the street began its steep climb that summitted at the oft-photographed view of Lombard as the "crookedest street in the world."

When she got to the top, Gina was breathing hard. Good. That's what exercise was—breathing hard. She stopped a minute to take in the view. In front of her, down in the valley, North Beach, the towers of Sts. Peter and Paul Church, and a slice of Fisherman's Wharf, with Telegraph Hill and Coit Tower beyond them. Behind her, the Golden Gate Bridge, the Presidio, and from this height the glint of the sun off the Pacific Ocean on the horizon as well.

She was aware of course that on a lot of days and nights—maybe even most of them—the fog could be so thick here that you couldn't see your hand in front of your face, but when the place conspired with the weather at a moment like this, Gina thought a person could live here for a hundred years and still not grow tired of it.

By the time she got home, down and up another hill and fifteen minutes later, she was ready for a shower. And when that was done, she put on some jeans and a pullover and went into her living room. Like the rest of the condo it was only as big as it needed to be, but very well appointed in an eclectic, comfortable style. A couch with a matching loveseat diagonally faced the brick fireplace with a Navajo rug in front of it. A pair of reading chairs—she had bought the second for David—bracketed the large front window. Built-in bookshelves rose to greet a ten-foot ceiling on both sides of the fireplace.

Now she went to the well-stocked, mirror-backed wet bar in the back corner of the room and took a very small, four-ounce plain leaded crystal glass off the shelf. David had given her a set of four of these, and she loved the feel and the look of them. Pouring an inch of Oban neat, she crossed to her reading chair, where she set the drink on the Chinese lacquered side table and picked up the notes she took when she'd talked to Stuart.

Caryn Dryden, it turned out, had lived a very full and complicated life, replete with personal and medical interactions, investment schemes, research opportunities and business connections. Stuart didn't know the details of most of it, but he'd done the best he could filling Gina in after she'd finally convinced him that if someone had in fact killed his wife, it probably hadn't been random.

Apparently, there were two unrelated areas of activity that had consumed his wife's time and energy in recent months.

The first was that she had been within a couple of months of opening a new, independent practice with a fellow orthopedic surgeon, Robert McAfee. The plans had been in the works for the better part of two years, but Stuart had picked up that something had changed in the past couple of months—he thought she might have been trying to bring in a third partner. She'd complained that she was short of cash, and evidently this third guy could bridge or mitigate the shortfall. But McAfee hadn't been happy. Wasn't happy. He'd been calling her day and night for the past month, threatening to pull out of the deal, but was already so financially committed that that would have been suicide.

Gina sipped her Oban and went on to read over her notes on Stuart's comments when she'd asked him why or how Caryn had run short of money. How did that happen if she was the money wizard who brought in the big bucks?

It was because, Stuart said, she was planning on making even more of the big bucks. Huge bucks. Fuck-you money, she had called it. Caryn had been involved for several years in the development and then the clinical trials for a new replacement hip, the Dryden Socket, which degraded at a much slower rate than the current state-of-the-art hip. The device was evidently very close to full FDA approval and, when approved, it promised to make gazillionaires out of all of its early investors. Of whom Caryn had not only been one, but the inventor as well. Apparently, this investment, too, had run into some kind of last-minute financial difficulties. The investment group's banker had come back to the original investors and offered something called mezzanine loans to hold the company over until government approval.

Stuart didn't know what mezzanine loans were, but Gina did. Very high risk and very short term, they were a common feature of a lot of deals that were close to viable but needed additional capital while the business geared up to profitability. Caryn had plunked more than two million dollars in cash into a mezzanine loan for the Dryden Socket within the past six months. Thereby leaving herself short on her new practice offices when there were the inevitable and unavoidable delays in construction and start-up.

Now, Stuart had said, with Caryn's death, McAfee's ass was saved, since Caryn had been well insured on the project. But the Dryden Socket was apparently still having some problems—serious enough that Caryn had called Jedd Conley's office to look into them. Although what Jedd had had to do with it was a mystery to Stuart.

Outside it had come to dusk. Gina finished her reading and her drink at the same time and sat back in her chair to consider what she thought she now knew. Listening to Stuart's recounting of the labyrinthine convolutions of Caryn's business life, she had by now concluded that murder, and neither accident nor suicide, was going to be a good bet in this case. Add to that Devin Juhle's comment at lunch that Caryn probably wouldn't be naked in a hot tub, thinking her husband was gone for the weekend, having a glass of wine with somebody she didn't know, and the bet became a near certainty.

And—the thought brought Gina up in her chair—if Caryn had told Stuart she wanted a divorce on Friday, would she have been naked in the hot tub with him?

Or maybe she'd just been alone relaxing and he'd unexpectedly come home.

But he hadn't gotten home until this morning. He had that gas station receipt to prove it. And having talked to Stuart all afternoon, Gina didn't think that he had paid someone else to kill his wife. All of which didn't mean he still couldn't be the target of a major investigation. But at least it did not appear that her client was guilty. At this early stage, that was about the best she could hope for.

Feeling good about the way things were going, she decided what the hell, she'd pour herself another small drink. Live a little.

She was back in the game with that rara avis, the innocent client. This was going to be fun.

Here is the fundamental irony of the wilderness experience: Its principal lesson is that we are not alone.

I am standing in the middle of a stream at the hour when the sun begins to clear the ridge out to the east. The shadow of the mountain recedes and reveals a world of vibrant color—beyond gray of rock and indigo sky, suddenly the field explodes into wildflowers—yellows and greens, reds and pinks and blues and whites. A movement out of the corner of my eye turns out to be a buff coyote stalking prey. Downstream, a deer stops for a drink. A jackrabbit breaks from its cover. Overhead, a hawk circles in a rising thermal. On the water, the hatch begins and the air above the stream fills with clouds of mayfly, or caddis, or mosquito.

I cast and a trout strikes.

There are no other humans in sight. From the direct evidence of my senses, there may be none on the planet. And yet my state of being is suffused with a sense of belonging in this place, at this time. I am in the midst of the dream of the Buddhist who, requesting a hamburger, says: "Make me one with everything."

One with everything.

It is singular that this experience of a healing solitude without any sense of loneliness occurs, for me, only in the wilderness. Perhaps it is because there are so few of the expectations of others to accommodate. Here I am responsible only to myself, only for my survival. A day or two out of the blandishments and distractions of daily life—away from the traffic and the small talk and the advertisements, away from the constant assault of vulgar and voracious media of all kinds—and I become increasingly aware of a deep sensory awareness that roots me to the here and now in a profound and fundamental way.

I am connected to the earth and always, immediately, to the present. I am an animal, both prey and predator, keenly tuned. I have no one to convince. There are no complaints. The interruptions are natural.

The fish leaps high in a flash of color, splashes back into its pool, begins a run that strips line and bends the rod. My concentration is absolute. The least slack in the line and the trout will throw the tiny barbless hook, and I will have lost my breakfast. Because make no mistake, if I manage to land it, I will eat this fish.

My appetites, out here, are simple and attainable. I don't need a raise, new clothes, gifts. Money can have no possible meaning. My music is in the stream, in the breeze, the crackle of a fire, the beat of my heart. I am empty of worry. And in this natural state, ironically enough, I get the closest to a feeling of identity with my fellow man.

This is the essence, and I am part of it.

In her reading chair by the front window, Gina put down the copy of Stuart Gorman's *Healed by Water* that she'd picked up at Book Passage after her dinner alone at the Ferry Building. To her surprise, she liked the book a lot. Stuart had absolutely nailed Gina's own feelings about the outdoors and the wilderness—that these things had been her salvation.

Solitude without loneliness. That was exactly what she felt when she went up to the mountains.

Her eyes covered the familiar terrain of her living room. Just after David had died, it had felt as though he had somehow imprinted himself on every object here—the books, his chair of course, the bar and its glassware, the loveseat—and his connection to these things had made her loneliness almost unbearable.

Up in the wilderness, there was nothing reaching out to snag her emotions and remind her of what was gone. Time she spent away from all of this, this *stuff*, lessened its painful hold upon her, until finally she realized that its ability to cause her anguish was all but gone.

She'd needed the wilderness to get to that point. She'd needed the long hiking days and the deep, empty nights for their solitude that seemed to lift the burden of the loneliness that adhered to all these familiar things in the city.

Getting up and walking over to the kitchen, she pulled a card from her purse and picked up the telephone, hoping perhaps to talk to Stuart about how he'd come to understand all of that. What had happened to him that had driven him outdoors? How, she wondered, had they sat together for most of the afternoon and had none of this even remotely come up?

But halfway through the phone number, she stopped and hung

the phone back up. She recalled that he was going to be with his daughter tonight, trying to make sense of what had befallen them. Calling him now would be an imposition.

Back in the living room, settling back in her chair, she pulled the book over to her, opening it again to her place. And then the telephone rang.

"Gina Roake, please."

"This is Gina."

"Devin Juhle. I hope you don't mind my calling you at home."

"I wouldn't have given you the number if I did. But you're working some long hours, Inspector. I'm gathering you got my message about Stuart Gorman."

"I did." He hesitated. "That was a pretty quick hookup, getting him on board as your client. I mean, after our lunch today."

This was gratuitous and Gina supposed she should have expected it. In any event, she wasn't going to dignify the unspoken accusation that she'd called Stuart as a result of what Juhle had told her at Lou the Greek's. She hadn't called him at all, but she'd let Juhle think what he wanted, since that's what he was going to do in any case. "Yes," she said. "The stars lined up just right on that one. I assume you're calling to set up an appointment?"

"I'm going to want to talk to him, yes. Sooner rather than later."

"Do you consider him a suspect?"

"A person of interest at this time."

"You know about his alibi?"

"I know what he's said, yes."

"And you don't believe him?"

"I'd like to go over some details he's mentioned, that's all."

"Well, of course, he's still upset. If you tell me what you need to know, I'd be happy to get the information for you."

"I think I'd rather get it from him directly."

"You don't want to give me a little hint about what this is about?"

"Just making sure I get the story straight. Plug up any holes."

This sounded ominous to Gina. Until this moment, she had been unaware that there was enough of a case for there to be any holes.

Gina knew how dangerous it was to have Stuart talk to the police again. If he said the wrong thing, or maybe even the right thing in the wrong way, she could watch him walk out of her office in hand-cuffs. She knew that many of her colleagues would be appalled by the idea that she'd let her client talk to the cops. But she still hoped she could deflect this investigation, maybe even avoid an arrest alto-gether, if they continued to cooperate. Juhle already had the most damaging parts on tape, and she'd be sitting right there if things got ugly. It was a calculated risk and she figured that she had to try. "I could call him and set something up for tomorrow at my office. Say ten o'clock, if you don't hear back from me."

"I was thinking you both might want to come down to the Hall and talk there."

Now Gina's alarm bells started to go off. The Hall of Justice meant a cold and threatening interrogation room off the homicide detail with both audio- and videotape running. But again, protocol and strategy demanded that she remain cool. "I think we'd all be more comfortable in my office, Inspector," she said. "Of course, you'd be welcome to record the interview. Or even videotape it, pro-vided I get a copy immediately. You're not planning to arrest Mr. Gorman, I hope?"

"I haven't applied for a warrant, no."

"You and I both know you don't need a warrant to arrest him. My question is, are you planning to do that or not?"

"I'm trying to keep my options open. I've got to talk to your client, and I want it all by the book and on the record, which means you're there with us. Ten o'clock will be fine. At your place. If I don't hear back from you."

"All right. I'll see you there."

NINE

WITH A PORCELAIN SAUCER RESTING ON the arm of his chair in Dismas Hardy's office, Wyatt Hunt sat back comfortably and sipped from his cup of freshly brewed coffee. It was Tuesday morning, about a half hour before the offices officially opened. In spite of that, in the space behind them a dozen or more employees had already started their workday. Hardy's office door was still open, and outside from the lobby came the sounds of phones ringing, Xerox machines humming, random bits of conversation.

They were waiting for Gina. Across from Hunt by the well-equipped coffee counter, Hardy finished pouring his own cup and turned around. "So when you talked to Juhle, you didn't let on you were working for us?"

"I don't believe it came up, specifically." Hunt sipped again, broke a grin. "Besides, I thought it might make for a stilted conversation. He asked if I'd seen Gina, and I told him not since lunch, which was technically true. It's not my fault he didn't ask if I'd talked to her. And he seemed to be in the mood—he'd been on Gorman all day and had nobody to talk to about it. This will shock you, but it seems his wife sometimes gets a little tired of cop talk at home."

"How could that possibly be?"

"I know," Hunt said. "Weird, but there you go. Anyway, he really wanted to tell somebody about everything he'd found out, and I happened to call."

"Lucky break for the good guys."

"That's what I thought. Maybe not so lucky for the client, though, unless you consider an eyewitness lucky."

"Sometimes it can be."

"I'm pretty sure this isn't one of those times, Diz." Hunt glanced toward the door. "Ah, the woman of the hour."

Gina stopped in the doorway. "Sorry I'm late, guys. Working the bugs out of what may be the new work schedule."

Hardy checked his watch. "I've got eight o'clock straight up, so you're on the dot. You want coffee?"

"As the predator wants the night."

Hardy gave her a look and said, "That'd be black, no sugar?"

"Sorry," Gina said. "I've been reading my client. The style rubs off. Sugar, please."

"How do you like him?" Hunt asked. "As a writer, I mean."

"He's okay. He says some good stuff. Kept me up till midnight last night."

"So I could've called you," Hunt said, "after my talk with Juhle."

Hardy handed her a cup and she turned to Wyatt. "So you got to him? What did he have to say?"

"I was just starting to tell Diz. He thinks he's got a case."

"With Stuart? How's he getting around the alibi?"

Hardy had crossed the room and propped himself against his cherry desk. Now he put in his two cents' worth. "Wyatt was just telling me about an eyewitness."

Gina slumped into a chair. "To what? The killing? He couldn't have killed her. He wasn't there."

"Well," Hunt said, "that may be a question." He placed his cup in his saucer and came forward on his chair. "Seems a neighborhood girl—lives right across the street, friends with his daughter—she saw him pull into his garage Sunday night. Then leave a couple of hours later."

"She *saw* him?"

"That's what Juhle says. His car."

"Which was it? Him or his car?"

Hunt looked the question over to Hardy, who said, "Who else would have been in his car, Gina?"

Hunt picked it up. "His story doesn't have anybody else driving his car, does it?"

Gina sat back in her chair. "Shit."

"Yes, ma'am," Hunt said. "And that's not including a few other things Devin kind of wanted to brag about."

"I'm listening," Gina said.

"Two domestic disturbance calls."

"*Two?*"

Hunt nodded. "One this summer, and when Juhle ran it down on the computer, he got another hit about five years ago. Your new client got himself arrested on that second one."

"He told me they'd never had a physical fight. I asked him specifically."

At his desk, Hardy frowned and crossed his arms over his chest. "Maybe he forgot."

"Did he also forget to mention the ticket he got last Friday night?"

Gina was sitting all the way back now, legs crossed. "*Friday* night?" she asked.

Another nod from Hunt. "Driving up to Echo Lake. Got pulled over by the Highway Patrol. Juhle found the officer and talked to him."

"He's been busy," Gina said.

Hunt agreed. "He thinks he's got a big, live one. They don't come around every day."

"So what'd the officer say? He remembered him?"

"Oh, yeah. No problem with that. He recognized the name. He's a fan too. Of Stuart's writing. Which is why he didn't arrest him."

"Oh, Lord." Gina shook her head in disbelief. "What was he going to arrest him for?"

"He told Juhle he would have thought of something. Disturbing the peace, resisting arrest, threatening a police officer . . ."

"He threatened him?"

"He swore at him. Close enough for most cops. But here's the bad part."

"That wasn't it?"

"Well, you decide. After the guy, the officer, recognized who Stuart was, he calmed down a little and told him about the awful fight he'd just had with his wife. That she'd told him she wanted to leave him. He told the guy he was heading up to the mountains because if he would have stayed down with her, he would have killed her."

"Those words?" Gina asked.

"According to Dev, pretty much verbatim," Hunt said.

Hardy broke in again. "And this guy Stuart, your client, Gina, he's coming up here when?"

Gina looked at her watch. "About an hour. Juhle's coming around at ten."

"Did Inspector Juhle mention anything about handcuffs?" Hardy asked.

"Last night he said he hadn't applied for a warrant." Gina's face was pure disgust. "Devin say anything about an arrest to you, Wyatt?"

"No. He wants more evidence. Apparently there are other issues?" A question.

"Oh, nothing important," Gina said with heavy sarcasm. "Only a three-million-dollar insurance policy, several more millions that he's going to get control over, to say nothing of a possible love affair with his dead wife's sister."

"You're kidding about that last one, right?" Hunt said.

She leveled her gaze at him. "Well, he denied it. And judging from what I've just learned since I got here this morning, that means it must be true."

When Phyllis buzzed into Gina's office and said that her client was out in the lobby, Gina said she'd be right out, but she didn't move right away. For the past quarter of an hour, ever since she'd come down from Hardy's office, she'd been sitting as far down as she could get in her deepest stuffed chair. Like Wes Farrell upstairs, she had no formal desk in her corner office. So she sat with her hands clasped tightly in front of her, trying to come to grips with the veritable tsunami of rage that had unexpectedly enveloped her in the wake of Wyatt Hunt's disclosures about her client and his rapidly deteriorating story.

She looked down at her hands. All of her knuckles were white, her joints stiff as she separated her hands and forced her fingers open. She brought her hands up to her face, pulled down on her cheeks. Finally, taking a deep breath, she whispered, "All right," and pushed herself up from her chair.

Oddly aware of her own crisp and echoing footfalls as she walked down the long hallway to the receptionist's station, Gina got to the lobby and pasted the semblance of a smile onto her face as she approached Stuart with her hand outstretched. "Good morning," she chirruped, falsely bright. "And right on time."

"Aiming to please," he said in his aw-shucks delivery, though it seemed to cost him. Stuart had shaved, combed his hair and put on nicer clothes—slacks and a pullover—but he looked, if anything, more ravaged than he had the day before, bleary-eyed and sallow complected. "The police show up yet?"

"Not for a while. If you want to follow me back this way . . ."

She wanted to avoid idle chitchat, so she turned and started walking. They reached her office and she preceded him through the door and crossed over to the ergonomic chair by the library table on which she kept her computer. Sitting down, she whirled around to face him. He was standing a couple of steps inside the room, hands in his pockets, reminding her of nothing so much as a dog waiting to be told what to do. She obliged him. "You want to get the door?"

That done, he turned back to the room. "Anywhere?" he asked.

She waved her hand. "Wherever. It doesn't matter."

He chose the couch, perhaps because it was facing her. Sitting back, ankle on opposite knee, he stretched his left arm out along the cushions and leaned back. "So," he said.

"So." Gina wasn't tempted to give him any help, but she waited for a long beat and when nothing came from him, she relented. Whatever he had actually done—and she was furious with him over what that might have been—he was the man she'd been reading last night, who had stirred something in her soul. "You tired?" she asked. "You look tired."

His shoulders heaved as though the question were funny. But there was no humor in the eyes. "I take a week off and sleep around the clock, I might get back to tired. But that's not looking too likely, is it? Not with Inspector Juhle on his way down here."

"Not very, no. You want some coffee?"

He shook his head. "I'm already three cups down. Any more and I'd float away. Anyway, it's nothing coffee would help."

Thinking that this might be an opening of some kind, maybe even a confession, Gina said, "So what is it?"

He exhaled heavily and shook his head, the picture of frustration. "Kym," he said. "My daughter. Our daughter." He met Gina's gaze. "You have kids?"

"No."

"Don't, then."

Gina gave a mirthless chuckle. "It's a little late. In any event, they're not on the agenda; I wouldn't worry. She's taking this pretty hard, is she?"

Stuart pinched the bridge of his nose. "I don't know what to do with her. I don't know what to do." Looking up, he said, "It's knocked her off the rails." Another sigh. "She and Caryn had some issues they hadn't worked out, and now of course they never will. When she left for college it wasn't very pretty between them. That's not making it any easier on her now."

"No, I don't suppose it is. Where is she now?"

"I left her back at the hotel. She cried all night and finally crashed sometime around six this morning, so I thought I'd just let her sleep. She ought to be all right for a few hours anyway." He hesitated. "Debra came by early, just in case, and said she'd stay until Kym woke up and be there for her. But this is killing Kym. I don't know what she's going to do. I don't know what I'm going to do with her."

Gina decided to douse him with a little reality. "Stuart," she said. "Did you tell her that you're under suspicion here?"

He couldn't have looked more startled if she'd slapped him, though he recovered quickly. "After you called me last night, I told her I was meeting you to talk with the cops today. So she knows as far as it goes. Which isn't very far. Today ought to be the end of it, right?"

Gina was tempted to ask him if he was joking with her, but she kept it straight. "Frankly, no, Stuart. I don't think today's going to be the end of it. There have been a few developments."

TEN

———

"BETHANY SAID SHE SAW ME? How could she have seen me?"

"She said she saw your car."

"She saw me pull into my garage?"

"Yes. Then leave a couple of hours later."

"So she saw Caryn's killer come and then go."

"That would be Inspector Juhle's assumption, I believe. And he came in your car."

"No he didn't. Not possible."

Deep inside, Gina was somewhat heartened by the unequivocal denial. Either Stuart was an extraordinarily good liar, or he was telling the truth. "Okay, leaving the car for a minute, let's talk about you and your wife not fighting, specifically about you never having hit her."

"Okay." Forward now on the couch, Stuart's blood was up. "What about 'never' don't you get?"

"I guess the part about the domestic disturbance call to the police last summer."

Stuart grimaced. "They found that already?"

"That's one question. A better one is, what about it? And as for them finding out about it already, I told you yesterday that they're going to find out everything about you, every little thing you've ever done, and they're going to drag it in front of the whole world, so it's way to your advantage to come out with it right up front—anything that's going to look bad when they bring it up later. Like, for example, hitting your wife."

The little tirade found its mark. Stuart shifted defensively back on the couch—legs crossed, arm out along the cushions, stalling for time while he decided what he was going to say. When he made the decision, he kept it simple. "I never hit her."

"She hit you?"

"No."

"But the cops came?"

"My busybody neighbor called them." A pause. "There might have been some noise. I did tell you we'd had some arguments."

"So you had this one time last summer when the police came?"

"And left. They just wanted to make sure nobody was hurt." He shrugged. "Nobody was. They went away. End of story."

Gina stared at him, her face set. "Okay. And that's it?"

"What do you mean?"

"I mean, is there anything else you think might be relevant to Inspector Juhle's ongoing investigation of *you*, Stuart, that your lawyer, if she wanted to protect you, might need to know?" Gina's tone had by degrees become more confrontational. Now she glared expectantly across the room and watched her client pretend to think until she could stand it no more. "You need a *hint*?" she snapped. "I could give you a hint."

He sat there, frowning. "Let me ask you something. Why are you being so hostile all of a sudden?" he asked. "What's that about?"

Gina couldn't come up with an answer right away. She sat back in her chair, gathering herself for a moment, before she finally said, "I read one of your books last night."

"The whole thing?"

"In one sitting, yes. *Healed by Water.* I liked it a lot."

Stuart's mouth turned up at the corners. "I didn't realize you knew that I wrote books."

"I'm your lawyer," Gina said. "I know everything. Get used to it."

"And that's what's bothering you? That you liked my book?"

"Not exactly," she said evenly, "but since you asked, I'm mad if your beautiful book conned me and you're really guilty. I feel personally abused when I find out an eyewitness saw your car coming and going just about when Caryn was killed. I can't figure out why you've got all these anger issues when you write about such spiritual, holistic stuff. I'm really pissed off if you're in fact sleeping with your wife's sister. I'm furious if you're as good a liar as you are a writer. I'm confused about your lack of reaction to your wife's death. I'm baffled and confused by cops coming to break up fights at your house when you say you've never hit your wife. Is that enough?"

"I can explain—"

"Not just yet, please." Her jaw jutted. "So yes, I think we can say that something is bothering me, that I'm a little bit hostile. And while I'm on it, I'm not in the habit of letting myself get fooled by men. I had a damn fine man for a good while there and I got used to it. So I'm afraid my guard might be down, and that makes me mad too. How's all that?"

"I didn't kill Caryn."

"Right. Okay, you've said that. Thank you."

"You don't believe me?"

She shrugged. Suddenly, and very much to her own surprise, she slammed her palm flat down on her computer table—a shockingly loud report, almost like a pistol shot in the closed-up room. "Jesus fucking Christ, Stuart! Do you think this is some kind of game, or what? Do you have any idea of how much trouble you're in right now? You don't think it *matters*, somehow that I don't need to know, that you got yourself arrested for domestic violence five years ago? Or

that you threatened a Highway Patrol officer last Friday night just before you told him you were getting out of the house so you wouldn't
kill your wife? What are you thinking? This is serious shit, and you are
hip deep in it."

"But how did they . . . ?"

Finally, the last of her reserve broke and she was on her feet. She'd
made no plan for it—it wasn't part of her usual repertoire or strategy—
but she was yelling at him. *"Goddammit, Stuart! It never happened is
not the same thing as they won't find out. Because they always find out!
What have I been telling you? It all comes out! Always! That's the way it
works."* Hovering over him, she straightened, then whirled and crossed
over to one of the windows. She parted the blinds, though she wasn't
really looking out at anything.

Gina had to get her anger under control. Letting out a breath
slowly, she closed her eyes, concentrated on the beat of her heart.
When she looked over at him again, Stuart was forward on the
couch, his elbows on his knees, looking at her as though he were
pleading for something—and maybe he was.

She summoned what calm she could and turned to face him.
"I'm sorry I raised my voice. That was unprofessional. I apologize."

He made some conciliatory gesture. "It's all right. People get mad."

She nodded. "Yes," she said. "They do." Gina crossed all the way
back to where he sat and lowered herself onto the opposite end of the
couch. She glanced at her watch, then over to him. When she spoke,
all the fight was out of her voice. "All right, Stuart," she said. "Inspector Juhle's going to be here in no time. Do you want to tell me about
the first domestic disturbance call? The one five years ago."

He was facing her, face drawn and pale, the fatigue around his
eyes almost painful to see. "It was just another fight. The first bad
one, really." He lowered his voice, ducked his head away from the admission. "I guess some dishes got thrown. One of them cut her a little. She was bleeding when the cops came."

"That's your version. So what's the police report going to say,
Stuart? What's the version the cops got?"

—

He inclined his head an inch. "I don't know. I never saw any re-port. I'm not sure what Caryn told them."

"But they took you downtown?"

"Yeah. Then Caryn came down and eventually they let me go back home with her. I took some anger management classes. The problem went away."

"Until last summer?"

Perhaps embarrassed, he looked down, shrugged. "I never did hit her. Not last summer, not before. Never."

"Okay." Gina was fairly sure that the distinction between Stuart hitting his wife and throwing a plate at her would not make much of a difference to a jury, if it came to him being in front of one, but if the exact type of domestic violence he'd committed mattered to Stuart, she'd let him live with his own conscience. For the time being, at least. "So what about this Highway Patrol guy?" she asked. "Did you threaten him?"

"No. I was pissed off, getting pulled over." A self-deprecating half-smile. "That anger thing again, I know. Every other driver on the road was speeding, and he pulls up behind me. So I mentioned that minor point when he got to the window. Probably I could have phrased it better, okay, but I didn't threaten him. I gave the guy my autograph at the end, so how bad could it have been?" He leaned in toward her. "Gina, listen, I've got a temper, okay. I work on it. Living with my two girls could try the patience of a saint, but the way I deal with it is to get away when I can. I'm not a violent guy, and I didn't kill Caryn, and that's God's truth. It'd do wonders for my peace of mind if I thought my own attorney believed me at least."

She just stared at him, unable and in any event unwilling to give him even a small part of what he wanted from her. The truth was that Stuart's peace of mind was about the last thing she cared about at this moment. There were much more pressing issues than her client's ten-der feelings, and they were rushing at her from all directions.

Finally, she checked her watch, crossed her legs, and sat back.

"We've got forty more minutes, Stuart, before Juhle gets here. We've got a lot of ground to cover, and we'd better get to it. You ready to tell me something I don't already know?"

After the interview, when Juhle and Stuart had both gone, Gina thought the knock on her door was probably Stuart coming back to fire her, or more specifically, to rescind her hiring. She wouldn't blame him if he didn't want to work with her after her attitude today. Although he would need some lawyer, that was for sure. The interview they'd just had with Juhle should have removed any of Stuart's doubts that his wife had been murdered and that he was the prime suspect.

Or maybe in the ten minutes since he'd left Gina's office, he'd had a chance to think about it and decided he didn't want to fork over her retainer of sixty-five thousand dollars in cash. This was a serious hunk of change. Other lawyers were both cheaper and less hostile, and maybe he'd decided to hire one of them. She almost hoped that he had.

She walked to the door and opened it, her game face on. Her two partners were standing in the hallway. Dismas Hardy said, "No arrest?"

Gina nodded. "No arrest."

Hardy broke a grin and half-turned to Farrell, his hand out. "Ten bucks," he said.

"I can't understand it," Gina said. They had all come into her office. Hardy and Farrell were on the couch where Stuart had been sitting, Gina in her deep chair. "If I were Juhle, I'd have arrested him. He can't need much more."

"No," Hardy agreed, "but it's cleaner if he gets an indictment first. And let's remember that next Tuesday is grand jury day. My guess is he's taking what he got here downtown and sharing it with the DA even as we speak. See if the grand jury is going to think it's enough. But he might even take another week or two eliminating other suspects. Case with this profile, he's going to want to get it right before it cranks up."

Farrell had slumped to nearly horizontal and had his feet up on the coffee table. Underneath he was certainly sporting one of his trademark T-shirts, but to the casual eye he was dressed like a working attorney—charcoal suit and maroon tie. "But whenever the arrest goes down, Stuart is signed on with us?"

"I gave him the papers to take home and look over," Gina said. "I absolutely low-balled him at sixty-five, and still I think even that money struck him as large. If I had to bet, I'd say he's in, but after Juhle finished, we didn't talk too much more. Stuart wanted to get back to his daughter, who is evidently pretty destroyed by all this."

"As who wouldn't be?" Hardy said.

Gina shrugged. "Well, apparently, Stuart himself." She glanced at Farrell. "I've seen people more torn up over the death of their dogs."

"Hey!" Farrell jumped. "Bart wasn't a dog. He was a person."

Gina gave him a tolerant smile. "My point exactly."

"How old is she?" Hardy asked. "The daughter?"

"Eighteen. Just started college up in Oregon. Was fighting with her mother when she left and hadn't patched it up."

"There's thirty happy years of therapy," Farrell said, "and that's if her dad didn't do it." This time he threw a quick glance at Gina. "And that's if her dad didn't do it," he repeated.

Gina returned his look with one of her own.

"I think, in his own subtle way," Hardy put in, "Wes is asking how you're feeling about your client's chances."

"Not exactly, Diz." Farrell pulled himself up to something resembling a normal posture, turned slightly to face Gina head-on. "I'm asking if your gut is telling you he's guilty or not."

Gina's face grew pensive. "My brain, the jury's still way out. It's too early."

Farrell pressed. "I didn't say brain."

"No, I know." She paused for a moment, took a small breath. "I guess at this point my gut wants to believe he didn't do it."

Farrell looked over to Hardy. "Told you."

"And," Gina went on, "now you're going to tell me how stupid and dangerous that is. Which I'm aware of. So." She addressed both of her partners. "What am I supposed to do, then? Not defend him?"

"No," Wes said. "Not believe him."

"I don't believe him or not believe him, Wes. I said that in my brain, the jury is still out. It's just the old sentimental slob in me wants to believe that sometimes men who are accused of killing their wives didn't do it. And especially men who write beautiful books about the wilderness and other issues close to my own heart."

Wes, whose own early legal career had been transformed by an extremely high-profile case where he'd won an acquittal for a friend and colleague whose protestations of innocence he'd believed and who'd turned out to be guilty, shook his head sadly. "Some people think the Marquis de Sade wrote beautiful books too," he said.

Hardy reached out and put a quick restraining hand on Farrell's knee. "She gets it, Wes. Really." Then, to Gina, "He doesn't want anybody to have to go through what he did. He's just trying to be protective."

Physically, Gina Roake was probably the strongest woman she knew. Three years before, she had shot and killed a man in a gun-fight. Now her stare had hardened. "I don't need to be protected," she said. "You both should know that by now."

"That's not the kind of protection I'm talking about," Farrell said. "I'm just telling you that if this goes to a full murder one trial, it's going to be your life for the next year or more. You're going to start to care about this guy, whether or not he's guilty, and I'm just giving you some friendly advice, based on my own experience, that you might feel better when it's over if you decide right at the beginning that he did it and work on that assumption."

"I've never defended an innocent client in my life, Wes. I'm down with the drill."

"Good." Farrell got himself upright. "Then there's nothing to worry about, and Diz and I are off to a gala luncheon at Lou's. Would you care to join us?"

Gina shook her head. "I just ate there yesterday. Once a week is my limit."

ELEVEN

———

"WHAT ARE YOU DOING?"

"When?"

"Right now."

"Nothing. I just woke up from a nap. Did you hear again from Juhle?"

"Not yet, which we can take as a good sign."

"Actually, I was just looking at an old AARP magazine somebody left here in the room, taking a quiz on how much I know about Michael Douglas."

"How're you doing on it?"

"Not too good. He's not married to Annette Bening?"

"Nope. That's Warren Beatty. Michael Douglas is Catherine Zeta-Jones."

"Get out of here. He doesn't look anything like her."

"His wife, Stuart. His wife is Catherine Zeta-Jones."

"I knew what you were saying. But then who's his famous father?"

"Here's a hint. Same last name."

"I don't know. John? Peter? Toby? Ryan?"

"The famous Toby Douglas?"

"Stephen? Isn't there a Stephen Douglas?"

"He debated Lincoln, so that's not it. How about Kirk?"

"Kirk Douglas! He's not old enough to be Michael's father, is he?"

"Must be, since he is. Or was. Any more Michael Douglas questions you didn't get?"

"Co-star in his first hit movie. I don't even know the movie."

"*Romancing the Stone.* Kathleen Turner was the co-star."

"Man. Do you know this much about the law?"

"At least. Possibly more. Some of it in Latin, even."

"Okay, then. I'm starting to feel better about you being my lawyer."

"Thanks so much," Gina said. "Is Kym with you?"

"No."

"Okay. What about Debra?"

"What about her?"

"I asked first."

"She went home after lunch when I said I needed to get some sleep."

"You get enough?"

"Couple of hours, at least so I'll make it through till tonight."

"So, you want to go out?"

"What do you mean?"

"I mean leave your room, get some air, take a walk? I could be there in fifteen minutes."

"And do what?"

"Talk."

"About what? More of all this?"

"Basically. You. Caryn. Stuff."

"Haven't we done enough of that today already?"

"Frankly, not even close."

"I'd want to be back here for when Kym gets back."

"That ought to be possible. You know, for a guy who's doing

nothing anyway, you're making this decision harder than it has to be. I'm talking a walk, a chat, we go wild, maybe a latte. Low risk."

"You can be here in fifteen minutes?"

"Or less."

"All right. I'll be ready."

The two girls used to do a lot of things together, but they'd drifted apart in the past couple of years. Bethany, a highly strung over-achiever, found that she didn't have the energy after her homework and other activities to keep up with Kymberly and her extreme mood swings. When Kymberly was down in the dumps, she was a total drag, often even talking about suicide, and then nodding off if they were trying to do quieter things together, such as studying or baking cookies, or just hanging out. On the other hand, when she was happy, she was recklessly crazy, invincible and immortal, and this was even harder to take—stealing things, making out with guys she didn't even know, doing drugs.

It got so that the only times they could get along easily was when they both were on a hill, skiing or boarding, and even then it was usually Stuart's presence with them that had made them comfortable. He was daredevil enough for his daughter, and controlled enough for Bethany. When the three of them were together, there was lots of action but he'd draw the line when Kymberly wanted them all to, say, ski off a cliff. But by now even those good times were a couple of years in the past, so Bethany was a bit surprised when Kymberly found her on campus at Galileo High School during lunchtime, just walked up to her as she was talking to some of her friends.

"Hey, can we talk a minute?"

"Oh God, Kymberly. Sure. I . . . I'm so sorry about your mom."

"Yeah." She was more nicely dressed than Bethany had seen her in a long time, although the expression on her face was strangely vacant. But then, Bethany reminded herself, she'd just lost her mother.

The two of them moved away from the other kids over to a corner of the courtyard. After they sat down on one of the benches against the building, neither of them talked immediately. Then finally Bethany said, "Are you okay?"

"Not really. It's not how I thought it would be. I didn't think it would bother me so much with Mom, you know. I mean . . ." Kymberly sighed heavily. "You know."

Bethany nodded. "I don't want to find out."

"You're right, you don't." Kymberly turned her head to look at her friend. There was a lot of unmistakable anger in her face now. "And now my dad's in trouble, mostly because of you."

"Me? What about me?"

"You telling the police you saw him show up at the house."

"Yeah, but I did."

"Okay, but he says he didn't do that." She stared long and hard into her friend's face. "Don't you get it, Bethany? If he did, that makes him look like he killed Mom."

"The cop I talked to said they didn't have any suspects yet."

"Yeah, well they got one now."

Bethany sat still for a long moment. "I didn't mean that. I mean, for that to happen."

"Well, what did you think was going to happen?"

"I don't know. I just answered his questions."

"Well, you gotta change your answers."

"How am I going to do that?"

"Just tell them you made a mistake. You remembered wrong."

"But I didn't, Kym."

"You had to, Bethany. It wasn't my dad. If you say it was, they're going to get him. You can't let that happen."

"But if . . ."

Kymberly slapped down hard at her own pants leg. "Listen to me! Forget the 'buts' and the 'ifs.' You've got to change what you told them. That's all there is to it."

"You mean lie?"

Kymberly, perhaps frustrated by her inability to get her message across more clearly, fixed her with another menacing glare. "Look, Bethany, it's pretty simple, okay. Either you lie, or . . ."

"Or what?"

"God, do I have to spell it out for you? Or something really bad is going to happen. Okay? Get it?"

The walk along the Marina from Fort Mason to Crissy Field is perhaps the most scenic stroll in a city justly renowned for its physical beauty. Today, with a cloudless, nearly purple sky above, the vista showed itself at its best.

Stuart and Gina were in shirtsleeves, hands in pockets, keeping up a pace. Before long they'd reached the deep green sycamore and pine hillsides of the Presidio. The pink-domed Palace of Fine Arts presided over the rooftops of the Marina District. To Gina's right, a forest of sailboat masts swayed gently at their berths, while beyond them the shimmering blue bay nurtured the rest of the fleet, a riot of billowing, multicolored sails cutting in and out of one another, flirting often dangerously with the huge transport and/or cruise ships that churned through the channel beneath the impossibly close rusty red cables and steel of the Golden Gate Bridge. In spite of all the full sails out on the water, here on shore only a breath of a breeze blew over them.

The Michael Douglas trivia had not by a long shot dissipated all of the friction between attorney and client from their morning session at Gina's office. Tension had thrummed between the two of them during Juhle's interrogation itself as Gina continually stepped in, answering—or more precisely, advising Stuart not to answer—many of the questions for which Juhle had already gotten answers the day before. Had Stuart loved his wife? Or hated her? Precisely when had she told him she'd wanted a divorce? What had been those exact circumstances? What time had he come home? Left Echo Lake? How much did he stand to inherit? And so on.

Neither Juhle nor Stuart had appreciated her efforts. It hadn't

helped that the only time Gina had thought it appropriate to cooperate fully with Juhle—when he'd wanted to take a saliva swab for
DNA—Stuart had strongly objected. In the end, Gina had prevailed.
A DNA sample was something that the police could get by search
warrant in any event. There was nothing to be gained by refusing to
provide one now. Nevertheless, something about it had galled Stuart
immensely, and his reaction had brought to a boil again the simmering anger that Gina had been fighting to suppress all morning. If he
was innocent as he said, why would he possibly object?

Finally, after Juhle had gone, they'd had the money discussion.
Sixty-five thousand down, cashier's check or money order, in her office as soon as possible, but no later than the end of the week. Gina
wasn't working for free, and this was going to be taking all of her time
if it went to a murder charge. Stuart could of course feel free to find
other counsel but, she cautioned him, "Like everything else, you tend
to get what you pay for."

Now, to the casual eye, they might have been a long-married couple power-walking for their exercise, making sure they got their hours
in, talking of mundane things—the house, the grandkids. But a closer
look would reveal a deeper intensity. Stuart had been telling Gina about
his daughter—the good and the rather more considerable bad of her.

"Well, which is it, if you had to choose one?" Gina asked. "Wonderful or difficult?"

"That's the thing. She's both. The wonderful part would be her
mother's incredible brains and drive and even a goodly portion of the
Dryden natural beauty. When she chooses to, she can be very, very
pretty, but . . . that leads us to the difficult part. In fact, everything
leads to the difficult part." He walked on. "I don't know how to say
this without it sounding pretty bad, but she's just never really been
easy in any way. We called her the Original High Maintenance Kid.
And that's when we were feeling good about her."

"Okay."

"Well, not really okay. You don't even want to hear about her eating habits, which ranged over the years from gorging herself early on to some pretty intense bulimia over the last couple of years. And let's not talk about mastering all the rudiments of hygiene—hair, fingernails, everything else. You know what she was wearing when she got in yesterday? Salvation Army camo."

"That's the style, Stuart."

"All right, but why does she wear that baggy shit when she could be . . . attractive? I just don't get it."

"Maybe she doesn't want to be attractive. Maybe the attention threatens her. I've got a friend who's the same way. She puts on a dress or wears a tank top and guys driving by crash their cars into things. I've seen it happen. She hates it. I don't think that's so abnormal."

"No, we haven't gotten to the abnormal stuff yet."

"Which is what?"

"The true mental stuff, which is really what nearly broke up Caryn and me a long time ago." Stuart gave Gina the extended version—how during Kym's adolescence, she'd tried their collective patiences with every kind of acting out in the book, until finally Caryn had decided that she suffered from "classic" Attention Deficit Disorder and should be on a regular, heavy regimen of Ritalin. "Problem was," he continued, "that I don't really believe in a lot of the versions of ADD that Caryn's high-end medical crowd tends to embrace."

"Embrace as what?"

"A one-size-fits-all explanation for high energy and disruptive behavior in young people. I thought that if my daughter needed attention so badly, maybe it was because she wasn't getting enough from her parents, myself included. So I started to take her places with me, the wilderness, the woods, the usual." He shrugged. "For a while, it seemed to help. And at least I wasn't drugging her."

"So what happened?"

"So, in the end, it turned out that, as usual, Caryn was more right than I was." Now he came to a full stop and looked Gina in the face. "The truth is we found out that Kym's bipolar, which used to be called manic-depressive. She does need to be on a regular dose of lithium, or she doesn't function right in the real world. And unfortunately, the classic situation, which she fits, is she forgets or refuses to take her pills. When she's on them, she's okay but everything in life is kind of low-key and boring, and she hates that. She wants the high of being manic. So she stops the pills and crashes and burns. You know that time . . ." But suddenly he stopped, looked out over Gina's head to the cloudless sky. "No," he said all but to himself. "Never mind."

But Gina put a hand on his arm. "Never mind what? What time?"

Stuart sighed and pointed to a bench next to the walkway. "You want to sit a minute?" And he told her what had really happened when the neighbors had called the police five years before, when "plates had gotten thrown."

Pulling a trick out of his writer's bag, Stuart had purposely used the passive voice when he'd told Gina about this before. The plates had gotten thrown all right, he said, and Caryn had gotten cut, but he hadn't thrown them—Kymberly had.

And Stuart and Caryn at least agreed that they weren't going to let their daughter be charged in the attack. Her life was going to be difficult enough—even if she got everything together and religiously took her medication—without the added burden of a criminal record. She'd gone off her pills again last summer, and this had precipitated the many huge and highly vocal fights between Kym and both of her parents.

The screaming between male and female voices that the neighbors had heard? It had been Kym and Stuart, daughter and father; not Caryn and Stuart, husband and wife. And when the police had come, he and Caryn had put on the act together, going along as though it had been them fighting—again, to protect their daughter.

He was sitting on the bench, canted forward, staring out into nothing in front of him. A couple of seagulls had landed in the grass across the path and were raucously fighting over a french fry. Gina cleared her throat. "You could tell this to Juhle, you know. He doesn't think you're a wife-beater, a lot of this goes away."

But Stuart shook his head. "It'd get out. Kym's got enough to deal with."

"It might not get out. Juhle can keep a secret."

"I don't know. I just don't know. Anything." He let out a lungful of air. "You want to be moving again?"

After they'd covered some ground, Stuart continued. "There's just so much guilt about every part of this. I mean, the truth is that Kym's problems—Kym herself, even—got so she poisoned everything with Caryn and me. Caryn went into her world of position and money and I just withdrew so I didn't have to confront it the whole time. When I was around, I'd try to be a good husband and father, I suppose, but I knew that I couldn't do anything to help my daughter, or to make things better with Caryn. It was just what it was. And I was too weak or, I don't know, too . . . too goddamn impotent to do anything."

"You thought it was your fault."

"It *was* my fault. I'm the one who originally wanted a kid so bad. If it had been up to Caryn, it never would have happened, and everything would have been better."

"Maybe not better, Stuart. Maybe just different."

"Another different couldn't have been worse, believe me. No, Kym was my genes. Without that, Caryn and I . . . shit. I don't know."

"And this is where all the anger comes from, isn't it?"

"Some good percentage, I'd say, yeah. Why do you think I had to go away to get 'healed by water'? But then I'd come home and Kym wouldn't have taken her pills and she'd explode at me for something trivial or absolutely imaginary, and the frustration would knock me sideways again. And then Caryn, of course, would blame me if I lost my temper."

Gina had her arms crossed. A breeze had picked up and blew the hair off her forehead. When she spoke, she kept her eyes out on the water. "You said Kym and Caryn were on the outs when she went off to school?"

"Yeah, that happened this past summer." Stuart went on to say that suddenly the sides had shifted and—even on her medication—Kym had begun to fight much more with Caryn than she did with him. She began to use street drugs, self-medicating, the doctors called it. Kym was showing up at home with CDs and jewelry and other stuff they knew she hadn't bought; things around the house began to disappear; she was having more or less random sex, hanging out with difficult friends, constantly ignoring her curfew. Caryn would not have any "daughter of hers" acting that way, since it reflected on her. And in this way Caryn, more than Stuart, had become the hated, the enemy.

And that was how things stood until two weeks ago when, a blessing for both parents, Kymberly had finally gone off to school.

TWELVE

STUART AND GINA HAD MADE IT down nearly to the Golden Gate Bridge, for the last couple of hundred yards walking in silence. But it was a more comfortable silence than they'd shared up until then. And Gina finally broke it. "So. Your book," she said, "*Healed by Water.*"

"Note the awkward silence," Stuart said, "while the author decides whether he should ask the reader for an opinion or not."

"I've already told you I liked it a lot. But it was more than that. When I finished it—it really touched me. I was just so . . . relieved, I guess is the word."

"About what?"

"About taking on a client who was intelligent and innocent. I can't tell you how good that felt. That I'd finally be able to put my legal talents to the service of someone who might actually deserve them." She kept walking, eyes forward, hands in her pockets. "I said something yesterday about losing my fiancé a few years ago. Well, since then, not that it matters to you, but . . ."

"Why wouldn't it matter to me?"

"I mean to your defense. In any event, since David, I've been having some trouble committing to things, to getting involved. And then suddenly, last night, I finished your book and was just so glad that I was going to get to do this. I mean, defend an innocent man. Do you know how many innocent clients I've had in twenty-some years as a lawyer?"

"I don't know. Ten? Fifteen?"

"Zero."

Stuart stopped walking, turned to face her. "You've got to be kidding me."

"No. You think that's unusual?"

"No innocent clients ever? Yeah, I'd say so."

"You'd be wrong. It's the norm, believe me. Public defenders, which is how I started, they get assigned cases out of the courtroom, and roughly a hundred percent of these people, they don't even pretend they didn't do what they're charged with. It's all just revolving doors, into and out of jail. They just want to cut a deal to lessen their time, or snitch out somebody to get back on the street, or convince a jury that whatever they did, yeah, they did it all right, but they can't be *guilty* of doing whatever it was because it just wasn't their fault. They were victims."

"Of what?"

"Anything you can think of, and probably a bunch you can't. Prejudice, bad childhood, Republicans, abusive spouses, drugs and alcohol, addictive personality disorder, sexual dysfunction, dumbshit syndrome, you name it. But whatever, the main thing is it wasn't their fault." Gina came to a full stop. "So anyway, last night the thought of getting to defend a righteously innocent client, it kind of filled me up with ... I don't know—motivation. Hope, maybe. Something to try for."

An hour later, as they got back to the Marina, Gina had more to work with. Although Juhle, in his zeal to connect Stuart to his wife's murder, to date hadn't seemed too aware of the maelstrom of drama that apparently swirled in all corners of the life of Caryn Dryden, Stuart had lived inside of it for years. Once he'd gotten his arms around the fact that Caryn had probably been murdered, he amplified quite a lot of the information that they discussed the day before, reinforcing Gina's impression that at least two other people might have had a motive to kill her. Besides those definite two, Stuart told her that he thought it possible that his wife had been having an affair, or maybe serial affairs. Which opened up another whole world of possibilities.

In Stuart's opinion, the most likely suspect to have killed his wife—and for all he knew, to have been sleeping with her too—was her main business partner, Robert McAfee, with whom she had been trying to open her new practice. As Stuart had intimated yesterday, Caryn was trying to bring in a third partner, Michael Pinkert—a mediocre though very rich surgeon. This was infuriating McAfee, who didn't want to work with Pinkert any more than he wanted to split their potential profits three ways. The selling point of the deal for McAfee had always been the efficiency and professionalism and synergy of him and Caryn working together. But Pinkert could bridge the money gap that was threatening their start-up. Caryn and McAfee had taken out insurance policies against their business start-up loans, and now with Caryn's death, McAfee would likely be able to open his own clinic and reap all the profits himself.

But even half of her own private clinic was nothing compared to Caryn's other major endeavor. She'd not just been your average, run-of-the-mill, dime-a-dozen orthopedic surgeon. Instead, she was a total joint surgeon, specializing in total hip replacement, or arthroplasty. Beyond that (as if that weren't enough, Stuart had said), she'd done her undergraduate work, and then a couple of years of graduate school before she transferred to med school, in polymer chemistry. Evidently in her spare time, Caryn had invented a new plastic cupside for the hip joint that marked a significant improvement in the plastic's unfortunate tendency to degrade in the body over time. PII, the company in whose lab she worked, had even named the thing the Dryden Socket, and after FDA approval, which was pending, it looked to become the worldwide gold standard hip joint. As such, projected sales would make it worth millions every year. But, as evidently was almost always the case when the FDA got near giving its final stamp of approval, some problems had surfaced.

Lately Caryn had been far more upset about "her" socket and her dealings with PII and the project's point man with the venture capital crowd—a Palo Alto investment banker named Frederick Furth, who'd arranged the mezzanine loan—than with anything about Bob McAfee.

As Gina had discovered last night, the mezzanine loan had left her cash-poor on her new practice offices when there were the in-evitable and unavoidable delays in construction and start-up. And the Dryden Socket apparently remained in limbo.

If these facts and alternative suspects did not directly impact the evidence that Juhle was collecting on Stuart, Gina knew that at least they would be useful in muddying the prosecutorial waters. At this stage, that would be its own reward.

Still some long blocks from the Travelodge, and with most of their legal business out of the way for the moment, Gina found herself coming back to Stuart's books, asking him which was his favorite.

"I like them all," he said. "They're all my babies, you know? But it's gratifying that other people like them too. I'm very lucky I get to do what I do."

"You do it very well. I identified with a lot of it, which I guess is what you're going for."

But Stuart shook his head. "No, I'm not really going for effects on the reader. I'm trying to get to something else. Sometimes I'm not so sure of what it is myself. Clarity, maybe." He shrugged, almost swallowed the next word. "Truth. That sounds arrogant, I know. But it's what I'm trying for. Something real."

"Well, you got that. You really did."

Shrugging that off, he cocked his chin at her. "If you don't mind my asking, what did you identify with?"

"Really, quite a bit of it. The analogy—you were talking about being in the moment, the step after step after step of, say, getting to the top; you had it from Guitar Lake to Whitney. I've made that exact climb three times now. How it's really not about getting to the top. It's about the thin air, the pain in your legs, the keeping on when you don't think you can . . ." Suddenly, she stopped. "I've done it, is my point," she said in a huskier voice, "but I haven't analyzed it very much, or expressed it the way you did. It was just something I needed to do. To get healed."

"Your fiancé who died?"

She nodded.

Stuart nodded back at her. "With me, it was the family. My family. What I had to get healed from."

"I picked that up."

"Not that I didn't find the experience of being married to a workaholic genius and raising an impossibly difficult child totally fulfilling. This is my great failing. And I'm not the kind of guy who can just ignore it, or have affairs, or be emotionally absent, or however else we're supposed to cope. But sometimes I just had to get away for a few days to find myself again, to hear some silence, to get the strength to recommit to coming back to it, when so much of it didn't seem that it would ever be worth it."

"For me," Gina said, "it was this whole . . . I guess it was the whole question of what life's about. And I couldn't get an answer here in the city. It was just too loud, too in-your-face. You know?" Then, "Of course you know."

"It's not particularly profound," he said. "We're all too much in it all the time. We've got to slow down, but we don't. But I didn't write it to try to teach anything. My goal was just to figure out for myself what worked and why it worked. That's what the writing's about— not the magazine articles so much, but the books. Figuring stuff out."

"Taking other people there too."

"Maybe, hopefully, that happens in the process if I write it right. Which I suppose is why the books sell. And that just shows that there must be a lot of us in the same boat. Maybe most of us."

"So." Gina hesitated, then figured what the hell. She wanted to know. "What about writer's block? Do you ever get that?"

"No. I don't."

"Never?"

Now Stuart broke one of his first true smiles. "I'm talking to a writer, aren't I?"

Gina lifted her shoulders, let them down. "Halfway through a bad legal thriller. Wondering how you get all the way to the end."

"Just keep going."

"Ha."

"Well, it's what I do. I suppose I get times where the ideas don't exactly flow, but the best definition of writer's block I ever heard was that it was a failure of nerve. It's not something outside of you, trying to stop you. It's your own fear that you won't say it right, or get it right, or won't be smart or clever enough. But once you acknowledge it's just fear, you decide you're not going to let it beat you, and you keep pushing on. Kind of like climbing Whitney. Except that if it's never any fun, then maybe it's something inside trying to tell you that you probably don't want to be a writer. You're not having fun with your book?"

"Not too much. Some. At the beginning. Then I got all hung up on whether anyone would want to read it and if they'd care about my characters and I started writing for them, those imaginary, in-the-future readers, whoever they might be."

"Well, yeah, but that's not why you write. You write to see where you're gonna go. At least I do. And in your case, nobody's paying you for your stuff yet, are they?"

"No. Hardly."

"Well, then just do it for yourself and have some fun with it. Or start another story that you like better. Or take up cooking instead. Or get up to the mountains more. But if you want to write, write. A page a day, and in a year you've got a book. And anybody who can't write a page a day . . . well, there's a clue that maybe you're not a writer."

"A page a day . . ."

"Cake," Stuart said.

They'd gotten to within sight of the Travelodge, and Gina recognized three of the local news channel vans double-parked in a row on Lombard Street. She put a hand on Stuart's forearm, stopping him in his tracks. "Looks like they've found you," she said.

"You really think they're here for me?"

"I think that's a safe assumption, yes."

"So what do we do?"

"You say nothing. I say 'no comment.' We get inside your room and close the door behind us and hope they go away. You ready?"

"I guess so. As I'll ever be."

"All right. Nice and relaxed. Let's go."

THIRTEEN

———

When Devin Juhle got back from his interview with Gorman at Gina's office, he was not in good spirits, and his mood wasn't much improved when, in spite of his discoveries the day before, Assistant DA Gerry Abrams wasn't moved to convene a grand jury to weigh his evidence just yet. In the first place, none of it was physical evidence. Abrams pointed out that an eyewitness seeing and possibly even identifying Gorman's car did not even under the most generous interpretation rise to the level of proof of anything about Stuart himself. And while the assistant DA found the two domestic disturbance calls compelling enough, these bore no direct relationship to the murder either.

Beyond that, forensics team boss Lennard Faro had come up with no fingerprints on the wine bottle, which Dr. Strout said was of a compatible shape to allow the inference, though not the absolute conclusion, that it was the weapon that had knocked Caryn unconscious. Microscopic traces of her blood on the label didn't hurt, either. There were partial fingerprints—not Caryn's—on pieces of the broken wineglass in the garbage disposal, and a complete and clear print on the one large shard they'd discovered under the hot tub, but none of the prints matched Stuart's or anyone's in the criminal data bank. Forensics had found a few drops of blood in the garage—still tacky—but whether or not it was Stuart's would have to wait for the DNA results, for which no one was holding their breath. Juhle had his reluctant swab of Stuart's saliva, all right, but the actual testing and results could take days. And even then, so what? Stuart's blood in his garage meant nothing. He could have cut himself shaving, or lacerated his finger on his workbench that morning or a couple of days before.

They just didn't have enough.

In Abrams' cramped third-floor office, Juhle, with a haunch on the opposite desk and sucking on a pencil eraser, sat staring between his two companions. "So what's it going to take, Gerry? We just ignore his motive?"

"Yeah but, you know, motive." Abrams shrugged. All of these law professionals knew that while motive was a nice plus if you could get it, by itself it meant next to nothing.

"Okay." In spite of his frustration, Juhle didn't want to appear to push. He kept his argument low-key. "We've got the history of domestic violence. We do have the girl identifying his car. If he acknowledges that he had the car with him all night . . ."

But Abrams was shaking his head. "She never said she saw him. It won't fly, Dev."

"It will if we can put him and only him in his car. He's more or less said the same thing, putting him there himself. In fact," Juhle's face lit up as he reached into his jacket pocket, "look at this." He passed the plastic evidence bag across the desk.

Faro, who'd been slouching by the door, moved up a few steps to take a peek. "What is it?" he asked.

"It's his alibi, but it just occurred to me that maybe it'll hang him."

Abrams opened the baggie and pulled out the crinkled piece of paper, holding it up. "Is this the original?"

"Yep. I got it this morning from him and his lawyer. They kept a copy."

"What is it?" Faro asked again.

"It's a gas station receipt from Monday morning, four fifteen a.m., from Rancho Cordova, up beyond Sacramento on fifty."

Abrams put the thing flat on his desk and, as Faro picked it up, assumed his thought position—feet up, hands templed at his lips. "What's this supposed to prove? Why'd he give it to you?"

"He says it proves he left Echo Lake at two a.m. It's where he stopped to get gas on the way back to town. But I'm thinking, what if he left the city after doing his wife, high-tailed up to Rancho Cordova and found this place so he could get the receipt and drive back down?"

"What's that get him?" Faro asked.

"If we believe it, it keeps him out of town until his wife's dead. So he couldn't have done it. But what it also does is prove he was in his car in Rancho Cordova at four fifteen a.m. Which means—if the timing works and we can place the car in San Francisco at the time of the murder, and we can—that he was the one driving it. It couldn't have been anyone else. We could make Bethany seeing his car the factual equivalent of seeing him."

Abrams kept his eyes closed, his lips moving unconsciously. Finally he said, "Even if the timing is right, it's still got problems, but with everything else added on, maybe it's getting closer."

"Rein it in, Ger," Faro said. "We don't want you going all enthusiastic on us."

"I like it," Juhle said.

"It might be a start," Abrams agreed, "if the timing's right. And we ought to be able to find that out in about two minutes." Pulling himself up straight, Abrams reached for his computer mouse and the screen on his desk lit up. "What's Gorman's address here in town?"

Juhle gave it to him. Abrams typed it in.

Faro moved over to look. "What're you doing?"

"MapQuest." Abrams drew the receipt closer to him and looked up again at Juhle. "And this is the address of the place he stopped at four fifteen? We know this?"

"Pretty certain," Juhle said. "I called them, and they've got a videotape running twenty-four seven which we'll be getting tomorrow. Stuart went in to get a Coke when he stopped. He ought to be on it."

Abrams typed in the address. Faro moved over as Juhle came around to look.

After about ten seconds, Abrams pushed his chair back and glanced up at his colleagues with a look of mild satisfaction. "Ninety-seven and a half miles. One hour, forty-two minutes."

Faro pulled at his goatee. "Only if he drove the speed limit, which nobody does."

"He might have if he'd just killed his wife and wanted to make sure he didn't get pulled over," Abrams said. "Which would have blown the alibi."

But Juhle was shaking his head. "It doesn't matter if he was speeding. Even if we call it almost twice that, say three hours, he left the house here at quarter to one. He could have been there at quarter to four. More likely it was probably closer to two hours, so he's at the ARCO station at three a.m., max."

Faro was leaning over Abrams' desk, consulting his copy of the original receipt. "Yeah, but that's too early. He bought his gas and his Coke at four fifteen."

This wasn't an impediment to the assistant DA, who suddenly had a clue he might be able to use. Hands at his lips, Abrams was matter-of-fact. "So he hung out up here for a while, Len, trying to decide what to do. Maybe he just sat in his car."

"Maybe." Faro pulled at his goatee. "I don't suppose I need to tell you guys that if he did kill his wife, going back home was dumb. He drives back up to his cabin and nobody would have known. She'd probably still be sitting in that hot tub right now, and nobody the wiser."

Juhle shrugged and said, "Not to sound clichéd about it, Len, but murderers have been known to return to the scene of the crime, make sure they didn't leave any clues laying around."

Faro wasn't going to fight about it. "I'm only making the point, Dev."

Deep in his thoughts, Abrams held up a hand, cutting off any more discussion. "Let's stay on point here, guys. Gorman left his home at quarter to one, he was in Rancho Cordova at four fifteen. Devin, do you have his exact address up at, where was it?"

"Echo Lake. Why don't you just try that?"

Abrams typed again, and they all waited again. "Call it eighty miles even. One and a half hours."

"Uh-oh," Juhle said.

Abrams opened his eyes. "What?"

"One and a half hours from two o'clock is three thirty."

"Yes it is, Dev," Abrams said. "And this means?"

What it meant obviously had jacked Juhle up. He crossed the tiny office, knocked on the opposite bookshelf a couple of times, and then turned back with a light in his eye. "Okay, follow me here. He drives up from San Francisco after doing his wife, all right, none of us have any problem with him hanging around killing time in Rancho Cordova until he gets gas and heads back down, right?" Without waiting, he went on. "But the same is not true if he's coming down from Echo Lake. This situation, he's on his way home. He's not going to kill forty-five minutes or more before gassing up. He's going to stop for gas and continue on his way."

"Maybe he left later than two," Faro said.

"Maybe he did, but he said it was actually a little before. He's got an extra forty-five minutes that just plain doesn't work, even if we use his own timetable."

Finally, Abrams sat up straighter and stretched. "I like this," he said. "This a jury can understand. If he left Echo at two and didn't get to Rancho Cordova until four, unless he got a flat tire or there was some traffic problem—we'd better check with the Highway Patrol and nail that down—then what was he doing? Whereas if he left the

city at one, he'd just wait around until he could put some space between him and the murder."

"That's it," Juhle said. "We get him to give us a sworn, clean and
specific timetable, we can hang him on it." He looked at his forensics
guy. "This doesn't sing for you, Len?"

Faro was back scratching at his beard. "No problem as far as it
goes," he said. "But still no physical evidence. Unless I'm missing it,
which I'm not."

Abrams flashed a disappointed glance at Juhle, clucked once, and
said, "Len's a spoilsport, but he's not all wrong."

Juhle returned to the homicide detail to find the place unusually
jumping. Normally, this time late on a weekday afternoon, a few
bodies might be sitting at desks reviewing transcripts of interroga-
tions, or writing up reports, or reading. Of the fifteen homicide inspectors in the unit, six would be a big number present at any one
time. But Devin had heard the low-volume but electric buzz out in
the hallway and he came in to pretty much a full house. There was a
little bullpen area just inside the entrance to the room, next to the
doorway to Lieutenant Lanier's office, perennially open but now
strangely closed. A couple of steps in, Juhle stopped.

"Dev!"

Darrell Bracco appeared from between the lockers that divided
the room. With a quick come-on-in hand motion, he got Juhle moving forward again. Nodding around at his colleagues stuffed among
the desks, Juhle threw a look toward his lieutenant's closed-up office.

"Hey, Darrell. What's going on? Marcel all right?"

"You didn't hear?"

"I guess not. What?"

"My old partner, Harlan Fisk? The supervisor? He got a tip at
lunch that the Fab Five is on the way over here. They're gonna do
Marcel. Is that perfect, or what? So till they get here, Sarah's in there
keeping him tied up."

"What do you mean, they're going to 'do' Marcel?"

"The Fab Five, Dev, the Fab Five."

"Right. But my kids aren't teenagers yet. Are they some band? I don't know them."

Rolling his eyes, Bracco leaned in toward him. "*Queer Eye for the Straight Guy*. They're going to do Marcel."

"What are they going to do with him?"

"Dev. Come on. Tell me you've never watched the show."

"Okay. I've never watched the show."

Overhearing the conversation, Emilio Thorsten butted in. "You gotta check it out, Dev. The show's a riot. These five gay guys, they find some prototypical straight—basically Marcel; I mean, he's perfect—who dresses wrong and wears the wrong shoes and glasses and lives in like a gym. And they fix him up. The house, the clothes, the look, the whole schmear."

"Gay guys do this? Why?"

"It's a TV show," Darrell said, "that's why. There's five of them. The Fab Five. They take some straight nerd and make him hip. Or more hip, anyway."

"And they're doing this to Marcel today?"

"Closing time, according to Harlan, who's never wrong. It's gonna be awesome."

Juhle had been in Homicide for six years and he'd seen worse attendance at mandatory call-ups. It occurred to him, not for the first time, that he was more than a little out of the loop among his peers. Not only had he never seen the show, he obviously hadn't been part of the grapevine of communication today that had connected every other person in the detail. "They're going to come with like TV lights and a crew and surprise Marcel?" he asked.

"That's the idea."

"Then I've got a good one too," Devin said. "A good idea, I mean."

"What's that?" Bracco asked.

"Somebody better get Marcel's gun off him. He's going to blow their asses off."

*   *   *

Supervisor Harlan Fisk missed on this one. After about an hour of progressively more disappointed waiting, Fisk called Bracco and told him his source had gotten it wrong. Fifteen minutes after that, six fully dispirited homicide teams had finally gone grumbling out of the detail and were on their way back to their beats, to their witness interviews, to their snitches, or to their homes. Marcel Lanier's door was open again, and the lieutenant appeared to have remained unaware the whole time of the gathering of his troops and their subsequent dispersal.

Devin Juhle had subpoenaed Caryn Dryden's home telephone records, but he wouldn't have those numbers for a couple more days. In the meantime, he sat at his desk with a list of the numbers he'd taken from her cell phone, which had an easily accessible record of the last ten calls she'd both placed and received. He punched in one of them.

"Hello." A young woman's voice.

"This is Inspector Juhle of San Francisco Homicide. Who am I speaking to, please?"

"This is Kym Gorman. Just a second." He heard the voice speaking to someone in the room with her. "It's the police." Then a man's voice. "This is Stuart Gorman. Who is this?"

"Mr. Gorman, this is Inspector Juhle."

"Jesus, Inspector, don't you guys ever give it up? Why are you harassing my daughter?"

"I'm not. I'm calling numbers from your wife's cell phone. Your daughter called her twice over the weekend and she called her back once. Did you know that?"

"No, not specifically. But last time I checked it wasn't a crime for a daughter and mother to talk on the phone."

"No, sir, it's not. I was just checking the numbers, finding out who your wife talked to in the last days of her life. Your daughter's was the first number I tried."

"All right, then, you've tried it." A pause. "Look, Inspector, she's having a bit of a hard time dealing with things right now, as you might understand. Would you mind please letting this go for a few days? Would that be too much of a problem for you?"

"No, I could do that."

"I'd appreciate it. I really would."

"All right, then. But you know, while I've got you, can you tell me one small thing?"

"You know what my lawyer says. I'd better not."

"But you've already said this one thing."

"Evidently I said a lot. And you've got it all on tape, right? Use that."

"All I'm talking about," Juhle went on, "is what time you left your place at Echo Lake. You said a little before two. I just wondered if you've had a chance to rethink that."

"Why?"

"Because I'm trying to get my timetable straight. You said a little before two last time. You want to change that now?"

Juhle waited through some silence until Stuart said, "No. It was a little before two. I'm pretty sure."

"There," Juhle said, "that wasn't so hard, was it?"

FOURTEEN

—————

KYMBERLY WAS HALF-WATCHING THE TURNED-DOWN television from the couch. She glanced at her father, slumped now in one of the room's reading chairs. "Daddy, are you okay?"

Stuart threw her a weak smile. "I think I'm finally running out of gas here, hon." He drew in a shallow breath. "I didn't know you'd talked to Mom over the weekend."

"Yeah, a little." After a hesitation, Kym shrugged. "Is that what the police wanted?"

"He mentioned it, that's all. What did you guys talk about?"

"Not much, really. I got her twice Saturday, but she was running around, so we only actually got to talk one time, on Sunday."

"What was she running around doing on Saturday?"

Another shrug. "You know. It was Mom. Something."

"She didn't say?"

Much as Stuart was striving to keep everything low-key, this question brought the beginning of a rise. Kym brought her eyes all the way away from the TV and over to her father. "What? Why are you looking at me like that? Do you think I'm trying to hide something from you?"

"No. And I'm not looking at you any way. I thought your mother might have told you something about what she was doing, why she couldn't talk to you, and that might have had something to do with whoever killed her, since it wasn't me."

"Jesus, Dad, are you saying . . . do you think it was me?"

Here we go, he thought. But said, "No. Don't be silly."

She sat up straight now, eyes growing wider. "You do! You think it could have been me, don't you? God, I don't believe this."

His hand went to his forehead. He'd learned that he could sometimes control the direction of his daughter's outbursts by refusing to continue the confrontation. "Kym," he said evenly, from behind his hand. "Let's not go here. I don't think that, and never could. I know you loved your mother. I'm trying to imagine who could have done what they did. And all I want you to believe is that *I* didn't have anything to do with it. That's all I want."

Miraculously, it worked. Kym seemed to pull back within herself for a second, then she nodded and got up from the couch, crossing over to him, kneeling down in front of him, her hands on his knees. "Of course I believe that. How could I not believe that?"

"The same way I couldn't believe it about you, sweetie. Never. Ever ever." Stroking her hair, he went on soothingly. "But with all those reporters who were out there . . . You saw them and you heard what Gina Roake said. They're going to make me the suspect because that's where the story seems to be right now. We should be ready for that. And not get mad. Getting mad isn't going to help anything."

"I know," she whispered into her hands, "I know that."

"I know you do," he said. "And that's why you're not going to be mad at me if I ask if you've taken your pills today."

She raised her face to look at him and nodded solemnly. "I started again this morning. I'm sorry. I felt so good at school I thought . . . but then I came down here. There was this party I heard about where a bunch of the new kids like me were going down to Santa Cruz . . ." She stopped. "I know. I'm sorry. I'm trying."

He let that go. It was going to have to be good enough.

"You went and saw Bethany? What did she say?"

"She said it was your car."

"But it couldn't have been. I wasn't here."

"I know. But she thinks it was, Dad. She saw it. It opened the garage door and pulled in. Who else could it have been?"

"Maybe nobody. Maybe she dreamed the whole thing. Did she notice the license plate?" Stuart had a personalized California plate that read GHOTI—a little private joke compliments of George Bernard Shaw. The "gh" sound from *laugh*, the "o" from *women*, the "ti" from *action*. So *ghoti*, if pronounced "correctly," spelled fish.

"She didn't say, specifically."

"Well, if she didn't see that, it wasn't my car."

"I know. But . . ."

"What I'm saying is that maybe she could try to remember that one little detail. Do you think she'd be willing to talk to me?"

"I don't know. I think maybe now it would scare her a little. I don't think she really got it that she was telling the police that it must have been you who killed Mom. Until I told her, and then she was all 'I didn't mean to say that.' Except she's sure it was your car."

"You know how many dark-colored SUVs there are? Black, green, blue, brown. Come on. And she never saw me, personally, did she? Get out of the car or anything like that?"

"No. But who else could it have been? I mean, who else had an automatic opener to get in the garage? That would mean Mom and . . . and somebody . . ."

"I know, hon. I know what it would have to mean."

At about eight thirty they'd finished dinner, and the suspect walked out of Izzy's Steaks & Chops with his daughter on one arm and his sister-in-law, Debra, on the other. Immediately, a swarm of news people closed in around them, cameras flashing, voices raised and demanding.

"Stuart! Give us a comment, huh?"

"Why'd you kill your wife?"

"How much was she worth?"

"How much are *you* worth now?"

"Who are these women?"

"You got a girlfriend, Stuart?"

Stuart finally stopped at the corner of Lombard and faced them. "I know you people are only trying to do your job," he said, "but I'd like to ask you all politely to leave me and my family to our privacy and our grief. On my left, this is my daughter, Kym, and this is my sister-in-law, my wife's sister, Debra. I did not kill my wife, and I'm going to cooperate in every way I can with the police in helping them to find who did kill her."

A reporter said, "You know that the police consider you the prime suspect. What do you have to say about that?"

"They're welcome to their opinion. You notice I haven't been arrested, though. If they had evidence, I'd be in jail. They don't, and they won't get it because it doesn't exist. I didn't kill my wife. That's all I've got to say. Now if you'll all excuse us."

"You saw the picture, of course?" Gina asked him on the phone.

"Me and Debra? They led the eleven o'clock news with it. Yeah, I saw it."

"Whatever you say, people are going to think she's the other woman, you know that?"

"Let them."

"It won't help you."

"All this public stuff is stupid, Gina. It won't hurt me if there's no evidence, and I don't see any evidence. Do you?"

"No, but it probably wasn't the smartest move in the world to rub that in Juhle's face on television, either."

"He'll get over it. Maybe it'll teach him not to share his suspicions with the media. He's going to fight me there; I'm going to fight him back. In fact, I'm half inclined to sue him for slander already. You do slander?"

Gina gave a little laugh. "Not this week. I've got a murder case that seems to be heating up. My client keeps talking."

"Freedom of speech. Use it or lose it. And speaking of which . . ." He told her about this earlier conversation with Juhle, the disputed time he'd left Echo Lake.

"And you told him maybe it hadn't been two?"

"No, I told him it was."

"Have I mentioned that the preferred term of art is just to say 'no comment'?"

"I tried. I tried."

A silence. And finally Gina said, "So how's your daughter?"

"She's a wreck. She cried all night. Her mom's gone and it's starting to sink in. That, and all the things left unsaid between them."

"That's hard, those unresolved issues."

"When she went off to Oregon to school, I told you about some of it today, they'd just had it out about what she was bringing up—or, more, what she wasn't bringing up. No makeup. One change of clothes. People up there weren't going to be shallow like they are down here, caring about all that external stuff. So, bottom line, she didn't even give Caryn a hug. She didn't come in and say good-bye. She just walked out the door. And the next thing she knows is her mother is dead. She's trying to find a place to put all that."

"Does she have somebody she can talk to? A regular counselor?"

"Are you kidding? A shrink a day, that's our motto. But I'm not sure that's what she needs right now."

"Is she taking her medicine?"

"As of today, maybe, if I believe her."

"Do you?"

"About as much as usual. Say, sixty percent."

Gina asked, "And how about you? How are you doing?" She waited. "Stuart?"

His voice was different. Gruff, unprotected. "It's started to hit me, too, I think. It's . . ." He sighed heavily. "It's hard. I get the feeling it's going to get harder."

"Missing her?"

It took him a second. "Caryn? Not really. Just this emptiness. Like the spaces around me are all too big or something. I'm all disoriented. I'm not saying it very well."

"You're saying it fine."

"I'm not. You remember how you said you were waiting for me to show some grief?"

"Yes."

"Well, I don't know when, or even if, that's ever going to happen." He paused, then went on in a rush. "What I've been hit by is this sense that what Caryn and I really had for the last several years—at least what I was convinced we had—was a commitment more than anything else. Certainly more of a commitment than actual love, whatever that is. We weren't going to cheat, I thought. We weren't going to embarrass each other. We were going to do as good as we could with Kymberly, try not to get in each other's ways, support each other's career choices.

"But somewhere along the way, it stopped being . . . being anything personal, really. We shared the house and were basically polite to each other. And I thought it would change back someday, maybe when Kym left, maybe later. But now I'm just starting to realize that even if she wasn't dead, that was never going to happen. And that's what I feel this emptiness about. It's like with her gone I'm suddenly allowed to feel what's been there and what I've been denying all along for five, six, maybe ten years. I know I should feel more grief, I feel guilty that I don't, but there it is. In some ways, I feel like I'm starting to wake up. How wrong is that?"

"It's not so wrong, although I wouldn't go out of my way to mention it to the press."

"I'll try to resist."

"And while we're on it, there's something else you might try to avoid around reporters."

"What's that?"

"Debra."

"I told you, there's nothing . . ."

"I know what you told me, but I'm talking about perception. She's beautiful, and whether or not you like it, her body language is claiming you. Wait up an hour and watch it again on the late news and you'll see what I'm talking about. She isn't there with you now, is she?"

"She didn't even come in, Gina. She left after we had dinner."

"Okay. And Stuart? She may be the nicest woman in the world. That's not my point. My point is the reporters have now seen her. So she's in the story. And if there's any way she could get a bigger part in it, that will happen without either of you doing anything. So, for the last time, there's no bigger part for her in this, is there?"

Nothing.

"Stuart?"

He sighed into the receiver. "What I've told you is true. We've never been involved. We've never had sex. Okay, clear enough?"

"Except that I hear a 'but.' "

Another pause. "Three years ago, when she was going through her divorce, Caryn suggested that I take her away from all the madness she was going through. So I took her up to the lake and we hiked around up there a while."

"How long?"

He hesitated. "Five days."

"Five days? You're in a loveless marriage and she's getting divorced. And nothing happened?"

"We didn't have sex, if that's . . ."

"*Of course* that's what I'm saying. Don't go all Bill Clinton on me."

"There's not. She would have . . . maybe she wanted to. Maybe I was tempted. I thought it was a good idea to cut off the last two days, and we came home early. I was married to her sister, for Christ's sake. We had a deal and I wasn't going to break it. And that's the truth."

"Swell. Who else knows you guys went up there? Who might tell?"

"Well, certainly her ex-husband, maybe some of her friends."

Gina's voice went flat. "So it's going to come out. And it'll be part of your motive."

"Except that nothing happened. And nothing is going to happen, I promise you. People can believe it or not."

"I'm not thinking about people in general, Stuart. I'm thinking about nineteen specific people on the grand jury. Or maybe twelve in a murder trial."

"I'll just tell them the truth."

"Stuart, you just told me the truth, and I'm not too sure it helped."

"Well, I don't know what else I can do. Did you hear what else I told those reporters tonight? Something else that was true?"

"What's that?"

"That I'm willing to cooperate with whoever it takes, even the police, to find who killed Caryn. In fact, just between you and me, maybe I'm going to try to find out myself."

"Not a good idea. This is why we have police."

"Except at the moment they think I did it."

"No, they're just saying you're a person—"

"A person of interest. I know, I know. And that means I'm the prime suspect as soon as they find something they can use as evidence. And then I'm in jail. I don't want to go to jail, even for a day."

"No. You're right there. You don't."

"Well, then, what's my option? Sit around and wait until Juhle piles up enough innuendo and hearsay to bring charges against me? Listen, Gina, if he's not looking for somebody else, then he's not looking for whoever did this, because I didn't. Have I mentioned that before?"

"A couple of times, I believe. And that brings us to some good news at last."

"What's that?"

"Your lawyer is starting to believe you."

FIFTEEN

———

THE TRAVELODGE DID NOT HAVE room service, so Stuart let his daughter sleep and went out to pick up breakfast and a newspaper. So at about 8:15, Stuart and Kymberly were drinking their Starbucks and eating croissants at the coffee table in his hotel room. His daughter turned a page of the paper, leaned forward over it for a minute, then looked up. "You've made *USA Today*, Dad. 'Writer Denies Implication in Doctor Wife's Death.' Oh, God. Nationwide."

"Can I see?"

She passed the pages over, and he scanned the article quickly. It wasn't long, maybe two hundred words in the Regional News section under San Francisco. Before he had a chance for any kind of a comment, the telephone on the side table next to the couch rang once and Stuart grabbed it. "Hello. Yes, speaking." But after that he wasn't speaking—he listened for a minute, at the end of which he said, "All right, thanks." Then sat holding the phone.

"Dad?"

Startled out of his reverie, Stuart smiled awkwardly at his daughter, then hung up and lifted his coffee cup to his mouth. "That was the police," he said. "We can go back home."

"Home," Kym said. "What's home going to be like now?"

He met his daughter's eyes, saw the incipient tears, and put his arm around her, bringing her in next to him, holding her as she broke.

Kym didn't think she could stand to be inside the house where her mother had been slain. She wasn't sure she could ever go back through that front door again. And fortunately, before they'd even finished their coffee, Debra had shown up unbidden at the hotel. She volunteered to take her niece shopping for some clothes (no argument about the shallowness of fashion this time from Kym) and then out to lunch someplace nice. After that, they could both go back to Debra's apartment, where Kym was welcome to stay with her as long as she wanted, and at least until the funeral. The medical examiner hadn't released the body, so they weren't sure yet when that would be. Certainly no sooner than next Monday.

So at a little before noon, after wandering aimlessly in the empty house for most of an hour, Stuart found himself alone upstairs at his computer in his small writing office next to his bedroom. He hadn't checked his e-mails since Thursday night, and now he was scrolling down through nearly a hundred of them. It did not appear that the police who'd searched his house so thoroughly over the past couple of days had opened his files, and this surprised him; but maybe they'd dumped his hard drive data onto a disk and taken it downtown to peruse at their leisure.

The correspondence was mostly predictable—fully half, in spite of his spam-blocking software, was unwanted, unsolicited mail of one kind or another; eight or ten were messages from people who'd enjoyed one of his books or others of his writings; both his agent and his publisher, offering any kind of assistance (but possibly not exactly heartbroken over the commercial possibilities of him being in the news); another twenty forwarded jokes that he routinely deleted; fifteen or so from people who'd heard about Caryn.

He had almost gotten to the bottom of the queue when he saw a familiar sender's moniker—TSNK—that brought him up short and caused his stomach to go hollow. Stuart had heard from TSNK before, twice. The first time had been a little over a year ago, a few days after *Sunset* had published a short piece that featured some of Stuart's favorite outdoor recipes for cooking trout.

At that time, he'd printed out the offending e-mail but then decided to ignore it. It had to be from some crank. Stuart hadn't considered calling the police or the FBI. He never even mentioned it to Caryn. Stuart, though, had kept the message, but he'd never had to go back and look at it to remember it in its entirety: *"It is bad enough when the ignorant kill God's and nature's noble animals in the name of food or sport. But when someone who glorifies himself as the friend and benefactor of nature does it, the crime rises to the level of evil. Now we know who you are. Punishment for your crime might come at any time. Prepare yourself. THOU SHALT NOT KILL."*

TSNK.

He'd heard from them, or him, or her, one other time four months ago, in the wake of another article he'd done—this one published in *Field & Stream*—on an albacore run he'd taken with a party boat out of Morro Bay.

The seventy-foot party boat had left the dock at midnight, and after a night running southwest for about sixty miles, they'd hit a good-size school of tuna. Although every one of the twelve other anglers hooked up, in the aftermath of bringing the fish aboard, Stuart had been appalled by the general greediness on the boat. The common attitude seemed to be that suddenly all of the boatmates were potential enemies, intent on stealing each other's catch. Two fights broke out, fists actually flung, when one of the mates tagged a bigger fish (they were all within three pounds on either side of forty!) as the catch of one man, when another was sure he had boated it.

Afterward, when the run was over, the men sat apart, guarding their burlap sacks of catch, lest another fisherman substitute his name tag to try to get more fish.

The story Stuart wrote for *Field & Stream* had been his knee-jerk solution to the rampant avidity. Wasabi and soy sauce in hand, he'd gone up to the first mate and asked him to bring up the largest fish Stuart had caught and cut up half of it—fifteen pounds of fillet—into sushi for breakfast for every man on the boat. The other half he gave to the short-order cook in the galley and told him to make as many variations of albacore as his heart desired to keep the crew and his fellow fishermen happy. So, besides the sushi, they'd all fed like lords on fresh breaded albacore, on seared sesame albacore, on garlic stir-fried albacore, and on albacore with butter, lemon and capers. By the end of the day, the men—even the earlier pugilists—were all friends, sharing recipes, tips and even tackle, trading their fresh tuna for each other's canned, planning other fishing trips as a group.

Stuart had thought it a very successful story about how an example of simple sharing could break the grip of irrational territorialism on a bunch of alpha males. TSNK apparently didn't have the same opinion: *"You've been warned once, and you have not heeded. Your influence could heal, and instead you choose to let it harm the helpless creatures of the deep. The albacore shall have their vengeance. THOU SHALT NOT KILL."*

This second time, Stuart did report the e-mail to the police, who directed him to the FBI, who in turn told him they would pass it either to Fish & Game or up the chain to Homeland Security as a possible threat from a terrorist organization. But Stuart had never heard another word about it from anyone, and in his heart he believed that the authorities considered the whole thing more or less a joke. And, in truth, he knew it was highly unlikely that Al-Qaeda cared much about whether he killed the fish he caught. On the other hand, there were organizations that did; if you said the word "terrorism" on U.S. soil before 9/11, you would have probably been more likely, and accurately, to conjure up images of Timothy McVeigh or the work of

PETA or the Earth Liberation Front than of Osama bin Laden and his followers.

These people were serious. And they, or someone perhaps sufficiently like them, had him in their sights.

In the emotional devastation he'd been enduring since last Friday when Caryn had told him she wanted a divorce, the thought of his most recently published article, an atypical foray outside of the fishing world in *Western Sportsman*, hadn't crossed his mind. Since he'd handed it in six weeks before, though, he'd worried sporadically that his tale of the boar hunt he'd gone on in the Sierra foothills might draw the attention of TSNK.

Now, the simmering of his all-too-familiar anger welling up again within him, he clicked twice on the message. It was dated last Friday, at 2:00 in the afternoon: *"The beasts of the fields are sacred unto God, and now you have taken to slaying them as well as their brothers in the waters. This is intolerable. We know where you live. There will be no more warnings. Soon you will suffer as your victims have suffered. TSNK."*

From her office, Gina placed a call to Wyatt Hunt, computer whiz. She was at Stuart's house a half hour later. "Is it possible Juhle missed this?"

They were in the kitchen, a room in which Stuart felt marginally comfortable. He was sitting on the counter by the sink. "Wouldn't he have told us if he saw it?"

"It may be why he hasn't arrested you."

"Well, there's one way to find out."

Gina placed the call from the kitchen phone and got the inspector on his cell phone. He was down in Hunters Point, interviewing another witness in a suspected gang slaying, but he wasn't making much headway—the homey ain't be 'membrin' nothin'. "No, I'm out on the stoop now, hoping nobody shoots at me. What's up, Gina?"

She told him, and read the latest message.

The bare fact of it made very little impact on the inspector. "It's an e-mail? No. We didn't download his files, but thanks for the idea."

"Devin, this looks to me like a threat to Stuart and maybe to his family. It says that they know where he lives. That it's the last warning."

"Are you sure he didn't go to some Internet café and mail it to himself?"

"Reasonably sure, yes. He got two other similar notes in the past year from the same sender. On the second one, he notified the authorities."

"When was that?"

"I don't know exactly. Four or five months ago."

"He could have been planning it back then. Set up the story."

Gina said, "Look, Inspector, I'm giving you the courtesy of this phone call. If you want to come here to look for yourself, my client would let you in without a warrant. It's your call."

"No. I'll be there. Don't erase anything. Don't touch anything. Give me an hour."

"One hour," Gina said, hanging up. She softened her tone to Stuart. "He was underwhelmed, but he'll be here. He doesn't think it's impossible you sent it to yourself."

Stuart's smile showed a few teeth. "They get an idea in their heads, they hold on to it pretty hard, don't they? Okay, so even forget this Thou Shalt Not Kill guy. Isn't Juhle looking at anybody else? Any other suspects?"

"I don't know. He should be. That's all I can say." She hesitated, looked out the window over his shoulder, came back to him, made an involuntary grimace.

"What are you thinking?" he asked. "Something."

"I'm thinking I'd like to see where it happened, if you could deal with it."

He took a beat, then said, "Sure," and boosted himself off the counter. "Out here."

The hot tub was still uncovered, still filled with water, although someone had turned it off, and the temperature was now tepid. They'd left the blackout blinds open, and the backs and sides of the neighboring homes and backyards were visible on all sides. Stuart dipped a hand into the water and stirred it.

Outside, the early autumn weather kept imitating summer. From a feeder by the back fence, birdsong punctuated the stillness. A smell of chlorine hung in the air, a hint of humidity. Stuart didn't turn around, but spoke quietly. "I'm starting to believe somebody drowned her. Somebody hit her on the head and pushed her under. I've got to find out who that was."

"We've talked about that, Stuart. That's the police."

A bitter laugh. "They're not motivated like I am." He turned back to her. "Now you want to ask: If I didn't love her anymore, why would it matter so much?"

"All right. That did occur to me."

"It's not so much Caryn. It's me. I'm the one who's going to have to live with the suspicion for the rest of my life, people thinking that I killed my wife. You think I want to look into my daughter's eyes and have her not be absolutely certain that I didn't do this? To say nothing of my friends, acquaintances, publishers. I can't have it. I won't have it." The small outburst seemed to settle something in him. "They're not locking me up. Whoever did this . . ."

"Whoever did it," Gina said, "will have made some mistakes, Stuart. When Juhle widens the net a little, he'll get to them."

"He's not looking. There's no net."

"There will be, though. I promise. It's only been two days and he's been spending his time eliminating you."

"*Wasting* his time eliminating me. And after four days, murders don't get solved, do they? Well, this one has to get solved." Stuart again put his hand into the lukewarm water. He kept it there, moving it slowly back and forth. "Okay," he said, as though he'd been arguing with himself and had reached a conclusion. "Okay, then."

Sixteen

———

Wʏᴀᴛᴛ Hᴜɴᴛ ᴡᴀs ᴜᴘsᴛᴀɪʀs ɪɴ ᴛʜᴇ small office, sitting at Stuart's computer. Gina and Stuart were packed in, standing behind him. "There's no way," Hunt was saying, "that you can identify where this came from."

"Can't we go to the server?" Stuart asked. "I mean, it's at Gmail dot com. Don't they have to have an account?"

"Sure, but what does that tell you? Nothing. There's no physical address. They probably signed up online, work out of a laptop. If it's in a public place, we could maybe locate the computer, but so what? They could be anywhere. But wait." Hunt held up a finger. "Another idea strikes. Hold on." His fingers danced over the keyboard. He stared at the screen, typed some more. Did it all again. Finally he pushed back, shaking his head. "Nope. An idea, but not a good one."

"What'd you do?" Gina asked.

"Googled 'TSNK.' Also 'Thou Shalt Not Kill.' Other than Bible sites, no record of anything like it, as you can see here. And if there's no record on Google, it doesn't exist. Maybe it is really just a lone crackpot, like you thought originally."

"But what's all this 'I know where you live'?"

A shrug. "Cheap terror tactics, that's all. They've written two of these before and done nothing, right? No attempt on you. The guy might be holed up in some cabin in Idaho or Maine or anywhere. Why should this time be any different?"

"This time," Stuart said, "my wife's dead. I think that's different enough."

"Of course," Hunt said. "Sorry. I wasn't thinking."

"It's all right," Stuart replied. "That seems to be going around. I wasn't thinking either the last few days. I'm only just starting to now." He looked over to Gina, back down at Hunt. "So what you're saying is that I could have done just what Juhle said, e-mailed myself from anywhere with this threatening stuff?"

"Essentially, right." Hunt swiveled halfway around toward the others. "Maybe if we found the actual computer this was e-mailed from, we could download the hard drive and prove the threat had come from that machine. But again, so what? We'd know who owned it. By itself, it wouldn't do us any good."

"Just to be clear, Wyatt," Gina said, "since we can't identify who sent it, Devin isn't going to be able to rule out Stuart on this, is he?"

"No. I don't think so."

"Wait a minute," Stuart said with some sharpness to Wyatt. "You know this guy?"

"What guy?"

"Juhle. Who both of you are suddenly calling Devin."

Hunt glanced up at Gina, shrugged. "Yeah. We go back. Why?"

"Because maybe he needs somebody he trusts telling him that I didn't do this."

Hunt coughed, made a noise in his throat, and Gina waded into the edgy silence. "Um, that's not really the way it's played, Stuart."

"I don't give a damn about how it's played, Gina. This isn't a game, it's my life."

Hunt, recovering, said, "Okay, it's your life, but Devin doesn't trust anybody that much. Not me, not his wife, nobody. He's a cop, he follows the evidence."

"In spite of the fact that he's got none on me?"

Hunt's shrug was a little more elaborate this time. "You're the spouse, sir. The spouse usually did it. That's where he's got to start."

"All right, then, but what about if there are other suspects? How about that?"

"He finds some evidence, he'll look at them. But he won't go chasing down another motive, not until he's eliminated you. And that's no matter what I say or do."

"So I'm guilty until proven innocent?"

"To Juhle, probably."

"I thought it was supposed to be the other way round."

Hunt gave him a flat look. "You see much else in life that works the way it's supposed to, let me know, and I'll buy stock in it."

Gina put a hand on her client's arm. "Listen, Stuart, Juhle might not think so, but you are at least being considered innocent, which is why you're not in jail right now. They don't have enough proof, and that's the nut of it. And of course I'm going to communicate all of Caryn's relationships to the inspector, and he may follow up on some or all of them. I may even lodge a complaint about the course of the investigation thus far with the DA, who happens to be a friend of mine. Of course," she added, "that'll go nowhere, but it might be a fun exercise."

"So meanwhile, what am I supposed to do?"

Gina and Wyatt exchanged a look that might have been conspiratorial or skeptical. "Most people," Gina said in a relaxed tone, "wait it out. See what happens."

"Well, call me a pain in the ass," Stuart replied, "but that's what I've been doing the last couple of days, and any more of it doesn't really appeal to me."

A few minutes later, they'd moved downstairs to the living room and along to the question of the garage door. Stuart had typically brushed off Bethany's testimony that it had been him in his car and wanted to concentrate on the bare fact of somebody getting into his garage, concluding with what he had up to this moment always taken to be obvious. "But that means it had to be somebody we know, or that Caryn knew."

"Excuse me," Gina said, "but hasn't that been the assumption all along anyway? She was, after all, in the hot tub, naked."

"She always went in the hot tub naked," Stuart said. "But now I'm wondering. We don't know that whoever it was went in the hot tub with her, or even drank that other glass of wine. It might have been Caryn, who knocked the first glass off onto the deck where it broke. So she got out and cleaned up most of it. Then her killer showed up, snuck up and hit her with the bottle, then pushed her under. It didn't mean she was having an affair with him, or with anybody."

"That's true," Gina conceded.

"Maybe she wasn't," Wyatt agreed quickly. Stuart perhaps needed that belief, and Hunt was inclined to let him have it. "But let's go back to the garage door. You're saying Caryn must have known her killer because he had a device or some other way to open the garage door, which she'd presumably given him, is that it?"

"Right," Stuart said.

"Well no, sorry, but not necessarily," Hunt said. "Lots of cars, nowadays, they've got buttons in the visor or the roof and you can set them to the frequency of your garage door so you don't need the little box. So anybody who'd ever been around your garage—a meter reader, a tradesman, the gardener, the garbage man, anybody—could have essentially stolen your frequency if they wanted to."

"So you're saying maybe this TSNK guy . . . ?"

"Not impossible," Hunt said. "Anybody."

Gina saw movement out the window and spoke up. "Here's Devin," she said.

* * *

Gina went to open the door and Juhle was one step inside, half-way through his greeting to her, when he stopped, glaring at Hunt. "Wyatt," he said with a measured calm, "what are you doing here?"

Hunt, standing with Stuart by the couch, shrugged. "Working too hard as usual." Starting off jovially, but when Juhle didn't respond, he said, "Gina had a computer question."

"So you've been on his computer?" Without waiting for a reply, his eyes now dark, Juhle spun back to Gina. "Did I dream telling you not to touch anything until I got here? Did you think that didn't include Wyatt?" Then back to Hunt. "How long have you been on this?"

Hunt shrugged again. "Gina called me and I drove right on out."

"I'm not talking this particular computer problem, Wyatt. You know that. I mean how long have you been involved in this case?"

"I just met him," Hunt said.

"Not what I asked," Juhle snapped.

But Gina stepped up into his space. "What are you getting at, Devin? I asked Wyatt to come out and look at Stuart's computer, see if he could tell where these threatening e-mails might have originated. That's all there is to it."

"No, it isn't. Wyatt's working for you while he's pumping me for information."

"No pumping was involved, Dev. You never asked. And for the record, I wasn't on anybody's clock. But while I'm on Stuart's case here, I've got to tell you this e-mail he's got is what I believe you inspectors would call a clue. And since you missed it and we're giving it to you so you don't wind up making a big mistake, maybe you could chill a bit on the accusations about whose side I'm on. I'm here for the same reason you are, Dev. Gina asked me. I think we'd all like to get a handle on who we're actually looking for. Caryn's killer. How's that?"

Juhle clearly still didn't like it. He threw a last malevolent glance at Hunt, another at Gina, even half-turned as though he would be going back out the door he'd just entered. But at last he got himself settled enough to talk. "So what have you actually got?"

Suddenly, though, and to everyone else's surprise, Stuart spoke up. "Before we get to that, Inspector," he said, "we should tell you about the garage door."

"What about it?"

Gina held out a flat palm, hoping to cut off her client. "Stuart . . ."

"No," he said. "This is relevant. Wyatt was just telling us how anyone . . ."

"Stuart!" Gina's voice cut through the room, brooking no dissent. "I mean it. We don't want to hear it."

"Maybe I do," Juhle said.

By now, Gina had moved up between the inspector and her client. "I'm sure you do, but you're not going to." She turned back to Stuart, making sure he was getting her message. Everything was strategy. Very little was truth. Let Juhle think that they'd found holes in his case, and let him convey that impression to the DA. "Now, Inspector," she continued, "I invited you out here to look at these e-mails. If you're interested, the computer's upstairs." She turned and started walking, and the men fell in behind her.

Hunt sat again at the keyboard and the rest of them huddled behind him in the small room. Hunt took them all back to the first e-mail. "And this was after what, again?" Juhle asked.

"An article in *Sunset*," Stuart replied. "Just recipes for cooking trout outdoors."

Juhle glanced briefly at the threatening e-mail. "Guy's obviously a nutcase."

"The point," Gina said, "is that it wasn't Stuart. He didn't send this."

"You got any way to prove that?"

From the console, Hunt spoke up. "That's the problem, Dev. We can't—"

But suddenly Stuart interrupted. "Excuse me, Gina. Permission to speak?"

She looked over at him. "Probably not. Not here, anyway."

"How about out there?" Stuart indicated the adjoining room. "It might be worthwhile."

"Okay." She spoke to the other men. "Give us a second, guys. Be right back."

Gina and Stuart were about five steps out of the room when Juhle started in. "I don't know if you've ever heard of it, Wyatt, but we've got this thing in law enforcement called obstruction of justice, where if you impede an investigation you can go to jail."

Hunt tapped idly at the keyboard. "Has somebody we know impeded an investigation?"

"Briefing a suspect's lawyer on the progress of an official investigation might even fall under aiding and abetting."

Hunt stopped with the keyboard, turned around. More impatient than angry, he laid it out straight. "Give it a rest, Dev. You know I work for Gina's firm, you knew she was representing Stuart. If you chose not to put that together, that's your problem, my friend, not mine. I never admitted nor denied anything about my involvement or lack thereof with Gina when we talked the other night, and you never asked, so what's the issue?" Juhle started to say something but Hunt held up a finger, stopping him. "And you didn't give me any information I wouldn't have known by the next day, anyway. None of which, I might add, convicts Gorman of anything."

"Taken together, it well might, Wyatt."

But Hunt shook his head. "Which parts, taken together? That he was pissed off at his wife? That he yelled at a Highway Patrol guy?"

Juhle shot back at him. "How about that he's got a history of domestic violence? Or that he's having an affair with his sister-in-law? That he's suddenly worth several million more dollars? That his neighbor saw his car pull into his garage? I know, I know, it might not have been him driving. But guess what? Who else could have been driving his car?"

"Except if it wasn't his car."

"Right. The neighbor girl who admits she likes Gorman also wants to nail him for murder, so she lies to put him at the scene. Come on, Wyatt, none of this speaks to you?"

Pointing at the computer screen, Hunt said, "Not as loud as this stuff. You don't really believe he sent these threats to himself?"

"No, he probably didn't. But I also don't see them as much of a viable threat."

"Except that the wife is dead."

A shrug. "He just as easily could have gotten his last message from this lunatic on Friday and realized it would be a good distraction. In fact, it just as well might have been the thing that made him decide that this was a good time to do what he needed to do with his wife."

Hunt rolled the chair back from the computer desk, crossed his arms, looked up at his friend. "It's unbelievable."

"What is?"

"How little any of what we actually know makes any difference. You realize that. It's all mind-set. You think because he's the spouse, he did it, so everything reinforces that. I know the same facts, and nothing proves he did it. Do you know for a fact he's boinking the wife's sister? I mean, do you have hotel receipts, pictures, anything real?"

"Not yet. We're looking."

"Very strong. It's all guesswork." Hunt looked up at his friend. "You know what this reminds me of, me and you? Remember when Cheney shot that guy last year, the hunting accident? So I'm out with some guys and one of 'em makes a joke about how dangerous it is going hunting with the vice president. And another guy across the table, knee-jerk, he says he'd rather go hunting with Cheney any day than get in a car with Ted Kennedy."

"That reminds you of me and you?"

"My point is that Cheney could have done anything, killed the guy even, and no matter what the facts were, his supporters didn't care. No matter what Cheney does, Ted Kennedy's always going to be worse. That's what I'm talking about. Fixed positions."

"Except I'm not fixed, Wyatt. I'm trying to build a case, and many elements of what I've found so far point to the same conclusion."

"Are you looking at anybody else?"

"Nobody else has popped up as too likely."

"How about the business partners?"

Juhle shrugged. "I've talked to three of 'em so far. Furth from her investment group down in Palo Alto, and her two medical partners, McAfee and Pinkert. And yep, there might be some motive, but also there's lots of alibi."

"Midnight Sunday night? Good alibis? That's a little weird itself, don't you think? I mean, if they weren't home sleeping."

"They were. All of them."

Hunt chuckled. "Well, there you go again. They have wives? You ask them?"

"One divorced, two blissfully married, and no. No reason to, not yet. Nothing points to any of them, Wyatt. You or Roake get me something that looks real, I'll look into it, I promise. Meanwhile, it's all Gorman all the time. Why? Because he did it, that's why. He's made some mistakes, guaranteed. I just haven't found any of them yet."

Gina was back at the doorway, Stuart behind her. "What haven't you found yet?"

Juhle didn't miss a beat. "Any way to tie these threats to a person or even a location. It's going to make it tough. What have you two been up to out there?"

Indicating her client, Gina said, "Stuart's got some diaries he keeps up, notes on his trips, pictures. Since we know the dates of these e-mails, he wanted to check if he was out in the wilderness when they got sent, which would pretty much eliminate him as the sender, right?"

"Possibly. And?"

"Well, the first date, August twenty-third, last year. He was in the middle of a six-day hike in the Bitteroots with two friends of his, one of them Jedd Conley. California Assemblyman Jedd Conley? Who probably wouldn't lie about whether or not they'd brought computers along. They didn't. Here's the photo of the three of them, identities and dates on the back." Gina thought the photo was persuasive enough as she passed it over to Juhle, three guys with loaded back-packs gathered around the hood of Stuart's SUV. "And Stuart didn't send these messages, Inspector. They're legitimate threats, and the last one appears to have been carried out."

Juhle took in that information with a stone face.

Wyatt Hunt twisted around to look at him and said, "Well?"

"It's a complication," Juhle conceded. "Except that the threats weren't really directed at Caryn, were they?"

Juhle having gone, the defense team was back downstairs in the kitchen. Hunt sat across from Gina at the table, his hands folded in front of him. From his perch on the counter, Stuart said, "Facts aren't going to make any difference, are they? Juhle's not seeing them."

Gina said, "He's going to have to deal with this latest stuff on some level. All things being equal, we bring these e-mails up in front of a jury, we've got a good leg up on reasonable doubt right there."

"Okay, but I don't want to keep talking about being in front of a jury. That means I'm arrested. We've got to keep it from getting to there."

"Granted," Gina said. "But we've got to be realistic too. And prepared."

"So what are you saying?" Stuart asked. "That he's going to arrest me no matter what? Even if he doesn't find any new evidence?"

"What do you mean, 'new'?" Hunt asked. "He doesn't have any yet, does he?"

"Not much physical evidence, no," Gina said. "And as I say, to-day might actually have slowed him down." She threw a glance at her client. "But realistically, we've got to be aware that it's not going to take too much more, Stuart. Maybe just the DA saying he wants to go for it. It's high profile enough that Gerry Abrams just might want the opportunity."

"Who's Gerry Abrams?"

"An assistant DA," Hunt said. "A tad ambitious, as Gina will attest."

She nodded. "Gerry does love a challenge."

"Terrific," Stuart said. "So what do I do in the meanwhile?"

Gina and Wyatt shared a glance. Neither of them had an answer for him.

SEVENTEEN

———

No, THANKS, HE DIDN'T HAVE MUCH of an appetite and didn't want to join Gina and Wyatt for lunch.

When they'd gone, Stuart paced in a cold fury from the hot tub on the enclosed porch in the back, out through the library, back into the kitchen, across the dining room and then the large living room and up the stairs to their—now his—bedroom. Down the hallway to Kymberly's room at the front of the house, he peeked through one of the two windows, through slats in the blinds, and noticed Bethany's window in the house directly across the way.

Her own blinds were open, the room's light thoughtlessly left on, and if he squinted through the still-bright noon sunlight, Stuart could just make out what appeared to be a poster on Bethany's bedroom wall. Scanning down, he got to Bethany's front door. Abruptly stepping back from the window, he realized how close the two buildings were—a hundred feet? Less? He could clearly read the greenish brass numbers of their street address set in the stucco next to the door. Bethany's identification of his car, even in the dark, would be credible if not compelling if she got it in front of a jury.

The thought of himself in front of a jury turned him around and brought him beyond the master bedroom to the back end of the house. There, beside his tiny office, in a closet filled with file cabinets, piles of manuscript pages, rarely worn clothing, and free samples of fishing and other outdoor gear he'd endorsed, he moved an old blanket and some sweaters and junk out of the way and got down on one knee. With the door open behind him for the light, he worked the combination on his safe, reached in and felt the old Crown Royal bag in which he kept his gun wrapped, and pulled it out.

As always, the Smith & Wesson 9GVE pistol felt heavier than he knew it to be. Its empty, unloaded weight was less than two pounds, but the thing always had what he considered to be a psychic heft that made up for its diminutive size. At four inches of barrel length, the gun was a short, snubby, recreational weapon that he'd bought on a lark long before his marriage and rarely used since. He'd bought it, basically, for fun.

But today, in his nonreflective mood, he stood with the velvet bag and its gun in one hand, its two clips and one box of bullets in the other, and crossed the room to sit at his desk. Moving his keyboard out of the way, he reached in and pulled out the gun. Doubly wrapped as it was in an old, oil-stained T-shirt, he unwrapped the package and set it down in front of him.

He always kept it clean and well oiled, and now he felt a modicum of satisfaction that it was ready to shoot. Checking the date on his nearly full box of 9mm bullets, he realized that he must have bought the ammunition on his last trip to the range at the beginning of the summer. More good news. He didn't want to have to stop and buy more bullets and face even the cursory questions of a clerk or, worse, possible recognition.

Pulling each bullet out individually, he checked them for external imperfections, but found none in any of the nine (eight for the clip and then, after racking a round, one in the chamber) that he slapped into the pistol's handle. Neither were there any bullet problems for the second clip that he slipped into the pocket of his Levi's.

The gun loaded now, the safety on and double-checked, Stuart stood up, and leaving his empty Crown Royal bag and half box of bullets on the computer table, he went back to the safe. Reaching in, he grabbed from a pile of fifty-dollar bills that he kept there for just such an emergency. Flipping through the money, it seemed to him that it was significantly less than he thought he'd put away, but there were still several hundred dollars all told, plenty to get by on for a while. Closing the door and twisting the combo lock, he went back to his computer, moved the ammunition box out of the way, and put the loaded gun onto the desk proper. In his ergonomic chair, he brought the keyboard back down in front of him.

On his e-mail screen, he stared at the latest threat for the briefest instant before hitting the Reply icon and typing his own message back. Out of habit, he reread what he'd typed for spelling mistakes and typos and, finding none, moved his mouse up to Send and clicked. The text: *"Come and get me, you cowardly son of a bitch."*

Satisfied, he turned off the computer, picked up his S&W, and carried it into his bedroom, where he placed it carefully on the made-up bed. He did not own anything but a generic belt holster, and had no intention of using that. Nor did he have a permit to carry a concealed weapon, and that is what he fully intended to do.

But first, he needed to throw some things together. He kept his travel duffel bag on a peg in his bedroom closet, and he put that next to the gun on the bed, then went to his dresser and pulled out a week's worth of socks and underwear. He didn't know how long this was going to take; at the moment, he couldn't have said with any specificity what "this" even was. His brain took him to the probable day of his wife's funeral—the following Monday or Tuesday?—but refused to go any further.

All he knew was that he wasn't going to jail—not for a week, not for a day, not for an hour.

In the bathroom, he gathered up a small selection of essential toiletries. He thought he might find himself having trouble with sleep over the next few days, so he threw in a truly ancient, perhaps no longer effective, half-consumed bottle of Dalmane sleeping pills that Caryn had needed for a while. And her remaining Vicodin, a few tablets.

Back in the bedroom, he rolled up another pair of jeans, four T-shirts, a lightweight fleece undershirt and two identical brown pullover sweaters. It was warm today, but you never knew. This was San Francisco, and it could be midwinter by dinnertime.

The telephone by his bed rang and he started to lift the receiver, but finally let it go until the machine picked up on the fifth ring. He heard a female voice downstairs on the answering machine, but couldn't tell who it was exactly. Debra? Gina? Kymberly? Some reporter? He couldn't say and didn't care.

Finally, in the new jangling quiet, he stood in his closet, staring at his hanging clothes. He needed a moderately heavy jacket that allowed freedom of movement, that would call no attention to himself, that would cover where he intended, should the need arise, to tuck his gun into his belt at the center of his back. He chose a gray-green front-zipping parka from Mountain Hardwear and wrapped the gun in it, then stuffed it into the duffel and zipped it shut.

Downstairs, leaving his duffel bag on the dining room table, Stuart went out to the hot tub area one last time. He leaned over the tub for most of a minute, but nothing in these surroundings stuck to him. He picked up no sense of Caryn's presence, of her ghost. There was only humidity and the faint whiff of chlorine, and a vast emptiness.

The house had a side door that led to a walkway along the fence at the edge of his property. Aware of the growing probability of reporters lurking—Juhle had reported a sighting on the street when he'd come by, as had Gina and Hunt earlier—and wanting to avoid them at all costs, Stuart went down through the garage and out that door, then along the fence into his backyard, a small wasteland of yellowing grass and untended planter beds.

Stopping on the grass and looking up at the back windows of his surrounding neighbors, he made sure that no one happened to be staring out just at that moment. Satisfied, he continued down to the end of the fence, where a gate opened into another steep uphill walkway between two other houses.

Coming out on Larkin, he walked downhill for three driveways and stopped at the fourth, taking one last quick look around for reporters or bystanders. No one. He already had his key out, and now he put it where it belonged in the garage door, turned it and opened the door up. Scarce parking everywhere in San Francisco, but particularly here on Russian Hill, had forced him to rent this place for his old black Ford F-150 pickup truck for about the last seven years, beginning at eighty dollars a month—a hundred and fifty now, and considered a bargain at that.

Throwing his duffel bag onto the floor on the passenger side, he slid in behind the wheel. He fished around in the glove box for his Leatherman tool, then got out with that and walked to the street, which was lined with parked cars. Picking out a vehicle at random, and making sure it didn't have the window sticker that identified it as one of the neighborhood cars, he squatted quickly down and removed the back license plate, replacing it with his own truck's plate. He went to the front and repeated the process. In less than three minutes, the new plates were on his pickup. One minute later, he'd backed out, closed and locked the garage behind him, and driven off in the direction of Jedd Conley's office in North Beach.

They sat drinking their coffees in the window of Mario's Bohemian Cigar Store, mostly a lunch-counter restaurant that sold cigars but only incidentally, at the corner of Columbus and Union. They were looking out at Washington Square Park with its contingent of tai chi classes, Frisbee-chasing dogs and, because of the sunshine, picnickers spread out over the grass.

But they weren't paying any attention to the scenery or to their drinks. Stuart had just told him that he was going down the Peninsula to talk to some of Caryn's business connections down there. Conley's face was drawn in concentration as he spun his coffee cup slowly in its saucer. "You want the truth, I don't think it's a particularly brilliant idea, Stu. You don't know anything about these guys, what they're like, and if one of them killed Caryn . . ."

"I'm going on the assumption that one of them had to have killed Caryn, Jedd."

"Not necessarily. Maybe it was this 'Thou Shalt Not Kill' guy."

Stuart went still for a second before shaking his head. "If it was him, he'll try for me next time regardless of what I do now."

"But you just told me . . ."

"I know, I know. And if it keeps Juhle off-balance for a day or two, it's all to the good. But look at this. In the first place, he doesn't quietly come into my home while I'm not there, and apparently without a weapon. No, he's at least got a gun. He's not coming to my house to stab me in my sleep. The guy's writing me threats on the Internet, for Christ's sake, Jedd. He's never going to risk letting me see him, or get me into some kind of hand-to-hand combat. If he does anything, he's going to shoot me, probably from a distance. Plus, he wants me, not Caryn."

"Maybe to punish you?"

"I don't think so. And there's no sign of a struggle, which there would have been. If she heard the garage door, and she would have, she would have thought it was me coming home early. And that would have got her out of the tub with a towel around her, at the very least."

"Maybe not. Maybe while you were gone she thought about the reality of you two getting divorced and changed her mind."

Stuart's mouth curved up, but it wasn't quite a smile. "That's a kind thing to say, Jedd, but that didn't happen."

"So what are you saying?"

"I'm saying she knew who it was. She was expecting him."

Conley suddenly seemed to remember his coffee and took a sip, then put the cup down with exaggerated care. "So you want to talk to who?"

"Everybody I outlined to Gina, the people Caryn did business with. All the other suspects. My other suspects, I should say."

"But you said they all had alibis."

"No. Juhle said that. They were all sleeping in their homes, apparently. Or maybe not. It could have been any of them."

"So what do you expect to accomplish?"

"I talk to them all, maybe I'll flush the one who did it."

"And then what?"

A shrug. "Play it by ear, I suppose. Break the guy's story, take it to Juhle. Or Gina."

"Or maybe, since he's already killed once, he'll just take you out too." Conley shook his head. "Listen, Stu, this is a bad idea. You said Gina's got an investigator working for her. He does this stuff every day, right? Questions witnesses, checks out alibis, huh? Let him do it."

"And meanwhile, what do I do? Sit around and wait for Juhle to come and arrest me?"

"You've got funeral arrangements, don't you? You've got Kym. You got Debra."

"I'm not spending any time in jail."

"Well, that's what Gina . . ."

"No!"

The vehemence of the answer brought Conley up short. "Hey! Easy." He straightened up in his chair. " 'No' what, Stu?"

"You're talking about Gina and her investigator, but the fact of the matter is that neither of their jobs have anything to do with keeping me out of jail. If I'm arrested, I'm sure they'll be great, but listen to them—all of them: Gina, Hunt, Juhle. Listen to them talk and you get the impression that the whole arrest scenario isn't really in anybody's hands. It can just happen when some kid of a DA gets a wild hair."

"But Gina's kept it from happening up till now."

"Not exactly true. It's either her or the fact that Juhle can't find evidence that I did it. In spite of my blabbing my guts out to him on day one." Finally, Stuart's features seemed to relax to a degree. "I'm not complaining about Gina, Jedd. I'm glad she's on board, for which I have you to thank. But I can't sit around and wait until somebody decides I need to be in jail. I've got to do something."

"Understandable." Conley cocked his head. "So you've come back to me? Not that I wouldn't help you in any way I can, but I can't really afford to get mixed up in this in a public way, Stu."

"I get it. Politics. Hanging out with a murder suspect is bad form. The help I want wouldn't be any more public than we are right now."

Conley finished off the dregs of his coffee, during which time he came to his decision. "All right," he said. "What are friends for? What do you need?"

Stuart cast a glance around the tiny restaurant, then leaned in across the table. "You said you'd talked to Caryn on Friday. You'd been working with her on some of the problems with PII and the socket. How serious were they?"

As though appreciating the question for the first time, Conley nodded almost imperceptibly, his eyes narrowed. "All things being equal, pretty serious. Evidently in some of the clinical trials, there'd been problems."

"Like what?"

Conley hesitated. "Like, apparently, people dying."

"Apparently? People don't apparently die, Jedd. They actually die. Did Caryn know about this? She must have."

"She was trying to understand what had happened first. There was ambiguity."

"How could there be ambiguity? People either died or they didn't, right?"

"Right. Sure. But these deaths happened after the study had been published, so due to the length of time before the problem showed up, there was some question about whether it was the result of the hip replacement or not."

"And Caryn was trying to find out?"

"Essentially, yes. You know as a public service my office looks into certain kinds of business fraud on behalf of some of our constituencies, and Caryn asked if . . ."

"Jedd. You already got my vote. I'm sure you did what you needed to do. But you're saying Caryn might have been threatening to blow the whistle on PII about these deaths. Which would cost all of the investors big money, wouldn't it?"

"I don't know if she'd gotten to that yet, but it . . . I'd say she was in the process of deciding what she was going to do."

"And who was she talking to about this? Besides you? The guy in Palo Alto, Furth?"

"Mostly, yes, I believe. Fred Furth."

EIGHTEEN

————

Elbow resting out the driver's side window, letting the warm and fragrant air swirl around him in the truck's cab, Stuart Gorman kept his pickup at the speed limit all the way on the "Country's Most Scenic Freeway," the 280 out of San Francisco down the forty-some miles to Palo Alto. He almost missed the small polished-granite sign indicating the headquarters of Sand Hill Equities Bank—a long, low, black glass building that appeared to be built directly into a tawny-brown hillside off Page Mill Road.

As he pulled into the parking lot, which was graciously shaded with olive trees, Stuart realized that his ride didn't exactly fit into the prevailing motif of luxury automobiles. He wondered about the location of the local dealership that obviously gave away all the Mercedes, BMWs, Lexuses and the random Porsche, since he figured there was no way that this many people could afford to buy them.

Parking far over to one side to retain a tenuous obscurity, he got out of the cab in the now-impressive heat and caught a glimpse of himself reflected in the building's surface: jeans, T-shirt, hiking boots.

He couldn't put on his jacket in this weather to cover his S&W. Which meant that the gun remained wrapped in the jacket inside his duffel bag.

So much for preparation. "Idiot," he said.

It didn't matter.

The receptionist somehow conveyed the impression that billionaires dressed any way they damn pleased. And when Fred Furth heard who was waiting outside in the lobby to speak to him, even though Stuart didn't have an appointment, he came right out.

In his mid-thirties, with a square jaw, perfect teeth, and an athlete's body molded into a two-thousand-dollar suit, he nevertheless managed to exude both sincerity and sympathy. "Mr. Gorman. Frederick Furth. Fred."

"Stuart."

Furth had a crushing grip. "It's good to meet you at last, although I wish it could have been under less difficult circumstances. We are all still devastated here about Caryn. And of course, anything we can do to help you . . ." He turned to his receptionist. "We'll be in my office, Carol. No calls, please. No interruptions. Mr. Gorman. Stuart. This way."

They walked in silence down a cool, wide, dove gray corridor and into a very spacious office made distinctive by a floor-to-ceiling window that covered two-thirds of the facing wall until it disappeared into the hillside into which the building had been built. Behind Furth's desk, the back wall—windowless—featured six inset computer terminals and two television screens, all of them on and, in the case of the TVs, with the sound turned down.

But Furth didn't head toward his desk, but instead to a seating area of functional leather chairs over where the room was brightest. As Stuart was sitting down, taking in his surroundings, the banker asked if he could get him anything. "If it helps you decide, I'm having coffee. Peet's."

"Sounds good," Stuart said. "Black's fine."

A high-tech, burnished-steel coffee machine claimed pride of place on the counter. Furth moved efficiently. He pulled mugs—not cups and saucers—down from the built-in cabinets, placed one under each spigot on the machine, and pushed one button. In less than a minute, the coffee was in front of them, and Stuart took a sip. "Thanks for seeing me. I know you must be busy. I probably should have called first, but I've been running on automatic for the past couple of days."

Furth waved that off. "I'd imagine so. I'd actually thought of calling you, but . . ." He paused.

"But you wanted to see if I got myself arrested first?"

A muted acknowledgment, shoulders slipping an inch, a quick twitch of an embarrassed smile. "Maybe a little of that. Sorry."

Stuart nodded. "For the record, I didn't kill my wife. The papers—everybody, in fact—seems to have it wrong. I wasn't there when it happened."

"All right," Furth said. "It wouldn't be the first time the media got things wrong. They need a story. For the moment you're the story. I've been there too. We can agree that it sucks. Now how can I help you?"

Stuart's drive down here had been an unraveling and evolving fantasy where he terrorized the men with whom Caryn had been involved, Furth the first of them. Now he was facing this charming and confident businessman in the flesh, and suddenly his very presence here struck him as somewhat ludicrous, even surreal. "To be honest with you, I'm not certain," he began. "I'm trying to get a handle on some parts of Caryn's life that I didn't know too much about. One of the first things I came across is I understand that she was having some issues with PII, financial and otherwise, and that you were the point man she talked to about all that."

"I'm not sure of everything you're talking about, but you're probably right. That was me. But if you're saying you think there's some connection between those issues and her death, I'd say you're wildly off the mark."

"I'm not saying that. Not yet, anyway. I don't even know what the issues were."

Furth killed a few seconds with his coffee, then put the mug down on the glass table in front of them and sat back in his chair, crossing a leg. It was the opposite of an antagonistic posture, relaxed and open. He seemed ready to talk. "You said 'financial and otherwise.' What's the otherwise?"

"I guess it would fall under ethics. She'd heard her socket had killed some people."

A cock of the head. "I thought you said you didn't know the issues."

"Not all of them. And I just found this one out an hour ago. So it's true?"

"Well," Furth said, "that's still to be determined. There are questions, certainly. And Caryn wanted them answered."

"Before final FDA approval?"

"That would have been her choice, yes."

"And what was holding that up? Getting answers?"

Furth brought his hand up to his Adam's apple and pulled at the knot of his tie. He cleared his throat. "Well, the company, PII, did the usual rigorous clinical testing, of course, as the FDA mandates on any new product, and the results of these tests assured the company and the investors that there was no problem with going into full production."

"Except that there was a problem?"

"Well, of course, when people die, you've got at the very least a perceptual problem." Now Furth uncrossed his legs and came forward a bit in his chair, a smile that begged for understanding. "But the fact is, the deaths were only reported long after the study period, so they were outside the study's parameters."

"But the people really did die, didn't they? Weren't there autopsies to find out why?"

"In some cases, yes, but the results were inconclusive."

"Inconclusive how?"

"In the way that blood clots can come from any number of sources. Not necessarily from complications of hip replacement surgery three to five years before."

"So these people, they died of blood clot complications."

"Basically, yes."

"How many of them?"

"To date, we've had formal confirmation of six. But you have to remember that this is out of over six hundred surgeries. So it's exactly in the ballpark of typical post-op clots, which is about one in a hundred. And remember that none of the patients were under sixty. The Dryden Socket wasn't causing those deaths. It was most probably the surgeries themselves. Typical complications. Tragic, of course, but typical."

"And what did Caryn think about that?"

Furth shrugged, turned his palms up, utterly forthcoming. "If you want the truth, I think she was just hypersensitive because it was her invention, with her name on it and everything. Once PII goes into full production, the numbers are going to be staggering. The profit numbers, I mean. She—both of you—were going to become very, very rich. I think the magnitude and reality of it made her nervous."

Stuart strongly doubted the truth of this. If anything, the opposite—that she would experience even a temporary setback in her pursuit of money—would be more likely to make her nervous. But there was nothing to be gained by voicing that opinion. Instead, he said, "So what was she calling you about?"

"She wanted me to intervene with PII. She thought they could solve the problem in two years or so, once they got a clear understanding of what it was. Again, from the late reports. Some more autopsies, that sort of thing."

"She wanted to put production on hold."

Seeing that Stuart seemed to understand and accept the basic issue, Furth sat back more comfortably again. "Essentially, yes. Which—I think you must know—well, you know about Caryn's mezzanine loan, of course?"

"Sure. The broad strokes."

"Well, hers wasn't the only one. And a delay of two years or more at this stage . . . I mean, some of the investors . . ." Another shrug. "I think you can see the problem."

"I think so." Stuart clipped out the response and realized that he was struggling to keep the outrage from his voice. "Caryn was threatening to blow the whistle on what she'd come to believe was a faulty product, and if she succeeded it would cost some people maybe millions of dollars. Isn't that about it?"

"I don't think she was quite to the point of blowing the whistle on anything. She just needed some hand-holding, the usual last-minute reassurance. She wanted to go forward as much as the next investor, I believe."

"She didn't talk to you about trying to postpone PII's production?"

"Not with any specificity, no. There really was just too much riding on all this. In another couple of months, both of you would have been smiling all the way to the bank. I'm sure of it."

Stuart felt that if he sat more than another minute or two under Furth's unyielding gaze with its unflappable geniality, he might be forced to come back inside the building with his gun and blow the guy away just on general principles. But there was one more avenue he needed to explore, if gently.

"So, Fred, let me ask—has a homicide inspector named Juhle called you?"

The change of topic didn't scare Furth. In fact, it seemed to put him on firmer ground somehow. Matter-of-fact, he nodded. "Yesterday. He asked what I was doing Sunday night."

"Let me guess," Stuart said. "Sleeping in bed."

"Eleven o'clock Sunday night, what would anybody be doing if you've got to be up at five thirty?"

"Five thirty?"

"Wall Street time. You're in the markets, that's when you're up if you want to make the six-thirty bell. But you already knew what I'd told him?" A question.

Stuart said, "I asked him if he was even looking for any other suspects—besides me—and he said he'd checked alibis with everybody on Caryn's cell phone. Which included you."

"So now you're asking me?" The question didn't seem to bother him, or maybe Fred Furth was so programmed for affability in his career that like Marie Antoinette he wouldn't show any anger or resentment even if he were facing his executioner.

"I mean no offense," Stuart said, adopting the tone, "but somebody must be lying about where they were if they killed Caryn, and I intend to find out who that was."

"Well." Again, palms up, unfeigned innocence. "It wasn't me. I'd say you could ask my wife or any of my three kids, but I'd really prefer you didn't see the need to do that. But because my heart goes out to you, it really does, I'll tell you more than the inspector asked. I barbecued a chicken on my new rotisserie. It was great, rosemary and lemon. Outstanding. And had half a bottle of wine—you know Chalk Hill Chardonnay? Awesome stuff. Then put the kids down by seven thirty—the oldest is six, so bedtime's always early. And I was sawing logs myself by nine. So no, I didn't kill Caryn. Besides which, I thought she was a great person. Smart, interesting, fun."

Stuart nodded, and suddenly found himself unable to speak. Evidently his wife had remained smart, interesting and fun to some people right up until the time she'd been killed. Covering his emotional lapse with a sip of coffee, Stuart put his mug down and got to his feet. "One more thing, if you don't mind? Did any of the other investors know she was working to get this postponement on going into full production?"

"Not that I know of. Not through me, certainly. Someone may have gotten some wind of it out of PII directly, but even that would have been unusual."

"Well." A chagrined look on his face, Stuart held out a hand. "Thanks for your time. Sorry for the questions."

"No problem," Furth said. "I wish I could have been more help."

The cab of Stuart's truck baked at close to one hundred degrees out in the lot. Opening both doors for cross-ventilation, he checked behind the front seat on the passenger side where he'd stashed his duffel bag and saw that it was where and how he'd left it and then, on second thought, brought it out and reached down to the bottom where he'd thrown in his little-used first generation cell phone. Going to stand in the shade of an olive tree while the cab aired out, he punched in his daughter's number.

"Hey, Dad. Where are you?"

"How did you know it was me?"

"You're kidding, right? You're in my address book. You call, your name comes up."

"Where?"

"On the window? In front? Hello? But let's play another game. Where are you?"

"Palo Alto. Talking to some people Mom did business with."

"What about?"

"What she was doing with them. If maybe it made somebody mad at her."

"Shouldn't the cops be doing that?"

"They're not, though. And I've decided I'm not going to get arrested, so it's up to me."

"What do you mean, you're not going to get arrested?"

"I mean pretty much the standard meaning. I'm not going to jail."

"Yeah, but . . . Dad, I don't think it's like they ask your opinion."

"No, I know. Which is why I wanted to call you and tell you how you could reach me if you need to. You've got my cell number?"

"Didn't we just do this? It's in my phone. How else would it know it was you calling?"

"Right. Yeah. Of course. But my point is that you can reach me anytime, but don't tell anybody you know where I am."

"Anybody? What about your lawyer?"

"No. I'll contact her if I need to."

"What about Debra?"

"You can tell Debra, but I don't really want to talk to her."

"Why not? She's being nice to me."

"I know that. She's a fine person, and I'm glad she's letting you stay with her, but I just can't talk to her right now, okay? And I promise I'll do what I need to for the funeral. But for now, I've got to do some things and maybe stay out of sight."

"But what if . . . I mean, if they say you're under arrest, they can just come and get you."

"If they can find me, which is why I don't want you telling anybody about my number."

"But they might shoot you. Don't they do that, for like resisting arrest?"

"Nobody's going to shoot me, Kym. I'm just laying low, okay?"

"I don't like it. I really don't like it, Daddy."

"Well . . ."

"What if they do shoot you, then what? First Mom, and then . . . I mean, what am I supposed to do if . . ." This, Stuart knew, was classic Kym beginning her downward spiral, and it was only going to get worse if he didn't stand firm.

"Sweetie, sweetie, sweetie. Hold up. Whoa. We'll be in touch all the time, you and me. I'm not going to confront any policemen, I promise. If they find me, I'll go along. But I really, really want to avoid that. I'm not going to let anybody kill me. Cops or anybody else."

"You know what you tell me whenever I say anything like that?"

"No. What?"

"Famous last words."

It took him the better part of five minutes to end that conversation on anything less than a disastrously negative note, but he kept at it until his daughter was at least giving lip service to respecting his decision. In the course of the talk, though, he asked her if she'd tried to reach him at their house earlier in the day and she'd told him no. Debra hadn't tried to call him either.

He'd been sure it was a woman's voice on the answering machine when he'd been packing, so it must have been Gina. Which meant there may have been a development. He considered it for a few seconds, and decided it probably wouldn't be profitable to talk to her in person, plus he was all argued out with his daughter, so he called his own home number to get the message Gina must have left.

But it wasn't Gina.

"Hello, this is Kelley Gray Rusnak from PII calling for Stuart. Stuart, I don't know if you remember me, but I was Caryn's lab assistant down here. You and I met a couple of times. I see what they're saying in the papers about you and Caryn, but you know I've read all your books and I just don't believe you're the kind of person who could hurt someone, especially Caryn. And I don't know, maybe you're already in jail, but I haven't heard that on the news yet and I probably would have, so I thought I'd try to reach you at your home number. I think maybe there's something you should know about that's been going on here, that Caryn was kind of worried about . . ."

NINETEEN

THE PII CORPORATE OFFICES AND LABORATORIES were located in the industrial flats, pocked by low-rise development, near the San Francisco airport. Kelley Rusnak seemed relieved to hear back from Stuart, but didn't want to talk about it on the telephone. Stuart convinced her to take some time off and meet him in half an hour at the Hungry Hunter, a steak house just off the freeway in San Bruno, perhaps ten minutes from where she worked.

The cab of the truck had cooled to mere lava, but Stuart barely noticed. Kicking himself for not having answered the phone in his house, when Kelley's information, whatever it was, might have done him some good in his discussions with Fred Furth or even Juhle, he was obviously speeding as he flew past a Palo Alto city police car waiting at the front of a line at a red light on El Camino. Slamming on his brakes, then jamming down a couple of gears, his eyes were glued to the rearview as the cop turned in behind him and lit up his red flashers.

A murder suspect driving a vehicle with a stolen license plate, carrying a loaded gun in the cab, Stuart put on his blinker and began to pull over. But the patrol car swung left around him. As it passed, the officer in the passenger seat wagged a finger at Stuart, but evidently they'd gotten a call to some event that trumped his traffic stop. Raising his own hand, acknowledging the warning with a wary smile, Stuart continued on the El Camino for another block before turning off the main thoroughfare into a side street—any side street. With his stomach churning and his head gone light with the close call, he wound his way through a neighborhood of mostly brand-new mansions, to the freeway entrance.

He was at the Hungry Hunter parking lot fifteen minutes later. It was past lunchtime now, and still an hour or more before happy hour was to begin, so there was no problem with parking. Stuart was rolling up his driver's side window when a knock on the other window almost made him jump. When he'd gotten Kelley's message, and even when he'd talked to her and set up this meeting, he hadn't been completely sure which of Caryn's lab colleagues Kelley was. But now, reaching over and unlocking the door, he recognized her right away.

She was an inch on either side of five feet tall, probably in her mid-thirties, with shoulder-length black hair and a faintly cherubic face, unadorned by makeup of any kind, even lipstick. "Do you mind if we just talk out here in your cab?" Although she'd already climbed in and closed the door behind her. Turning to face him, she let out an anxious breath, tried a mostly unsuccessful smile and said, "Hi."

"Hi. How are you doing?"

"I'm a little nervous, to tell you the truth."

"What about? Coming to see me?"

"Not just that, but that, too, yes. Driving over here, I even thought somebody might have been following me. They passed by and went on the freeway, but still . . ."

"Why would somebody be following you?"

"No reason, really. And they probably weren't. But things have been so weird lately, and then with Caryn . . . I'm so sorry about her. She was really . . . really special. I still can't believe it."

"I'm having some troubles with that myself." Stuart turned and looked around behind them, out over the parking lot. "Well, Kelley, we seem to be the only ones out here. If you want, we could go some-place else, or just drive. Whatever you want."

She shook her head. "No. I'm sure this is all right. I'm just being paranoid." A quick smile. "Which of course doesn't mean that they're not after me."

"Who would be after you?"

"Well . . . I guess whoever might have been after Caryn."

"We're talking concerns about the Dryden Socket, right?"

She nodded.

Stuart took a beat, then rolled his window down again and rested his hands on the bottom of the steering wheel. "Just before I called you, I was visiting with Frederick Furth down in Palo Alto," he said. "You know him?"

"By name, sure. He was Caryn's go-to guy for the money stuff."

"Right. He told me that Caryn was just having some last-minute jitters, that's all. It was nothing serious. You don't agree with that?"

"Not even a little bit. That's just not true. She was going to try to stop them from going into full production if she could. At least that's what she told me last week."

"But why, Kelley? Furth told me about the problems that didn't make it into the clinical studies, okay, but—"

"Those weren't 'problems,' Stuart. They were deaths."

"Right. Furth acknowledged that. He wasn't trying to hide any-thing that I could see. He said you're always going to get a certain percentage of deaths in any major surgeries like these from various complications. Post-op clots. That kind of thing."

"Right. A certain percentage. Did he happen to tell you what that percentage was?"

"He said about one in a hundred. Which is what's coming back from these clinical trials. I think he said they've had six deaths in six hundred surgeries, something like that, which is right in the pocket for this kind of surgery in general."

She was looking at him in disbelief. "He told you one in a hundred? He's off by a factor of five."

"How could that be? I mean, all this stuff is published, isn't it? It's public record."

"Right. And so far—so far—it's true they've had those six confirmed deaths that have been in the first published studies, the ones that came in just a little too late. I suppose you've heard about that since that's what all the fuss has been about. The late reports. Except what Mr. Furth left out is that these aren't the only studies reporting fatalities. They're just the only ones that have been vetted and published so far."

"And Caryn knew about others?"

"Of course. She's the inventor. She wanted to see the earliest drafts. Which evidently they tried to keep from her too. And pretty successfully."

"Who did?"

"Furth. The money people. And of course Bill Blair. Our CEO? Once we pulled through the first round of clinical trials, they were all gung ho for full production, but Caryn had gotten some calls from docs she knew that had had problems. She even had a couple of her own patients show some disturbing signs. And it worried her."

Some of these details rang with a distant familiarity in Stuart's mind. He was sure that Caryn had mentioned some of this to him back when she was first starting to test her new socket, her concerns about every aspect of the product. But he hadn't paid very close attention.

Caryn was all about problems and their solutions. She was the original girl who cried wolf—everything was a crisis, a problem, a challenge. Their daughter wouldn't eat dinner one night and Caryn would harangue his ear off about how Kym was borderline anorexic or bulimic. If a patient had a rough night's sleep after surgery—and almost all of them did—Caryn would worry it to death. Until finally Stuart, feeling it was out of self-defense, just finally shut her off. He couldn't listen to any more "what ifs." She'd talk and talk, one critical topic—money, the state of health care, polymer chemistry, her patients, Kymberly—flowing seamlessly into the next, and each one fraught with danger, possible failure, alternatives to consider.

Exhausting. Constant and exhausting.

Until he was left nodding, pitching in with the occasional "Uh-huh."

But now, sitting here with Kelley, he realized that many of the things that engrossed Caryn might in fact have been damned interesting, even compelling. Certainly, the details surrounding the Dryden Socket were fascinating—and incredibly important—to him right now at this moment. But back when it had been a part of Caryn's daily existence he had been tuned out, deaf to the songs that gave meaning to his wife's life.

It had not all been her shutting him out, at least not at the beginning. He'd been equally complicit, perhaps more so, in the dissolution of their intimacy. The thought hit him, suddenly and unexpectedly, in a wave of regret and loss and brought him up short, his hand suddenly at his forehead as though pressing away a migraine.

"Stuart? Are you all right?"

He nodded at her. "I'm sorry. My mind just went out. Where were we?"

"Clotting," Kelley said. "Hypercoagulability."

"Sure," Stuart said, "I was going to say that."

"You're teasing, but it's a real thing. It's what Caryn was trying to fix."

"Could a layperson understand it if he wanted to explain it to his lawyer, for example?"

"I think so. You know that the basic problem Caryn set for herself was to find a plastic for the cup-side of the hip that didn't degrade, right?"

"Generally, yes."

"Okay, so she knows polymer chemistry inside out. She discovers this one particular type of high-density polyethylene—"

"Whoa, Kelley. We're dumbing it down, okay?"

An impatient pout, then Kelley continued. "High-density poly-ethylene *is* dumbed down, I'm afraid. You don't want to hear the technical name. Bottom line is she found a plastic that worked in animal trials. As you know."

"What wasn't working before?" Stuart asked.

"The basic problem? Some people, Caryn included, believed that the industry standard plastic was the proximate cause of even the one percent of blood clots. And even worse, over time the plastic elutes a chemical—"

"It does what?"

"Elutes. Produces. A chemical that dramatically increases coagulation in some people. It's called 'small particle disease'—there's a layman's term for you—and it's often fatal."

"And that's what Caryn was trying to avoid?"

"Right. She thought, or hoped anyway, that she could drastically reduce that one percent clotting number, maybe down to one in a thousand cases, or less. So I think it's important to understand that even if Mr. Furth was correct on the fatality number he gave you, and he's not, the Dryden Socket at one percent failure was no improvement over what we've been doing for years. And in fact, Caryn was most of the way to convinced that it was worse."

"How much worse?"

Kelley bit at her lower lip and took in a deep breath. "Maybe a lot. Maybe as much as five percent. Those are the preliminary figures from studies that aren't completed yet. Five in a hundred deaths."

"From the same thing? Small particle disease?"

"No. In fact, we've done several coagulation cascades and this is kind of the opposite, where we're seeing the creation of multinucleated giant cells which, essentially, become osteoclasts that eat bone."

"Eat bone? Not good, I'm guessing."

"It is bad. It's going to be much worse, though, if PII goes into full production."

"But if they know this, why would they go ahead with it? I mean, they've got to realize that they're looking at lawsuits forever. They'd be killing themselves."

"Not if they could get the problem fixed soon enough. They could take orders, start some cash flow going, have the delay later in the process rather than sooner. Caryn was already working on it, narrowing down some other options . . ."

"Another plastic?"

"Right. And pretty sure she was on the right track. She told me she thought we had a good chance to solve the problem in two years, maybe less. But it's a time and money game with PII. They're evidently strapped pretty badly right now, and if there's more delay before the FDA gives them a green light . . ."

"I know about that. At least I know that Caryn put up a lot of short-term money . . ." Stuart, struck with another insight, drummed his hands on the steering wheel. "Which would mean that at the time she did the mezzanine loan, she must have believed PII was going into production pretty soon, right? And was okay with it."

"But she wasn't okay with it. I know she wasn't." A silence settled in the cab. Finally Kelley said, "Look. She thought the money she gave them was to buy time for her research. That was her clear understanding. Except then she found out they weren't reporting the negative studies and planned to go ahead anyway."

"And when did she find that out?"

"I'm not sure exactly, but recently. Certainly by last week. She was down here, I think it was on Wednesday, and had evidently just gotten word from Mr. Furth that the FDA was days or weeks away from approval, and she was having a fit about it. She went into Mr. Blair's office and he told her that the deaths had occurred after the study was completed and therefore they shouldn't technically affect the FDA's ruling, which was going to send PII stock through the roof. And meanwhile she should just keep up her work on the next generation."

"How did she respond to that?"

"How do you think? She told him it was unconscionable and that if he went ahead, she was going to go to the newspapers. It was her name on the socket, and she wasn't going to allow it to hurt people."

"So what did Blair do?"

"He backed down a little, evidently. At least that's what Caryn told me when she came back out to the lab. They were all going to have another meeting this week and see if they could all come to some decision that made everybody happy. But she wasn't too optimistic."

"And the meeting was supposed to be this week?"

"Probably today," Kelley said. "She usually came down here to work on Wednesdays. Except of course now there won't be—" She stopped abruptly as her eyes teared up. For a few seconds she fought the urge to cry. At last, swallowing, gathering her strength, she went on. "So you see why I felt I had to talk to you?"

TWENTY

Assistant District Attorney Gerry Abrams showed up uninvited at Devin Juhle's desk in Homicide at a little after four, when Juhle had just gotten himself arranged to write up an incredibly depressing witness interview he'd had with a despondent mother in a case he was following up on after he'd left Stuart Gorman's house. Abrams breezed by the lockers across from him, knocking on the top of one of them to announce his arrival. When Juhle looked up, he started right in, the soul of enthusiastic good cheer. "I must say you look a bit peaked, my good man. I've been thinking about Gorman, and I predict it'll cheer you right up."

Juhle threw his pen down on the desk, relieved after all at the respite. He pushed himself back in his chair and crossed his arms over his chest. "You know who I've been thinking about, Ger? Fidel fucking Rayas, that's who. Wondering why we've got to waste time and money on a trial for the son of a bitch."

"Because, my son, as I'm sure you know and appreciate, he's innocent in the eyes of the law until proven guilty. Who is he?"

"Christina Hidalgo's boyfriend. Also, p.s., the killer of her son, age five months."

"Shook him, did he?"

Juhle nodded. "Maybe a bit more than that. Although he's on his way to convincing Christina that it wasn't his fault, at least enough that she won't testify to it. He didn't really shake him. He just picked the kid up, trying to quiet it down, and then he just stopped breathing. Maybe because his skull got cracked. Somehow. Falling off his bed, maybe."

Abrams closed the gap between himself and Juhle's desk and plunked himself on a corner of it. "Tell her if it wasn't him, the only person that leaves is her. That ought to bring her right around."

Drawing a deep breath, fully disgusted, Juhle let out a string of matter-of-fact profanity. "I want to just shoot him right now," he concluded. "I swear to God, I do."

Abrams nodded. "I couldn't agree more, Dev. Really. The saddest thing about life here in San Francisco is there's no chance getting a death penalty. Maybe you could arrest him and accidentally slam into a telephone pole while you're driving him downtown. Guys like Fidel, I bet they're too macho to use their seat belts. You're going fast enough, he's toast."

Juhle perked up, straightened in his chair. "You know what, Ger? That's not a bad idea. Cost of a car against a murder trial, the city wins big time. I could get a medal." Juhle took a breath, seemed to shake the evil thoughts off his body, changed the subject. "So what were you thinking about Gorman? I thought yesterday we didn't have any evidence? You get something I don't know about?"

"No. But I watched the news last night."

"The fox?"

"His wife's sister. You saw her, then?"

"She was hard to miss. Va-voom, huh?"

"At least. But you put her in the mix, suddenly we might be at a tipping point."

"Is she in the mix? Were they together?"

Abrams fairly beamed. "Why I love television. Noon news, just breaking. Her ex-husband says they went up to his cabin—that cabin again—for nearly a week. Alone together."

Juhle whistled, impressed. "But wait," he said. "There's been another development beyond that, not saying it's going to un-tip you, but you need to hear about it."

"What's that?" Abrams listened while Juhle explained about the TSNK e-mails. When the story was over, he said, "He's going proactive, that's all. Trying to give us something else, get us off him."

"That's how I read it too," Juhle said, "but it was a pretty good press. His lawyer and her investigator."

"Who's the lawyer?"

"Gina Roake."

Abrams brightened. "Roake. I don't recall her ever doing a homicide before. I should ask around. If she hasn't, it's something else to consider. The call on whether or not to bring him in is close enough. If he's got a first-timer defending him, odds on us go up. Maybe only slightly, but with everything else that might be enough."

"So what were you thinking about that brought you down here?"

"What we actually had." Suddenly the assistant district attorney was on his feet, pacing between Juhle's desk and the lockers. "Look, we've been going on about the lack of physical evidence, and there's no doubt that's a problem. The question is whether it's insurmountable. With this woman, finally—the sister-in-law—I'm starting to believe maybe it isn't."

"I'm listening."

"Okay, you're a jury. You hear about Gorman leaving the lakes at two o'clock in the morning. Squirrelly right off the bat, no? He takes way too long to show up at Rancho Cordova. And by the way, I did check and there were no traffic problems. Any way you cut it, there's lost time in there. It makes more sense that he drove up from the city after the murder. Then he's got a neighbor—and not just any neighbor, someone who's going to be a hostile witness for us and *his daughter's friend*—who puts him and his car at the house. He's doing CPR on a corpse in full rigor when the first squad arrives. Then there's the money. And finally, now, the other woman. This thing sings like Pavarotti."

"You're preaching to the choir, Gerry. But you're the DA. You've got to make the call."

Abrams' eyes flicked at the ceiling, came back to Juhle. "We don't do something, he's gonna walk. Are you expecting more from the morgue or the lab?"

"Nope. We could always get surprised, but . . ."

Abrams crossed back to the lockers one more time, his finger tattooing the echoing metal, trying to make up his mind.

Just at that moment, the telephone on the desk rang. Juhle held a finger up to Abrams and picked it up. "Juhle, Homicide." He all but came to attention in his chair, straightening up, grabbing for his pen. "Yes, Mrs. Robley," he said, "go ahead. I'm listening." And as he listened, his face clouded over until it was set in darkness. "Yes, ma'am," he said. "Should I talk to her? No. Sure. I understand." After another minute of monosyllables, Juhle hung up and looked over at Gerry Abrams. "Bethany Robley's mother," he said. "The son of a bitch sent his own daughter to threaten Bethany to change her testimony."

This wasn't good news for the witness by any means, but it brought a cold smile to Abrams' face. "We've just tipped, Dev. Go talk to her on tape. Nail it down. Then let's go find us a judge, get the sucker in jail while we've still got the chance."

Robert McAfee greeted Wyatt Hunt in the doorway of the newly built warehouse-like structure on Geary at the eastern edge of Japantown. The site of the city's soon-to-be-completed Total Joint Clinic was not in a low-rent neighborhood by any stretch, and its now-sole principal betrayed a distinct pride of ownership as he shook Hunt's hand.

McAfee, dressed more like a construction worker than a doctor, in heavy work boots, tan denim pants and a black and gold Giants windbreaker, looked young and fit enough to play with the big club. He had all of his hair, and none of it was gray above a subtle widow's peak that bisected an unlined forehead. With his piercing gray eyes, strong nose, good teeth and day-and-a-half stubble, he was as handsome as a movie star. He also accepted without question, and without looking at the proffered business card, Hunt's description of himself as a defense investigator looking into the death of Caryn Dryden, offering only, "But I already talked to one of your partners, whose name escapes me, I'm sorry."

"Devin Juhle?" Hunt volunteered, willing to take advantage of McAfee's lack of distinction between police and defense investigators. Hunt had done what the Penal Code required—identified himself and given the witness a business card. What the witness chose to believe after that was not Hunt's problem.

"That was it. Juhle. I told him I was asleep on Sunday night, which I was. Though of course I was devastated to hear about Caryn. I still am. But I don't know what else you need to know from me. I hadn't seen her since last Thursday. Surely I'm not a suspect, am I?"

Hunt loved it when he was mistakenly taken for a policeman. He answered with an open, guileless look. "Until somebody's arrested, the field's technically open, but you were home in bed when the murder occurred." He phrased it as fact, although he knew from Gina that McAfee was Stuart's pick as most likely suspect which, if true, meant the alibi was bogus.

"That's right."

"So my real interest is that as Caryn's business partner, you might know something about her and either not know that you know it or not realize its importance."

"Okay, that's possible." McAfee's smile came and went haphazardly. Hunt's presence and questions clearly were rattling him. "But I thought you'd more or less settled on Stuart?"

"He's in the mix, Doctor, but as I said there's been no arrest yet. The media's made up its mind, if it has one, but there are some questions."

Hunt's intention wasn't to let his cop impersonation intimidate the witness; he wanted to get him relaxed and talking. He looked over McAfee's shoulder to where construction sounds could be heard and put some enthusiasm into his tone. "I love these infill projects. I live in a converted warehouse myself down on Brannan. How close are you to being finished here?"

"Well, now, with Caryn gone, that's all a bit up in the air. If you'd like a quick tour while we talk, I'd be happy to show you around a little."

"That'd be great. I'd like that. Thanks."

McAfee's relief at leaving the immediate subject of Caryn's death was palpable. He turned to indicate the reception area. "Well, where we are here, this is pretty much finished." He led Hunt behind the counter, showing off the stations, the computer outlets, the phone bank.

"How many patients were you planning on handling?"

"We hoped to get up to eight a day."

"Eight a day? That many people need new hips?"

"And shoulders, and knees. And yes, even hips alone, eight a day, at least."

"You and Caryn were going to do four operations each, every day?"

Perhaps this struck McAfee as funny. Perhaps he was still nervous. At any rate, he had a loud, uninhibited laugh, though he cut it off after the first couple of notes. "I'm sorry," he said, "but no. We hoped to be able to bring in associates, fellow orthopedic specialists, and have them on staff here within a year or two. Any one doctor shouldn't do more than one total joint surgery in any given day. Although there are some who try."

Hunt decided to take a risk. "Michael Pinkert?"

The name stopped him, wiped the joviality from McAfee's face. "Yes, he'd be one of them. Have you been talking to him?"

"Not yet."

"But obviously you know that he'd been in some negotiations with Caryn."

"And with you, right? You want to talk about it?"

Clearly, McAfee didn't. He looked back over his shoulder quickly as though considering whether he should take his inquisitor on the next leg of the clinic tour, but finally flashed another false smile and leaned back against the wall. "You have to understand that Caryn and I, we went back as far as our residencies together. She was an incredible woman—smart, driven, a workaholic really, like me. With so much going on in her brain all the time. It was—she was—a joy to be around. Not that everybody saw that part of her, of course. She could be very . . . abrupt, I suppose. And short-tempered. Impatient with stupidity, that was all."

"She wouldn't have liked me," Hunt said, trying to keep his witness at least marginally on his side for as much time as he could, which he was afraid wouldn't be much longer.

"I think you're being modest, Inspector," McAfee said. "In any event, what I'm getting at is that she and I were an immensely compatible team from very early on. We shared the same work ethic, the same approach to our practices. Dr. Pinkert has a different philosophy than either Caryn or me. I didn't see him working well with us."

"Don't take offense at this, Doctor, but were you and Caryn intimate?"

McAfee let out a breath, and with it went some of the confidence in his posture. "I should have expected it would come to this," he said mostly to himself. Then he nodded. "For about a two-week interval about twenty years ago. No, more like eighteen. Soon after Kymberly—her daughter—was born. She and Stuart were having troubles. The girl was evidently . . ." He shook his head. "Anyway, she decided she wasn't going to leave him or end the marriage back then—I don't know why—but she and I . . . we both realized it was a mistake." Meeting Hunt's eye, he said, "I know this looks bad, but we haven't been together since then, and that's the truth. We were friends and business partners, that's all."

"And suddenly she was betraying you by asking Pinkert to join you both on this clinic?"

"Well, not betraying me. That's a bit strong. We disagreed about it, sure, but . . . I didn't kill her, Inspector. I wasn't her lover anymore."

"You're saying she had one?"

"I can't say for sure."

"But still, you think it's true?"

McAfee wrestled with the question for a moment.

"The reason it's important," Hunt said, "is if she was having an affair, her lover might have been her killer. I'm not looking for a name, Doctor. Just a yes or a no."

Finally, McAfee nodded. "All right, then, I'd say yes. Although who it is, or was, I don't have any idea. But I think so."

"Why? Anything specific?"

"Nothing I could put my finger on. But as I told you, I knew her very well and for a very long time. You pick up on changes. Sometime last summer, she changed."

"In what way?"

"Well, over the past couple of years, she'd become grim. It was all money and business, or responsibilities with her family, and she did it all with a kind of lockjawed determination. She wasn't going to let it beat her that things were hard, that life was work and nothing else." He shrugged, took a beat. "Then her daughter—have you met Kymberly?"

Though he hadn't, Hunt nodded.

"Well, on top of everything else, Caryn was going through a particularly difficult time right around Kym's graduation. Very difficult. I'd hold her hand—not literally—but I'd listen to her complaints. She was at the end. Evidently Kym had a new boyfriend she'd started sleeping with and she was staying out all night and doing drugs and stealing things and for a while there, Caryn seemed to lose the ability to cope with it all. She felt it wasn't ever going to end, that her home life with Stuart and Kym was this chain around her neck that was choking her, and she'd never get it off."

"So what happened?"

"So one day, suddenly, she came in here and she was . . . I don't know how to describe it other than radiantly happy. Really like her old self. The change was so dramatic, I had to ask her what had happened."

"And what did she say?"

"She said she'd just realized how beautiful she was. I told her that of course she was, and she just smiled at me and said I had no idea. That was all. Except that after that she started to take more care with her looks—not that she needed to, but . . . I don't know how to put it, exactly. She looked more obviously attractive—bought some new clothes, wore her makeup differently, smiled more. She had more energy for her work. She was just different."

"And not because anything changed at home?"

"No. I'm sure of that. Rather the opposite, in fact. I remember she found out Kym had pierced herself in a very private area around this time, and rather than agonizing over it as she would have a few months before, she was almost breezy. She said, 'I've just got to give her a home until she goes off to college. I owe her that much. Then I'm free.' And never a word about Stuart. It was like he simply ceased to exist."

Hunt pulled out the small tape recorder he kept in the pocket of his sports coat. "I'm not so hot at taking notes," he said, echoing the disengenuous and universal theme. "You mind if I record what we say? I want to make sure I get it exactly right."

"No. Go ahead."

Satisfied, Hunt looked up. "Let's cut to the chase, Doctor. Do you think it was Pinkert?"

Again, the unexpected guffaw; again, cut off quickly. "I suppose I just inadvertently gave my answer away." In all seriousness, he continued. "I'd be surprised if it was Mike."

"Why?"

"First, you've got to know him. He needs to lose fifty pounds. Caryn hates extra weight on people. The other reason might be me. When Caryn and I had our thing, one of her big worries was that word would get out around the hospital. She told me that if she was going to do that again, it wasn't going to be with anybody she worked with. She didn't want gossip. She didn't want to hurt her husband.

She just needed to do what she had do to. Maybe that's a small thing, and maybe she changed her mind, but I think she stuck with it."

"You think she had other affairs?"

"Well, at least two. Which eliminates any moral objection to the idea, doesn't it? So it would have been a matter of convenience. I'd say probably." As though just remembering, McAfee snapped his fingers. "Are you really interested in seeing the rest of this place?"

"Sure." Hunt followed McAfee through a door into a long hallway. Since McAfee had never asked him to turn it off, he checked to make sure his tape recorder was still working. It was.

As they took the tour, it was evident that construction was well along. The internal walls separated administrative and medical offices from waiting areas and from operating theaters. The rugs weren't down yet, but the lighting was installed, the place about half painted, most of the equipment and furnishings still to come. But to Hunt it felt like a mostly unfurnished medical complex, not a warehouse anymore. When they got down to the far end, Hunt said, "Looks pretty close to done. When are you opening?"

McAfee crossed his arms over his chest, proud of what he'd wrought. "I'm shooting for the first of the year, give or take a couple of weeks. I start hiring staff in the next week or two."

"So everything's a go?"

"Pretty much. There's always last-minute problems, and I'm sure there will be on this, but all in all I'm fairly confident."

Hunt decided to take the gloves off. "Pretty big change in a week, isn't it?"

McAfee's face went slack, then reddened. "What do you mean by that?"

"Well, I mean, obviously, last week you were fighting Caryn over a partner you didn't want in the business. But you needed his money to keep construction going. Now both those problems are gone. Also gone is an original headstrong partner who was giving you nothing but headaches. How much life insurance did you and Caryn take out on one another?"

"I don't have to answer that. And I resent the hell out of the implication. I loved Caryn."

"How much insurance?" Hunt repeated. "It's in the public record. If you make me look for it, I might get cranky. How much?"

"Two and a half million."

"Each?"

"Each."

"And when's the last time you saw Caryn?"

"Friday, here. No, Saturday morning. I ran into her at the hospital where we both had patients. We barely spoke."

"Because of the tension between both of you and Pinkert?"

"No. Because we were busy looking at patients. I just told you that."

"Yes, you did. But it seems to me that if you're having all of these issues, you might have talked about them a little."

"We'd just done that the day before. She finished before me at the hospital on Saturday and left. Maybe to go see her lover. I don't know. But we didn't talk."

"All right. What about Sunday?"

"No, I didn't see her on Sunday."

"What did you do Sunday night?"

"I already told your partner . . ."

"That you were asleep. I'm talking earlier. Dinnertime. Where did you have dinner?"

"I don't know. I'd have to think."

"Go ahead. Take your time."

Hunt pulled out his notebook again. Ostentatiously flipped pages, grabbed his pen. "Sunday," he said curtly, "three days ago."

McAfee rubbed his hands together. He forced a painful smile. "I'm just not remembering. I'm drawing a complete blank. Sunday, Sunday . . ."

"Sunday," Hunt said. "You were in bed by eleven. Maybe your wife would remember."

He shook his head. "We're divorced. I'm living by myself out on

Fillmore. I'm really drawing a blank here, though. Just a second. Do you mind if I make a phone call?"

"Not at all."

McAfee pulled his cell phone from his belt and said "Office" into it. A few seconds later, he started talking. "Marcia, hey, it's me. What's my calendar got me doing on Sunday, last Sunday? Sure, I'll wait a minute." That nervous come-and-go smile. Then, "Nothing? No, I'm sure I did something. I just can't . . . okay. Okay. Thanks then. Bye."

Clicking off, he shrugged dramatically. "I guess I'm going to have to think about it. Whatever it was, it wasn't too memorable."

"Doctor, didn't Inspector Juhle ask you about this?"

"Sure. I told him I had surgery scheduled Monday morning, so I'm sure I was in bed."

"He didn't ask about before you went to bed? What kind of car do you drive?"

"A Toyota Highlander."

"That's an SUV, right?"

"Yes."

"What color?"

"Black. Oh wait, Sunday, there it is! I had the kids."

"You had the kids."

"My three kids. I'm remembering now. We went over to Tilden and swam in the lake, had a picnic. We bought a lunch at that deli in Montclair." McAfee wiped at the sheen that had developed on his forehead. "Yeah. Then we all went to Spenger's—you know, in Berkeley?—for dinner, and then I dropped them back with Jenny, their mom, it must have been about eight. Eight thirty. Just dark, anyway. God, how did I not remember that?"

"I don't know," Hunt said. "So you left the kids at eight thirty. And then what?"

"Then I went home. It had been a long day—you know, three young kids. And I watched a little TV, then went to bed. Probably around ten. Just what I told Inspector Juhle."

"Alone?"

"Yes, of course."

"Okay, Doctor, thanks a lot. You've been very helpful." And Hunt folded up his notepad, put it again in his back pocket and started up the long hallway on his way out.

TWENTY-ONE

————

GINA HAD STARTED OUT TYPING ON the computer in her office, thinking to take her client's writing advice and get in one page for the day and to have fun with it. It seemed as though she'd been writing for about fifteen minutes when the phone rang.

When she glanced down at the bottom of her screen and saw that she'd been lost in the work for almost two hours and had written five pages, she was so shocked that she didn't hear the next couple of telephone rings and finally had to grab hurriedly at the receiver, hoping she hadn't missed the call.

"This is Gina Roake."

"Ms. Roake. Inspector Juhle." Gina noted with a tingling sense of alarm that she'd ceased being Gina and Juhle was no longer Devin. Something about their relationship had shifted. "I wonder if you're with your client right now?"

"No. I'm at my office."

"Yes, ma'am. That's where I called you. And Mr. Gorman isn't with you?"

"No."

"Do you know where he is?"

"To my knowledge, he's still at his house. That's where I left him right after we were all there together this morning. What do you want to see him about?"

"I've got a warrant for his arrest."

Gina felt her head go light; something went out of her shoulders. "That's not possible. Since we saw him this morning?"

"That's right."

"What's changed, Inspector? This doesn't make any sense."

"It makes sense to Gerry Abrams, and that's good enough for me." Juhle didn't have to explain anything to her at this point—they had their warrant. But he couldn't help gloating a little. "Did you know that your client and his wife's sister went up to the mountains together alone for a week?"

"Yes, but—"

"So now we've got the bad timing on the drive down from his cabin, the money, and another woman in the picture. I also just heard from Mrs. Robley, Bethany's mother. Did you know about your client threatening her if she didn't change her testimony?"

"I have no idea what you're talking about. Stuart didn't do that. He'd never do that."

"Well, Bethany says he did. His daughter delivered the message. It took Bethany a few sleepless nights to help her decide she had to tell her mother. Abrams says we've got enough. He wants him in custody, and I don't blame him."

"But . . . this is crazy, Inspector. I know Stuart didn't threaten anybody, much less a young girl. And he told me all about Debra. They weren't up there a week. It was five days. And they didn't . . . oh, never mind about that." Gina realized how ridiculous she sounded making excuses. "You're bringing him downtown?"

"As soon as I find him. You're sure you haven't heard from him?"

"Of course I'm sure."

"Because there's another thing you might want to consider."

"It won't change the fact that I haven't heard from him, but what's that?"

"When nobody answered the door at his house, I let myself in and found half a box of nine-millimeter ammunition out on his computer table. His dresser drawers were mostly cleaned out, and so was the bathroom cabinet. As soon as we're off the phone here, I'm going out with an APB that your client's on the run and should be considered armed and dangerous."

"Well, before you do that," Gina said, "have you tried his daughter? She's staying with Caryn's sister. Maybe he went over there to see them."

"Do you know where that is?"

"No. I'm sorry."

"No number?"

Gina had his home telephone number, and she'd reached him at the Travelodge yesterday, but—another failure—she hadn't bothered to get his cell number. She was badly out of practice, and her client was likely to suffer because of it. "The sister may be listed," she said. "The last name is Dryden."

"I'll look into that," Juhle said.

Another thought struck her, and Gina asked, "What about the reporters who were camped at his house? Didn't any of them see him leave?"

"There's a way out through the garage. A gate in the fence opens onto a walkway between a couple of houses out of the backyard."

"He was just avoiding the reporters," she said. "He'll be with his daughter, I'm sure."

"Well, I'll tell you what," Juhle said. His patience, thin to begin with, was clearly just about worn through. "Why don't we both keep looking? But if I don't hear from you or him by, say, five o'clock, I'm putting out the bulletin."

"That's only an hour from now, Inspector."

"That's right," Juhle said. "So we'd better get looking, shouldn't we?"

*   *   *

"Jedd, this is Gina. I'm sorry to bother you at your office, but I'm in kind of emergency mode here. Have you heard from Stuart lately?"

"You can bother me anytime you want, Gina. Would lunchtime today count as lately?"

"You saw him at lunchtime? Where?"

"Over here in North Beach."

"Do you know where he is now?"

"No. But he said he was going down to Palo Alto to talk to some of Caryn's investment people. I assume that's where he went. What's the emergency? About him?"

"Only that they've issued a warrant for his arrest, and now they think he's on the run, armed and dangerous."

"Armed and dangerous? Stuart?"

"Evidently he left some ammunition out at his house and Juhle found it."

"Stuart owns a gun? He had a gun when he was with me?"

"I don't know about that. It sounds like it, though. I just wondered if you had a way to get ahold of him. He needs to know what's happened, and especially that he's wanted."

"He thought it might get to that, even without good evidence. That's why he took off."

"He told you that?"

"Word for word. He said he wasn't going to jail. The cops weren't looking for who might have really killed Caryn, so he was going to on his own. For the record, I told him to let you and your investigators do that, but he wasn't much convinced."

"Jedd, he's got to come in. He could get himself shot. I've got to talk to him. Do you have any way to reach him?"

"I've got his cell number, and you're welcome to it, but from what he was telling me today, you're not going to have an easy time talking him into coming in, especially if that means he's spending any time in jail. He was pretty firm on that."

"Jedd, they've got the warrant. He's going to jail."

"Not if they can't find him."

"Jesus, Jedd. On top of everything else, he doesn't want to be in the middle of a manhunt. Things are bad enough as it is."

"I hear you. I do, Gina. But he thinks he can get somewhere the police haven't gotten to with his own investigation."

"Well, he's an idiot then. I've got good investigators. Stuart's met one of them, Wyatt Hunt. He just got a load of dirt today on Caryn's business partner. We're all over this case."

"I believe you. But Stuart doesn't care about that. He doesn't have faith in the system, Gina. He doesn't think the innocent naturally go free. He thinks mistakes happen, this arrest warrant being a perfect example. He doesn't want any part of the process."

"It's too late for that, Jedd. It's started without him. Now the trick is to contain the damage. And if he doesn't show up on his lawyer's arm in the next few hours, everything from here on out is going to be much worse. You know that."

"I know that. You know it. Do you want me to call him first? Try to talk some sense into him. At least he'll probably pick up if it's me."

"There's a heartening thought." Gina considered for a second. "All right, but promise you'll get right back to me."

"As soon as I'm off, regardless of what he says. I'll give it my best shot."

"I know you will. And Jedd?"

"Yo."

"Not that I didn't appreciate it and all, but next time you've got an innocent man referral for me to defend, maybe you'll want to resist the urge."

At seven thirty that night, with no dinner inside her, Gina was driving south on the Bayshore Freeway on the way to San Mateo, where Stuart was staying near Coyote Point in Room 29 of the Hollywood Motel. Jedd Conley hadn't had any luck changing Stuart's mind, and neither had Gina in a second long talk with her client from her apartment. In spite of that, she still entertained some hope that the face-to-face discussion she'd talked him into might make him come around.

But the knot in her stomach and nervous tic in one of her eyelids were better indicators of her odds.

Dusk was well-advanced by the time she knocked quietly on the door, which faced a two-lane road perpendicular to the freeway and along the edge of San Mateo's municipal golf course. A light was visible in the room through the venetian blinds; a shadow moved across it in response to her knock, and then she was standing looking up at her client, who had his cell phone to his ear, motioning her in, closing the door behind her.

"My daughter," he mouthed all but silently.

Nodding, Gina moved into the room and sat in a chair beside a linoleum table against the wall. The room was large, with two queen beds and a half-kitchen behind her in the back. Stuart went back to the near bed and sat propped with the pillows he'd piled against the headboard.

"That wasn't your fault, hon," Stuart said. "That was between your mother and me. It didn't have anything to do with you."

Gina watched her client as he listened some more, his face a mask of pain and regret. Grimacing at something his daughter was saying, he brought his free hand up to the birthmark near his eye and rubbed it mechanically. "That's just how she was with everybody. No, *especially* the people she cared about. She was just one of those insecure people who needed what she did to matter more than who she was. So if she wasn't accomplishing something . . . I don't know . . . something tangible, like her inventions or her operations . . . well, the rest of it didn't have as much meaning to her. Yeah. That was me, too. Well, of course it hurt, but by that time you and I were just getting in her way. I know she was your mother, hon. I know it's not fair . . ."

Stuart looked across at Gina, gave her a distracted nod and held up a finger, asking for another minute or two. Nodding, she half listened to a long-suffering father trying to explain the inexplicable to his devastated daughter. With something of a shock, she suddenly saw the handgun in full view out on the stand under the reading light between the two beds. To take her eyes off it, and to give Stuart a bit more privacy with Kymberly, Gina stood up and walked back into the half-kitchen, where she poured herself a glass of water.

The sight of the gun had roiled her stomach anew and, now having drunk the water, she put the glass down and leaned against the counter, arms straight and with her weight on her hands, her face up, her eyes closed. She exhaled heavily, telling herself that the sudden stab of nerves was irrational, yet recognizing it for what it was. It was fear.

What had she been thinking?

Before in her life, she had only defended guilty suspects, and now here she was alone with her client and his gun, with a warrant out for his arrest for a murder.

Drawing a deep breath, her eyes still closed, she sighed again.

The words seemed to explode in her ear, directly behind her. "Are you all right?"

She brought a hand to her chest and whirled on him. "Oh my God. You scared me to death."

"I'm sorry." He flicked on the kitchen light overhead, the blessed brightness dissipating the shadows. "And I'm sorry about the phone. I had to talk to Kymberly."

"I heard. She's having a rough time?"

"My heart's breaking for her. She doesn't understand why Caryn didn't love her. She wants to have a chance to ask her one time. What she did wrong."

"What Kym did wrong? Why would she think she did anything wrong?"

"It's a little circular, isn't it? Because her mother had stopped loving her. It wasn't just Kym not saying good-bye to Caryn when she left to go to college. Caryn didn't make any effort to say good-bye to her, either. She was all just 'Thank God that's over and she's gone. Now I can get on with my life.'"

"Was she that hard, really? Kym?"

Stuart searched the corners of the ceiling for an answer. He ran a hand through his hair. "I don't have anything to compare Kym to. Maybe all kids are hard on their parents, or their marriages. All I can say is she sucked the energy out of both of us. I kept thinking . . . we both thought that somehow it was our fault. That we'd spoiled her. But really, I don't think it was that. From the beginning, she was just so hard."

"But isn't that the norm?" Gina asked. "Everybody says once you have kids, your life is never the same."

Stuart met Gina's eyes. "That's true, but there are degrees. Most of our friends, back when we had mutual friends, they'd joke about how their lives had changed. But there was always good to go with the bad. With us, from early on, it was always waiting for the other shoe to drop. You know, Kym didn't sleep through the night until she was four years old! You know how tired you get with four years of no sleep? She was in diapers until she was almost eight. I mean . . ." But he couldn't find the words. He shook his head, trying to shake the memories. "Sorry."

"There's nothing to be sorry about. It must have been difficult."

He almost laughed. "Difficult's a good word. So now, how am I supposed to console her? She drove her mother away. That's the truth. She wore us both down until Caryn just gave up. Maybe she would have come back to caring about Kym after she wasn't living with us full-time anymore, but now Caryn will never get the chance for that. And it's just killing my little girl." Suddenly, he checked himself, apologetic. "But you didn't come all the way down here to talk about Kym."

"I'm happy to talk about Kym. Whatever you want. Obviously you're still trying."

He shrugged. "What am I going to do? She's my daughter. I love her. But Lord, sometimes you wonder when it's going to get better. If things are ever going to improve."

Gina was leaning back against the counter in the narrow kitchen. "Maybe the first step is believing that they can."

He gave her a weak facsimile of a smile. "That would be a pretty thing to think." Then, perhaps not meaning to sound so dismissive, he added, "But maybe you're right."

"I am right, Stuart. It happened with me. A year ago I would have told you I was a lost cause. I'm not. Change is not only possible, it's the only possibility." Gina had him listening, and she pressed on. "You know, Stuart," she began, "you're the one who told me you don't want to live with suspicion hanging over you for the rest of your life. Has it ever occurred to you that getting legally cleared, getting an acquittal, is the best way to put that suspicion behind you, once and for all?"

"You want to ask O.J. about that?"

"He's the exception that proves the rule."

"Okay, but who's to say there won't be another exception? Or, worse, I'm the innocent guy who pulls life in prison for the crime he didn't commit. No thanks."

"And so you think this—what you're doing now—is helping your case?"

"You mean doing my own investigation?"

"I mean being on the run. Any chance you have of ever getting reasonable bail in this case evaporates if the cops have to run you down."

He shook his head. "Being on the run is a nonissue. It goes away if I find something." He came forward. "Listen. I talked to both Fred Furth and Caryn's lab assistant today at PII. They both say that there's something seriously going wrong with the Dryden Socket and Caryn was blowing the whistle on it, maybe as early as this week. She was really going to make a stink about it."

"And—this is your theory?—that because of this, somebody killed her to stop her?"

"I think it's absolutely plausible."

"So do I. So what?"

"What do you mean, 'so what'? It's a strong motive."

"Agreed. Strong motive. And again, so what? Do you have a specific person in mind who had a way to get into your garage? Then have a glass of wine with your wife—"

"That's not how it happened!" Stuart snapped back at her, his voice rising. "He snuck up on her and hit her from behind."

"Do you know that? How do you know that?" Gina pointed a finger at him. "No, you don't know that, Stuart. In fact, the much more likely possibility is that whoever it was didn't come over with the intention of killing her. He came over to have sex with her."

"No! She was . . ."

But Gina pressed ahead. "Don't be ridiculous! Listen to yourself. Think about the reality, not what you wish might have happened to spare everybody's delicate feelings. She was naked in the hot tub. He got there because they'd been having an affair for a while and that's what they'd arranged. You with me so far?"

"You don't know any of this."

"I know it as much as you know anything about the motive. Forget the motive for a minute. The *facts* point to him being in the tub with her, and for the obvious reason. She knew you were going to be gone. Kym was already gone. She had the house alone, and they set it up together. They were being romantic, having a glass of wine. Everything was cool. And then they had some disagreement about something—probably not something like the Dryden Socket, which had been simmering for weeks or even months. Something personal, some change in their status quo. Maybe she told him she wanted to stop, and she told him this was their last time. Maybe anything. The point is, he couldn't deal with it. So he got out of the tub, went behind her, did what he did, and got out of there."

His face set, Stuart nodded. "All right. Suppose we go with that. The problem is, Juhle thinks that mystery man must have been me. Same scenario, exactly. She told me she wanted the divorce and I lost it and killed her. Except that I didn't. It wasn't me."

"Right," Gina said. "I'm giving you the benefit of the doubt on that part. In fact, I don't think it was you, Stuart. If it was you, I don't think you would have come back down the next morning. You never would have done the CPR. And mostly, I don't think you would have done it to Kym."

He looked across at her. "Never," he said. "Never."

"I know. But my real point is, you're not going to get to any of this yourself. Not solo. Not even with me and Wyatt looking. And certainly not while the police are trying to find you. Who's going to talk to you once the word is out in the news? There's no chance."

"So what am I supposed to do?"

Gina drew a breath and held it for a minute. "You're supposed to come in with me, Stuart."

He glared at her defiantly. "I can't do that."

"You have to," she said. "There's no alternative, if you don't want to be taken by force when they find you, which they will. And then, if you don't actually get shot when they come to arrest you—which is not impossible—then you start off not only as a murder suspect, but as an armed fugitive, in which case you're in twice as deep shit as you are now."

Stuart stood unmoving. "I know there's something going on with the socket."

"Ya-fucking-hoo," Gina said. "I'm sure you're right. And there's also something going on with Bob McAfee. Wyatt had a long talk with him today, and his alibi isn't as strong as Juhle would like to have us believe."

"Then why have they decided to arrest me?"

She stared at him. "Are you kidding me, Stuart? Nobody's that naïve. Not even you."

"What?"

"You send your daughter to talk to a critical prosecution witness. She conveys the message that her testimony is inconvenient. What does that look like to you? You're lucky Kym's not in jail herself right now for witness intimidation." Her client's unyielding and uncomprehending expression pushed her into a rage. *"Goddammit to hell, Stuart! They think you're dangerous. Get it? Dangerous. Killer on the loose. Armed. Threatening witnesses."* Gina shook her head. "What the hell is the matter with you? Do you understand that the first cop that sees you will be ready to shoot you dead?"

"But that's not . . . I mean, none of that is . . ."

They could go around like this forever. Gina reined in her anger, controlled her tone. She had to close the deal. "Look, Stuart. The good news is that we can get a hearing in ten days, and if they don't have their evidence by then, the judge might not hold you to answer at trial."

"*Might* not." Stuart held out his hands, pleading with her. "I don't get it. Even if they really think it was me, why would they go ahead if they've got no way to prove it? Why wouldn't they wait?"

She shrugged that off. "You want more? Beyond all of the above? Okay, you're a name. Your wife was important. When important people get killed, the public wants to see somebody charged, and if nobody is, the DA comes under fire. So Gerry Abrams is protecting the reputation of his boss. And at the same time, if Abrams convicts you, he makes his name."

"So it's just politics? Stupid city politics?"

"Politics. Ambition. Bad luck. You name it. But whatever it is, these are the cards we got dealt, and the only choice is to play them. I'm sorry, Stuart, but there it is. That's why I came down here tonight. There's no other option. The alternative—you hiding out this way—only puts off the inevitable. And you have to believe me, it would be much, much worse."

"I could leave the country."

"You could," Gina agreed. "Never see your daughter again, live with the constant fear of extradition, have everybody in the world believe you killed Caryn. Then your passport expires. What do you do then? You want to do that?"

Stuart closed his eyes; his body sagged. Finally, he looked over at her. "I don't know if I can do jail, Gina. The idea of being with those guys scares the shit out of me."

"I know. I don't blame you. But there's a separate section in the jail, outside of the general population, called Administrative

Segregation, Adseg for short. It's where they keep at-risk prisoners. After you surrender, I'll try to make sure that that's where you wind up."

"Surrender?"

"Just a word, Stuart. Just a word."

"Shit."

"I couldn't agree more."

TWENTY-TWO

———

GINA PARKED HER JETTA IN HER space under her building and, making sure that the garage door had closed behind her, took the inside stairs to the back door of her condo. Walking up the short hall, turning lights on all the way, she went directly to her kitchen and opened the freezer section of her refrigerator, where she had a stash of commercially frozen dinners as well as several labeled plastic containers of her own preparations.

The largest of these was a deep, square Tupperware holder with a piece of tape on the side that read LASAGNA/SAUSAGE and she pulled that out, took off the cover, re-covered the dish with a paper towel and stuck it in the microwave, setting the timer for ten minutes. She walked over to the bar area and flicked on the radio which, since David, she'd kept tuned to classical.

To the strains of a flute and guitar performance, she went to her bedroom, took off her clothes and got into a hot shower. Gina considered herself a no-nonsense person, and never more so than when she showered. In five minutes, she was clean and dry again except for her hair, which she toweled for half a minute, then combed out damp. From her dresser, she grabbed an old comfortable pair of blue jeans and one of David's white button-down dress shirts, washed over the years now to a frayed near-translucence, soft as silk.

Back in the kitchen nook, barefoot, she opened one of the straw bottles of Chianti that she'd bought at Cost Plus a month before, and poured herself a glass. She laid out a regular setting, complete with placemat, cloth napkin, fork, knife, pepper and salt, Tabasco and Parmesan cheese on the small table by the front window, and had just finished watering her early blooming Christmas cactus in its tiny pot on the same table when the microwave beeped.

She brought the steaming lasagna over to her place. It wouldn't be cool enough to eat for a few more minutes, but Gina sat down anyway, picked up her wineglass, took a healthy drink from it. The guitar and flute on the radio had given way to chamber music, perhaps a Mozart concerto. She sat back, let out a long, deep breath and took another sip of Chianti, smaller this time, and started going over the events of the last couple of hours in her mind.

She'd finally convinced Stuart that he had no choice, that he had to give himself up. In his presence at the motel, she'd called Juhle on his cell phone and told him that she was ready to surrender her client. How about tomorrow, say 10:00 a.m.?

She also wanted to make clear to the inspector that Stuart was not now and had never been armed. He'd simply taken some money from his safe for random expenses and had to take out the box of ammunition to get at it; then in his haste to get out on the road he'd forgotten to put it back. He'd snuck out the back way to avoid reporters, not to evade capture. Aside from those small lies, she'd basically told Juhle the truth of what Stuart had been doing all day—talking to people who might know something he didn't about Caryn. He hadn't been running from the police and from his arrest; he hadn't even heard about the warrant. They'd be at the Hall of Justice at ten o'clock sharp the next morning.

The lasagna—one of her specialties—was cool enough to eat. She took a bite, closing her eyes and savoring it, glad she'd made it with the hot Italian sausage rather than the mild, the sauce from the vine-ripe fresh tomatoes she'd picked up last month at the Ferry Building.

All in all, she thought, the night had been a success, a definite win for the home team, although Stuart wasn't quite seeing it in that light yet. But Gina had no doubts that getting him into custody, especially given the weakness of the case against him, was by far the best course of action he could take, albeit still one fraught with risk. Indeed, though, it was the only one that made any real sense.

More than that, in making the argument to him, in dealing with his very real and legitimate concerns, in the intensity she had to draw upon to prevail, she recognized a flame of passion in herself for the law and for her work that had lain as a near-dead ember for the better part of three years. That had been part of the general malaise and shutdown she'd experienced after David's death. But if nothing else, tonight had validated her return to her vocation in an immediate and gratifying way.

This was the right thing for her to be doing, the best use of her time and talents. Over her client's reservations and even violent disagreement, and whether he saw it or not, she had already done him a world of good. If she had not prevailed, if Stuart had become the object of any kind of real manhunt, when there would have been no question that he was in armed flight from prosecution, his prospects could have been terminally dashed. And she had prevented that. It felt good—better than good. A breath of fresh air after too long underwater.

Ten thirty.

The dishwasher cycles competed with the background music turned down low on the radio, but Gina was aware of neither. Her second glass of wine was still full on the reading table next to her. She was in her reading chair by the living room's front window, having already read through all of her notes and other miscellany in the folder she was keeping on Stuart. The thin blue volume of the ever-popular California Evidence Code now lay open on her lap. She made it a point to read it through once a year as a discipline. She'd gone through nearly two thirds of it at this one sitting, and though she would have denied that it was pleasure reading, it wasn't by any means a chore.

This was the nuts and bolts of her work. Lawyers talked in numbers—Penal Code sections, Criminal Code, Evidence Code, numbered Jury Instructions. It was the language, and she was as immersed in it as she would have been in cramming her rusty Italian if she was planning a vacation to Cinque Terre.

At first she was not sure whether it had been anything at all that had caught her attention and made her look up. Dishes rattling, settling in the dishwasher? She scanned the room, saw nothing that caused the noise and was about to go back to her book, when here it was again, unmistakable. She glanced up at the clock on her mantel, frowned and dog-eared her page. Though her front-door entrance was slightly recessed from the street and not visible from her front windows, she looked through those windows anyway and saw that someone had parked illegally on the sidewalk directly across the street. So she crossed over and used the peephole, then turned the dead bolt and opened the door.

"Hey." Jedd Conley in his business suit, hands in his pockets, projecting—for him—an unusual reticence. "Is this a bad time?"

"It's a bit of a surprising time. But no. I mean, it's okay." She pointed out behind him. "Is that your car? You'll get a ticket, parked there."

But Conley shook his head. "Legislative plates. Not automatic, but most cops recognize them and cut some slack. I think I'll be safe."

"So what can I do for you? Are you all right?"

"I'm fine." A quick, nervous smile. "Slightly uptight, maybe."

"You want to come in?"

"That'd be nice. Thanks."

She stepped back, opening the door, letting him in. "So what are you uptight about?"

"Life. My work. The usual. I don't know why I said that, though, why that came out." He let out a breath, tried another smile that didn't quite succeed. "I'm fine."

"Okay, good, then that's settled. Can I get you a drink? I've got a little of everything."

"Some scotch wouldn't be bad."

"It never is. Maybe I'll join you." She was moving behind the bar. "Have a seat somewhere. Is Oban okay?"

"Oban would be perfect."

"Perfection is my goal," she said. "Ice?"

"In a single malt? Surely you jest."

She shrugged. "Some do. Though for the record, I don't either." She had her special glasses out on top of the bar, filling them about halfway, a good couple of shots each, and carried them over to where he was sitting on the couch facing the fireplace. "Public health notice," she said, "leaded crystal. Drinking from these glasses could cause health problems and may impair your ability to operate heavy machinery."

"God forbid," Conley said. "I think I'll risk it."

"Brave man." She handed him his drink.

Holding the glass up, checking the generous pour with obvious satisfaction, he clinked her glass. "A woman after my own heart." Drinking a little, he settled back. "Thank you. I'm happy to inform you that you've attained your goal."

"My goal?"

"Perfection."

"Well," she said, surprised at the flush she felt rising in her face, "my pleasure."

When she'd finished with Stuart's folder, she'd tossed it onto the coffee table; she hadn't really noticed, but the picture of all the pals from the Bitterroot camping trip had slid out most of the way. Now Jedd picked it up, turned it over. "This has to do with Stuart's case somehow?"

"I don't know," she said, "probably not." She explained about the threatening e-mails, and Stuart's contention that the picture proved he hadn't sent them to himself, since he'd had no access to a computer.

"Or anything else," Jedd said. "But don't get me wrong, it was a great trip. At least till the ride home."

"What happened on the ride home?"

"My damn car threw a rod. Cost me two grand. I didn't feel right about asking my fellow campers to chip in, but they could have offered. It put a slight pall on my memory of the trip. But still"—he put the picture back into the folder—"I guess it was worth it. Getting away is always worth it."

"Yes it is." Gina by now was seated at the far end of the couch, and she turned to him. "So what can I do for you, Jedd?"

"I don't know, really. I was out at one of Horace's endless events tonight just over at the Fairmont—you know Horace Tremont?"

"Not personally, but of course."

"You know he's my father-in-law?"

"I remember reading about all that when you got married. Your wife is Lexi, right?"

"Right. The lovely Lexi." He smiled, but his inflection put an ironic spin on the words. "Anyway, it seems that Horace and some other of his kingmaker friends wanted to feel out my interest in running for the Senate."

"The U.S. Senate? Would you want that?"

He shrugged, at least feigning nonchalance. "It's something to think about. I'll be termed out next year in the Assembly. I'm going to want to do something. I don't know, it might be fun. We'll see. It's a long way off. Anyway," he continued, "when the meeting broke up, I got to wondering how things had gone after you talked with Stuart. Since I was so close to you up here, I took a chance and drove by and saw the light on and thought you might be up."

"I'm surprised you knew I still lived here."

He shrugged, smiled. "Tell you the truth, I wasn't a hundred percent sure until I saw your name in the mail slot. But I don't think I could have imagined you anywhere else. The place looks great, by the way. Terrific furniture. Cool art. I don't even remember the bar."

"That's because it wasn't here the last time you were. I remodeled about ten years ago, then added some stuff for David, even though we spent most of our time together at his place."

"Well, you always had great taste. It's beautiful." He raised his glass, toasted her and drank a sip. "So," he said. "Stuart. How'd it go?"

Relieved to turn away from the personal stuff about herself, Gina took a sip of the scotch. She felt herself begin to relax. "Finally, okay. It took the phone call, then a trip down to San Mateo and a lot of convincing, but he's coming in and giving himself up tomorrow, ten o'clock. Very reluctantly, I might add. But he'll show."

"You must have been persuasive as hell. When I talked to him, he wasn't spending any time in jail, period."

"Well, he's not that much better, but I got him to go along."

"How'd you do that?"

Gina smiled. "My usual. Equal parts charm, guile and threats. I made him an offer he couldn't refuse."

Conley enjoyed the phrase. "I thought he was a grieving widower."

"Not that kind of an offer, Jedd." She lifted her legs up onto the couch and tucked them under her. "So the Senate thing? Is that what you're uptight about?"

Conley paused, threw her a direct look. "You don't let much get by you, do you?"

"You'd be surprised. You said it was work and life. Running for the Senate seemed to qualify."

"Well." He sipped his drink. "Sometimes the profile is difficult to manage, that's all. It gets inside you." Apparently making up his mind to tell her about it, he went on. "As for uptight, I had to let go my assistant today and if history's any judge, she's going to slap me with some kind of bullshit lawsuit, when the plain truth is the woman was just incompetent and couldn't do the job. But you fire anybody nowadays, you become the bad guy. You know this. Hell, everybody knows it, and still it goes on." He sighed in frustration. "Anyway, it's done now. I'm just hoping I documented everything correctly. We'll see what happens."

"Well, if you need a lawyer . . ."

He chortled quietly. "I'll keep you in mind, thanks. Maybe she won't do anything. Because God knows I made sure I never did anything even remotely suggestive around her. If there's one thing I've learned in life, if you're going to mess around, you don't dip your pen in the company inkwell. If you choose to mess around at all, that is." He drank off some more of his scotch.

A silence, pregnant with their mutual history, gathered in the spaces between the low-volume tinkle of piano music from Gina's radio.

Jedd finally looked down the length of the couch at her. "You know, Gina, I said it the other day when you came to the Travelodge, and I meant it then, but I'll say it again. You haven't aged a day in twenty years."

"Not true," she said, "I've aged about twenty years, and I feel every one of them."

"Well, you don't show them. No makeup, hair still wet . . . and look at you right now. You're just incredible."

She gave him a long and piercing look. A smile tickled the corners of her mouth, and then slowly she shook her head from side to side. "I don't think so, Jedd. Nice try, but it wouldn't be a good idea."

"It was never a bad idea with us. If memory serves, and it does."

"Yes, it does. But it would be now. A bad idea."

"Why? What would be different?"

"You being married, for one thing."

"Lexi wouldn't ever have to know. We used to be pretty discreet, if I recall."

"But I would know, Jedd. A girl's got to have a few rules, and not sleeping with married men is one of mine."

"Okay, we won't sleep."

"No," she said.

He wagged his head back and forth. No hard press, but he was enjoying the game. "It doesn't really seem right."

"It does to me, I'm afraid." She finished her Oban and got herself upright, off the couch. "I'm flattered, Jedd, really. You've made my week. But no's got to mean no."

"Fair enough, if you really mean it." He was up, then, closing the small space between them, standing in front of her. "I'll make a deal with you. If you can still say no after one small kiss, I'll take it as your final answer."

She looked up into his eyes, confident enough, amused enough, to give him a full smile. "My momma didn't raise no fools, Jedd. Now you can either finish your drink and go, or you can go right now, but we're not doing this. Any little part of it. You need to go home and kiss your wife."

"She'll be in bed."

"So wake her up."

"Come on, Gina. It's not about her. It's about you and me."

"There is no you and me, Jedd." Ducking around him, giving herself room, she stopped behind the couch. "If you leave your wife, after the divorce is final, I might let you buy me a drink, and we'll see where that might take us. But even then, it's not a promise. It's a maybe."

"You're a cruel woman, Roake."

"I am," she admitted. "And getting crueler all the time." Crossing over to the door, she put her hand on the knob and turned back to face him. "Now, are you going to finish your drink first or just walk?"

Accepting defeat with a nod, Jedd toasted her silently again, and drained his drink. Placing the glass carefully on the coffee table, he got to the now-open door and stopped. "You can't blame a guy for trying," he said.

"Well, you can a little bit," she said. "Good night, Jedd." With a gentle shove, she moved him along until he was outside, then closed the door behind him and, with a sudden emphasis, she threw the dead bolt hard enough to make sure he heard it.

It took Juhle about an hour with his cell phone–tracking technicians to trace the approximate location from which Gina had called him to arrange Stuart Gorman's surrender the next morning, and most of another hour to arrange for two SF police officers and their squad car and some San Mateo County SWAT-team backup to meet him when he closed in for the arrest.

Cell phone technology possibly hadn't been much a part of the normal police arsenal the last time Gina had worked a major case, but now Juhle thought that everyone in the crime business must know that it was child's play to pinpoint a locale from a phone call. Wyatt Hunt had told him in passing that Gina had been out of the game awhile, and that Stuart was her first murder case ever, but even so he was amazed and happily surprised when she called him on her cell phone in Stuart's presence.

And especially after the hardball she'd been playing with him on the interview and everything else, he wasn't in the mood to be doing her any favors anyway. And if Gina thought that Juhle could know the whereabouts of an armed suspect who was the object of a murder warrant and knowingly let that person remain at large for even one extra minute, she had another think coming.

So no sooner had Juhle gotten off the phone with Gina than he told his wife that he'd be out late, and put some wheels in motion. The cell tower site gave him a confined area to search. All the district cars started checking out parking lots for vehicle license numbers—by now, the plates Stuart had stolen had been reported. The result was that at 11:21 p.m. Juhle flashed his badge at the night clerk at the Hollywood Motel, showed the man a recent picture of his suspect, and was told that the man he sought had checked in this afternoon under the alias of Stuart Ghoti. The clerk specifically remembered because he paid cash, which he did not see too often. He was in Room 29, around the corner and about halfway down the block.

Now, just after 11:30, Juhle had the street blocked off in both directions by the San Mateo County presence, and had his own San Francisco team of two officers out of their car, accompanying him to the motel room door. All of the men had their holsters unbuttoned, ready for action.

Stopping at the door, Juhle listened for a minute and heard the low hum of a television that also cast its flickering glow on the window blinds. He figured he had enough adrenaline flowing now to pull a locomotive uphill, and tried to gather himself to get control over his emotions and excitement, but it was a losing battle. For one last time, he considered other options, such as having one of his backup people call the room. Or even simply knocking on the door and announcing himself. But he'd already rejected those options— Stuart Gorman might try to flee through them all in one of those situations; he might learn that he was surrounded and, panic-stricken, commit suicide with the gun that Juhle believed in his heart that he still and had always had with him.

No, the thing to do was what he'd decided to do. A no-warning storming of the room. None of this bullhorn, come-out-with-your-hands-up bullshit. They had the "door opener," a massive, cylindrical metal weight on chains. One swing at the flimsy motel door would be all it took. Looking side to side at his two acolytes, he nodded.

The wood shattered as if it were balsa, the door flew backward, and Juhle followed it in, hitting the light switch just inside.

Stuart, a deer in headlights, leaning back on pillows set up against the headboard, took in the situation in a heartbeat, then threw a lightning glance at the pistol that was still out next to him on the bed table.

"Don't even think about it!" Juhle yelled. "Put your hands over your head! Now!" Juhle was crab-walking straight toward him, his gun centered right between Stuart's eyes to make sure he had his complete attention. Three steps later, Juhle had Stuart's gun in his left hand, his own in his right. His backup team was already all the way across the room, on the far side of the bed, their own weapons out, leveled at the suspect.

For a long moment, time froze. No one moved. The television nearly masked the sound of the men's heavy breathing.

Finally, Stuart said, "You're making a mistake."

"I don't think so," Juhle said. Then added, "Being a smart guy, you probably already figured this out. But you're under arrest. You have the right to remain silent . . ."

TWENTY-THREE

———

AT 9:00 A.M. SHARP ON WEDNESDAY, September 28, nine business days after Stuart Gorman was arrested on a charge of first-degree murder, with a cheerful "Good morning," his attorney walked into the reception area outside the office of San Francisco District Attorney Clarence Jackman. Gina, in high dudgeon at what she took to be Juhle's lies and even betrayal, had scheduled this appointment on the morning after Stuart's arrest. His preliminary hearing was scheduled for the next day in Judge Cecil Toynbee's courtroom, Department 12.

Jackman's secretary was a large, handsome, light-mocha-skinned woman in her early forties named Treya Glitsky, whom Gina knew very well, both professionally and socially. Treya's husband, Abe, was deputy chief of inspectors in the Police Department and also the best friend of Gina's law partner, Dismas Hardy, so it was a tight circle.

"And a good morning to you too." Treya looked over from her computer and broke a welcoming smile, getting up out of her chair and coming around her desk to hug her visitor. "Clarence is expecting you," she said, then added more quietly, "but I wanted to warn you that he had Gerry Abrams in here yesterday afternoon for a good while."

"To brief him?"

"I'd assume. Or just bring him up to speed. This thing's gotten big in a hurry, hasn't it?"

"It's crazy," Gina said. "You get a little celebrity buzz, you'd think the world revolves around it. But it's also, between you and me, the reason Clarence has to step in and call this thing off. It's going to be an embarrassment to him."

"Well," Treya said, "Gerry's been beating his own drum pretty hard too."

"Don't I know it."

Indeed, it would have been hard for anyone to miss. Since the arrest, the media had been having a field day with the story of the new-age outdoor writer and his brilliant doctor wife. And Gina had no doubt about the source of the dozens of leaks that fueled the nearly endless recaps and updates. Over the past two weeks, Gerry Abrams had become almost a household name in San Francisco, as had Stuart Gorman. And of course, this had increased Gina's profile as well, even if her mantra throughout it all had been that she had no comment except to say that her client was innocent, and would be acquitted if there was a trial.

But still, she had to admit that the constant barrage of media analysis was taking its toll on her confidence. While it remained true that the physical evidence pointing to Stuart's guilt was, in her opinion, light to nonexistent, nevertheless she found herself on several occasions over the last couple of weeks blindsided by one or another reporter's fresh recapitulation of all the circumstantial evidence. And—she had no need to remind herself because it remained a truism throughout her entire career—circumstantial evidence was sufficient to convict.

Gina had used her own spies in the Hall in the past couple of weeks to find out when Abrams was scheduled to appear in court, and she'd come down and sat in the gallery during two of his hearings. He had, to her mind, a scary amount of charisma and a persuasive style that, for all of its homespun sincerity, could not disguise the obvious intellect. She knew that a prosecutor such as Gerry Abrams could present his circumstantial case with such a strong narrative that it could quite literally trump a complete lack of physical evidence.

In fact, the pervasive onslaught had actually brought her back to some significant doubt about Stuart's factual guilt or innocence. By the time she'd come to the motel in San Mateo and talked him into turning himself in, she'd come to have faith in her client's story. All of his explanations and actions, even including going out to interview Caryn's business colleagues, had seemed convincing to her. But in the relentless prose of the print media and the endless analysis of the radio and TV pundits, the consistency of Stuart's guilty scenario was viscerally so powerful that it had literally, several times, made her sick.

And now on Stuart's behalf she was about to take another huge professional and personal risk. She hadn't been lying or making any kind of false threat to Devin Juhle when she'd referred to the DA as her close, personal friend. In fact, she'd been a member of Jackman's informal "kitchen cabinet," meeting regularly on Tuesdays for lunch at Lou the Greek's, for most of his administration. She considered him a fair, just, good man, and one with whom she shared a real friendship. The fact that he had apparently gone along with this prosecution, even to this point, filled her with a deep sense of foreboding. If he had serious misgivings about this case, he was keeping them private. But she knew that this wasn't Jackman's style. If he didn't believe in the case, he would have counseled—or ordered—Abrams to abandon it.

When she'd all but demanded this appointment after Stuart's arrest, Jackman had been uncharacteristically impatient, as though he found Gina's position—that her client was truly innocent—somehow distasteful. He'd granted the meeting, she felt, as a personal favor, rather than a professional courtesy. And this was another source of real discomfort.

Now she heard the door open behind her and turned to see her old friend, the city's chief prosecutor—all six feet four, two hundred and fifty pounds of him—standing in the entrance to his office. As always, Jackman wore a perfectly tailored suit, today in a dark blue, with a light pink shirt and muted blue tie. His face, though smiling in greeting, was a slab of jet-black granite under a tight gray buzz cut. He tended to speak very quietly, but the pitch of his voice was so deep, it seemed to resonate in her bones when he said, "Aha! And here's my favorite defense attorney now."

If Gina was Jackman's favorite, she would not like to imagine how the scene would feel to someone he liked a little less.

It was all low-key and ostensibly cordial, of course. Clarence didn't go to his power position behind his desk, but he made sure Gina was comfortably seated in the upholstered chair out in the living room section of his office, that she had a fresh cup of good coffee, that business and her health were both good. Preliminaries out of the way, he got himself situated on the leather couch across from her, coming forward with an open expression, elbows on his knees. "Now, Gina," he began with the voice of God, "how may I help you?"

"I guess the best thing you could do, Clarence—for me, for my client Mr. Gorman, and maybe for you yourself—would be to drop this insane prosecution, at least until Gerry Abrams gets some evidence that might tie my client to the crime of killing his wife."

Jackman's face was set in a patient neutrality. "I take it you're convinced of Mr. Gorman's innocence."

"That's not the point, sir. The point is that Mr. Abrams and Inspector Juhle have worked this case from the beginning with a presumption of Mr. Gorman's guilt, and not his innocence. And without that presumption, that illegal and unethical presumption of guilt, there is simply no case against him."

Jackman, nodding thoughtfully, said, "What about the neighbor girl who saw his car?"

"Excuse me, sir, but she allegedly saw his car. She never saw him, Clarence, because he wasn't there. The People have to prove he was there. I don't have to prove he wasn't. That's exactly what I'm talking about."

"And your client's threats to her?"

"He never made threats, Clarence."

"That's not what she said. It's not how she felt."

"He never saw her."

"I hope you're not denying that his daughter did see her. Twice."

"To find out what she really saw. That was all."

The DA appeared to be considering her words. "All right. Let's even, between you and me, grant that. How do you explain the attempt at CPR?"

The question was unnerving. Jackman had apparently been thoroughly briefed on the details of the case. He'd been prepped by Gerry Abrams and looked like he was going to be ready for her objections. But she wasn't going to roll over without a fight. "Frankly, I don't know what made him do that. Panic, frustration, a last-ditch hope? Her body was still warm, remember. He just couldn't give up without trying something."

"And the domestic violence? His arrest some years before? What about those? Inadmissible? Irrelevant?"

"Maybe both, really. But the truth about those, Clarence, is that both times the police were called out to their house, it was because of fights they were having with their daughter."

"Says he."

"Well . . . yes."

"Have you talked to the daughter about that? And even if you have, don't you think that if it could have a bearing on saving her father from going to prison, she might decide it's okay to lie about that? This is the same girl who went across the street and threatened her neighbor, right? I can't see that a little perjury for her father's sake would bother her much." Jackman pushed himself back into the couch and straightened his back. "I am not prejudging your client, Gina, but you keep referring to the lack of evidence in this case, and I'm not at all certain I agree with you."

"I'm talking about physical evidence."

"I understand that. And of course that's the strategy for your position. But it's also one that either denies the existence of or willfully ignores a rather substantial circumstantial case."

"If it was so substantial, Clarence, why didn't Abrams take it to the grand jury first?"

Jackman raised his shoulders, then let them fall. "He didn't want to wait to call them into special session. He was concerned about your client's flight risk. He became convinced—because of the weight of circumstantial evidence that he and Inspector Juhle had amassed—that your client needed to be in jail."

Gina opened her mouth to respond, but Jackman cut her off before she could say a word. "And I must add that your client's behavior after he found out about the warrant—harassing private citizens, carrying a loaded firearm . . ."

"On that, Clarence, if Juhle hadn't broken our deal, that gun would have been back in Stuart's safe the next morning . . ."

"Ah, but as it was, it turned out that your client had the gun with him at the precise time that you were telling Inspector Juhle he didn't." For the first time, Jackman's tone grew firm. "You don't lie to policemen, Gina. You're an officer of the court. I don't know what you were thinking. What if Juhle had gone to make his arrest and somehow acted on your assurance that Mr. Gorman was unarmed? Does the potential for disaster there escape you?"

Chastised, and justly so, Gina still held her ground. "We made a deal, Clarence. If Juhle broke the deal, how is that my fault?"

"Because his mandate is not to keep deals with defense attorneys. His mandate is to arrest murder suspects when a judge has seen fit to issue a warrant. If he can do that before the time you arranged, that's what he needs to do. We don't let suspected murderers go have a latte until it's to their convenience to appear for their arrest. We arrest them. Surely this is obvious enough."

"Surely it's equally obvious," she retorted, "that with so little evidence, Gerry Abrams hurried this arrest so he could get his name in the paper, Clarence. That's what that is about."

Jackman's voice rumbled. "That allegation is beneath you, Gina. Mr. Abrams has never before been a hound for the press. He has a consistent and unified theory on this case. I talked to him at some length just yesterday and he is convinced that the—granted, heavily circumstantial—evidence allows for no other conclusion, beyond reasonable doubt in his mind, that your client killed his wife."

"That's just a knee-jerk prosecutor's reaction, Clarence. You know that."

If he did, he didn't acknowledge it. "Well," Jackman sighed. "If his evidence is flawed or inconclusive, it seems to me that it's to your advantage. You pressed for an early preliminary hearing—tomorrow if I'm not mistaken, right?—and no doubt that request has hampered and will hamper the People's ability to build an impregnable case." He spread his hands out. "I don't really know what you'd like me to do, Gina. Which is how we began here today. I'm not going to overrule Mr. Abrams. He's built a case that will either fly or not on its merits. That's how we do it."

"Stuart's an innocent man, Clarence. Someone else killed his wife. Not him."

"That's why we have trials, Gina. And hearings. Mr. Abrams has to prove that, and it's your job to stop him if you can."

"Maybe, but it shouldn't have even been allowed to get to this stage. They have nothing. This is just wrong, Clarence."

She realized at once that she'd gone too far. Jackman's nostrils flared briefly, a tight-lipped smile came and went. "Well . . ." Rubbing his hands together, Jackman's face cracked in a parody of a smile as he got to his feet. "Maybe mine is just another knee-jerk prosecutor's reaction," he said, "but I only see one suspect in this picture, Gina.

And I also see a defense attorney who's perhaps feeling the pressure of her first murder trial walking a very thin ethical line of her own."

"Clarence, I'm not—"

"You're not presuming upon our years of cooperation and friendship and making a personal appeal to the district attorney to subvert the system and dismiss charges that have been brought by this office in a timely and legitimate manner?"

"No, I'm—"

"Ah, good then. I must have been misunderstanding you. I hoped I was." Somehow Gina was standing by now too, and Clarence was moving her, hand on her elbow, toward the door. Then he had his hand on the doorknob. "Show us what you've got at the hearing tomorrow. I'll keep a close eye on the evidence. Your client will get a fair hearing, Gina. That's what he's entitled to, and that's what he'll get."

TWENTY-FOUR

——————

UNDERSTANDABLY, JUHLE'S BETRAYAL ON THE ARREST deal also knocked the bottom out of Gina's well of credibility with Stuart. How in the world, he wondered aloud to her in angry terms at his very first opportunity before the arraignment and bail hearing, could she possibly have been ignorant of the fact that Juhle would trace her location by cell phone? Surely this was a standard police procedure, done every day? Surely she should have known about this, and avoided such a telephone call at all costs? And if she did know, why did she trust Juhle not to do it? Was she stupid or naïve? Because clearly she was one or the other.

Then, she should absolutely have known that her assurance to him that he would be able to peacefully turn himself in on their timetable was chimerical at best and negligent at worst. Not only was his decision to surrender based on that faulty presumption, but his very life was immediately and directly threatened. If he'd had his wits about him enough to actually reach for the gun right at his tableside, there was no question either Juhle or one of his backup officers would have shot him dead. Surely, this was malpractice if ever there was such a thing.

As if that wasn't bad enough, she'd talked him into agreeing to something he desperately didn't want to do, and also she'd done it in a way that had actually, and dramatically, hurt his case, and the perception of his guilt. In fact, although Stuart never used the gun, the mere fact of his possession of it created a sea change in the tone of reporting on the case. Why had she not warned him to get rid of the gun before she made the phone call?

Before, the killing was newsworthy because of the personalities and profiles of the principals; Stuart's marginal fame; the usual glamorous smorgasbord of money, complicated business issues, and sex. And although Stuart was clearly the front-running suspect, in most of the early stories, there was a sense of debate: Did he or didn't he? What were the pros and cons? How much evidence, really, was there, and what did it matter?

Since the arrest and its details—the flight to a motel room, registering under a false name, the loaded gun within an arm's reach on a table next to the bed—had become public, the presumption of innocence, or even the suggestion of possible innocence, was no longer in the mix. And this, of course, made it easier to believe in Stuart's "threats" to Bethany, and even in his "threatening" visits to Fred Furth and Kelley Rusnak, in spite of these latter witnesses' statements to the contrary. It didn't matter if they had felt threatened during their talks with him; Stuart's very presence was a threatening act. The talking heads and columnists got it right: an armed murder suspect with an all-points bulletin out on him calls on you while you're working, there's an element of threat.

But beyond even that, the near-ubiquitous perception that Stuart was at the very least no better than every murder suspect the Hall had entertained over the years had other immediate and personal consequences.

The first of these was bail. Normally there is no bail in a murder case, or at least no bail that anyone could reasonably be expected to make. But occasionally, especially when there may be issues of self-defense or of lofty community standing, a judge will grant bail of, say, a few hundred thousand dollars. Which of course in Stuart's case would have been doable. But at the bail hearing, Gina could hardly argue with any credibility that her client wasn't a flight risk. Everybody in the courtroom, and most certainly the judge, knew that he'd already tried that once.

First, the judge simply denied bail. Then, when Gina quite correctly pointed out that some bail was required in a noncapital case, the court promptly set bail at $20 million.

Secondly, and more upsetting especially to Kymberly than almost anything else, was the judge's refusal to allow Stuart, even accompanied by armed sheriff's deputies, to attend Caryn's funeral. From Stuart's perspective, this was pure spite, and an indication of how reviled he'd come to be among the regular denizens of the Hall.

Not that any of this would necessarily be admissible or deemed relevant at the hearing or trial. But for a million understandable reasons it all played hell with Stuart's confidence in his attorney. Also with Kym's and Debra's. After living with his confusion and doubts and anger for nearly two weeks, when he came in to see Gina in the attorney's visiting room at the jail, Stuart had finally made the decision to put it to her directly: Why shouldn't he let her go and get himself another attorney with more experience? Didn't she think it might be better for his chances if she simply withdrew?

So now, having just been chewed up and spit out by her friend the district attorney, Gina found herself fighting for the job she now wanted more than anything else in her career, more than anything in her life, in fact, since she'd prayed for David Freeman not to die.

Stuart's question itself didn't surprise her; she had expected something like it or stronger, an actual dismissal, for some days now. But if he was going to give her a chance to talk herself back into his trust, and the question implied that he hadn't made up his mind definitely to fire her, she was going to take it.

"First," she began, "I admit I screwed up the arrest itself. How it went down was my fault. I should have taken the gun from you, and I should have made the call to Juhle from my office. All of that is true, and I'm sorry."

Stuart sat a few feet down from her on a plain wooden chair, limp as a puppet with cut strings, looking lost in his bright-orange jumpsuit. He had already lost some weight in jail. The deeply tanned skin showed a distinct pallor under the hollowed-out cheeks. "I hired a supposedly experienced criminal attorney who was comfortable enough charging me sixty-five thousand dollars to take the case," he said.

"That's true. But it's also true I told you that I'd been out of practice for a while and that sixty-five is a discounted rate for this kind of case. And by the way, how much of that have you paid me up to now?"

The answer, which they both knew, of course, was—none of it.

"And yet I'm still here, aren't I? Every day." She held up a hand. The point spoke for itself: She was committed to him and to this case. "All I'm trying to say is that a murder case is the major leagues, and once in a while they throw at your head. I didn't expect Juhle to do that, but he did. He won't catch me off guard again."

Gina hated making excuses for herself; she was, in fact, fairly intolerant of them in others as well. David's motto, borrowed from Churchill she believed, and which she'd long ago adopted, had been "Never complain, never explain." And it had served her well too. Yet here she was, begging this man she hadn't known a few weeks ago to understand her and to forgive her for what she'd done.

So she was forcing the words out, but her body language betrayed no weakness. She sat at the room's one long table, an elbow resting on it, her legs crossed in a relaxed posture. Her confession concerned her technical failure, but there was very little mea culpa. "So we took a hit, Stuart. My fault more than yours, but there it is. But I didn't screw this up all by myself. I didn't let Kymberly talk to Bethany, and if you had bothered to tell me that you were going to let her, I would have pointed out what a truly terrible idea that was. I didn't run from the police. And as for the gun, you seem to forget the reason they found it on you is that you refused to give it to me."

"All right, fine," Stuart said. "I'll accept all that. But why should I have to keep paying the price for it now?"

"Well, the easy answer is you don't have to, Stuart. You say the word, and I'm gone and that's the end of it." Her bulldog expression dared him to call her on it if that was his decision. She wasn't going to show any sign of wanting or needing this job. She could take whatever he could dish out. But when his eyes fell away from her gaze, it seemed to her to be a small retreat. She still had some control over her fate here; for some reason, perhaps only inertia, maybe a fear of the devil he didn't know, he was reluctant to pull the trigger and tell her he was going to go with another lawyer.

"The thing is, Stuart," she said, "I don't know if you can tell or if you care, but I'm pretty angry right now. At Juhle mostly, but also at Gerry Abrams and even Clarence Jackman. They didn't have to play your arrest the way they did. I was being cooperative. We were coming in the next morning, and they knew it. So it was all macho bullshit."

"Pretty effective macho bullshit, though."

"Sure. Sometimes it is. But now I know where they're coming from. I know how they intend to play it. I've been doing this— defending people in Superior Court—for twenty-some years. I'm on great terms with the judges and bailiffs and clerks, and don't let yourself believe that doesn't matter. We get into court and Mr. Abrams and Inspector Juhle will, I hope, suddenly discover that I'm a bit of an old pro myself. And now I'm an old pro with a grudge and a score to settle, and I don't intend to make it pretty." She paused. "If you'd like me to stay on."

"Given that, are you sure you'd want to?"

"Yes, of course. I thought I'd made that clear. But while we're talking and before you make up your mind for good, there's one other thing we've got to get straight."

Stuart sighed and scratched at the stubble on his neck. "What's that?"

"Well, with all respect," she mustered her calmest voice, "I understand how you feel about the arrest and then me telling Juhle you weren't and never had been armed. That was a mistake too. If I hadn't told him you'd never taken the gun, okay, we're arguably in a much better position right now. So that's strike two on me.

"But the problems haven't been all on me. I didn't take the gun in the first place. *You* took the gun, and that's why you had it with you. That's not anything to do with me. If you remember, I wanted to take it home with me that night, get it out of your hands. I pleaded with you to let me have it. That was my advice. But you overruled me."

"I thought I might need it."

"Right. That's what you said. Your ecoterrorist friend might have followed you somehow. But the point is: why you're in all this trouble right now, it isn't all me. It isn't even mostly me. I wish it were. But I need you to see that so much of this is what *you* did. Talking to Juhle that first day. Deciding to take your gun with you. Sneaking out through your back door. Stealing license plates. Using a phony name. Asking Kymberly to talk to Bethany . . ."

"She did that on her own."

"Maybe. But that's not what Bethany said she told her."

"She got it wrong, then." Stuart put both of his hands up to his forehead. "God, God, God." He looked across about four feet of space to where Gina sat. "So remind me. What are we arguing about?"

"About whether I keep my job or not. You've lost a lot of confidence in me, and I understand that. I wouldn't blame you, Stuart. But I'd like you to be sure that it's me, after all. Not just these shitty circumstances. And don't get me wrong, they're plenty shitty. I didn't predict any of this happening, and maybe I should have."

He nodded, then grew quiet for nearly a full minute, until he finally took a deep breath. "Help me out here, Gina. Kym's all over letting you go. So's Debra."

Gina shrugged. "It's not their call, Stuart."

"But then who do I go with? Jedd Conley? I don't know any other lawyers."

"I do," Gina said. "I could recommend any number of them. Though probably not Jedd," she added with a trace of humor. Then, in all seriousness, "Either one of my partners would take you on, and they're both excellent."

"But," he said. "I hear a 'but.' "

"No you don't. They're good guys and good lawyers with lots of experience. And they almost certainly wouldn't suffer from the incredible handicap of believing you're innocent. Wes—one of my partners—even told me, 'Whatever you do, don't start believing he's innocent. He'll just break your heart.' "

"Sounds like a sweetheart."

"He is." She met his eyes. "He's just another pro who's seen it all before. He often says he doesn't believe anybody except his dog. He loves his dog, though."

Stuart cocked his head. "What about your David?"

The question quickened her somehow. "What about him?"

"I mean, with his clients. Didn't he ever believe they were innocent?"

She took a moment before shaking her head. "His rule was he'd never ask and never let them tell him. It was one of the first things he always told his clients. 'I don't want to know. All I want to know is what evidence they've got and if I can make the jury doubt some or most of it. That's the job. Whether you did it or not doesn't matter to me.' "

"He didn't really feel that?"

"Oh, yes he did. Really for truly. With his whole heart."

"And what about you?"

"Well"—she felt herself break a rueful smile, and it surprised her—"you're watching me break new ground. If I had come to this from a different angle, I don't know what I'd be thinking. Probably that, like everybody else, you don't get all the way to arrested if you're not guilty. As I say, that's the professional approach."

"This time I really do hear a 'but.' "

"Yep," she said. "You do." She raised her eyes and stared him full in the face. "But in this case, I don't believe you killed Caryn." Lowering her voice, she went on. "Wes may be right, I'll get my heart broken over it, but I don't think so."

"I won't break your heart," Stuart said.

"See? There I go believing you again." She met his eyes, all business. "But look, this is full-disclosure time. You know this is still my first murder case. You know that so far, to say it hasn't gone well is an understatement. There's some chance that even though I'm watching a lot more closely, and I'm a lot more pissed off, I might get sandbagged again. You might be better served with one of my partners or any number of other pretty good lawyers in town."

"Guys who'll believe I did it."

"Probably. But most wouldn't care to know, one way or another."

Stuart met her eyes again, but briefly, then abruptly he got up and walked over to the glass block wall that ran along one side of the room. He stood there for a few seconds before nodding to himself and turning around. "I didn't kill Caryn, Gina. I didn't love her anymore, but I didn't kill her."

"I know that. I believe that."

He closed his eyes for a second with obvious relief, then opened them and met her gaze straight on. "I think that's the most important thing."

"I think so too," Gina said, "though we're in the minority."

"I'm comfortable in the minority," Stuart said. "That's where I spend most of my time, anyway." Crossing back over to his chair, he pulled it around, up closer to Gina, and straddled it backward. "So this hearing tomorrow?" he said. "How bad is it going to be?"

The conference room at Freeman, Farrell, Hardy & Roake was a large oval with floor-to-ceiling windows and a set of glass double-doors looking out on a small, grassy roof garden and similar large windows facing the main lobby. The idea had looked terrific in the architectural plans, and even when the remodel had been completed. But in practice it soon became obvious that the place was a fishbowl. Everybody walking by could clearly see who was inside and often exactly what was going on in there around the huge circular table. In the land of attorney-client privilege and secret negotiations, this did not turn out to be a plus for the business.

To rectify the situation, David Freeman had ordered several large potted trees to be delivered—dieffenbachia, palms, some citrus—to partially block the view, or at least mitigate the lack of privacy. Over the years, more greenery had been added—giant ferns, rubber trees, a California redwood that now scraped the thirty-foot ceiling. Bringing potted flora to the office became an unspoken trophy moment for Freeman and his associates after a win in a big case, and the room came to be known as the Solarium.

And here, today, technically a few minutes after the close of business, Gina had her discovery folders and yellow legal pads spread out on the table in front of her. She turned at the knock on the side panel of the door.

"Hey, Wes. Come on in."

"Don't let me bother you," he said. "Gert and I are just passing through."

She nodded absently as her partner—his T-shirt today read TAKE THE MESSAGE ON YOUR BUMPER—AND STICK IT!—led his Labrador back behind Gina, through the room and out onto the grassy lawn where they'd put in the memorial bench for David. In another minute, the outside door opened again and they were back inside. "Poor girl," Wes said, "I thought she was going to die if she didn't get outside to pee. But there's no way I bring her down here before Phyllis leaves. I don't see her as a dog person, do you?"

Gina straightened up in her chair. Her shoulders rose and fell. "Wes . . ." She motioned to the many piles of paper surrounding her.

"You're busy, I'm sorry."

"The hearing's tomorrow."

"Gorman?"

"That's the one."

"Is it as bad as the papers make it look?"

"Close, but Wes—"

He held up a hand. "Got it. You're working. I'm out of here. Come on, Gert. Gina still likes you. I'm sure she notices that you're not even on a leash. She's just busy."

Gina looked over, shaking her head wearily, but unable to suppress a small smile. "Sorry, Gert," she said. "Good dog. Very impressive."

"What's impressive?" Dismas Hardy suddenly appeared behind Wes and Gert.

Gina finally put her pen down, pushed her legal pad a few inches away. "What's impressive is how anybody gets any work done around here." She turned to face her two partners. "Guys. Hearing tomorrow. I'm a little overwhelmed."

"Gorman," Farrell said to Hardy.

"I guessed," Hardy said, then turned to Gina. "He pay you yet?" Since he'd become managing partner of the firm, he kept a pretty firm eye on the bottom line.

"He's had a little trouble getting to the bank," Gina said. "In fact, he's had a pretty tough couple of weeks in general. Maybe you've read something about it in the papers."

Hardy broke a grin. "That would be no, then?" A little more serious now. "So bring him a blank check in jail."

"I'm not worried about getting paid, Diz. He's good for it."

"Not if he did it," Farrell said. "Gert, sit! Anyway, Gina, you kill your wife, you don't get to collect the insurance on her. It's one of those dumb rules."

"Yeah, well, he didn't kill his wife, so it won't be a problem."

"Uh-oh," Farrell said.

Gina sat back in her chair. "Just because you believed a guilty client who lied to you, Wes. That doesn't make it a general rule of the universe. Innocent people get arrested and go to trial and get acquitted."

"Right," Farrell said. "All the time. When was the last one exactly, though? I forget. Was that Scott Peterson? Oh no, that's right. He was guilty."

"I believe Mr. Hardy here has seen a few innocent clients, if I'm not mistaken."

"Well, he got some of them off, anyway."

"Hey!" Hardy struck as quick as a snake, punching Farrell's shoulder. "They *were* innocent, that's why."

"See"—Farrell, rubbing his new bruise, turned to Gina—"it's sad. He still believes it."

"It's easy to believe things if they're true," Hardy shot back.

"I'm just saying, Gina, don't get your hopes up."

"No, you wouldn't want to do that. You wouldn't want to believe anything good was ever going to happen."

"Okay, then," Wes said, "as long as that concept is clear." He looked down at his dog. "C'mon, Gert, she's going to be all right. It's time for us to go home."

Dismas Hardy stood in the doorway for another moment and made sure that Wes and his dog had gone up the stairs, then he stepped inside the Solarium and closed the door behind him. "So how's it looking?"

"Bad enough." Gina flashed him a weary, hopeful, evanescent smile. "Then this new discovery I got an hour ago." Discovery was, of course, supposed to be all of the evidence that the prosecution had collected in a case—police reports, witness testimony, forensic and medical records, photographs, everything. Gina had gotten the first box of these records from Gerry Abrams' office within two days of Stuart's arrest. The rest of it—further transcripts with witnesses, more police write-ups, whatever came in—tended to arrive in dribs and drabs. "If I didn't keep getting ugly surprises, I'd be happier."

Hardy pulled up a chair next to her. "Like what?"

She grabbed at a manila folder and passed it across to him. As he turned over the photographs contained in it, she explained their significance. "Juhle went up to Stuart's mountain retreat at Echo Lake with a warrant last week. He thought he might find some evidence of deliberation or premeditation. I'm thinking he hit the mother lode."

Hardy turned the picture over. "What happened here? It looks a hurricane hit the place."

"Either that or some guy named Stuart."

"You didn't know about this? He never mentioned it?"

"It's never come up."

Hardy was flipping through the folder, his second time through. "This is the wife, I presume." He held up a close-up of a smiling woman in a frame behind a web of shattered glass. Another picture showed a table and chairs knocked over or lifted up on their sides, ly-ing in a scattering of broken plates, bowls and other glassware; in an-other, the mattress was halfway off the bed, its stuffing coming out. "Well," Hardy held up the bed picture, "at least now you know why he couldn't sleep. I couldn't get comfortable with the bed like this ei-ther." Then, seriously, he asked, "Have you talked to him about this yet?"

"No. I just got it this afternoon after I'd spent half the day with him. And oh, did I mention my charming half hour with Clarence this morning too?"

Thinking it might be better news, Hardy took the bait. "How'd that go?"

"I can't decide which part was worse, my ethical failings or my in-competence." She gathered the folder of pictures back to her, then sighed deeply. "He was as mad at me as I've ever seen him, Diz. It was bad, maybe irreparable."

"I doubt that," Hardy said. "He's eaten me for breakfast a few times and we're still pals. He'll get over it if you will."

Gina nodded, the picture of glumness. "Let me ask you some-thing, Diz. You're up on this case, right?"

A shrug. "Just what's in the news."

"What's it look like to you? Honestly."

Hardy killed a second or two admiring the ferns, then came back to Gina with a somber look. "I might be wrong," he said, "but since your Px"—a preliminary hearing—"has a probable-cause standard of proof, which is a long long way from a reasonable-doubt standard, bottom line, the judge holds him to answer." This was legalese, telling Gina that she was going to lose tomorrow and her client was going to have to go to a full trial. "Of course, that's assuming I'm a reasonable mind, which is not a slam-dunk assumption. But if you'll grant me that, then you've got a reasonable mind with a strong suspicion that a crime has been committed and that your client committed it. And that's what the statute mandates."

"Even without any physical evidence?"

Hardy's brow went dark. "What are you talking about? They got physical evidence up the wazoo. An autopsy. Probably a murder weapon. Pictures of a torn-up cabin, plus a strong motive, an eyewitness, prior domestic violence, a bunch of lies your client told, and—oh wait, before I forget—he grabbed a gun and took off before the police could get him in jail. Did I leave out anything? Of course he did send his daughter to threaten a witness too, but maybe that was her idea. Your client's going to trial, Gina. You better get used to it." Hardy gave her a shrug. "You asked me." On a less confrontational note, he added, "You got anybody else to point at?"

Gina shook her head no. "Wyatt's talked to Caryn's business partner, whose life got way better when Caryn died. Plus, he had an affair with her a while ago. His alibi is weak too. But we can't put him at the scene. He even provided fingerprints to Wyatt—voluntarily—and no match. Beyond that, there's nobody else close except maybe this guy who sent Stuart a couple of threatening e-mails. His car is what's killing us; the neighbor girl seeing it."

Hardy reflexively corrected her. "You mean *saying* she saw it."

"I didn't say that? I thought I did."

"No, what you said was, 'The neighbor girl seeing it.' And not to beat on you when you're down, that's the kind of slip that'll kill you."

"You're right. You are so right." Gina's face went blank, her voice hollow. "You know," she began, "Stuart wanted to fire me this morning.

I talked him out of it. I'm thinking now that maybe that was a mistake, that I'm not ready for this."

"Everybody feels that way, Gina. It's performance time. You'll rise to it like you have before a hundred times."

"But never in a murder case."

Hardy embodied nonchalance. "Same rules, same procedures, same people in the courtroom. You'll get your sea legs and be fine. But let me ask you one."

Sighing again, she nodded. "All right. Shoot."

"You believe your man didn't do it, right? He's factually innocent. And forget about Wes. You don't have to explain why to me, if it's good enough for you."

"Okay. Yes. He's innocent."

"So use that. If he's innocent, what really happened? What's your theory on the case?"

Gina pursed her lips, looked into the middle distance. "She was expecting somebody. He came and they had a disagreement about something important. No, more than important—life-altering. Somehow she was going to ruin this guy's life. So he had to kill her."

Hardy contemplated that for a moment. "So she was having an affair?"

"Yes."

"Definitely?"

A beat, then, "Yes."

"Okay, then, there's your case. So here's ten cents of free advice: Prove it."

TWENTY-FIVE

IT WAS STILL DARK OUT WHEN Gina heard her morning *Chronicle* hit her front door and, since she wasn't sleeping anyway, reached out in her pajamas and brought it in. The end of the balmy spell, prefigured for the past several days by increasing winds and scudding cloud cover, was now reality enough that the paper was wrapped in plastic to keep it dry, and although the actual rain hadn't begun to fall, clearly it was going to be wet and cold.

Gina had stayed at the office with her discovery folders until nearly nine o'clock, then packed them up in her lawyer's briefcase. Thinking it might bring her luck and wondering all the while at the same time if it was a good idea, she had taken a taxi to the Rue Charmaine, the restaurant directly under David Freeman's old apartment on Mason, one block straight downhill from the Mark Hopkins Hotel that had been their favorite. Rick came out of the kitchen and showered her with attention. Then, in a custom long-established by David, Rick first determined what wine she'd be drinking—in this case, a half bottle of Gevrey-Chambertin—and then brought her several small private special dishes that did not appear on the menu, to match the wine.

Home by eleven, wrestling with all that surrounded her case—Stuart, David, Juhle, Clarence, Caryn's phantom lover (and killer?)—she finally fell asleep sometime after 12:30, the last time she remembered glancing at her clock.

Until she was looking at it again at 4:15, wide awake.

When the paper hit the front door, it was the excuse she needed to throw off her covers. She knew she wasn't going back to sleep today. Might as well not fight it.

In her single-mindedness since Stuart had been arrested, Gina had neglected to do any grocery shopping, and now the pickings in her home were slim. She told herself that this wasn't smart if she was to have the energy she was going to need in court, but that wasn't going to help her this morning. Nothing remotely resembling a meal spoke to her from the pantry shelves. But she had one frozen teriyaki rice bowl left in her freezer, and not really in the mood for it, she nevertheless put it in the microwave and started the coffee going, six cups' worth.

Returning to the kitchen table, sitting down, opening the paper, she felt some undefined sense of relief that, at least for today, Stuart was off the front page. Although ironically enough, she thought, here was a picture of Jedd Conley and his wife on page three, at some fundraising event, with an accompanying article about his anticipated run for the U.S. Senate. He was still being coy and hadn't definitely committed, but obviously someone—one of Horace Tremont's political allies, no doubt—had floated the rumor to see how it played on the street. Judging from the article, it was going to play pretty well.

Thinking back to the night he'd put the make on her ten days before, Gina shook her head in a kind of disgusted wonder. She didn't hate or even dislike Jedd. In fact, to the contrary. But why, she wondered, was it always these guys with a kind of slippery personal morality who got drawn to high-level politics? And, all too often, elected?

It drove her nuts, which is why she rarely allowed herself to think about it. But seeing the story now in the paper, she resolved that if Jedd did decide to run, she wouldn't vote for him. Even if he was charming, sexy, discreet. It wasn't going to happen.

The timer on the microwave sounded as Gina finished the first section of the paper. She turned it over as she was getting up. Stirring the rice absentmindedly, she brought it over by the coffee machine, put it down and poured herself a cup with a spoonful of sugar. On automatic, coffee in one hand, rice bowl in the other, she returned to her seat at the table, noticing that outside, it was still dark.

The cup stopped halfway to her mouth and she put it back down softly, staring at the familiar name under the headline in the regional news that had caught her eye:

APPARENT SUICIDE IN FOSTER CITY

Police in Foster City are treating as a probable suicide the death, apparently by sleeping pills, of a woman found yesterday in her bed in the Harbor Creek Condominium complex. Kelley Gray Rusnak, 34 years old, and unmarried, had been a laboratory specialist for the San Bruno medical technology company, Polymed Innovations, Inc., for the past 11 years. When she failed to appear or call in her absence at work last Friday, and then this Monday, her employers became concerned and notified the police. William C. Blair, PII's president, said, "Kelley was one of our most reliable employees and when she didn't call in sick, we were very concerned that something bad must have happened."

Fully clothed when found, Ms. Rusnak, police say, appeared not to be the victim of foul play. Blair acknowledged that he had heard reports from the victim's colleagues that she had been depressed in recent weeks, and had recommended that she seek counseling. An autopsy is pending.

Funeral arrangements have not been announced but the family asks that in lieu of flowers, contributions be made to . . .

*   *   *

Gina knew that rain or shine or fog, Wyatt Hunt usually started his day early with a jog from the warehouse in which he lived near the Hall of Justice, out to the Embarcadero, then north to Maritime Park, and back. He didn't answer his phone at home when she called him, so she left a message and, her breakfast and coffee forgotten, ran to her room and got changed into her well-worn jogging outfit and tennis shoes. She would run across town, down California and Market, and cut him off. If she missed him, she'd go by his place.

She didn't miss him. At 6:15, Gina ran at his side, slowly enough through the light drizzle that they both could talk. "She was going to be one of my witnesses, Wyatt. She was one of the two people Stuart saw down the Peninsula. He wasn't fleeing from the arrest, but going down to talk to these people and find out what they knew about Caryn's business. I tried to subpoena her, but couldn't get the damn thing served."

"Well, now you know why."

"This has to be related to Stuart, and to the Dryden Socket somehow," she said. "She told Stuart something was seriously wrong with the product."

"So she killed herself over it? Why would she do that?"

"I'd be surprised if she did."

"But you just said . . ."

"I said the cops in the paper were calling it a probable suicide. I'm calling that pretty unlikely. I mean, two deaths in two weeks, and the women were partners in the same project? This doesn't raise a flag for you?"

They jogged on together. "It's a definite question," Wyatt said.

After a few more steps, he added, "I could look into it, but it would be an expensive fishing trip. And how's that helping Stuart in the here and now?"

"Yeah, I know. It's not."

They'd gotten pretty much to the end of the line, where the asphalt of their running path ran into the breakwater a few hundred yards beyond the Maritime Museum at the corner of Ghirardelli

Square. Out on the open water, the bay was a churning mass of gray-green, studded with whitecaps. The cloud cover was dark, thick, unbroken and low over the Golden Gate Bridge, the wind gusty and fitful. Without discussion, they turned and put the wind at their backs, now allowing it to push them along, making it easier to talk too.

"Okay," Gina said, "let's leave Kelley and go back to Caryn. Do you think she was sleeping with somebody?"

Wyatt huffed. "Probably."

"Diz says that's our killer."

"He's probably right."

"So who do we got?"

"Actual names? McAfee. Maybe Pinkert. The guy down in Palo Alto—Furth. Conley . . ."

Gina came to an abrupt stop. "Conley? You mean Jedd Conley?"

Hunt, keeping up his pace, jogging in place, shrugged. "Sure, why not? They talked on Friday. Maybe they made a date for Sunday night." Seeing Gina's reaction, Wyatt said, "I'm just throwing out possibilities, Gina, everybody we know she talked to. I don't know if anybody's even asked Conley if he's got an alibi. I could find out quick enough."

"You ought to do that." Gina went back into her jog, Wyatt falling in beside her. "Eliminate him, if nothing else. But whoever she was seeing, they had to meet up somewhere. They had to plan it. Somebody might have seen them or heard something."

"Maybe not," Wyatt said. "Not if it was Doctor Bob."

"McAfee?"

Wyatt bobbed his head. "Lots of places to hide out in their new clinic space. It would have been a piece of cake, Gina, as long as they mostly didn't want to do it laying down. The same would hold true of Pinkert, too. Even if she didn't like fat guys."

"Who said that?"

"McAfee."

"Well, she liked Pinkert enough to ask him to be her partner. What's his alibi?"

"I don't have one for him, either. McAfee basically just said it was no chance."

"Okay, we should get that too." They ran in silence for about half a block, then Gina went on. "I'd like you to put in all the time you can on this, Wyatt. Go back to the hospital and start with the assumption that Caryn was having an affair. See what you can find."

"Do you have her phone records?"

"They were with the discovery docs. I haven't done much with them."

"I'll want them."

"Done. What else? But think fast." They'd gotten to the Ferry Building, the foot of Market Street. "This is my turnoff." Both of them came to a halt, neither breathing hard.

"I've probably got most of the rest. I'll call your office if I need anything else."

"You won't forget the alibis. For everybody."

"Right," Wyatt said. "Everybody in the whole world."

The whole Kelley Rusnak situation refused to go away, but before Gina had even gotten home from the run—walking up the steep grade of California Street on the way back—she got to thinking about something that struck her as anomalous in the news story, and that led her to what she thought was a pretty good idea. By the time she was in her kitchen, she was sold on it.

It was still early, just after seven o'clock, but she had no compunction about making the phone call to another longtime acquaintance who was also a member of Jackman's kitchen cabinet. Jeff Elliott was the columnist who wrote "CityTalk" every day for the *Chronicle*, and Gina had what she believed was a legitimate scoop.

Jeff had been conspicuously silent to date on the Gorman case, probably because he didn't deal so much in innuendo as in hard news, he wasn't starstruck and he had friends—Jackman and Gina—on both sides of the matter. He was also generally regarded as a class act who didn't feel the need to spin the truth for a headline. Wheelchair-bound now with slowly advancing multiple sclerosis, he already had his column and his byline; he had nothing to prove, and he usually avoided trolling in the turbid waters of slander and leakage favored by so many of his Fourth Estate colleagues.

He picked up on the second ring, apparently awake for hours. "This is Jeff Elliott?"

"Jeff, good morning. It's Gina Roake."

"Back in the fray too," he said. "I must say I appreciate the personal invite, but I was already planning to attend."

"Attend what?"

"Your hearing today. That's what you're calling about, isn't it?"

"As a matter of fact, no. Not really. Although I've got a story that might be related."

"Might be?"

"Probably is. I just don't know how."

"Which is where the ace investigative reporter comes in."

Gina thought, no wonder Jeff was so universally well-liked. "Exactly," she said. "I'm guessing you've seen the paper today. I'm further guessing you've still got it within arm's length. Would I be correct?"

"It's almost scary," he said. "Okay, I've got it. What?"

"Second section, page six, under Digest."

She heard him turning the pages over the phone. "So we're not in the City?"

There was no mistaking his disappointment. Jeff drew his columns almost exclusively from within the boundaries of the City and County of San Francisco. Interesting news might happen elsewhere, but if it wasn't on his turf, he usually passed it along to someone else.

So Gina spoke up quickly. "I'm predicting we're going to get here pretty fast. You see the suicide in Foster City?"

"Got it. Kelley Rusnak?"

"That's her. Lab assistant at PII. Guess who she was the assistant to?"

"Don't say Marie Curie. She's not old enough."

"Caryn Dryden."

"Stuart Gorman's wife." Although Jeff had not yet written a column about the case, he knew that the hearing was scheduled for this morning, and he knew the principals by heart.

"Correct. Although you notice the article doesn't mention that. It also doesn't mention, perhaps because the reporter had no way of knowing, that I'd tried to subpoena Ms. Rusnak for Stuart in the preliminary hearing." Gina paused for a second, letting Jeff absorb the fact. "You also might notice that the spokesman for the company isn't some personnel person, somebody with HR, it's the CEO himself. William Blair. Talking about being worried about a lab assistant because she missed two days of work? This in a company with over a hundred and fifteen employees on site."

"Okay." Jeff was following her.

She went on. "The reason I know all this, and the reason I wanted her to be my witness, is because on the day that Stuart Gorman was arrested last week, he got a call at home from Kelley Rusnak, and then met her in some parking lot down the Peninsula."

"What did she have to do with him?"

"Nothing, directly. She'd only met him a few times. But she gives him a reason to be down the Peninsula other than running from an arrest warrant. She also thought something about the work they were both doing at PII might have had something to do with Caryn's death." A long silence ensued, during which Gina read Jeff's mind. "I don't blame you for considering that this is me trying to get another version of events out in front of the public, Jeff. But two things. First, I just wouldn't do that. You've known me a long time. That's not my game. Second, all this is easily and independently verifiable. You call Bill Blair, ask a few questions, you like his answers, you leave it alone. But I don't think you will like his answers. I think there's an enormous story here."

"About what? These two women?"

"Some of that, yes. But more about the project they were working on. Have you ever heard of the Dryden Socket?"

"No."

"Well, sit tight and hold on." She gave him a succinct rundown of what she'd learned about Caryn's invention, the incredible profit it was poised to make, the problems with the clinical trials, the late reporting, Caryn's threats to expose PII's behavior, the pending FDA approval, the mezzanine loans, Fred Furth and his venture capital group. "And now they would have us believe that this young woman kills herself?" she concluded. "I think Bill Blair is at the very least involved in some kind of cover-up. He wants that socket to get to the market with FDA approval, and he's going to hide the negative test results."

"How's he going to do that? Clinical trials, they're public documents."

"Right. But these results came in after the trials were completed. Technically, they're not part of the approval process. Now apparently they're coming in mostly as questions to PII. 'Could this death or this clot be from the socket?' So if there's no whistle-blower on the inside, like Caryn or this poor girl Kelley, nobody gets to find out about what's going on."

Jeff hesitated, then said, "You're right about one thing. This changes the complexion of things around Gorman. If I put it out and any part of it's true . . ."

"It's all true. You can check it all yourself, as I'm sure you will."

"Of course. But if this is any part of your case, with the coverage you're already getting, what I'm saying is it's going to go national in a heartbeat."

"That would be a nice bonus, I admit. Get another version of things out there in the ether. Plus, something else might shake loose. This case needs another suspect in a bad way. What do you think?"

Jeff took most of thirty seconds, a very long time, before he said, "I like it. Up to Caryn Dryden's murder, anyway. But I still can't understand why this girl killed herself. If she was whistle-blowing on this . . . unless someone threatened her somehow . . . but even then . . ."

Gina cut him off. "That's the part I can't figure out either, Jeff. And with my case heating up the way it is, I can't even send investigators out to look. There's no time, and I've got other priorities. But I'm sure there's something here, something big, and it would be an incredible coincidence if it wasn't somehow connected to my case. I just can't see how."

It wasn't until she'd hung up that another thought struck Gina. The cover-up scenario she'd just described so eloquently to Jeff Elliott would benefit anyone who held stock in PII or stood to gain from the timely approval of the Dryden Socket. With Caryn's death, the ownership of all of the family's PII stock, as well as the huge negotiated return on Caryn's $2 million mezzanine loan, would all go to Stuart.

Other suspects, as she'd hoped aloud to Jeff Elliott, might in fact shake loose—Bill Blair, Fred Furth. But if one were inclined to view her client as guilty to begin with, and this seemed to include the whole world at the moment, then she'd just set in motion an investigation that would only give Stuart more, not less, motive.

Her stomach tightened and she fought her way through the cramp with shallow breathing, then shakily stood up to go in, take a shower, and get into her courtroom clothes.

TWENTY-SIX

———

A COVERED BUT OPEN-TO-THE-AIR corridor extends from the back door of the Hall of Justice, past the jail on the left and the morgue on the right, and ends at a parking lot reserved for police and other official vehicles. Today at 8:15 a.m. the walkway was wet and windswept and Gina was hurrying, head-down, to get to the jail to meet with her client. She nearly walked into the young woman who stepped into her path. "Oh, I'm sorry, I . . . Kymberly? What are you doing out here in the cold like this?"

"I tried to see my dad, but they won't let me in."

"That's because it's early for visiting hours. But what are you doing here? Your father said you'd gone back to school."

She shrugged. "School's bullshit." She gestured to the jail. "They're letting you in, aren't they?"

"Yes. But I'm his lawyer." The girl didn't look good. She was in flip-flops, a pair of torn blue jeans, and a camouflage sweatshirt with a hood. Weather? What weather? She hugged her arms to her body. The hollows under her eyes were dark enough to be bruises. Her shoulder-length hair hadn't seen a brush or a comb since she'd last slept, which might not have been recently. "Are you okay, Kymberly?"

"I'm fine."

"What did you want to see your dad about?"

"Nothing."

"Have you eaten anything today? Are you back staying with Debra?"

"Maybe. I don't have to tell you where I'm staying."

"No, that's true. But I need to be able to find you if you're going to testify."

"Who said I was doing that?"

"Didn't your dad tell you about that? You remember. We'll need you if Bethany starts talking about how your dad threatened her."

"She probably won't, though. That's bogus."

"I know, but she might believe that's what happened."

"I doubt it. She's not stupid."

Gina gave up. "All right. But just to support your dad, it'd look good if you were in the courtroom. And then if it came up, we could use you."

"Sure, that's what you guys do, isn't it? Use people. So feel free. Walk all over me if you want."

"I won't do that. I'm trying to avoid having to issue you a subpoena and if you're just there with us, I wouldn't have to." Exasperation played over her features but Gina, trying to stay nice, took another tack. "So. Are you getting enough sleep? You look very tired, Kym."

"So do you."

That was enough. Gina decided to confront the overt antagonism straight on. "Why are you being so rude to me?"

"Because you're screwing up and it's hurting my dad. You ought to quit."

"I offered to do that yesterday. Your dad decided to keep me on."

"Why would he do that?"

"Because I believe he's innocent. Most other lawyers probably wouldn't. He seems to think that's important." Gina, much more heavily dressed, nevertheless was starting to feel the chill, and knew that Kymberly must be near freezing. She pointed to the door that led to the jail. "I'm cold standing out here," she said, putting it all on herself. "Let's go inside."

The lobby was all glass block and industrial linoleum, as welcoming as a bus station. But it was dry and there was no wind—an improvement. Gina walked over to the plastic bench against the right-hand wall and sat at one end. Kymberly took the other, as far from Gina as the bench allowed.

"So you've taken some more days off school? Do you think that's a good idea?"

The young woman turned on her. "School? What do you care if I'm in school? What am I going to do in school?"

Falling into adult mode, Gina tried to give her a reasonable answer. "Whatever you were doing there before this happened with your mother, Kymberly. You had plans then. Don't lose them over this."

Kymberly rolled her eyes. "Right. Here's the thing, though. How about if I never went to school in the first place?"

"Is that true?"

"*Is that true? Is that true?*" Mocking Gina's tone. "Why? Is that such a shock? Nice little Kymmie didn't do what her mommy wanted? What do you think? Like school's going to do me a lot of good, right? I'm going to be a better person? Give me a break. Like all that education made my mom such a sweetheart."

Shaken by this information, Gina barely trusted herself to breathe. She wanted to know more, but knew that if she betrayed that fact to Kymberly, the girl would stop talking. Her expression neutral, Gina looked across at her. "But you wanted to see your dad today?"

"My dad's okay. I wanted to tell him how important it is he gets off on this."

"He knows that."

"No, he doesn't. Not if he's willing to gamble on you just because he likes you."

"What do you mean, likes me?"

"Finds you attractive. How's that? Clear enough?"

"Did you ever think it might be because I'm a good lawyer?"

"How would he know? What've you done good yet?"

Gina opened her mouth but found no words.

Kymberly shook her head. "Just like with Mom."

"What's just like with your mom, Kym?"

"It's the way his brain works. He *decides* he's with Mom, and so he stays all those years, even when she drives him out of the house for weeks at a time and gives him nothing back. He *decides* he likes you, so now he's keeping you on. It's just who he is. Even if you're not doing the job he needs done."

"I'm trying to do that job, Kymberly. I really, truly don't believe he killed your mother."

"It's not *believing*, don't you understand? I *know* he didn't do it."

One of the jail's admitting officers glanced over from where he stood behind the counter. "Everything all right over there?"

Gina held up a hand—everything was under control. Turning back to Kymberly, she said, "What does that mean? You 'know' it. How can you know it more than I do? Is there something specific you should tell me?"

The questions stopped Kym abruptly. She looked first down, then across to the admitting counter, then at last back to Gina. "I just know him. I just know him." Shaking her head as though to clear her thoughts, she said, "You've got to keep him out of prison. He can't go to prison! Don't you understand? *That can't happen!*"

Tears welled up and brightened her eyes. Gina reached out to touch her and offer her some comfort, but suddenly she bolted up and, with an anguished sob, broke for the door. Gina, immediately on her feet, got outside only in time to catch a last glimpse of Kym as she disappeared around the edge of the building.

*   *   *

In the attorney's visiting room, trying to shake off her reaction to Kym, Gina heard the knock from the deputy and a second later was standing up, preparing herself to look strong for her client as Stuart appeared at the door. When she saw him, though, she could feel something go out of her, out of the forced animation in her face. "Where are your dress-out clothes?" she asked, her voice sounding hollow and shaky, even to herself.

"Dressing out" was a courtesy afforded prisoners going into trial. They were allowed to wear their own clothes and shoes instead of the orange jail jumpsuit and paper slippers. The idea was to minimize the bias that jail garb creates for a jury. That wasn't the rule at prelim, where there was no jury to be prejudiced. Nevertheless, Gina had over the years tried to dress out her clients as often as she could, if only for the tiny psychic lift it might give them, the nod to dignity. From time to time, her requests to dress out her client for prelim had been granted.

Expecting the same result with this latest request, she'd gone to Stuart's home over the weekend and brought a couple of changes of clothes down to the jail. She'd never received notice to the contrary, so it really hadn't occurred to her that the courtesy would be denied in this case. But here was Stuart now, not just in the typical jail orange jumpsuit, but a red flight-risk jumpsuit, shackled hand and foot.

She seemed to be taking it worse than Stuart, who actually struck a faux-modeling pose for an instant, flashing a smile at her. "I thought I'd go for something bold in red," he said, then shrugged as though it were of little import to him. "I asked the guards when I should change, and they said it wasn't happening."

"Christ." Gina leaned back against the table.

Stuart came and stood about a foot in front of her. "Hey, it's okay."

She looked up at him. "Not really, Stuart." But all the weight of the morning again bore down on her, and she hung her head. "Christ," she said again.

He touched the side of her arm. "You all right?"

Finally, she looked up and met his eyes. "It's just been a monster of a morning. You're going to want to sit down."

Kelley Rusnak hit Stuart pretty hard. Like Gina, he in no way believed that she had killed herself. She had not been depressed when he'd been talking to her. Quite the contrary, she had been outraged, eager to help right a wrong, ready for a fight. There must be more to the story that hadn't come out yet, that would perhaps be discovered at the autopsy. Gina told him about her call to Jeff Elliott, that he was going to try and follow up on the story if he could. That if they got lucky, it could broaden the case away from him; although since Stuart still stood to gain from any Dryden Socket profits, that effect might be mitigated.

"Of course," he said. "You wouldn't want unmitigated good news."

"Don't worry about that." They were both on the hard wooden chairs at the long table, and Gina knocked on the tabletop. "Okay, that brings us to number two. Again, not pretty."

"How many do we got?"

"Four. First was Kelley. Second, these." She opened her briefcase and took out the photos of the Echo Lake cabin that she'd shown her partner in the Solarium just last night.

Stuart took them, and it seemed to take him a minute to recognize the first picture for what it was. When he finally did, he swore under his breath, then quickly flipped through the bunch of them. "Where'd they get these?"

"Juhle got a warrant and went up to your place."

Stuart took in a deep breath, then let it out in a rush. "I got really drunk," he said. "I've always said I was furious." Then, "Can they use these?"

"I'll try to have them excluded, but if I were the judge . . ." She stopped.

"You'd say they spoke to my state of mind. I think I would too. Okay," he said, "we're now officially even."

"In what way?"

"Well, the problems with the arrest? We can put that on you. But these pictures? I bet I could have remembered what I'd done up there and had somebody go by and clean up a little."

Gina nodded at him. "I bet you could have too."

"It's just with finding Caryn and all . . ."

"I get it. And that's going to be my argument back at them. You had all the time in the world to get back up there and clean it up good as new, and it never occurred to you because you hadn't done anything to make you think you needed to clean it up. That's really okay."

"Yahoo." He sat back in his chair and crossed his arms. "So what's number three?"

"Number three," she said, "is Kymberly."

He showed nothing but perplexity. "Kymberly? What about her?"

"She was here this morning."

"Where?"

"Here. At the jail. She wanted to see you, but they wouldn't let her in. It was too early."

"Bastards."

"It's a jail, Stuart. There's visiting hours."

He sighed in frustration, then suddenly the obvious question hit him. "Wait a minute. She was down here? What about school? Debra told me Kym just went back up after the funeral. She can't be missing this many classes." He brought his hand to his forehead, squeezed at his temples. "God. I've got to talk to her. Is she coming back later? Will she be at the hearing? I've got to see her."

"Stuart." Gina kept her voice low-key. "The thing is, she just told me she never went up to school in the first place."

The confusion played all over his face. "What? Of course she did. I talked to her up there that first week every day. I mean . . ." He stopped, stared at Gina, completely at a loss.

"You called on her cell phone, didn't you? Or she called you?"

"She never went up there?"

"That's what she said."

"So what . . . where is she staying?"

"I don't know. I'd guess somewhere in the city. Maybe a boyfriend's? I don't know."

"You didn't ask her?"

"Yes, I did. She told me it was none of my business. She wants me off the case. She says I'm no good for you. You'll wind up in prison. She got very upset. *Very* upset. Then ran out, crying."

Stuart took it in with his arms crossed, his chin on his chest.

"Evidently," Gina said, "and this is number four, you're keeping me on because you've got some kind of a schoolboy crush on me. And if that's the case, that's a bad reason. I will get you through this hearing and then help you find another attorney."

He sat still for several more seconds before he opened his eyes and looked across at her. "My wife has just been killed, Gina. No offense to you—you seem like a terrific person—but no matter what my daughter says, I'm not in the market. I never said anything remotely indicating that I've got any romantic thoughts about you or anybody else, because I don't. It's just too soon. I don't have any feelings at all, if you want to know the truth, except this . . . fear over how all this is going to turn out. This is so entirely the kind of thing that Kymberly might imagine and make real for herself. Is she taking her pills? Did you ask?"

"I didn't ask. If I had to guess, I'd say no."

He sat with it for another moment. "She never went up to college at all?"

"Unless she was lying to me this morning."

"Which, I hate to say it, we can't rule out. Could you call up there and check? Reed College in Portland."

"Of course. I can do it right now."

It didn't take five minutes. Kymberly had never checked in at the college. They'd already given her dorm room to another student on their waiting list.

Stuart all but talked to himself. "So she might have been here—I mean, in San Francisco—when she talked to Caryn on Saturday and Sunday."

For a long beat, Gina sat frozen to her chair. "What did you just say?"

"When?"

"Just now. That Kym talked to her mother on both Saturday and Sunday?"

"Yeah," he said. "I told you that." He leveled his gaze at her. "Didn't I? I must have told you that."

"I'm sure I would have remembered, Stuart. This is the first I'm hearing about it. What did they talk about?"

"Kym never said. I never asked. We got off the topic."

" 'Kym never said,' " Gina repeated. "You never asked." A long and disappointed sigh.

"I thought she was in Portland," Stuart said.

"Right. That's what you thought. What do you think now?"

"I think I'm a fucking idiot. It never occurred to me she might be down here. Where did she . . . ?" He ran his hand up through his hair. "Oh, never mind. God." With a hangdog look he said, "I'm killing us here today, aren't I? First the cabin pictures, now this."

Gina was frustrated and furious with her client's consistent failure to understand his own plight, but she wasn't about to beat him up again over it. He seemed to be doing a good job of that on himself. She simply shrugged. "You didn't know," she said. "How can you help that?"

"I could have thought about it. About all these things. I don't know what else there might be, but suddenly I'm afraid I haven't given it all to you. Which puts you in an awful place."

She wanted to say that wherever it put her, it was better than where he was. Instead, she forced a nonchalant smile. "I'll live. And tell you what," she said. "If anything new comes to you, don't worry about repeating yourself. I'll deal with the redundancies. How's that?"

Enough with the recriminations and the hand-holding, though, she thought. "Meanwhile," Gina went on, "it would be good to know what Kym talked to Caryn about. If she comes by to see you again maybe you could ask her? Or . . . hey—"

With a little flourish, she handed Stuart her cell phone and after a slight hesitation, he punched in his daughter's number. She wasn't picking up, and he said, "Kym, it's me. Gina tells me you came by to see me this morning and they wouldn't let you in. Maybe you could be in court today—Department 12, nine thirty. And then we could have a visit after that. If you need to get a message to me, it's okay to go through Gina. I just want to know that you're all right." He closed the phone and handed it back. "I didn't want to mention the calls to Caryn until I'm with her."

"Probably a good idea."

For a brief second, there was eye contact between them, but both attorney and client looked away. The unspoken thought that hovered in the air was too dangerous to voice: there was every chance that last Sunday, Kymberly had finally told her controlling mother that she wasn't going to school. Perhaps she'd come to the house and told her in person. It would not have been pleasant. In any event, Kymberly would know considerably more about some of her mother's thoughts and actions on the last day of her life than anyone else.

It was, Gina knew, even possible that Kymberly was in some way involved in Caryn's death. She sensed that her client was wrestling with the same thought, or maybe he'd already decided how he was going to deal with it.

"Stuart," she said, "you remember how you took the heat for Kymberly on those domestic disturbance calls? You said you had done it when you knew it was really her."

He shook his head. "I'm not saying I did it in this case, though."

This was, of course, technically true. But the fact remained that while he was under suspicion, his daughter was not. To what length, she wondered, would Stuart go to protect Kym? Would he even hide something from Gina and sacrifice himself if that were the choice?

But before she could frame the question, the deputy knocked on the door and announced that they were out of time. They were shackling the jailed prisoners together for their short walk over to the Hall of Justice and its courtrooms.

TWENTY-SEVEN

————

PEEKING OUT FROM WHERE SHE AND Stuart were waiting in the cell that served as a holding tank behind Department 12, Gina could see that, as advertised, it was going to be a full house, even by the standards of the busy prelim courts. The courtroom itself was a utilitarian space, completely windowless. With its old blond furnishings and high ceiling, it had the feel of Gina's old high school library. The gallery featured theater-style seating with about eighty chairs. Once the judge had gotten rid of the normal crush of business, fully three fourths of them would be cordoned off for the media. Every seat was already taken, and though there was very little standing room, the back wall accommodated those willing to deal with the discomfort.

Gina recognized several talking-head types from the networks, as well as some local print reporters, including Jeff Elliott in his wheelchair in the center aisle. She might have expected it, but didn't, and was therefore happily surprised to see both Dismas Hardy and Wes Farrell there on the defense side to lend their moral support. Jedd Conley sat a row in front of them, chatting amid the hum to Debra

Dryden, who was there on Stuart's "side" of the gallery. As a witness—albeit a hostile one—for the prosecution, Debra along with all the other witnesses would have to leave the gallery as soon as the first witness was called, but at least Stuart would see her in the courtroom, showing her support, when he came in.

There was no sign of Kymberly.

Gina wondered at the rest of the crowd on "her" side of the gallery—people she'd never seen before. Trial groupies or lookie-loos, she thought, until she noticed that a couple of them in the front row were holding what appeared to be various copies of Stuart's books. Fans, she realized, and the sight of them for some reason cheered her slightly.

The other side was just as crowded, but Gina didn't recognize anyone except the medical examiner, John Strout; Len Faro from the forensics team; Devin Juhle; and Bethany Robley and her mother. Besides Faro, several uniformed policemen filled in the entire third row of spectators. In front of them, inside the bar rail, Gerry Abrams was officiously arranging folders while making easy small talk with one of the bailiffs.

She turned around to face her client, who hadn't much enjoyed being chained to twelve other inmates who had walked in their paper slippers, now wet, into the back door of the Hall and around to their cages behind the respective courtrooms. He sat slightly forward on the concrete bench that afforded the only seating in the cell, looking as though he didn't have a friend in the world. She looked down at him. "I think we've got some fans of yours out there," she said. "They're holding your books."

"My books." Stuart shook his head. "Talk about a different world." Then, suddenly, he seemed to perk up himself. "Did I tell you I got a message from my publisher yesterday? You'll never guess."

"Your sales are going through the roof."

"No fair," he said, "you guessed. Not exactly through the roof, but they're going back to press with all of them. Can you believe that?"

"Sure. From the one I've read, they should. It's a great book."

"Yeah, well, I'm afraid the sales don't have much to do with the literary quality of the books themselves. In fact, Gina, here's a great idea. Maybe we want to string this whole trial thing out even longer. Time we're done, I'll be rich."

"You're already rich, Stuart. And we've got to talk about money, by the way. I'm going to need a check from you soon. My partners are getting a little antsy."

He cracked a small grin. "Maybe we ought to wait and see how things go out there in the courtroom today."

"That," she said, "is a really bad idea."

"Hear ye, hear ye! The Superior Court, State of California, in and for the County of San Francisco, is now in session, Judge Cecil Toynbee presiding. All rise."

Toynbee was relatively new to the Superior Court bench, and completely unknown to Gina. When he came through the door at the back of the courtroom, she thought there must have been a mistake and some law student had run off with the real judge's robes. But no, the fresh-faced, clean-shaven young man ascended to his chair, peered out over the courtroom, and smiled at one and all with an unfeigned enthusiasm. Gina felt as though she could almost hear him thinking, *This is so cool.* He leaned over and greeted his court reporter, a decades-long veteran named Pat Crohn, and then sat down.

And clearly he wanted this prelim.

Instead of doing the expected, sending out this long prelim to another courtroom set aside for the purpose, he did the opposite. He quickly reassigned the other fifteen matters on his calendar, dividing them up among the other half-dozen prelim courtrooms. He was going to keep this one for himself.

And Gina thought she knew why. This wasn't going to be a typical hearsay prelim with police officers reading the statements of witnesses into the record. True to his word, Jackman was giving her a real shot, a real look at the evidence in the case. The prosecution was going to call the actual witnesses to these events, and even more extraordinarily, Abrams had told her that she could call any defense witness that she wanted. This was going to be the real deal, and Toynbee wanted to watch it come down.

Now Gina, sitting down at the judge's cue, put a hand on Stuart's arm and gave it a little squeeze, trying to impart to him a confidence she didn't quite feel.

A preliminary hearing was different from a trial in many ways, not simply because of the standard of proof required. From a strategic standpoint, neither side gave an opening statement. The prosecution would simply begin by calling witnesses, whom the defense could cross-examine. Motions were rarely filed in advance. Judges would rule on the fly. Gina had no fewer than half a dozen objections to what she expected the prosecution to present, and a good ruling on any of them could help out considerably, even if it would not likely affect the outcome.

The judge, comfortably seated now, looked again with satisfaction at the gallery for a moment. Casting his eyes down in front of him, he appeared to be scanning over some pages. The hum in the gallery picked up for a minute and then gradually subsided on its own. When it was perfectly quiet, Toynbee raised his eyes and nodded to Ms. Crohn. "Let's call the case, Pat," he said with great amiability.

Amiable or not, though, Toynbee wasn't proving to be much of a friend to Gina and Stuart. In the next ten minutes, she asked formally to allow her client to dress out, at least from now on. She asked to have him unshackled. If he couldn't be unshackled, she asked at least that he shouldn't be chained to his chair. She asked that photographers, and particularly TV cameras, be barred from the courtroom. Since witnesses were not allowed in court except while testifying, but Juhle, as the investigating officer, would be permitted to remain throughout the prelim, she asked that he be required to testify first.

And so it went: "Denied."

"Denied."

"Denied."

By the fourth or fifth denial, Toynbee actually seemed to be straining to put a more-or-less friendly spin on the things: "I'm afraid that's another denial, Ms. Roake. Sorry."

The gallery behind her tittered with either sympathy or humor, or both. Gina leaned over and whispered to Stuart, "For the record, I didn't think we were going to get many of these, but I had to try." Stuart's response, as he stared straight ahead with his hands folded in front of him on the defense table, was a continual, tiny nod, as though he were humming a tune in his head.

At last that part of it was over. Gina closed her eyes and released a silent sigh of relief, trying to remind herself that she really hadn't expected any different result, although she'd harbored small hopes on a couple of the motions. But she consoled herself with the fact that at least Abrams hadn't simply brought his case before the grand jury, when no defense attorneys, and no judges even, were allowed to be present. It was a truism that by using the grand jury, a district attorney could "indict a ham sandwich."

Nor had Abrams simply called Juhle to recite the statements of the witnesses. At least at this preliminary hearing, Stuart wasn't automatically going to a murder trial. Gina would have a chance to cross-examine the prosecution's witnesses, raise doubt, even call witnesses of her own. Beyond that, she'd get a chance to see the kind of case that Abrams was going to present, as well as a preview of the witnesses and evidence he would use at trial, if it came to that.

Not that she had much doubt of the eventual result—given the probable-cause standard, a trial was virtually inevitable. But that was, as David Freeman used to say, one of the many beautiful things about the law: You just never knew exactly what was going to happen. You kept firing your best guns and—who knew?—you might hit something and do some real damage.

But now Gerry Abrams was on his feet, rearranging yet another folder, calling his first witness, Dr. John Strout. As her partner Dismas Hardy had reminded her just the night before, the prosecution only had to prove two things to succeed at this hearing: that a murder had been committed, and that the probable person who had committed that murder, at least enough to bring a "strong suspicion to a reasonable mind," was the accused. So Abrams' decision to call Strout was both expected and expedient. With one witness, the prosecution would get half of its job done—prove that there had been a murder. Except this case wasn't so cut and dried.

The cause of death had always been drowning, and the DA only could get to murder by comparing the wine bottle they'd taken from the garbage can in Stuart's kitchen to the fracture in Caryn's skull. She thought calling Strout was going to give her an early opening.

She came forward in her seat, her nerves and the failure of her motions forgotten.

Strout had been the medical examiner in San Francisco for so long that his very presence on the witness stand—especially for the professionals in the courtroom, the lawyers and the judge—met the gold standard of instant credibility. Tall, ascetic-looking, his white hair thinning but still slightly longer than conventional, Strout was every inch the picture of the country doctor in whom families would unhesitatingly place their trust. (In reality, of course, he was an urbane forensics wizard whose collection of torture instruments argued for a less benign characterization.) Over the course of his forty-year career he'd probably spent a total of a full year actually testifying while sitting on the hard wooden chair in the witness box.

The inherent drama of the situation—pronouncing upon the exact cause of a violent death—had long since clearly lost its power over him to enthrall. Looking at him now as he took the oath, Gina thought that if he were any more relaxed, they'd have to wake him up.

Gerry Abrams wore a pale green suit, yellow shirt, brown tie, dumb clothes if there'd been a jury, Gina knew—way too flamboyant—but probably not an issue here. He came a few steps out in front of his desk to her left, greeted the good doctor, and started right in.

"Doctor Strout, could you please give your name and occupation for the record?"

They were under way.

"John Strout. Chief Medical Examiner for the City and County of San Francisco."

"And how long have you held that position?"

Normally, without great cause Gina would not intrude early and out of turn in any proceeding; it tended to annoy judges. But this time, she felt she could start making some friends in the courtroom. "Your Honor," she said, "defense will stipulate as to Doctor Strout's qualifications."

"Thank you, Ms. Roake. Mr. Abrams?"

Abrams turned to her and nodded his thanks. "Doctor Strout," he said. "You did the autopsy on Caryn Dryden, the victim in this case, did you not?"

"I did." With his accent, the phrase came out, "Ah dee-id."

"Would you please tell us your findings and the clinical observations that support them?"

Among his other attributes, Strout was thorough. He began with the delivery of the body to the morgue, still in the final stages of rigor, still warm due to its immersion in the hot tub. At Abrams' prompting, he talked about the blood tests he ran that indicated a blood alcohol level of point one one and also the presence of the narcotic pain reliever Vicodin. He described the depressed fracture behind Caryn's ear, to which Abrams said they'd return in a minute. Finally, Strout's unequivocal finding was that the cause of death was drowning.

"Now, Doctor," Abrams said, "could you talk for a minute about the time that death occurred?"

"I could," Strout replied, "but I'm not sure I could get it all done in a minute."

Strout was enjoying himself as best he could. Time on the witness stand could get stultifying if you didn't break it up. The gallery behind Gina showed its appreciation with this tiny joke. Toynbee smiled too, still obviously delighted to be where he found himself. Then, back to business, Strout ran down the various permutations surrounding death in a one-hundred-and-five-degree bath, its effect on both the onset and relaxation of rigor mortis, core body temperature, and how these issues affected the calculation of time elapsed since death.

"But you were, in fact, able to calculate the time of death, were you not?"

"Fairly precisely, I would say."

"More precisely than if she hadn't been immersed in hot water?" Clearly, Abrams and Strout had rehearsed this moment.

"Yes, sir. Slightly more so. She died between about eleven forty-five and twelve forty-five the night before."

"Thank you, Doctor." Abrams then went over to what was usually the evidence table in the center of the courtroom, although today there was very little on it. He picked up the wine bottle that Strout had referred to earlier. It was distinctive enough to be recognizable: The label said it had held Edna Valley Chardonnay. Abrams had it entered as People's One, then handed it to Strout on the stand. "Do you recognize this bottle, People's One, Doctor?"

"I do."

"When did you first see it?"

"Inspector Juhle brought it to the morgue."

"At his request, did you compare it to the injury on the victim to determine if it could have caused that injury?" In this most clinical of settings, Caryn was "the victim," and would be until the prosecutor used her name in front of a jury to humanize her at trial.

"I did."

"What did you find?"

"It was a perfect fit."

"Could you explain that further?"

"Sure. Earlier, I had shaved the hair from the scalp to expose the fracture, which was pronounced and clearly defined. I compared it to the shape of the bottle and concluded that the bottle could definitely have caused the fracture."

"But Doctor, couldn't any bottle of this size and shape have caused an identical injury?"

"Of course. Any object could have caused the injury. But it would have had to have been the size and shape of this bottle."

"Doctor, was the blow to the victim's head enough to render her unconscious?"

"Yes. Certainly enough to stun her for some period of time, perhaps enough to knock her out."

"So the blow itself didn't kill her?"

"No. As I said, the cause of death was drowning. There was water in her lungs. She was definitely breathing when she went underwater."

"Thank you." Abrams turned to Gina. "Your witness," he said.

Twenty-eight

————

Gina took what she hoped was an invisible deep breath, pushed her chair back, and got to her feet. Her legs, much to her relief, felt strong. (Dismas Hardy had cautioned her to watch out about standing up too fast or moving too far away from her table before she felt her sea legs come in under her.) Wasting no time, she walked to the center of the courtroom. "Good morning, Doctor. Did you say that the blow from the bottle to the victim's head rendered her unconscious?"

"No. Not exactly. I said it could have."

"It could have. But not necessarily did?"

"No, not necessarily."

"Was the blow hard enough to fracture the skull, Doctor?"

"Yes."

"Doctor, how long before being submerged in the water did Ms. Dryden sustain this injury?"

"I don't know."

"Well, wasn't that fracture associated with the bloody wound on the scalp?"

"Yes, it was."

"And would that injury have bled after she sustained it?"

"Yes."

"Now, typically, when you have a bloody injury, you can see by the clotting and scabbing how long the victim survived after the injury, isn't that true?"

Strout threw a glance over to Abrams. Neither of them was smiling now. "In some instances."

"Well, what you mean, Doctor, by 'some instances,' is that if there had been significant scabbing, an injury like this could have been sustained hours, or even days, before the drowning, isn't that so?"

"No. I don't think days. If able to do so, the victim would have sought medical attention after receiving this injury."

"But certainly hours? Correct? Because this body was submerged in water, any evidence of clotting or scabbing would have washed away, right?"

"Correct."

"So for all you know, Caryn Dryden could have sustained this injury hours before she was submerged in water. Isn't that the truth?"

"That would be accurate."

"Now also, Doctor, you can't say that she was struck with the bottle, as opposed to striking the bottle with her head. Correct? Let me be clear. You don't know if someone hit her with the bottle or if she stumbled and fell and hit her head on the bottle."

"I'm not sure that's a likely scenario. We're talking about an awful lot of force here."

"Are we, Doctor? This injury was in front of her ear, was it not? Right at one of the thinner parts of the skull?"

"Yes."

"So, Doctor, it is true, is it not, that you cannot rule out the possibility that Ms. Dryden, for example walking on a slippery floor, full of alcohol and Vicodin, stumbled and hit her head on a bottle of wine that she was carrying?"

"Well, no, I can't absolutely rule that out."

"And by the way, Doctor, when you say the blow was enough to render her unconscious, I think you've already said it would not necessarily have done so."

"True."

"So having inflicted this injury on herself, she could have recovered from being stunned and thrown the bottle and the broken glass she was carrying into the trash compactor, true?"

"I can't absolutely rule that out."

"Well, Doctor, when you say you can't absolutely rule it out, what you're saying is that you can't rule it out. Correct?"

"That is correct. I can't rule it out."

"All right. Leaving the fracture and the bottle for the moment, let me ask you what, if anything, you found on the victim's body that indicated someone had pushed her under the water?"

"I'm sorry?"

"Other bruises, finger marks on her shoulders? Tissue under her fingernails? Other signs of a struggle?"

"No. There were none of those."

"So, is it not entirely consistent with the medical evidence that Ms. Dryden could have injured herself and, not realizing the extent of the injury, got into the hot tub, passed out, and drowned?"

"Well, counsel, I think anybody with this kind of an injury would have sought medical attention after a very short period of time if they were able to do so. It would have been a very painful injury."

"Doctor, what is Vicodin?"

"It is a prescription drug."

"And isn't that precisely the sort of prescription drug that a person might take if they'd just suffered a very painful injury?"

"Yes."

"Thank you." Although she knew exactly what her next question would be, Gina paused for the judge's benefit, consciously frowning as though she were confused. Most uncharacteristically, Strout was showing small signs of discomfort. Shifting in the chair, straightening his rimless bifocals, adjusting his collar. He was so nearly always infallible, and considered so, that this type of minute questioning was a rare occurrence. And clearly an unwelcome one.

If she were in front of a jury, Gina would have slowed down even more at this point. She wouldn't have wanted to stack her own credibility against the kindly and obviously very knowledgeable older gentleman. But here she had no such concerns. Even though she believed that Caryn Dryden had been murdered, she needed to nail down the fact that the testimony of San Francisco's medical examiner in no way proved that point. "All right, Doctor," she said, "moving along to the question of the victim's sobriety at the time of her death, you've testified that her blood alcohol level was point one one, is that true?"

"Yes."

"And this level is considered legally drunk in California?"

"Yes."

"In fact, isn't the legally drunk standard actually quite a bit lower, at point zero eight?"

"That's true."

"So Caryn Dryden wasn't just drunk, was she? She was smashed."

"Objection!"

Gina knew this was coming from Gerry Abrams even before she'd finished saying her last words, and was frustrated that she'd allowed herself to get carried away and say them. She didn't want anything to get in the way of her flow, her rhythm.

Judge Toynbee didn't even have to think about it. "Sustained," he said.

Gina came right back at Strout. "Doctor, you've already said the victim also had a narcotic in her blood, did she not? Is the use of alcohol contraindicated with the use of Vicodin?"

"Yes."

"And why is that?"

"Because they're both central nervous system depressants."

"And when someone mixes Vicodin with alcohol, what is the result?"

"It varies depending on the dosage of each, but certainly lethargy, respiratory depression, maybe extreme somnolence, skeletal-muscle flaccidity." He shrugged. "It can bring on a host of problems up to and including cardiac arrest."

"And incidentally, Doctor, certainly the sort of thing that might make someone slip and fall down? Right?"

"That's right."

"Now, in your vast experience, and excluding Ms. Dryden, have you seen deaths that you attribute to excessive alcohol and drug consumption combined with hot tub use?"

"I have."

"Can you explain?"

"I sure can." He sat back in the witness chair, crossed one leg over the other and gave a short course on the dangers of alcohol abuse in conjunction with extended time in water that was above 104 degrees: respiratory failure, collapse of the central nervous system. He ended with, "But that's not what killed the victim in the case. She drowned."

"So you've testified, Doctor. But in this case, is there any way you can state with certainty that the victim, inebriated as she was and with Vicodin in her bloodstream, did not simply pass out and slip under the water, where she drowned?"

"No. I cannot state that unequivocally. I can't state it at all." Strout could barely keep a straight face. He'd just been subjected to as good a cross as any in his career. He had to give the devil her due. This was still probably a murder, though his testimony had done little to prove it.

But as he liked to say, this was his favorite sort of problem: somebody else's.

Abrams' original battle plan had probably been to use Strout to establish the murder and make the connection between the bottle, the skull fracture, and the drowning. Then, never considering the possibility that Gina would do to Strout what she'd just done, he'd call Lennard Faro from the CSI team to establish the provenance of the bottle, the so-called foundation—what it was, where it came from, how it was relevant—and then move on to his heavy-duty motive evidence. Maybe Gina's cross-examination of Strout had left him shell-shocked; in any event, Gina was pleasantly stunned when Abrams gave her the gift of calling Faro to the stand and putting him through his very short paces.

Gina knew exactly how to take advantage of this strategic error. "Sergeant Faro," she began, "you said that you found this wine bottle in the trash compactor in the kitchen, is that right?"

"Yes, ma'am."

"And you took it out and labeled and bagged it and sent it to the police lab for analysis?"

"Well, not exactly like that. As I said earlier, I took the whole garbage bag to the lab and on my instructions, they took out the bottle and any other relevant items."

"And by 'relevant items,' you mean shards of glass in that same trash compactor, do you not?"

"Yes. We compared those pieces with a part of another wineglass we found under the hot tub, and they matched."

"I see. And did you find fingerprints on any of these glass pieces?"

"Yes."

"Did you find Stuart Gorman's fingerprints on any of these glass pieces?"

"No, we didn't."

"Did you identify whose fingerprints they were?"

"No. They didn't appear in our database."

Having gotten all she could from that topic, Gina moved on. "Now. The bottle and the broken glass were in the trash compactor bag together, is that correct?"

"Yes." Faro didn't seem to know where she was going with this line of questioning, and this suited Gina fine.

"Was there anything else in the trash compactor bag, Sergeant?"

"Any more glass, you mean?"

"No. I mean anything at all."

"Well . . . sure. I mean, it was for garbage. There was other garbage in it."

His tone and attitude induced a small buzz of laughter from the gallery. He was trying to play the question as ridiculous.

"And did you ask the lab to analyze this garbage as well?"

The onlookers out in the theater seats, now somewhat primed for drama from Gina's earlier performance with Strout, had been listening quietly, even intently, but at this question, another low hum of laughter rippled through the gallery.

Thinking everyone was laughing at Gina—perhaps they were—Faro couldn't quite hide a quick and confident smirk. "Did I ask the lab to analyze the rest of the garbage?" he repeated.

"Right. That's my question."

"For what?" Still playing it for a laugh.

Gina shrugged. "I don't know. Evidence?"

Realizing that even if Gina's question was ridiculous, she was serious about it, Faro sat up. "I was with the lab techs and watched as they went through the whole bag. We got the bottle and other pieces of glass, but there wasn't anything else to look at."

"Just garbage?"

"Yes. Just garbage."

"Hmm. Were there fingerprints on the bottle?"

"No. It had been wiped."

"Now, by wiped, you mean that someone had taken a cloth or some other material and rubbed along the surface, presumably to remove evidence that was found there, right?"

"Yes, correct."

"Can you distinguish between an object that just doesn't happen to have any usable prints on it, and one that has been deliberately wiped down?"

"Yes, we can. Typically an object such as a bottle will have something on it, unless it's been washed down or wiped. Dust, debris, smudges, partial prints—even if those partials aren't good enough to give us an ID. And that's particularly true on a surface such as glass, which is a good medium to hold fingerprints. We found nothing like that on this bottle. In the absence of evidence that it had just, for example, been washed, it would appear that it had been wiped before it was put in the trash compactor."

"But there was still blood on it, isn't that true? Caryn Dryden's blood."

"Yes."

"So the wiping wasn't completely successful, was it?"

"No. Some microscopic traces had soaked into the label. And whoever wiped the bottle failed to remove them completely. But I have to tell you that otherwise, he did a pretty darn good job."

"Let me ask you this, Sergeant. Was there any indication in the trash bag of what had been used to wipe the fingerprints off the bottle? And presumably some of Caryn's blood, as well?"

"Like what?"

"Like Kleenex, or paper towels. Maybe a dish towel."

Faro looked confused. "Well, there might have been some paper towels, but there wasn't any sign of blood on them."

"But do you remember any such towels specifically?"

From behind her, Abrams objected. "Relevance, Your Honor. Where is this going?"

Toynbee said, "I think I see where this is going. I'll listen to a few more questions. Overruled." Then he pointed a finger at Gina. "I said a few, Ms. Roake."

"Yes, Your Honor." Back to Faro. "Sergeant, were there paper towels in the trash?"

"I don't specifically remember. Probably."

"If so, though, are they still available for analysis?"

"No. As I said, it was just garbage. After we went through it, we tossed it out."

"Of course, Sergeant, you are aware you could get DNA from a paper surface, such as a paper towel?"

Seeing the trap, Faro hesitated.

Gina went right on. "So if someone indeed used that bottle to hit Ms. Dryden, and that same person wiped the bottle, at the same time that they were removing their fingerprints, they could have been leaving their DNA, isn't that right?"

"Yes." Suddenly Faro's jokes about garbage weren't feeling so funny.

"But you didn't either save or analyze any of those materials, did you?"

Faro's eyes darted over to Abrams, out to the gallery. This was the crux of the matter—he hadn't collected the most important evidence.

"Sergeant, your answer."

It took him nearly a full minute, which is a long and eerily silent time in a packed courtroom, until finally he shook his head and said, "Uh, no."

"And if you had retained that 'garbage,' as you called it, and we had the paper towels used to wipe the bottle, we might be able to know whether my client was the person who'd wiped it down, wouldn't we?"

"Objection. Speculation."

It was, but Gina didn't care what the ruling was. She'd made her point.

From the bench, before Gina had even turned around to go back to her table, Toynbee tapped his gavel and called for the lunch recess. Standing at her place in front of the witness box, Gina let Faro walk by her and turned to watch him stop to say a few possibly uncharitable words to Gerry Abrams.

She waited until Faro had let himself out through the bar rail, then on an impulse she walked the few steps to the prosecution table. Abrams was standing, head down, arranging his folders, but after a moment looked up. "Well," he said, "looks like you drew first blood."

"It's a bad case, Gerry."

He shrugged. "It's what it is. And I wouldn't get my hopes up if I were you. It's still going to go to a jury."

"Without a murder? You're kidding yourself."

Another shrug. "We'll see. It's still a murder—you got nothing to rule it out, anyway."

"True, but traditionally, you're supposed to be able to prove it."

"I intend to. And a jury will buy it. Your man's guilty. Get used to it." Dismissing her out of hand, he turned and walked through the gate in the bar rail out to the gallery, where he cracked some joke that got the uniformed policemen chuckling.

Gina stood rooted, paralyzed with a sudden spike of anger. These guys, she thought. What were they basing their prosecution on if it wasn't the facts of the case? Because surely the facts as she'd seen them couldn't support anything approaching the bedrock certainty with which Abrams, Juhle, even Jackman obviously felt that they were right. Could it be that it was just a question of arrogance? She had the feeling that the pursuit of Stuart did not spring from any sense of justice, but from a belief that he was vulnerable, convictable, and that was all that mattered—he'd be another notch in the belt, that was all. A career step for Gerry Abrams, a timely closed case for Devin Juhle, proof that Clarence Jackman's administration was equal-opportunity in prosecuting those who broke the law.

Here they were, in the midst of a well-attended, high-profile hearing. The State's apparatus for punishing the guilty was in full array, the district attorney's position set in stone. And yet she had just shredded their contention that a murder had even been committed at all, and gotten a straightforward admission that they hadn't collected the strongest possible evidence that might have tied Stuart to what had happened, whatever it had been.

And still, obviously, on a fundamental level none of this mattered to the prosecuting team. It wasn't personal, either to them or about Stuart. Nor should it be, she knew. She was fine with that in the normal grinding mill of the legal system, where most of the time there was no real question of the defendant's culpability. But the problem with that was that it seemed to create this mind-set that was literally blind to the concept that someone could get into the system and be innocent.

Perhaps this was really what Wes had been warning her about all along. You don't get involved with people you believe to be innocent, because the fundamental function of the law wasn't to dispense justice. She'd said it herself not long ago: It was about conflict resolution.

You say he's guilty, I say he's not. Let's decide this case and get on to the next one before lunch, because we've got five more of them this afternoon. Justice was nice. Something everyone hoped for and even usually attained. But it was fundamentally a by-product of a system designed effectively to settle disputes short of clan warfare. If a conflict could be resolved by a conviction, and that was apparently the case here, then a warm body who could be convicted was all the system demanded. And once those wheels were set in motion, they inexorably rolled on.

Perhaps Farrell was right after all—it shouldn't matter this much. It was business. The job was to provide the best defense the law allowed, period. But she suddenly saw with great clarity that even the best defense might very well fail, and if that happened, this case might wind up consuming years of Gina's life. To say nothing of Stuart's.

She couldn't let this case be about conflict resolution, a simple verdict. It was going to have to be about the truth.

TWENTY-NINE

THE MEDICAL OFFICES FOR MOST OF the doctors who worked in Parnassus Hospital, and this had included Caryn Dryden, were on the upper three floors of the six-story building. It took Wyatt Hunt the better part of a half hour, starting with the information booth on the first floor, to wade through the bureaucracy, the hospital administration, and then the various nurses' and scheduling stations upstairs before he finally found himself in the staff canteen and lounge on the sixth floor, stirring a paper cup of coffee, pulling a plastic-and-metal chair up to a table across from a young woman named Cindy Delgado.

Cindy was probably in her early thirties. Short and slightly overweight, she wore a neat blue knee-length skirt and starched white blouse. Medium-length curly black hair framed a lovely face made prettier by the easy and bright smile with which she'd greeted Wyatt when he'd introduced himself to her at her station down the hall a few minutes ago.

She wasn't smiling, though, as she stirred her own coffee and said,

"It's such an incredible waste. She really was one of the best doctors, and I'm not just saying that because she's not here anymore. You know, trying to say nice things? With Caryn, everybody acknowledged it right from the beginning. It's so hard to believe that something like this can just happen to somebody like her. Out of nowhere, in the middle of everything, and then boom, your life is over."

"Well, it didn't just happen to Caryn, though. Somebody made it happen."

"I guess that's true." She sipped her coffee. "So. You said you're working for Stuart's lawyer. Does that mean you don't think he's guilty?"

"I don't think much of anything yet, Cindy. We're trying to understand a little more about Caryn's life. Do you think Stuart could have killed her?"

The directness of the question brought her up short. "I don't know. I've just been hearing about it everywhere, you know. From what they're saying, it seems like he might have."

"Do you know him? Stuart?"

She shrugged. "Not really. I've never actually said hello to him or anything that I remember. He didn't come up here too much. If ever, really. So no, I can't say I know him."

"How about when you first heard that Caryn had been killed? Do you remember your thoughts then? Your very first ones?"

She shook her head. "Just that I couldn't believe she was dead, that it had to be some mistake. But of course it wasn't."

"How about when you heard that it was a suspected murder?"

"I don't know. I'm sorry. I guess I didn't really think anything except maybe it was a break-in at her house or something like that. And then they started talking about her husband."

"So you had no reason to doubt it was Stuart?"

"Like what?"

"Like maybe something that was happening here at the hospital. Something you might have heard or seen, or simply known. Were you and Caryn friends?"

"Outside of work? No. I don't think she had too many friends outside of work."

"Okay, then how about here? How long had you worked for her?"

"Four years."

"Exclusively?"

"Well, no, but mostly. I kept her book."

"And you got along well?"

"Really well. We just didn't do things together outside of work."

"So in all that time, didn't you ever share any personal stories?"

"Some, I guess. But really, not too many. Her daughter and my son, once in a while."

"What about them? Were they together? Are they?"

Cindy smiled broadly. "My son is seven. Her daughter is eighteen. No. Just mom stuff. But beyond that, she was a very busy person. One appointment to the next, boom boom boom. Then off to surgery. Time is money, you know."

"She'd say that?"

This brought another smile; it wasn't a bad memory. "Every day, I bet."

Wyatt, half finished with his coffee, had nothing. Cindy Delgado seemed to take the world at face value and was clearly not a gossip. If he was going to get any useful information here, he was going to have to push her. Pushing his cup to the side, he leaned in over the table. "Cindy, let me be honest with you," he said. "Caryn's husband is in trouble. He swears he had nothing to do with her death, and my boss believes him. She thinks Caryn was having an affair."

In a couple of seconds, Cindy's face went through a range of expressions. Initially, immediately after Wyatt's words, the suggestion—the very concept—obviously caught her off guard. Her vivid eyes registered first surprise, then perplexity, and finally some kind of resolution. But, covering well, she only said, "Why does your boss think that?"

Wyatt shrugged. "When they found her, she was naked in her

hot tub. There were two wineglasses. Caryn knew Stuart wasn't going to be home that night. My boss thinks she invited somebody over."

"So you're saying that person came and killed her?"

"That's our working hypothesis, yes." He lowered his voice. "Cindy, when I first mentioned this, you thought of something. I saw it in your face."

"No, I—"

"For what it's worth, some of the other doctors who knew her thought Caryn was seeing someone too. Starting sometime in the past few months. Did you notice any change in the way Caryn was acting, or seemed to feel about herself, back then?"

Cindy's coffee cup was on the table in front of her and now she reached out and started to turn it slowly, staring at it as if it were a crystal ball. Without looking back up at Hunt, she said, "One day I opened the door to her office to deliver some X-rays. I thought she'd gone out to her new clinic, otherwise I wouldn't have just gone in. Anyway, she must not have heard me come in and I heard her say 'I love you too.' And then she hung up and turned around and saw me standing there, and it was like all of a sudden she was scared to death. She actually went white, saying I'd startled her, and then she blurted out, all panicked like, 'That was Stuart.' And I kind of made a joke of it and said, 'I would hope so.'" Now Cindy looked straight at Wyatt. "But maybe, I'm thinking now, it wasn't."

"So who, thinking now, was it?"

She thought another minute, biting her lip. Stopping herself, she went on. "But no, that would mean . . ." The perplexity was back in her eyes as she stared across the table at Wyatt.

"It would mean he killed her."

"No! I didn't say that!"

"No, you didn't. I did. Cindy, this is too important to fool around with. Who are you talking about?"

"I can't imagine that. I mean, Bob's got a family and—"

"Bob McAfee? I thought he was divorced."

"Yes, but the three kids. He's still in their lives. He couldn't have killed anybody."

"Guys with children kill people every day, Cindy. How well do you know him?"

"To talk to, you know. Like all the doctors here, maybe a little better because he was around more, setting up the new clinic with Caryn."

"Would they have had an opportunity to get together here?"

"What do you mean?"

"I mean physically get together. Conduct an affair. Here in the hospital."

Maybe Wyatt was going too fast, but he had Cindy talking about an uncomfortable topic and he didn't want to give her time between his questions to think about whether or not she should answer them. She kept twirling her paper cup in front of her, avoiding Hunt's eyes. "Well . . . I mean, it's a building full of rooms with beds in them. What do you think?"

"So did you notice a change in Caryn's behavior over the summer?"

"A little bit, maybe. But mostly I just thought she was feeling all gung ho about her clinic and her invention—you know about that?"

Hunt nodded.

"Except then both those things got complicated again."

"She talked to you about them?"

"A little bit. The last couple of weeks she was pretty uptight, so I asked her."

"And what did she say?"

"That it was just business stuff. Maybe she'd spread herself too thin."

"Did she say anything specific about McAfee?"

"Not that I remember."

"How about Doctor Pinkert?"

"No," she said.

"No what, Cindy?"

"No, I don't think they were personally involved. Bob, maybe. Doctor Pinkert, I'd have to say no." With that, Cindy broke out of her uneasy trance. She stopped turning her cup, she glanced at the clock on the wall, double-checked it with her watch. "Uh-oh. I really should be getting back to my station." She pushed her chair back and started to get up.

"Could you do one or two more questions?"

With a small sigh, she settled back into her chair. "Just a couple, though. Okay?"

"Okay. Thank you. You kept her book. Was that just for her medical appointments and surgeries?"

"Mostly."

"But you'd have to know about her other activities so you avoid scheduling conflicts, right?"

"Sure. Of course."

"So is there anybody else she saw on a regular basis? That was in her life, if you will."

"Well, you mean all that stuff down the Peninsula? There was Mr. Blair at PII, the president, you know. And Kelley, her lab assistant, and Mr. Furth, who was her broker. She liked him, I know."

"Mr. Furth?"

"Yes. She thought he was really hot. I mean, she joked about it." She brought her hand up to her mouth. "But I probably shouldn't say that, should I? I don't mean she was having an affair with him. She just thought he was cute."

"Cute, maybe, but with a good alibi, so you don't have to worry about getting him in trouble." However, at her mention of Kelley Rusnak, Wyatt felt he owed Cindy some information in return for all of her cooperation. "This is not good news, but I should probably tell you. Maybe you've already heard, but Kelley, Caryn's assistant, apparently killed herself late last week."

The young woman's mouth hung open, her eyes flat. The fact nearly decked her.

"There's no apparent connection to Caryn," Wyatt continued, "at least that we've heard about yet. But it's a pretty big coincidence, if nothing else."

Finally, Cindy found her voice again. "She wasn't murdered too, then?"

"Apparently not," Wyatt said. "Sleeping pills."

"Man!" Cindy was shaking her head in disbelief. "I don't like this. This is too weird."

"Nobody likes it, Cindy. But we don't know what it means, if anything."

"Well, it's got to mean something, don't you think? She didn't just randomly kill herself a couple of days after Caryn for no reason, did she?"

"We don't know, Cindy. We just don't know. You'd think there might be some connection, but we don't know what it is. But while we're still on PII, maybe you can tell me something about Jedd Conley?"

"Who?"

"Jedd Conley. Assemblyman from San Francisco. Evidently he was looking into some of the issues with PII for Caryn. Do you know if they talked a lot? Or met up somewhere?"

Still obviously shaken by the news about Kelley Rusnak, Cindy took a beat before she said, "I don't really even know the name. He's not in my book." She looked into Wyatt's face. "God, I still can't believe about Kelley."

"I know."

Cindy took a deep breath, let out a long sigh. "Wow." After a long moment of reflection on the tragedy, suddenly she remembered to check her watch. "Oh God," she said, "I've really got to get back to work."

While he was at Parnassus, Wyatt took the opportunity to go down one floor and see if he could get a minute with Dr. Michael Pinkert. Even though no one seemed to consider him as a fitting candidate for Caryn's lover, the fact remained that he saw quite a bit of her and that she thought enough of him to invite him to join her and McAfee as a co-equal third partner in their clinic. So it would seem on the face of it that he could have had no motive to kill Caryn, since she was the one fighting McAfee for his inclusion in the clinic and its profits.

In fact, though, Wyatt realized that Pinkert fit as perfectly as any of the other possible suspects into Gina's theory of the case—that she was in the hot tub with her lover and took that moment to tell him of a decision she had come to that would have struck him, at the very least, as an immense personal betrayal. Something that perhaps would have a profound financial impact as well and that might, in fact, ruin his life entirely.

It took no imagination at all for Wyatt to hear Caryn telling Pinkert that she'd decided McAfee was right. They couldn't afford to take him on. So she reluctantly was withdrawing her offer to him as well as her physical favors. If, added to this, Pinkert also suffered from the neurosis of the month—chronically low self-esteem anyway because of a weight problem—and had become infatuated with Caryn, only to be summarily dumped after all the financial and personal promises he'd made to her, the risks he'd taken for her, Hunt had no doubt that there was plenty of motive here for murder.

Wyatt's luck and timing couldn't have been better. Pinkert was between surgeries, in his office. When his scheduling person told him that there was someone who wanted to talk to him about Caryn Dryden, he came right out and brought Wyatt back into his office with him.

"Sorry about the accommodations," Pinkert said. Besides the doctor's own chair by his tiny desk, the only place to sit was on the paper-covered examination table.

"No problem." Wyatt boosted himself up onto it. "I appreciate your seeing me without an appointment."

"If it's about Caryn, I'm going to be available if it's possible," he said. "I'm still in shock, if you want to know the truth. I've already talked with the police, so you must be with Stuart's team."

"That's right. That's not a problem for you?"

"Not at all. Why would it be?"

Wyatt shrugged. "You were close to Caryn. If you thought Stuart killed her, maybe you wouldn't want to help out his defense."

But Pinkert brushed that off. "Not a problem. I find that if you tell the truth, things tend to sort themselves out. Now, how can I help you?"

Physically, Pinkert came as advertised. Probably closer to fifty years old than to forty, he needed to lose some serious weight. And yet he didn't strike Wyatt as obese so much as soft—a man who because he'd always been the class geek and always studied had possibly never done a lick of hard exercise in his life, and whose sedentary nature had gradually caught up with him. The handshake outside had been weak, with the skin of his hand feeling almost bloated, stretched over too much flesh, as were his cheeks and the folds in his face around his protuberant eyes. His lips were outsize too—purplish, wet and swollen, though this didn't appear to be a function of fat but of heredity, which made Hunt wonder, since the trait was singularly unattractive. He would have thought that people with those lips would have had more significant trouble finding a mate than their competitors, and that over time they would have selected themselves out of the gene pool.

But apparently not. Beauty, obviously, continued to be in the eye of the beholder. On Pinkert's desk, Wyatt couldn't miss the large framed wedding photo of the doctor and his wife, even at a glance a really lovely Asian woman. Next to that formal wedding shot was another framed headshot of the wife. She had a particularly beautiful, model-quality face. Above the desk on the wall a more recent professional photo showed him and his wife and the four kids, two boys and two girls. The corkboard on the wall was a collage of maybe fifty snapshots held in place by pushpins—more family life—everyone smiling, healthy, happy.

"You've got a lovely family," Hunt said.

"Thank you. It's my greatest blessing." He followed Wyatt's gaze over to the pictures and let them replenish him for an instant. But then, solemn, he turned with a small sigh and said, "Now. Caryn."

"All right. Let's start with the clinic. I gather you're out of that now."

"It appears so. They needed my capital, and now Bob McAfee doesn't."

"How do you feel about that?"

"Well, disappointed, of course. I think the name-brand recognition Caryn was going to get because of her Dryden Socket was going to be a terrific marketing tool for the clinic. So I thought it was a tremendous opportunity. But there'll be others. All in all, it was a good learning experience. If Doctor McAfee does well with it, I might open a clinic of my own someday and this will have shown me how it could be done."

"So there's no hard feelings?"

"Not really, no. Not on my part anyway. It was just a business decision."

"All right. Do you mind if I ask you about your relationship with Caryn?"

A small, patient smile. "Did I kill her, do you mean?" But he held up a hand, stopping Wyatt's response. "It's all right. Obviously, if Stuart didn't, you're trying to find out who did. So my answer to you is that I liked Caryn very much, and respected her as a doctor. You may not know, but I've already told the police that I was at home on the night she was killed. My wife and I are hooked on *Masterpiece Theatre*. Sunday nights. Nine to eleven. We never miss it. Especially *Jericho*. We love *Jericho*. Of course, that means it'll probably be canceled." He threw a quick glance over to his wife's picture. "And I know, that leaves the time after eleven. I've told the police I'd be happy to take a lie-detector test if they felt they needed one, but I had two surgeries that next day, Monday, and to be fresh and rested for them, I needed to sleep, and that is what I did."

Wyatt didn't feel like he needed a lie-detector test. He believed

Pinkert implicitly. But there were still a few questions. "Doctor, let me ask you this. Did you get any indication that Caryn was involved with anyone else besides her husband?"

"That assumes she was involved with her husband."

"Yes it does. She wasn't?"

"Well, at least not the way I am with my wife."

"How do you know that?"

"You pick these things up. He's a rather well-known authority on fly-fishing, you know, and a couple of years ago, Kiyoko gave me a fly rod for Christmas, so I asked Caryn if I should perhaps talk to him about getting lessons, or how to start, or any of that."

"And what did she say?"

"Well, it was the strangest thing. She just looked at me for a long minute, like she wasn't exactly sure what I was talking about, until she finally just shrugged at me and said she could give me his e-mail. That was her entire response." His torso heaved as he took a breath. "My point is that I was fairly excited about the whole idea, and usually, you know, well, my experience is that if someone shows an interest in your spouse's specialty or expertise, you tend to show a little excitement yourself. I mean, when people come to me about Kiyoko's paintings—she does incredible Japanese block prints—well, you see, I'm doing it there. But with Caryn and Stuart . . . with her, really, there just wasn't anything like that. It was like she didn't want to be reminded that he was in her life. Very odd, I thought."

"All right," he said, "so was she involved with anyone else?"

Pinkert's smile struck Hunt as sad. "I really couldn't say at all. I never saw her outside of a medical environment, and she was always strictly professional in that context. Beyond that, I spend my time either with my patients or with my family. I find that's plenty. So I tend not to notice little personal things that might be going on right under my eyes. Kiyoko makes fun of me about it, that I'm such a nerd, but I can't really help that. It's who I am."

"I wouldn't worry about it," said Hunt. "You seem fine to me."

"Well, I'm happy," Pinkert said, the large, unfortunate, ugly mouth turning up in a cheerful smile. "And happiness, I believe, is the key. Don't you think?"

"Your mouth to God's ear," Hunt said.

An hour later, Wyatt Hunt was in North Beach. Jedd Conley's office was on Powell between Stockton and Grant, around the corner from Moose's, one of everybody's favorite restaurants. So since his next stop was Conley's, he took the opportunity to eat a real lunch at one of the best bars in the city. He ordered a simple Moose Burger, which bore little relation to the fast food item of the same name at your local burger stand, consisting as it did of freshly ground prime beef, grilled over mesquite—blood rare in defiance of the food police and their ubiquitous threats of *E. coli*—on a freshly made sourdough bun, with lettuce and tomato and onion (grilled, if requested) and a pickle made on the premises.

Sated, Wyatt walked back out into the drizzle and turned left. Turning left again, he walked uphill for half a block until he came to the storefront whose etched front window announced that it housed the offices of the Assemblyman for the 13th District of California.

Inside, a counter divided the well-lit space. Two doors in the back indicated the presence of some private suites, or possibly one big one. A large poster of a beaming Jedd Conley commanded one wall. It was surrounded by smaller framed shots of the assemblyman posing with what looked like at least one representative of each and every demographic unit San Francisco had to offer, which made for a crowded wall. The opposite wall featured an enormous map of the city and also the official framed photo of Arnold, which struck Hunt as somewhat incongruous since the Governator was a Republican.

"Can I help you?" A sweet-looking, matronly woman in her mid-fifties had gotten up from one of the two desks behind the counter. The other desk was clean, with only a computer terminal and a telephone. The woman seemed to be the only person here, which Wyatt thought surprising until he realized that Conley's main office was in Sacramento. This was merely a satellite office he used as a local base.

And in turn, this gave him an idea and an opening, since he realized that walking in and announcing that he was looking to establish an alibi for Conley in a murder case probably wouldn't get him a whole lot of cooperation.

"Well, I don't know, really," he began with a self-conscious, tentative handshake. "My name is Wyatt and I'm a graduate student in poly sci out at San Francisco State, and I'm thinking about doing a report kind of like . . . well, do you know William James's book called *The Varieties of Religious Experience?*"

The woman looked at him warily. "I'm sorry, but no, not really. This is Assemblyman Conley's office. Maybe you want to go to the Archdiocese."

"No, I don't think so. I know it's Mr. Conley's office. And it's all right not knowing about William James," Wyatt said. "I only said that because I'm thinking about my report and calling it 'The Varieties of Political Experience.' So you see, it's not entirely stupid."

"No. It doesn't sound stupid. Actually, that sounds very interesting."

"Well, I don't know yet. I hope it will be. But I thought I'd come down and talk to somebody who was in the business, so to speak, and see if I could get a good place to start. You're not too busy, are you? I don't want to bother you."

The woman ostentatiously looked over Wyatt's shoulder, then turned around both ways and came back to him smiling. "I think I'll be able to squeeze you in," she said. "My name's Maggie Even. Long 'e.' And I wish it was Evans too, but it's just not. It's Maggie Even. When I was dating Jack, my husband, I used to tell all my friends, 'What I'm going out with him for—my plan is I'm going to get even.' And I did. Jack, I mean. Now it's my name too. Little did I know." She shook her head. "Anyway"—she put out her hand again—"Maggie."

"Wyatt."

"That's what you said."

"Just to let you know it hasn't changed." He grinned at her. They were now pals. "Anyway, I was hoping to get some record of the kinds of stuff Mr. Conley does in the course of, say, his average month. Like fund-raising, or talking to groups—everything, really."

"Well," Maggie Even said, "we've got a little problem because I'm just a volunteer until they hire another full-time person and I'm pretty new here myself. But if you want to come around"—she indicated the hinged opening in the counter—"I'm pretty sure I could find a record of his appointments somewhere."

THIRTY

———

TODAY'S SPECIAL AT LOU THE GREEK'S was Salt-Baked Merides—
oven-roasted baby smelt over rice, served with a searingly spicy sweet
red sauce on the side. The consensus at Gina's table—herself, Hardy,
Farrell and Jeff Elliott in his wheelchair—was that possibly because
she had done essentially nothing to a fresh and delicious single ingre-
dient, Chui had conceived and executed her best-ever Greek/Chinese
meal. The novelty of the unexpectedly excellent food brought the
table to silence for a moment, and this served to punctuate the end of
the shoptalk that had been going around since they'd come over from
the Hall—mostly about Gina's stellar performance at the morning
session.

Now Jeff Elliott said, "So Gina, after we got off the phone this
morning, I did a little research and Googled the Dryden Socket, then
got Bill Blair on the phone before I came down here. He didn't seem
all that happy to be hearing from me."

Gina put her fork down. Turning to her two partners, she quickly
filled them in on the Kelley Rusnak suicide and where it either

intersected or not with Stuart's case. When she'd finished, she turned back to Jeff. "Talk to me."

"Well, first, I'm sure you're going to like this, but the main thing I had to understand is that no matter what I might have read online or anywhere else, 'There is nothing wrong with the product. It sailed through the clinical trials. It's already been used on hundreds, soon to be thousands, of happy patients. Ninety-nine percent of the alleged problems came in long after the trials were complete and the reports written. And those reports haven't been vetted yet either. So there's no story.' "

"So you thanked him for his time and hung up," Hardy said.

"I really wanted to, but force of habit, danged if just one more question just kind of slipped out before I could stop it."

"What was that?" Gina asked.

"I asked him if it were true that Kelley Rusnak and Caryn Dryden had both been working on the socket. And whether or not their two deaths in the past two weeks might have been in some way connected to their work at PII. Or to each other."

"That would have been the part he didn't like," Farrell said.

Jeff nodded. "Not too much, you're right."

Gina normally would have tolerated if not joined the banter, but today she was all attention. "So what'd he say?"

"That Caryn had been murdered, and Kelley had been depressed and was a suicide. There was no connection between them."

"But Stuart told me she wasn't depressed at all."

"Have they done the autopsy on her yet?" Hardy asked. "If not, I'd call down to San Mateo and see if you can talk somebody into putting a rush on it."

"I've already done that this morning," Gina said with a resigned shake of her head. "I called the homicide DA and asked him to call the coroner. They were either going to get to it right away or else they weren't."

"I know somebody in the coroner's office down there," Farrell said. "No promises, but I could make a call."

"That'd be good," Gina said. "If Kelley's a murder, then she was killed when Stuart was in jail . . ."

"That's a good alibi for him," Jeff said.

"Better than that," Hardy said. "Two murders makes it way harder to pretend they're not related. Even for Abrams, I'd bet."

"That's a beautiful thought," Gina said, "but old Gerry's hung his hat on Stuart, Diz. He's not going to let another murder get in his way."

Jeff wanted to get back to his point. "But here's the thing about Blair, guys. I pushed a little bit about why he didn't see fit to mention anything about Caryn Dryden in his statement to the press about Kelley. He said, and I quote, 'Honestly, it never occurred to me.' "

"Did he say, 'At that particular point in time'?" Farrell asked. "I love it when they add that at the end."

Gina ignored Wes. "But that's got to be a lie," she said to Jeff.

"Obviously. And since I had him lying anyway," Jeff continued, "I thought I'd see if he had anything to say about his relationship with Caryn."

"Did he have one?" Gina asked. "Personal, I mean."

A shrug. "They showed up together a lot on Google. They evidently did a lot of show and tells for investors, and not just in Silicon Valley."

"They traveled together?" Gina asked. "Overnight?"

"At least. I didn't have the time to go looking for hotel reservations and airplane tickets, but there'll be a paper trail and maybe witnesses if you send somebody to look into it."

"So what did this guy Blair say?" Hardy wanted to know. "About their personal relationship?"

"They had none," Jeff said. "Naturally. Everything between them was pure business. She was an immensely talented inventor and scientist, and he was a marketing and sales guy. Although of course he was devastated by her death."

"Maybe we ought to send Wyatt down and see if we can get him to have a talk with this guy," Hardy said. "Find out where he was when both these women were killed, or killed themselves, if only to tell it to the judge in there."

"Not that that's going to matter too much at this stage," Farrell, ever helpful, added.

Struck by the phrase, Gina turned on him. "What do you mean by that, Wes?"

Farrell meant no offense. "I mean you'll have all these answers by the time you go to trial. You don't really need them for this hearing, where they're not going to make any difference anyway."

"Well," Gina said, "what if I'm not willing to concede that just yet? That this hearing is a lost cause, I mean. I killed them in there this morning."

"Yes, you did," Farrell agreed. "I never meant to imply that you didn't."

"But I'm going to lose anyway?"

Farrell held up his hands. "Hey, you might not."

Kymberly Gorman was smoking marijuana with her boyfriend, Trevor Stratton, in the Volkswagen camper van in which they'd lived for most of the past weeks, except for the few days after her mother's death when she'd stayed with her aunt Debra. The two young people were parked at almost the precise spot where Wyatt Hunt and Gina Roake had turned around during their jog that morning, in one of the parking spaces where Beach Street dead-ended beyond the Maritime Museum at Aquatic Park. Although in theory a two-hour parking limit applied, in practice it was a good place to lay low, since very few cops ever ventured down the foreshortened street, and even the meter maids typically avoided the tight turnaround at the end, preferring to shoot up Polk Street for easier pickin's. Kymberly and Trevor's parking place was also less than six blocks from the Gorman/Dryden home, currently unoccupied.

Trevor Stratton was twenty years old. At six feet tall, 175 pounds, he was a well-built, good-looking kid in a slacker kind of way, at least when he got cleaned up. But like Kymberly, mostly he didn't see the need for that. Today, for example, he wore a wispy three-day stubble. His long hair was blonder than it was brown. Sporting tattered jeans and year-old ruined red tennis shoes, he was exactly the kind of guy Kymberly could never bring home to meet her mother, which made him perfect.

Not that it had been that hard, but Trevor had helped talk Kymberly out of actually attending college when she'd been on the verge of going away. He himself had started at university last year at USF, and had completed most of his freshman work. But his parents back in Illinois had never flown out to visit him, or asked to see his grades, and he realized that they never would, so he stayed for the summer, bought the van, and told his parents that he was living in an off-campus flat. So they sent him $1,500 checks for food and rent every month, which he picked up at a friend's apartment. It was a pretty great existence most of the time.

Except for having to deal with Kymberly's moods and stuff. But most of the time she was up for sex, and her whole attitude was radical and kind of cool. Plus she was a lot prettier than she thought she was. Really pretty, in fact. Trevor got a lot of points with most of the guys he knew for just being with her.

Except now, and for a couple of days now, she was in one of those difficult moods. Manic to the max. He didn't think she'd slept more than an hour or two per night since the funeral, when she'd been so depressed. Then this morning, deciding she needed to visit her father in jail. And that hadn't worked out, except to make her cold. Then they'd come out here with the van and had a few hits—trying to slow her down—but instead she got it in her head that they needed to play some music for tips, so they'd broken out his conga drum and guitar and walked down to the cable car turnaround. He'd strummed his acoustic guitar and sang a bunch of his own monotonic songs while she'd slapped the drum tirelessly for a couple of hours.

When Kymberly got going on something, she had tremendous energy. He had to give her that. And they'd made nearly twenty bucks, which was definitely worth it. But all of it had been in the steady drizzle, and while Trevor had worn his rainproof parka, he hadn't been able to talk Kymberly out of her flip-flops and T-shirt with no bra, which probably didn't hurt the tips.

But now, back in the van, she was whining again, still wound up and endlessly needy. He might have to try to talk her into taking some of the lithium, although it brought her down and got her off her high, when she'd get as boring as she was exciting now. She'd probably sleep for a couple of days if he did that, so he thought at least they ought to get it on one more time before she checked out.

"I just want to get some more clothes," she was saying. "I'm cold."

"Just use the blanket there, Kym. Here, let me wrap you up."

But she shrugged that off. "Too hot, too hot, too hot. Aren't you listening to me? Plus it smells bad. What did we do with those clothes I got with Debra? Did I leave them with her?"

"I don't know. I didn't see them."

"You did too!"

He shook his head. "You never brought them back here."

The suspicion was back in her eyes. Lately this seemed to be her fallback position with him. Not trusting him. When in truth he was the one providing for her—this ride, her food, her dope, her drink, her needs. But this was the thing, he knew, that made her so difficult at certain times and so kind of fascinating at others. You just never knew what her reality was going to be. And suddenly, now, she sat up, her stoned eyes flashing in anger at him. "You sold them, didn't you? That's what you did, Trev. You turned them back in at the store for the money."

"No I didn't, Kym. You never brought them back. You left them at your aunt's."

"I wouldn't have done that. I liked those clothes."

"You said you hated them."

"I did not. You're making that up." But something about it

seemed to strike her as possible, if not actually true, and she shifted gears in that infallible way she had. "Let's just go up to the house."

"I don't think that's a good idea."

"Why not? Nobody's there. I've got my old clothes in my room, in my closet. I'm really cold, Trev. I'm not kidding. I don't want to get sick."

"You don't get sick from being cold. That's an old wives' tale."

"I don't care about that. And I don't believe it either." She was patting her pockets, feeling around in the pile of blankets and other stuff on the mattress with her. "Where are my keys? You're not the boss of me. I'm just going."

"Kym." He picked up the blanket from behind her and tried to wrap it around her shoulders. "We can't go up to your house. We just can't do that."

She grabbed at the corner of the blanket and pulled it off her again. "Where are my keys? Did you take my keys, too?"

"I didn't take them. You gave them to me."

"So give them back now. Do you even know where they are?"

"Yes."

"So where are they? You have to tell me. They're mine."

"They're ours, Kym. And they're in a safe place. Can't you leave this blanket over you, please? Just until you warm up. Then we can talk about it."

"But I want to go to my house and get my clothes."

"Kym. Your mother was killed there. Remember that? You said you'd never be able to go in there again."

"But I could now. My mom's not going to . . ." Whatever the evanescent thought was, it had vanished. She sighed and said, "Anyway, you could come with me."

"I can't go in there, Kym. I can never go back in there. Don't you get that? If somebody saw me and knew that you were with me and then they got my fingerprints somehow, they might put me in jail."

"No! You can't go to jail, too!"

"I know. I know. But if anybody saw us there Sunday . . ."

"Nobody saw us, Trev. It was in and out; I know the combination, we hit the safe, take the money . . ."

"We should've taken all of it. And the gun, too."

"No! That would have really been dumb. I know my dad. He wouldn't have known exactly how much he'd put in the safe, but he'd notice if all of it was gone. And we don't need the gun. What do we need a gun for?"

"We could have sold it someplace. And there was just so much more there, Kym, for the taking. Stuff they never even would have missed, I bet. But now that chance is gone forever. We should have got more when we could."

But then she had that faraway look in her eyes again, and she went silent, now reaching for the towel and pulling it tightly around her, smell or not. "I knew you wanted to go back. It's so lucky you didn't go back." She reached out and touched his leg. "You didn't, did you? Go back."

"Of course not, Kym. You know I didn't. I told you that."

She recited the explanation as though she memorized it: " 'I stayed with Jen and you went to Jeremy's and bought this weed instead,' " she said.

"Right. With the money we got from the safe. And luckily I didn't go to your house, 'cause whoever was there might have . . . I mean, I might have got in the way too."

"Like Mom did."

"Right. Just like that. But that's why I can't go back there now. They might think somehow I had something to do with your mother. Which I did not, Kym. I swear to God, I didn't."

Kymberly nodded and nodded, until the movement became so pronounced that it turned into rocking. A tiny, frail humming started deep within her and in a few seconds had turned to a full-throated keening that Trevor had to muffle by pulling her against him and holding her to his chest, rubbing her back, smoothing her hair, whispering soothingly to her. "It's okay, now, it's okay." And then, just as suddenly as the moaning had come on, it broke into a cathartic sobbing that wrenched at her chest and seemed to involve her whole body.

"Don't leave me," she cried. "Please please please don't leave me."

Trevor continued to stroke her back. "I never would," he whispered close to her ear. "Never ever ever."

"Kym, this is Gina Roake again."

"How did you get my number?"

"Your father tried to call you this morning on my cell phone, so the number's on it."

"Okay. What?"

"Are you all right?"

"You always ask that, you know that?"

"I'm sorry. Bad habit. It sounds like you've been crying."

"What if I was? My mother's just been killed. I guess I can cry if I feel like it. Is that okay with you?"

Gina thought that there was no winning with this young woman. Biting her tongue, repressing a sigh that she was certain would be misinterpreted, she summoned her most neutral voice and said, "I'm on my way back to your father's hearing, and I have a question for you."

"I might not know the answer." She said something else that Gina couldn't pick up.

"What was that?"

"Nothing. I was talking to somebody else. What's your question?"

"When you talked to your mother on that last Sunday, did you tell her you weren't going to school?"

"No. Why would I do that?"

"I don't know. I'm just asking. Your father wanted to know too."

"Why do you always say, 'your father,' like it was this big formal thing? Why don't you just call him my dad?"

"Okay, Kymberly, your dad wanted to know what you'd talked to your mother . . . to your mom about. If it wasn't about school."

"Money. To tell her I was going to need money."

"Wasn't she sending you money?"

"Yeah, but that was directly to the dorms. I told her I met some people and we'd decided to rent an apartment instead, so she should just send me the money directly."

"And what did she say to that?"

"What do you think? That she wasn't going to do that."

"Did she say anything else?"

"The usual. Was I taking my pills? I shouldn't leave the dorms. Blah blah blah."

"So that was the whole talk?"

"Pretty much. She had to go out as usual, so she cut it short."

"Did she say where she was going?"

"She said she had an appointment."

"Did she say with who?"

"No. It was just the usual. 'I've got an appointment.' Covers for everything."

"Kymberly," Gina said. "Would you please try to remember if she said anything about who she was meeting. It might have been the last person to see her alive before she was killed. It might even have been her murderer."

Nothing again from the daughter. "She said she had an appointment, that's all. Hey, is my dad there? Can I talk to him?"

"He's in a cell behind the courtroom right now, Kymberly. He left you a message that maybe you can come see him this afternoon during visiting hours. He'd like that."

"Yeah, well," she said. "I don't know. You can tell him I took one of my pills. I'm getting a little tired. I'll see how I feel."

And without another word, Kymberly hung up.

Gina sat at the defense table, waiting for Stuart to be brought in. Judge Toynbee had declared the lunch recess a little early, and now a long afternoon loomed before her. Though it shouldn't have made any difference, she was acutely aware that the rooting section of her lunch mates had all gone back to their regular jobs. The fact that Dismas Hardy was going to try to get in touch with Wyatt Hunt and assign him to get some facts about PII and Bill Blair didn't quite make up for the irrational feeling Gina had that she'd been abandoned. Ridiculous, she knew. She was a big girl. But the show of support in the morning had been unexpected and very nice. She glanced back. Debra Dryden was still waiting in the hallway because Abrams had subpoenaed her and she had to stick around. In spite of Debra's strong and positive feelings for Stuart, to Gina she really didn't feel like much of an ally. And Jedd Conley's appearance this morning had evidently been token as well, since now there was no sign of him.

On the prosecution side, however, the only evacuees were the morning's two witnesses, Strout and Faro. At this very moment, Abrams was talking animatedly with Juhle, Clarence Jackman, and a couple of the uniformed cops who'd been out there all day. Suddenly, a general laugh broke out in the group, no doubt someone with a joke. Guys sure could find a way to laugh just about anytime, she noted. And, in fact, what wasn't for them to laugh at? They sure didn't have to prove much at this hearing; they were a united team; nothing was that serious anyway; it was a man's world.

Gina abruptly turned her back on the gallery, thinking *fuck that noise.* She wasn't going to let herself get sucked into that negative thinking. She might be alone here, all right, but she was a damned competent lawyer who'd beaten many a man before. And, she told herself, this time she had the truth on her side. *Okay, guys,* she thought, *I'm ready. Bring it on.*

THIRTY-ONE

———

BY ITS NATURE, A PRELIMINARY HEARING tends to be short on narrative thread. There is no real opportunity for or tolerance of argument.
In theory, the proceeding marshals and presents the evidence against
a defendant in such a way that it speaks for itself. This structure, cou-
pled with the probable-cause standard of proof, allows both sides to
play a little fast and loose with witnesses and even, sometimes, with
physical evidence, since no formal explanation of the relevance of the
various elements of a case is required in advance.

This would probably be good for Gina when it came time to present her own alternative theories of her case—the connection of Caryn
Dryden to Kelley Rusnak and to PII, the inadequate police interroga-
tions of alternate suspects with strong motives and into Caryn's financial
and personal lives, the rush to judgment on Stuart because he was the
spouse—but it made it difficult to know how to deal with a prosecution
witness such as Officer George Berriman of the Highway Patrol, a well-
groomed, good-looking, friendly man on the sunny side of thirty.

Over Gina's continuing objections on relevance, Berriman's

testimony put into the record that Stuart had been upset when he'd
been pulled over on the Friday night before Caryn's death and that
he'd said he was going up to the mountains for the weekend, because
otherwise he might kill his wife, with whom he just had a bad fight.
There wasn't anything Gina could do. It was what it was. Not devastating, but very far from helpful. But she thought she could make a
small point or at least put in a dig to Abrams.

"Officer Berriman"—she stood again in the center of the courtroom—"in the course of your average working day, do you pull over
many people and give them speeding tickets?"

"Sure. That's a big part of the job."

"And you've testified that Mr. Gorman was very upset when you
pulled him over, is that right?"

"Yes."

"Well, let me ask you this, officer. Do you run into a lot of people
who are ecstatically happy that you've pulled them over to give them
a speeding ticket?"

A ripple of low laughter ran through the gallery behind her as
Berriman told her no.

But she barely waited to hear him say it before she all but waved
him away with a curt, "No further questions." Without moving, she
looked up at the bench.

The judge took the cue. "I think I hear a relevance objection
from Ms. Roake. I'll let it in for whatever it's worth, which I have to
say isn't much."

Buoyed by Toynbee's rebuke to Abrams, Gina went back to her
table fighting to hold back any sign of smugness or confidence, but
when she sat next to Stuart, she leaned over and whispered. "We're
now three for three, which makes them oh for three."

"Okay, at last you've convinced me," Stuart said. "I'll cut you
your check. You're hired."

Before calling his next witness, Abrams introduced as evidence the tape
of the 911 call Stuart had placed after discovering Caryn in the hot tub.

Gina of course had obtained a transcript of this with her discovery documents and was familiar with the actual words, but hearing it played back in the courtroom underscored even more dramatically the absence of any sense of grief. Stuart's voice—calm, rational, detailed, matter-of-fact to a chilling degree—couldn't have sounded less like a panicked husband who'd just come home to discover his wife dead.

Abrams didn't dwell on the tape, but called his next witness, Captain Allen Marsten from the Central Police Station, the first police officer on the scene, who did his own damage dealing as he did with Stuart's attempted CPR on Caryn while she was in a state of full rigor mortis. His testimony was certainly relevant and gruesomely powerful, with him entering through the open door (in other words, Stuart hadn't started trying to resuscitate his wife until after he had called 911 and then opened the front door), easily persuading Stuart to give up on the artificial respiration, describing the contorted position into which Caryn's body had stiffened.

Particularly effective was the wrap-up, which Gina knew was a preemptive assault on what would be her only argument—that Stuart had been so overcome with emotion after he'd discovered his wife in the hot tub that he had tried to breathe life into her even though it might have been apparently hopeless.

"So, Captain Marsten," Abrams said. "After the defendant stopped with his attempt at artificial respiration, what did he do next?"

"Well, he stood up, pulled a towel over the body, and asked us if we'd like some coffee."

"Coffee?"

"Yes. He said there was a fresh pot he'd made before he discovered his wife. Sergeant Jarrett and I both told him no thanks."

"Was the defendant crying or otherwise visibly upset."

"No, sir."

"All right. What did he do then?"

"He told us he could use another cup, and walked into the kitchen."

"Did he look back at his wife's body at all?"

"No, sir. He just went inside and poured himself a cup of joe."

Gina stole a glance up at Toynbee just as he allowed himself a piercing gaze at Stuart. Obviously, Marsten's testimony, unadorned as it was, had made an impression on the judge. He was looking at Stuart as though he'd never seen him before.

After this strangely powerful lead-in, Abrams called Devin Juhle to the witness stand. His testimony, based to a large extent on her client's own conversation with him on that first morning, was relevant and potentially damning.

Over an hour and a half, it all came out. It began with Stuart's direct testimony—captured on tape and transcribed—starting with the divorce ultimatum, Stuart's various admissions about the troubles in the relationship, the financial ramifications of Caryn's death, and the couple's marital history, including his interviews with the neighbors who'd told him about the two domestic disturbance calls to the home. It went on with Stuart's suggestion to Juhle about about the Vicodin upstairs and the 105-degree hot tub. Then Bethany Robley and her unwavering identification of Stuart's car on the night of the event, plus the threats to her delivered on Stuart's behalf by his own daughter.

Gina objected that they couldn't tie the alleged threat to Stuart, but . . .

After that, Abrams backtracked to the warrant Juhle had pulled on the cabin and the havoc wreaked therein, talked about the discrepancies in the timing of the drive from Echo Lake, offered his own scenario of a more plausible late night/early morning drive from San Francisco to Rancho Cordova and back. Then Abrams fast-forwarded Juhle through to some of the details of the arrest, Stuart's apparent armed flight down to a motel in San Mateo, the loaded gun in Stuart's possession when Juhle broke in the door to make the arrest.

In all, it was exactly the kind of narrative, from a highly skilled and experienced witness, that Abrams was prohibited from delivering himself. The prosecutor didn't have to say "consciousness of guilt," a formal legal construct that sometimes could possess the power to convict. His witness's testimony eloquently delivered the message.

This was the way it was supposed to work.

But remembering David's rallying cry that defense work wasn't for wimps, when Abrams turned to her after he'd finished and said, "Your witness," Gina gave Stuart, next to her, a couple of confident pats on his forearm, then briskly rose from her chair and strode to her place in the middle of the courtroom.

After a respectful nod at Toynbee, Gina then directed her attention over to Juhle, who sat relaxed in the witness box. "Inspector Juhle," she began, "your testimony about Stuart's timetable on the morning after the event was based on the discussions you taped that morning with him, isn't that correct?"

In an effort to humanize her client to the court, Gina would always try to refer to Stuart by his name, whereas the prosecution would always call him the defendant, or even simply "defendant," without the "the." These little honorific games might be silly and may or may not have ever made an actual difference in a verdict, but attorneys for both sides tended to feel that they could only ignore them at their own peril.

". . . was based on the discussions you taped that morning with him, isn't that correct?"

"Yes, it is."

"He told you he left his cabin at Echo Lake at around two a.m., isn't that right?"

"He actually said it was a little before two."

"Ah, a little before two, thank you. Now would you please tell the court how you came into possession of the receipt from the gas station in Rancho Cordova indicating that Stuart pumped gas there at four fifteen a.m.?"

"You gave it to me."

"So I did," Gina said. She thought the point would be clear enough to the judge. As Stuart's lawyer, she wasn't about to hand any evidence over to the police if she thought it pointed to his guilt. "And did you have occasion to discuss with Stuart the discrepancy in time that you brought up in your answer to Mr. Abrams?"

"Yes, I did. I asked him if anything had held him up on the drive down from his cabin that could account for the extra time. And he said no."

"Did he elaborate beyond that?"

"Yes. In a later statement, after he was in jail, he said he must have been wrong with his initial guess of when he left."

"In other words, his earlier statement about his timing was an estimate. Not, as you testified earlier, definite?"

"Objection, Your Honor. Calls for conclusion."

It did, and Gina knew it, but she didn't care. Toynbee sustained the objection, but she went right on. She knew that there was precious little she could do about Stuart's admissions that he and Caryn weren't getting along, or about the kind of money he stood to come into upon her death. And she'd deal with the neighbors and Bethany Robley's testimonies when they were on the stand. But she knew that the entire consciousness of guilt edifice that Abrams and Juhle had so carefully constructed, and that had made Juhle's testimony appear so formidable, was largely built on sand. And she intended to kick the foundations out from under it.

"Inspector Juhle, on the morning of Stuart's eventual arrest, did you have occasion to see him at all?"

"I did. At his house."

"Did you go over there to serve your warrant for his arrest?"

"No. We didn't have the warrant yet."

"You didn't have the warrant yet. This was the day the warrant was issued, was it not?"

"Yes."

"But you didn't have it yet. Then why did you go over there?"

Juhle shifted in the chair, his first real sign of nerves. "You called me on your client's behalf, and asked me to come over to look at some e-mails he'd apparently received."

"E-mails? What was the nature of these e-mails?"

"They were apparently threats to your client."

"What kind of threats?"

"Death threats."

"From whom?"

"I don't know. Someone who signed himself 'Thou Shalt Not Kill.' "

"How many of these e-mails were there?"

"Three."

"And when did my client receive the last one?"

"On the Friday before . . . before. The Friday before," he said.

"Before the event, you mean?" Gina wasn't going to refer to Caryn's death as a murder since the prosecution had been unable to prove that it was.

Juhle clearly hated this "event" business. "Yes. Before the killing."

"So two days before the event in question, Stuart had received an e-mail threatening him with death? Is that correct?"

"That's what he said. It's what it looked like."

"And what did you do with this information, Inspector?"

"I didn't do anything. I thought it likely that your client had sent it to himself."

"And the other ones as well?"

"Yes."

"Including the one during the week he was wilderness backpacking with a California assemblyman and another friend in the Bitter-root Mountains?"

Juhle shrugged. "He could have had anyone send it to him."

"True," Gina admitted. "But again, Inspector, this was possibly exonerating evidence in this matter, just like the credit card receipt from Rancho Cordova, that Stuart voluntarily shared with you, isn't that right?"

"For what it was worth," Juhle replied, "which wasn't much."

"Move to strike, Your Honor," Gina said. "Nonresponsive."

"Sustained."

"Just yes or no, please, Inspector," Gina added. "Spare us the editorializing."

Abrams was on his feet. "Your Honor . . . !"

"Now hold on, both of you!" Toynbee said. "We're not doing this. You both know how to ask questions and make objections, and you'll do it from now on. Clear?"

Gina bit back her reply—that nothing Stuart had given to Juhle appeared to have any worth to him because the inspector had already made up his mind ahead of the evidence. But she didn't want to get into a pissing contest, not when she had a better way to bring him down. "Inspector, while you were with Stuart on this same morning, the day of his arrest, did you inform him that he was a suspect?"

Juhle broke a tolerant smile. "He already knew that."

"He did. How? Did you tell him?"

"I assumed he'd read the papers. He'd hired a lawyer."

"All right." Again, Gina wasn't going to argue the merits, though they were on her side. She had Juhle without them. "And so, because Stuart was a suspect, you ordered him not to leave the city, to stay in your jurisdiction, isn't that correct?"

The first signs of anger coming off him like tiny sparks, Juhle flicked a look at Abrams before he came back to Gina. "No, that's not correct. We hadn't decided to arrest him yet."

"So Stuart was an unconstrained citizen, free to go where he liked?"

"Technically."

"Not just technically, Inspector. Absolutely. He could have taken a plane to another country and not been disobeying any order of yours, isn't that true?"

Juhle took a while to answer. Finally, he got it out. "I suppose so."

"You suppose so. And do you also suppose, Inspector, that Stuart was fleeing when he eventually did hear about the arrest warrant?"

"I don't know about that."

"You don't?"

"But I assumed so. I went back to his house to pick him up on the warrant and found open and mostly empty dresser drawers and discovered half a box of ammunition out on his desk. I made the assumption he'd armed himself, which turned out to be true. He also snuck out of his house and didn't respond to calls to turn himself in when we did get the warrant."

"Ah yes, the famous 'armed and dangerous' we've heard so much about. Isn't it true, Inspector, that Stuart legally owned the weapon you recovered from him?"

"Yes. It was his gun."

"And when you broke into his room at the motel in San Mateo, did you see this gun?"

"It was on the end table next to his bed."

"In other words, in plain sight? In other words, it wasn't a concealed weapon, was it?"

"Not at that time, no."

"To your knowledge, did he at any time carry it concealed on his person?"

"No."

"And you've just finished telling us that he had received repeated threats on his life. True?"

"Yes."

"All right. When you broke in, did he reach or lunge for the gun?"

"There were three men pointing guns at him, yelling, 'Don't move!' He didn't move."

"No, he didn't." Gina turned and quickly walked back to her table, ostensibly for a sip of water. In fact, she didn't want her aggressiveness to get the better of her and she needed a little time to frame her last few questions from this key witness. When she was back in her place, the calm tones of her voice came as a bit of a shock even to her. "Inspector Juhle, to recap. Stuart did not know he was a suspect in this event. There was no warrant issued for his arrest when he left the city to interview some people on his own in connection with this event . . ."

Behind her, she heard the scrape of Abrams' chair, and the objection. "Calls for a narrative, Your Honor, and assumes facts not in evidence."

Toynbee sustained the objection, as she knew he would, but at least she'd put the reason for Stuart's trip down the Peninsula into the judge's consciousness, and that had been her intention.

Juhle saw his one shot and took it. "And of course, he stole license plates from another car and put them on the truck he was driving."

This, Gina knew, had been just another flat-out mistake on Stuart's part. Of course, Stuart had correctly suspected that there'd be a warrant out for his arrest shortly, and had developed the strategy to avoid detection and identification. But she wasn't here to argue that point—Toynbee would have to factor it in and draw his own conclusion.

Gina pasted on a tolerant smile, kept any rise out of her voice. "Yes, he did, Inspector. Would it be fair to say that this case has attracted about as much media attention as any case in recent memory?"

"It has had some."

"Well, you know, don't you, Inspector, that the press has been hounding Stuart since the day of his wife's murder?"

"I don't know about 'hounding.' "

"Well, how about following around with cameras and microphones in groups of five and six every time he walked out his front door? You know they've been doing that, Inspector, because you've seen it, and because we've complained about it to the Police Department."

"I'm aware you've made those allegations."

"Could it be, Inspector, that Stuart didn't want to have his truck followed by an aggressive pack of reporters who didn't leave him alone?"

"Objection. Speculative."

"Well, Your Honor," Gina said. "Mr. Abrams wants you to draw one conclusion about this license-plate business, but I'd like to suggest that there is a far more sensible one obvious to anyone who knows the facts."

"What's sauce for the goose, Mr. Abrams. I'll let it in for what it's worth," Toynbee said. "Which once again, Ms. Roake, isn't much. Let's move on."

"Now lastly, Inspector, and still on the subject of Stuart's alleged flight to avoid arrest. Can you please tell the court how you came to learn of Stuart's presence at the Hollywood Motel in San Mateo?"

This was going to be bad, and Juhle knew it. "I traced a call made from a cell phone and made its location."

"And what was the nature of that call, Inspector?"

Juhle, hamstrung, couldn't bring himself to describe it. Behind Gina, she was aware that the entire courtroom was still, hanging on Juhle's response. But it wasn't forthcoming. After a long moment, Gina broke into the silence. "Isn't it true, Inspector," she asked in her gentlest voice, "that that call to you was made by Stuart Gorman's attorney, who had heard about the arrest warrant and wanted to arrange her client's surrender the next morning at ten o'clock? And that you agreed to accept such a surrender?"

Juhle's eyes kept flashing between Abrams and Gina. Finally, Judge Toynbee leaned over from the bench and addressed him directly. "We're going to need a yes or no, out loud, Inspector."

"All right, sorry, Your Honor." Juhle brought himself back to Gina. It still took him another few seconds until he finally mumbled it out, just audibly. "Yes. But you and I both know, Counselor, that a lawyer is supposed to surrender a wanted client immediately. And just because I told you I'd be around if your client decided to come in later didn't for a second mean that I was going to stop looking for him. This was a murder warrant, not an invitation to drop by the Hall of Justice."

Gina felt she could allow him the little rant. She ran through the notes she'd been balancing in her mind. Stuart's alleged consciousness of guilt was based on knowing that he was wanted and acting on that assumption by arming himself, carrying a concealed weapon, and his flight from prosecution. Satisfied that she'd touched all the bases, she now made a small bow to her witness. "Thank you, Inspector. No further questions."

The short recess was over almost before it had begun. Stuart didn't even leave the defense table, but asked Gina if he could borrow a pen and one of her yellow legal pads. When she got back from her bathroom break, he didn't look up immediately, but continued until he got to a good stopping place.

"What are you doing?" she asked.

"Writing a few notes. I got an idea."

"I'll take anything you've got."

"From where I'm sitting, you don't need any help. I'm almost starting to feel like we're going to beat this thing." He saw Gina try to hide the grimace. "You don't think so?"

"I hope so," Gina said. She half-turned to make sure no one was hovering near them, within listening distance behind the bar rail. Coming back to him, she spoke sotto voce. "I think we're all right up to now, but just about everything they've talked about so far, even Juhle, is just interpretation of facts, not the facts themselves."

"No. You beat him on that one."

"Not really, Stuart. Maybe I did get Toynbee to see another alternative and plausible explanation for the timing. And consciousness of guilt isn't flying too high either. That, unfortunately, leaves guilt itself. And that's where Bethany Robley comes in." But Gina didn't want to entirely deflate Stuart's newfound hopes. It was surely true that she'd stymied the prosecution's efforts up to now, and if Bethany Robley was like the other witnesses so far, then Gina might allow herself some hope about the results of this hearing, but not until then. Meanwhile, they had to get through Bethany. Gina put on a false face. "But I've got a plan that might do some good, so we'll see. Meanwhile"—she pointed to the legal pad in front of him—"what's your idea?"

He was covering the page with his hands. Casually, but definitely. "Nothing, really. It's not about this, anyway, I mean us here, what we're doing now. It's just a few random thoughts."

"Well, if you get so you'd let somebody read them, I'd be interested."

"You don't have to say that, you know." He indicated the pages. "This is just for me."

"Not for your readers?"

"Well, them, too." He paused. "I mean, there's the people who read me, but then there's the people who surround me in my life. And traditionally, those people aren't really into what I write. It's just not . . . it just wasn't that important." He broke a tentative grin. "Or relevant, as you lawyers would say. It wasn't that relevant to them."

Gina said, "You mean her. Caryn."

Stuart smiled, looked away, let out a breath. "I got used to it."

She was silent for a beat. "How about if I really would like to read it? If I just like the way you write."

"Well." He drew another breath. "That might be nice."

Bethany Robley, looking terrified and sleep lagged from her days of insomnia, came up to the bar rail down the center aisle on her mother's arm, though her very large mother didn't seem a logical choice to be steadying her daughter, since she herself was walking with the aid of a cane. As she passed into the courtroom proper, Mrs. Robley let go of Bethany's arm, watched her walk on for a couple of steps, then suddenly lurched to her right, just behind Gina's back, and got ahold of Stuart's jumpsuit at the shoulder, pulling him back in his chair toward her. *"How dare you threaten my daughter! How dare you!"* She brought up the cane with her free hand and swung it overhand, Stuart taking the hit mostly on the arm as it glanced off the side of his head.

Immediately Toynbee was gaveling the courtroom to order, yelling for the bailiffs. Some of the media people in the front row were up and clearing out of the area, while Gina turned one way to see what was happening behind her then the other to get out of her chair and somehow try to restrain this crazy woman. Stuart, stunned as the rest of the people in the room, turned in shocked surprise. *"Clair, wait!"*

"Mom!" Bethany yelled. *"Stop!"*

But Clair Robley wasn't waiting or stopping. Swearing violently at Stuart now, in a mad rage, she pulled him off his chair and all the way back to the rail and repeatedly swung at his head with the cane as he tried to cover and defend himself. She was still swinging when the bailiff who'd been guarding the entrance got his arms around her and managed to hold her relatively still, which allowed the other two bailiffs time to get in range to restrain her further.

It was all over within thirty or forty seconds. Mrs. Robley still held by the three big guards, a crying, near-hysterical Bethany now back beyond the bar rail in the first row of the gallery, trying to get to her mother. Gina was helping Stuart get up from the floor. Once to his feet, he righted his chair himself, collapsing down into it. There was a lot of blood coming out of his forehead at the hairline.

The judge kept slamming his gavel. "Order," he kept saying. "Order. Order."

THIRTY-TWO

————

THERE WASN'T MUCH CHOICE. THE BAILIFFS took Clair Robley into custody. Stuart had to get some medical attention for his bleeding head. Poor Bethany, rattled into hysteria, was in no condition to testify. Judge Toynbee recessed the hearing for the day.

With today's plan A, the hearing, suddenly scuttled, Gina's plan B, after only a little thought and all the success she'd had with Abrams' witnesses, was to return to her office to start organizing her notes for the eventual 1118.1 motion for a directed verdict of acquittal that she'd have to file when the prosecution rested after presenting its case in chief at the trial. True, this might still be most of a year away—although she was going to try to shorten that time if she could—but the morning had provided just too many opportunities to take this case apart board by board. And while her arguments were still fresh in her mind, she wanted to commit them to paper.

Of course, if they got to trial, Abrams would be a lot more careful to prepare Officer What's-His-Name from the Highway Patrol again. And Faro wouldn't try to be cute about the garbage.

But Gina wanted to be ready to pounce if any hint of these weaknesses made their way into the trial. As it stood now, the prosecution's case looked like it was all going to come down to Bethany Robley's testimony. In all, Gina was somewhat heartened—Bethany had never seen Stuart that night and, better yet, had never even said she had. So it came down to the car, and from what she'd seen in discovery, she'd never mentioned Stuart's personalized GHOTI license plate.

But as it happened, Wyatt Hunt called Gina's cell phone to report in on his morning interviews soon after she got outside the Hall of Justice and into the continuing drizzle, and it looked as though Gina's immediate implementation of plan B was going to have to wait as well. Here was Gina's chance to go down the Peninsula and personally meet up with William Blair, and she wasn't about to pass it up.

So Hunt picked her up out in front of the Hall in his MINI Cooper at a few minutes after three, and as they swung around the Hall and back onto the freeway going south, he said, "I thought this hearing was going to run all day. What happened?"

"Mayhem." She gave him the short version. "I've never seen anything like it."

Wyatt shifted into the freeway traffic, enjoying the story. Like most other of his fellow professionals in the field of criminal justice, Hunt found that his sympathy over any one person's individual misfortune—Stuart's, Bethany's, Juhle's—usually got subsumed in the pure joy of the absurdist theater of it all. "I wish I'd been there. A cane?"

"Big ol' cane." In retrospect, Gina was beginning to see the humor in it herself. "Pretty soon now they're going to have to rig the Hall with cane detectors."

"I can see it," Hunt agreed. "First no metal, then no cell phones with cameras, now no canes. I bet shoes are next." Wyatt put on his announcer's voice. "Coming soon to a jurisdiction near you, the Naked Courtroom. For security reasons, you must leave all your clothes at the door."

"And people think trials are ugly now."

They drove on in a companionable silence. The windshield wipers slashed back and forth, the drizzle picking up into something approximating real rain. After a minute, Wyatt looked over at her. "So did Devin get to talk before they called it off?"

"He did, but I'm thinking about now he's wishing he didn't. His version of things started out good, but it was all spin."

"I told him that too."

"He should have listened to you."

"Always, though he rarely does. It's tragic, really. I'll have to go over to his place and make fun of him."

But Gina shook her head. "I'd give it a couple of days, Wyatt. Seriously. It wasn't pretty. Not for him, anyway." After a small hesitation, she said, "So how'd your morning go?"

"Good. McAfee's still in play. And even though Mike Pinkert's basically got the same alibi as McAfee—in bed, except he was there with his wife—I believe him. Unless my gut is completely useless, he's just not in it."

"You don't believe McAfee?"

"Not completely. And I still like his motive more than anybody else's. Tonight I'm going to talk to the people in his condo building, see if anybody saw him go out or come in around eleven. Meanwhile, I've got to say that Pinkert's pretty much out of contention. Oh, and while we're on it, so's your Mr. Conley."

"He's not my Mr. Conley, Wyatt. He's everyone's Mr. Conley, maybe soon everybody's Senator Conley. He's alibied up?"

"Greenpeace fund-raiser with like five hundred people at the Marina Yacht Club. Unless he's got a body double. Some politicians do, you know."

Another thought that struck Gina as funny. "Not Jedd, I don't think," she said. "So, do you know where we're going now?"

"PII, right?" He pointed at the terminal screen in his dashboard. "I got it on the navigation system before I picked you up."

"Of course you did," Gina said.

Hunt nodded. "We aim to please."

*   *   *

Bill Blair wasn't in at first, and Gina thought that was instructive in itself.

Then Wyatt said to his secretary: "That's a shame, because Ms. Roake had some questions for Mr. Blair on the Kelley Rusnak matter. Kelley was supposed to be Ms. Roake's witness in the Caryn Dryden murder hearing. Anyway, she'd like to keep this private and hoped to give him a chance to answer a few questions. But if he's not around, she'll have to take her questions to Jeff. That's Jeff Elliott of the *Chronicle*. And see if he can get some answers for her. So if Mr. Blair's not here, I guess he'll just have to read the paper tomorrow and respond to that."

Though she was a woman, the secretary reminded Gina of the William H. Macy character in *Fargo*. Smiling miserably at both of them, she swallowed a couple of times, then said, "Let me just run and check to see if maybe he's gotten back when I wasn't at my desk."

Gina almost said, "Yah, shure," in that great Frances McDormand Norwegian accent, but stopped herself in the nick of time. "That'd be nice," she said. "Thanks."

Less than two minutes later, they were making their introductions to Mr. Blair, a short heavy man of about forty-five, with small eyes and colorless hair combed into a very short pageboy.

His corner office seemed almost to sulk behind its tinted windows on this gray afternoon. Fluorescent lighting overhead gave the room an impersonal feel that wasn't much mitigated by the view of the enormous parking lot outside, the lack of even mass-produced "art" on the two remaining walls. A massive light oak desk was piled high with neat stacks of papers and documents—a small sign of order perhaps hiding a larger chaos? A couple of self-consciously modern chrome-and-leather chairs sat on industrial carpet facing his work space, and Blair indicated that his guests take them, then went to his own chair behind the desk and sat down.

Gina wasted no more time. "Mr. Blair," she began, "thank you for seeing us without an appointment, but time is short. Kelley Rusnak was going to be a witness for me in Stuart Gorman's hearing on the murder of his wife, which is going on in San Francisco this week. Kelley met with Stuart down here about two weeks ago. She told him she might be in some kind of danger because of her involvement with the Dryden Socket."

"Nobody murdered Kelley. Apparently she killed herself."

"Apparently," Gina said. "Did you know Kelley well?"

Her reply, and then the following question, both seemed to surprise him. "We're a small company, but no, not really more than anyone else. Less than some. She wasn't management, after all."

"I noticed, though, that you gave the statement about her death. Is that the company policy?"

"Well, fortunately, until lately we haven't had to have a policy on that. In this case, we needed a statement for the paper, so I ginned one up. I'm afraid I don't really see anything particularly sinister about that." With one hand, he moved one of the piles of paper to a new location about a quarter inch from where it had been. "I told all this to Mr. Elliott this morning. You're trying to muddy the waters surrounding your client. Laudable in an attorney, I suppose, but actually fairly tedious for the rest of us."

So, Gina thought, the gloves were coming off early. She gave him a saccharine smile. "Be that as it may, the reason Mr. Elliott was interested in the story had little or nothing to do with my client, but with the cover-up around the Dryden Socket that both Caryn and Kelley were trying to expose."

He shook his head, his lips tight. "There is no cover-up, Ms. Roake. I don't know how these rumors get started, but there is no problem with the Dryden Socket. It's a remarkable device that marks a major improvement in the technology of hip replacement. The FDA will be issuing its formal approval any day now, and we're gearing up for tremendous worldwide demand. If we thought the product was harmful, do you imagine, one, that the FDA would give its approval and two, that we'd be so foolish as to go ahead with increased production, with all the lawsuits that a faulty product would entail?"

"One," Gina didn't miss a beat, "the FDA would give its approval if they never got wind of problems because they occurred after the formal closure of the clinical trials. And two, you would if you needed immediate cash, had huge overseas orders that you could fill first, and were already working on an improved product that you could have in the pipeline before too much damage was done." She leaned back in her chair, looked over at Wyatt, back at Blair. "This issue isn't going to go away. Some folks have suggested the possibility that Caryn Dryden was killed to shut her up."

"Don't be absurd."

"Do you remember what you might have been doing on the night Caryn was killed?"

"I don't even know what night Caryn was killed."

"It was Sunday," Wyatt Hunt offered helpfully. "Three weeks ago."

Blair scrunched his tiny eyes, the muscles in his cheeks working steadily. "This is beyond the pale," he said. "I have no idea what I was doing three weeks ago on a Sunday night. I'm quite certain, though, that whatever it was, it wasn't drowning one of my longtime stars." Suddenly he pushed back his chair and got himself onto his feet. "I'm afraid this meeting is going to have to come to an end," he said.

"The issue isn't going to go away," Gina said as she stood up.

But Blair didn't move. Safe behind his desk, he stood almost at a military attention. "I have nothing further to say to you," he said. "And you are not to return to these premises, or I'll have you removed. Go be ridiculous in the courtroom where people have to put up with you. And while you're at it, you might brush up on the libel laws before you start spreading any more vicious lies."

THIRTY-THREE

WYATT DROPPED GINA AT HER SUTTER Street office. The now-constant rain hadn't speeded up the commute any, and they didn't get back until about four forty-five. It had already been a long and exhausting day. Was it only this morning that she'd learned of Kelley Rusnak's death? And gone jogging with Hunt? It seemed impossible.

As she was coming up the stairway to the firm's main offices on the second floor (they'd expanded the first-floor offices to accommodate an influx of new associates and a new word processing department), a wave of exhaustion suddenly washed over her. She actually stopped a few steps short of the top and put her briefcase down, wrestling with the idea of simply turning around, catching a cab for home, and maybe even squeezing in a short uninterrupted nap before the inevitable written or dictated recap of her day at the hearing. And then of course she'd also want to go over all of her discovery again to be sure that nothing escaped her in the continuing crush of events.

Plus, she'd be needing to review Bethany Robley's statement so she'd be ready for her cross-examination tomorrow. Or, at least, she hoped it would be tomorrow. Clair Robley's courtroom attack on Stuart today might have repercussions beyond those anyone expected, and she had to be ready for them, too.

And then she needed to check on Stuart, to see how seriously he'd been hurt. And make sure she got Wyatt's latest news after he and his crew interviewed the people about McAfee's alibi. And then she had to remember to call Fred Furth, whom she'd subpoenaed along with Kelley to corroborate Stuart's explanation of why he'd "disappeared" down the Peninsula.

And maybe segue somehow from Furth's testimony into some of the PII issues. And then . . .

Stopping herself, she realized she was already beginning to spin out of control. She had to keep her focus. The minute her mind started to relax—even standing in her stairwell—a half dozen other ideas, chores and responsibilities assaulted her consciousness. Maybe she'd manage a few hours of sleep before dawn, but that was all she could realistically expect, or allow herself.

She picked up her briefcase and finished her climb.

Only to be greeted by Phyllis as soon as the receptionist saw her. "Ah, Ms. Roake." In the rarefied and humorless world of the firm's ancient spinster of a receptionist, attorneys did not possess first names. "Mr. Farrell wanted to see you the minute you got in. On the Gorman matter. Shall I tell him you're on your way up?"

Gina looked across the lobby to the stairs leading up. In her present state of fatigue, the dozen or so steps suddenly seemed as insurmountable as the final ascent to the peak of Whitney, or Shasta, or Kilimanjaro, all of which she'd summited in the past three years. But there was nothing for it—Wes wanted to see her right away about her case. But she still couldn't quite get herself to move, to start the climb. In her short hesitation, staring wearily over at the steps, Phyllis read her mind and, in response, cleared her throat. "If you won't be needing it up there, you could leave your briefcase behind the counter here with me. I'll keep an eye on it."

Gina's briefcase, of a kind specially built for lawyers in trial or other litigation, was more than a foot thick and, loaded as it was with reference materials and other law books, her file folders, copies of all the discovery, Wyatt Hunt's interrogation tapes and other junk he'd collected in his investigations, and so on, it weighed more than twenty-five pounds. If she was going to be forced to make the ascent to Farrell's lair, at least she could do it without carrying the added weight.

Smiling weakly, she put the briefcase down and pushed it behind the counter. "Thank you, Phyllis. That's a good call."

A crisp nod. "I'll tell him you're on your way."

It wasn't, after all, such a long or difficult journey. Ten steps across the lobby, fourteen stairs, another few steps to Farrell's well-decorated door. In keeping with his T-shirt motif, Farrell had much of his office door covered with liberal bumper and otherwise tasteless stickers, sometimes both at once: SOMEBODY GIVE BUSH A BLOW JOB SO WE CAN IMPEACH HIM; LAWYERS, GUNS & MONEY, THE OIL HAS HIT THE FAN; MY LAST GOOD CASE WAS ANCHOR STEAM BEER. But Gina had already read them all and today they didn't even register. She knocked once, cracked the door. "You decent?"

"Probably not. Come on in. Watch out Gert doesn't escape." Wes was over by his refreshment counter, watching espresso drain into a tiny cup, and turned as she entered. His T-shirt today read A FRIEND WILL HELP YOU MOVE. A REALLY GOOD FRIEND WILL HELP YOU MOVE A BODY.

"Phyllis said you looked like you could use some coffee," he said.

"How much you got?" Gina asked. "She's a dear, that woman."

"Actually," Wes replied, "company secret, but she's a robot. And the next generation, supposedly, they're making them with person-alities. I can't wait." He handed her the demitasse. "So guess what? Kelley Rusnak was probably murdered."

The cup stopped halfway to Gina's mouth. That had been her as-sumption all along, but it was nice to get the formal verification, and the vindication.

Farrell leaned back against the counter. "My guy down in Redwood

City called me about an hour ago. Kind of an interesting sequence of events, actually. His theory, anyway. You want to hear it all?"

"As opposed to what? Half of it?"

"Don't get snippy," he said.

"Don't ask dumb questions and I won't. All of it. Yes, please."

"Okay. The first thing a little weird was she had three mostly undissolved pills—Tylenol with codeine—in her mouth."

"Undissolved. How could that happen?"

"Well, one way, somebody could put them in her mouth after she was already dead, or close to it."

"Again, though, why?"

"Maybe because that was the only drug she had on hand with the prescription made out to her. The empty bottle was next to her bed where they found her, which is why they initially thought it was straight OD. But it wasn't. Why? No codeine in her blood."

"None?"

"Zero. She died from an overdose of Elavil, also called amytripti-lene. Which is a prescription antidepressant."

Gina put her untouched coffee down on the table, lowered herself onto the couch, absently stroking the dog who'd come over. "But let me guess. There was no bottle for this stuff in her place, with her name on it?"

"Right. But wait, listen, it gets better. The other thing she had on board was Rohypnol."

Gina knew what that was. "The date-rape drug."

"Exactly. And she could have taken it herself, of course, techni-cally, but the odds are she didn't. My guy thinks somebody was with her and got it into her drink. Then when she was woozy, popped her full of amytriptilene. She would have been feeling funny anyway, dizzy and/or sick. Maybe he told her it was aspirin. They're tiny pills, and it looks like he gave her a lot of them. So the roofie"—the street name for Rohypnol—"kept her from waking up as she went into tachycardia from the amytriptilene. And after she was out, somebody tried to throw off the investigation—at least for a while—by trying to force some codeine down her throat as well."

"That's a bizarre way to kill someone," Gina said.

Wes shrugged. "Maybe sometimes you've just gotta take what's available."

"No," Stuart said. "Kym used to take amytriptilene. It was one of the first things we tried, but her current doc put her on lithium and it seems to work better. At least when she takes it the way she's supposed to."

Gina's fatigue was forgotten. She was still running on the adrenaline rush she'd picked up in Farrell's office. Kelley Rusnak's probable murder eliminated the last shred of doubt. Stuart hadn't killed Caryn. Two women working on the same project for the same company had now been killed within three weeks of each other, and the idea that these murders were unrelated was too much for Gina to swallow.

And not only were they related, in all probability they were committed by the same person. The Dryden Socket had now become the center of Gina's case, and ironically enough, it was still no formal part of it; there was no evidence about it, no testimony related to it. She doubted if Gerry Abrams had ever heard of it.

But what it meant for Stuart, of course, was that he was innocent. Gina thought she might even get Wyatt Hunt to persuade Juhle to give the matter some of his attention. But that would be for later, if at all.

Now it was seven thirty and Gina had still not gone home, but rather had cabbed directly from her office down to the Hall of Justice again. She and Stuart were in the semicircular main Attorney Visiting Room at the jail—the glass block, the long table, the two chairs. Stuart had sustained several bruises on his arms and a couple more on his head, along with the one gash at his hairline that had bled so prolifically, but all he had to show for it was a two-inch-square bandage on his forehead. "So why do you want to know about Kymberly and amytriptilene?" he asked her.

Gina considered her response, then decided she had to give it to him straight. "Because Kelley Rusnak died of an overdose of amytriptilene."

A confused frown passed over Stuart's face. "I don't see the connection. What could Kelley's suicide have to do with Kymberly?"

"I'm getting ahead of myself," Gina said. "As it turns out, Kelley wasn't a suicide after all." Carefully leaving nothing out, she filled him in on Farrell's information. "Anyway," she concluded, "amytriptilene is a link. I wanted to see where it might connect."

"You're not saying you think that Kymberly could have had a part in any of this?"

Gina looked hard at his face, tortured now by this possibility. "I talked to her before the afternoon session today, Stuart," she said gently. "I asked her what she'd been calling Caryn about on that last weekend. She told me she asked her for money, and that Caryn turned her down. You realize that if you're in jail and Caryn's dead, she's going to have nearly unimpeded access to all of your money."

"You can't believe any of this."

"What I'm wondering, Stuart, is why you can't. Once Caryn was out of the way, who was the only person standing in the way of the Dryden Socket coming out on schedule? Kelley Rusnak. When Kymberly visited you here in jail, did you mention your visit down to Kelley? Did you tell her what you'd talked about?"

"I told a lot of people. Everybody who came by. I wanted it clear. Kelley and Furth were proof I wasn't running and hiding from Juhle." He ran a hand down the side of his face. "She could never have killed her mother. And she didn't have any amytriptilene anyway."

Keeping her calm, Gina asked, "Were her expired prescriptions refillable?"

Suddenly slamming his hand flat on the table. *"No! Goddammit! No!"* Out of his chair now, he grabbed the back of it and Gina thought for a moment he was going to throw it in his fury, but he got himself back under control enough to look her in the eye and say, "We're not going there, you hear me. We're not doing this."

Abruptly, he turned from her and walked as far away as he could get. In the far corner, he stood with palms pressed against the glass block, his head down. After a long minute, Gina got up and walked over behind him. She touched his shoulder, her palm flat against his back. She felt his shoulders heave once, then again. Then they gave way altogether in a series of smaller, silent quakes. In the presence of such abject and obvious pain, memories of her own agonies over David Freeman—when her resolve and her spirit just broke—came swelling up over her, making her head swim, tightening her throat.

She didn't trust herself to move. "All right, Stuart," she whispered. "All right."

Since she was never going to get anything like a night's sleep in her life again anyway, when Wyatt called her at home at ten thirty, she told him he could stop by and talk to her in person on his way back to his place. When she opened the door, he grinned wearily and said, "We've got to stop meeting like this."

But that was as light as it got before it got heavy again. Before he'd even gotten a chance to report on Bob McAfee, she told him about Kelley Rusnak and her fears about Kymberly. "At least now we know why she's laying so low. Why she didn't want to come to the courtroom. I need you to find her, Wyatt. I need to find out where she was and what she was doing last Friday. Drop everything else. I've got her cell number. If she picks up even for a few minutes, Juhle can somehow get at least her approximate location."

"Maybe Juhle can, Gina, but I'm not sure I can get him to do that for us."

"Could you call in a favor?"

"From Devin? After what you did to him on the stand today? Probably not."

"Well, I need to find her. Maybe if you tell Devin about Kelley being murdered?"

Hunt shook his head. "Not in his jurisdiction. He's not interested."

"He's got to be. Kelley's got to be part of Caryn. He has to see that. It's still his case. Here's his chance—if he solves the mystery, he can still be a hero. If it turns out it doesn't make any difference, he's still the dedicated cop who spares no effort in the pursuit of the truth."

Clearly, from Hunt's expression, he thought it was an extreme long shot, but he finally shrugged. "What the hell. Can't hurt to ask. You mind if we sit down?"

Gina, who'd been on a tear of intensity for longer than she could remember, felt the tension in her break. "Sure, I'm sorry. I'm a little wound up. You feel like a drink or a beer or something?"

"Why? Do I look like one?" He waved it off. "No, I'm good," he said. "But with all this talk about Kelley and Kymberly and how everything's all got to be related, I hope you haven't given up completely on the good Doctor McAfee."

Gina rolled her eyes. "Don't even tell me. Why?"

"Because it appears that he forgot to mention taking his car out of his garage sometime around ten or so the night Caryn got killed."

"You're kidding me."

Hunt held up three fingers. "Scout's honor."

"Somebody specifically remembered that? Three weeks ago? How'd that happen?"

"Young love to the rescue once again." He had his little pocket notepad out and was flipping the pages. "Here you go," he said. "Lloyd Phipps and Abby Loran, number 17-B, same building as McAfee. In fact, Lloyd knows him enough to borrow stuff. The ID is rock solid."

"Okay, what about them?"

"Abby moved in with Lloyd that night, so they remember the date. They're still doing weekaversaries. It's kind of cute. Anyway, there they are, down in the garage, moving up the last carload of her stuff, and McAfee comes out, says he's having trouble sleeping, he's going down to buy some Ovaltine . . ."

"You're making this up."

"I'm not. It's what happened."

"Did they see him come back?"

"No."

"No, of course not." She closed her eyes and let out a sigh. "So I'm going to have to subpoena them. And McAfee, too."

"Shouldn't be a big problem," Hunt said. "I've got their addresses at work. I told them it might be happening. Didn't bother either of them. Of course, I could have told them I was the grim reaper and it wouldn't have bothered them much either. Long as they could go together."

"Young love," Gina said wistfully.

"You really can't knock it," Hunt replied. "It's a beautiful thing."

THIRTY-FOUR

––––––

GINA WAS IN HER OFFICE BY six o'clock the next morning, and worked straight through until eight thirty, when she took a cab down to the Hall of Justice. She spent the time drawing up subpoenas for her new potential witnesses from Wyatt Hunt's travels last night. Whether or not he succeeded in finding Kymberly today, Gina also wanted to have a subpoena ready for her, not only to see if she could get to the critical amytriptilene and PII issues, but far more prosaically in case she'd need Kymberly to rebut Bethany Robley's version of the threatening conversation. While she was at it, though for different reasons, she also wanted to be able to call Fred Furth and Bob McAfee if the need arose.

Though she fully intended to spend some quality time figuratively holding Stuart's hand in the cell behind the courtroom before what was likely to be a devastating, and in any case upsetting, day of testimony, with all the last-minute preparation, she never got around to it.

* * *

It probably wasn't technically cuttable, but the tension was thick in the courtroom. Predictably, the news outlets—both print and video—had a banner opportunity with Clair Robley's courtroom attack of the defendant who'd threatened her daughter, and they weren't going to let it go by. The *Chronicle*'s lead headline had screamed, "Disorder In The Court," and some sneaky reporter had obviously gotten past the guards with his photo–cell phone intact, and had caught a dramatic, albeit uncredited, photo of the cane coming down on a cowering Stuart Gorman.

Probably in large part because of this, the soon-to-be-seasoned Judge Toynbee had ordered a secondary screening of every person who would be allowed in the courtroom for the morning's session, and the line of reporters and lookie-loos had stretched the length of the second-floor hallway and down the stairs into the Hall's lobby. It would be fair to say that none of the people in this queue seemed patient and tranquil. As a matter of fact, building security had to be called to break up three shoving matches of rivals fighting for their space, and a sketch artist for one of the cable news stations got himself arrested at the door to the courtroom when the errant F-word escaped his lips, directed at the guard right at the courtroom door, leading to denial of the artist's access, which in turn impelled him to throw a right hook at the cop's face.

Backstage, it wasn't much better. As soon as both Abrams and Gina were in their places at their respective tables, Toynbee called them back to his chambers and told them both that until further notice they were under a gag order: Pointedly he ordered Abrams to stop his leaking to whomever it was, and then he stunned Gina by expressly forbidding her to share her opinions of the case with Jeff Elliott. (His "CityTalk" column on elements of the PII story and how they might relate to Stuart Gorman's hearing had appeared in the morning edition.)

Gina, though chastened, nevertheless felt emboldened by her new knowledge about the probable murder of Kelley Rusnak, and tried to open a discussion with the judge concerning the relevance of

PII issues to the matter at hand. Unfortunately for Gina, in his free time yesterday afternoon, Toynbee had reviewed the proposed testimony of Bethany Robley and had found it reasonably compelling. Clearly, in spite of the incredible unlikelihood of Kelley's and Caryn's murders being unrelated, Stuart still seemed very much the main suspect in Caryn Dryden's murder in Toynbee's mind. This was disconcerting, to say the least, and made Gina wonder if the judge was somehow privy to information she'd not been made aware of.

She was about to find out.

When she walked into the courtroom from behind the judge's bench, she was immediately struck by the hostility in the air. It was ugly back there, the gallery packed with many more people than there had been yesterday, when it was merely SRO. Abrams still had most of his usual allies: Jackman for the second day in a row, when his presence in a courtroom was normally a newsworthy event on its own; more uniforms; the neighbors she recognized as witnesses; Bethany Robley today in the front row, next to an obviously angry black man who, Gina thought, must be her father.

She wondered about the psychology of the mob. Stuart, after all, was the one who'd been attacked. And yet, somehow, this crowd seemed, if possible, more weighted against him than the one yesterday. When the bailiff opened the back door and let Stuart into the courtroom—this was before Toynbee had taken the bench—the ominous rumble behind her in the gallery was enough to make the hairs on Gina's neck stand up. What was that about? she wondered.

Her client still sported the bandage from yesterday's attack, and looked positively worn down and exhausted. They should feel sympathy for him, if for anybody. At least, Gina thought that until she realized that most of these people undoubtedly still believed that Stuart had killed his wife—after all, he'd been arrested for it!—and on top of that, that he'd threatened this young, sweet, shy, A-student witness, whom the *Chronicle* had also profiled that morning.

For his part, Stuart got to the table and paid no attention to the gallery, instead leaning over and whispering to Gina, "I'm so sorry about last night. I didn't mean to yell at you. You're the only one holding this together. I'm just not ready to accept Kym as any part of this. Can you understand that?"

Her jaw set, Gina could only nod. Just.

"Miss Robley," Abrams began. "Would it be okay if I called you Bethany?"

She answered in a small voice, her voice shaky, her eyes darting over to Stuart, out to her father, back to Abrams. Terrified. "That would be fine," she said.

"Bethany, would you tell the court what you were doing at around eleven thirty on Sunday night, September eleventh, of this year."

"Sure." But she hesitated before beginning, chancing one more look at all these adults who were either tormenting or supporting her.

In the last couple of weeks, especially since those terrible first days before she had told her mother about the threat to her that Kymberly had delivered, she had come to some fundamental decisions about who was on her side and who wasn't. Before, she had always liked Mr. Gorman—enough to be comfortable calling him Stuart, for example—but she'd always known that when he lost his temper, he could be terrifying.

The time that stuck in her mind the most was once when they all were skiing and this snowboarder came from out of nowhere from behind them and smashed into Kymberly, going pretty much full speed. After Stuart made sure that his daughter wasn't seriously injured, he skied down to where the boarder had fallen, moaning in the snow. Bethany would never forget not only the look in Stuart's eyes, but the true sense she had that he was going to stab the kid with his pole. As it was, he picked him up—an adult-size kid—and yelling and swearing at him the whole time that he ought to watch where the fuck he was going, he slammed him back down onto the hard-packed snow a couple of times before he got himself back under control.

He had talked about it half the way home, too, saying he wished he had hurt the kid more. He'd missed his chance. But at least he'd intimidated the snowboarder enough to get his address and phone number, in case there were complications with Kymberly. He told the girls he was still considering looking the guy up and hunting him down. Bethany thought at the time he was mostly kidding, blowing off steam—but even so, it wasn't funny kidding. She believed he really might do it.

Now she dared a quick glance at this man who, she'd convinced herself, had absolutely clearly told her that if she went ahead and testified against him, something really bad was going to happen to her. That was all the proof she needed that he'd actually killed his wife.

Watching the young woman's hesitation as she assessed the danger Stuart posed to her, as she then turned and waited for the nods of assurance from Gerry Abrams and from her father, Gina suddenly felt a stab of panic. She had studied and well knew the psychology of terror—from the Stockholm syndrome, where hostages came to admire and even love their captors, to a situation such as this one.

Gina's instinct now told her that Bethany had come to the unshakeable conclusion that Stuart was a dangerous man who needed to be put away, and that was all there was to it. In the past ten days, that nascent belief had grown to a dead certainty within her. The stress and responsibility placed on her, her willingness and even need to please her protectors, and the intense coaching she'd received from Gerry Abrams and her parents—there was much literature documenting that factors such as these could actually conspire to change Bethany's wiring, down to the level of her synapses, and this in turn might affect the actual details in her memory. Her certainty about what she *must have seen* in her mind might now be indistinguishable from what she actually *had seen*. And if that were the case, they were in big, big trouble.

Gina leaned over and whispered to Stuart. "Don't look back at her. And no matter what she says, stay cool."

And now, on the stand, Bethany brought her gaze back to the

center of the courtroom. Getting a confident nod from her protector, Gerry Abrams, she began. "Well, I was doing homework in my room, but it was getting to be about eleven thirty, which is my bedtime. I closed my books and was going in to brush my teeth and get ready for bed when I looked out my bedroom window and saw a car pulling up to the house across the street. And then the garage door coming open."

"Did you recognize the car, Bethany?"

"Yes. I'd ridden in it many times. It belonged to my neighbor across the street."

"And do you see that neighbor in the courtroom today?"

Desperate to break up the rhythm of Bethany's testimony, Gina recognized an early opportunity and stood up. "Objection. I'm sorry, Your Honor. Vague. Does counsel mean the neighbor who owns the car? Because there's been no testimony that the witness saw the driver of the car that night."

"Obviously," Abrams responded, "the question calls for an identification of the neighbor who owned the car, and I'd ask that Ms. Roake be admonished not to interrupt the testimony of an already-uncomfortable witness with frivolous objections."

If nothing else, the objection had succeeded in slowing things down.

Toynbee, whose earlier sunnier disposition seemed in the light of his own current intensity as though it must have been an apparition, was not thrilled with the exchange. "All right, both of you," he said. "That's strike two. Ms. Roake, your objection is overruled. The question was obviously proper. Mr. Abrams, when I need your advice on how to run my courtroom, I'll ask for it. I swear to you, if the two of you don't settle down, somebody's going to walk out of here with a lighter pocketbook."

Abrams went apoplectic. "Your Honor, I haven't done—"

The judge glared, grabbed his gavel and slammed it down, shutting him up. "I've ruled on the objection, Counselor," he said in a firm tone. "You may continue questioning your witness."

Gina was going back to her table. Behind her, she heard Abrams ask the judge if the court recorder could read back Bethany's testimony so he could take up where she had left off. As she'd hoped, Gina's objection and the argument around it had made Abrams lose his place. After a minute, the recorder had found the spot. "Mr. Abrams: 'Did you recognize the car, Bethany?' " she intoned. Then, "The witness: 'Yes. I'd ridden in it many times. It belonged to my neighbor across the street.' "

Abrams, back in his place, said, "And do you see that neighbor in court today? The neighbor who owned the car?"

She pointed to Stuart without looking at him. Abrams, back in his place, said, "So you recognized the car, did you not, Bethany?"

"Yes, I did."

"Could you describe it, please?"

"Yes, it's a black Lexus SUV."

"Is there anything else distinguishing about this car?"

"Yes, there is."

"And what's that?"

"The license plate."

Next to her, Stuart shifted in his chair and started to say something. Gina quickly put a hand over his forearm, leaned into him, "Not now," she whispered harshly. But in fact Gina, too, had a very bad feeling. In all the transcripts that Gina had seen of Bethany's testimony in her discovery, she'd never once mentioned the license plate, or the fact that she'd seen it.

Abrams was going on. "What about the license plate, Bethany?"

"It's a personalized plate. It says G-H-O-T-I."

Next to her, Stuart said, "That's bullshit! She couldn't have seen that."

Gina squeezed her fingernails into his forearm. "Shut up. Suck it up."

Toynbee was glaring at the small disturbance they made, his gavel poised to fall. But Stuart managed to calm himself. Gina eased the pressure on his arm. Toynbee lowered the gavel and again turned his attention to Abrams, who smiled at Bethany and said, "Are you absolutely sure, Bethany, that these were the letters you saw on the license plate as it turned into the driveway across the street and into the garage?"

With a last defiant glare at Stuart, Bethany nodded to Abrams and said, "Yes, sir, I am."

In spite of Gina's many objections, some of them merely for the sake of disturbance, Abrams and Bethany went on to establish that the same car had pulled out of Stuart's garage at a quarter to one, but the real damage had already been done. The prosecution had presented firsthand eyewitness testimony from a credible person who was giving false witness although, Gina believed, she might truly believe that she was telling the whole truth and nothing but.

Before Abrams was finished with her, Bethany also delivered an emotional recasting of the so-called threat from Stuart that Kymberly had conveyed. Gina's strenuous objection that there was no evidence tying whatever Kym might or might not have done to Stuart was for naught. At trial, she knew, the prosecution would just drag in Kym and impeach her if she had claimed it was her own idea. But for now, the evidence was coming in even without that necessary foundation, and there didn't seem to be a damn thing she could do about it. In the telling, Bethany came all the way to tears, and Toynbee had to call a short recess to let her regain her composure. After that, she testified that the message from Kymberly contained an explicit warning from Stuart that if Bethany went on the stand to testify against him, something very bad was going to happen to her. She'd had to miss two days of school, pretending to be sick because she was so afraid of going out of her house.

And then, luckily, the police had arrested Stuart.

Gina had her work cut out for her. She came to her position before Bethany in the middle of the courtroom and gave her a warm smile, which the witness did not return. "Bethany," she began, "when did you first give your account of the night of September eleventh to Inspector Juhle?"

Now Gina's mission was precisely the opposite of her strategy during Abrams' direct. This time she wanted to get Bethany talking freely so that something unguarded and unrehearsed might slip out. "I don't know exactly. I think it was the next day. The day after Caryn died."

"And you told the inspector the whole truth, didn't you? You didn't hold anything back?"

"Yes, I told him the whole truth."

"And you knew that Caryn Dryden was dead, and how important this was, so you tried to be as helpful and complete as you could, isn't that right?"

"Yes."

"Now, during that conversation, were you aware that Inspector Juhle had a tape recorder going?"

"Yes. He asked my permission before he began."

"So the entire conversation, as far as you know, is on tape, right?"

"Right."

"Did he ask you any questions before he turned the tape recorder on or after he turned it off?"

"Just whether I agreed to have the tape on, but nothing else."

Gina continued. "Now, that conversation was just a short while after Caryn's death, and a lot has happened since then, hasn't it? Scary things, like your talk with Kym and having to testify here today. Do you think your memory might have been a little better back then than it is today?"

"Well, my memory is pretty good today."

"But if you said something on the tape, and you say something different now, don't you think it would be more likely that what you said on the tape was right, just because of the amount of time that has passed and the things that have happened?"

"Probably so."

"And in that first discussion, did you tell Inspector Juhle that you recognized Mr. Gorman's car?"

"Yes. That's what he was asking about."

"And you identified it as you have today, as a black Lexus SUV. Kind of a smaller sport utility vehicle?"

"Yes."

"Did you tell him what the license plate was during that conversation?"

"Yes."

"Bethany. Has anyone given you a copy of the tape to listen to, to prepare for your testimony?"

"Yes."

Nodding, Gina walked swiftly over to her table and pulled some pages from the open folder she'd left there. "Bethany, I've got here a transcript of that original talk, and I'd like you to take a look at it for a minute—it's not long—and point out for the court where you told Inspector Juhle about the personalized license plate."

"Sure." Happy to cooperate, Bethany took the papers in her hands and began looking through them.

Gina turned and stole a glance at Gerry Abrams, who was busily arranging his own materials and didn't meet her eyes.

For all of her inexperience with murder proceedings, Gina was very familiar with most of the games attendant in criminal proceedings in general. She was certain that she was dealing with one of the most common of these now. Since all transcriptions of testimony had to be included in discovery, which the prosecution then had to give to defense counsel, sometimes discussions with crucial witnesses happened, as though by inadvertence, "off tape." This meant that critical testimony, such as the kind Bethany had presented here, could be shaped and even created out of whole cloth and remain outside of the record until it could be dropped as a surprise to maximum effect at a trial or hearing.

Now Gina turned again to face the witness. Bethany's brow had clouded and she was turning pages, trying to find what wasn't there. Finally, she looked up. "I'm sorry," she said, "I'm afraid I don't see it here."

"That's correct," Gina said encouragingly. "You don't." Gina read from her own copy of the transcript. "And Inspector Juhle asked you specifically how sure you were, didn't he?"

"Yes."

"So, from the transcript now, Inspector Juhle says: 'I guess I'm just asking how sure you are.' Then you say, and here again I'm quoting from the transcript: 'What? That it was Stuart? I don't know. I told you I didn't see him. But if he was driving his car, it was him. Because that was his car.' "

Bethany gave a small nod.

"And Inspector Juhle asks, 'How did you know that?' To which you answered, 'I don't know. I just knew.' " Gina lowered her pages. "Bethany, wouldn't this have been a good time to mention the license plate?"

"Objection, speculation."

"Sustained."

Gina thought she'd try again. "Bethany, when you gave this first interview, did you remember that you'd seen the license plate at that time?"

Now Bethany threw a quick worried glance at Abrams. "Well, yes. Of course. You mean, did I remember at the time Inspector Juhle asked me that first day if I'd recognized the license plate the night before?"

"That's right, Bethany, that's what I'm asking."

"Yes."

"And yet when Inspector Juhle asked how you knew this was Mr. Gorman's car, you answered that you didn't know how, you just knew, is that right?" Bethany's eyes were glued on Abrams behind her and so, without pause, without turning around, Gina looked up at the judge. "Your Honor," she said sharply, "would the court please instruct Mr. Abrams not to give nonverbal cues to the witness during my cross-examination?"

Abrams nearly screamed. "Your Honor, it is unprofessional and highly unethical for Ms. Roake to make an accusation like that when she knows there is no basis for it."

"Your Honor," Gina shot back, "I object to Mr. Abrams telling me what I know or don't know."

Toynbee pointed, his glare now a constant feature. "And I object to the two of you treating my courtroom like a nursery school. That's a hundred bucks each, and it gets much worse very fast."

Gina gladly accepted the fine. It was worth it because it gave her just what she wanted. The acrimony and confusion of these battling adults had dissolved any sense of security that Bethany might have built up over the lunch hour. Now Gina went back to her desk, took a drink of water to calm herself down, then came back at the witness. "You didn't know how you knew about the car, Bethany, you just knew. Wouldn't you have known it was Mr. Gorman's car because you recognized the license plate?"

"I guess so. Yes."

"And yet you didn't mention that to Inspector Juhle?"

"Objection. Asked and answered."

"Sustained."

She pressed on. "Bethany. Do you remember the first time you mentioned the license plate to Inspector Juhle, specifically?"

"Not exactly. I'm not sure."

"Because I've looked through all the transcriptions of your interviews with both him and Mr. Abrams, and you've had five of them. Did you realize that?"

"I didn't know it was that many."

"And I bet you've talked to your mom about this a lot, too, haven't you?"

"Yes."

"And you never mentioned the license plate in any of those conversations, did you?"

Silence.

"When was the first time you mentioned the license plate to anyone, Bethany. Do you remember?"

"I said I didn't exactly."

"Your Honor!" Abrams again. "Counsel is badgering the witness."

"I don't think so," Toynbee said. "Overruled."

"So do you remember, Bethany, the exact time? Was it, for example, after you came to believe that Stuart had threatened you?"

"No! I knew it before then. I knew it right away."

"Then why didn't you say anything about it?"

"I don't know. I guess I didn't know how important it would be."

Gina paused to compose herself. Despite her best efforts, she found herself enraged. "Bethany," she asked, forcing a pleasant expression, "I read in the newspaper this morning that you've got a grade point average of four point two, one of the highest in your class, don't you?"

"Yes." Perking up a bit.

"And Inspector Juhle asked you specifically how you recognized the car, didn't he?"

"Yes."

"And you knew it was an important question, didn't you?"

"Well, not exactly."

"Well, you knew that you recognized the car because of the license plate, right?"

"Yes."

"And you were telling the whole truth, right? Not holding anything back?"

"Yes." Her voice smaller.

"But Bethany, isn't it true that right up until today in court, you never said during any of your other taped interviews that you remembered the license plate? Isn't that true? How could a smart girl like you not recognize the importance of that information?"

"Your Honor!" Abrams called out in outrage. "This is badgering heaped upon insult!"

Damn right it is, she thought. And every word on purpose.

But as Toynbee sustained the objection, Gina nodded meekly. "I'll withdraw the question, Your Honor."

*   *   *

Without Kymberly Gorman available as a witness to refute Bethany's testimony on the alleged threat, Gina didn't think she could make any points revisiting the subject. Clearly, whatever words Bethany had heard, she'd interpreted as threatening. That was her reality, reinforced by her mother's acceptance of it, steeled in the forge of yesterday's attack on Stuart, and Gina couldn't really see any point in trying to change it. Without having accomplished much with Bethany, Gina reluctantly dismissed the witness.

She very much expected Abrams to call as witnesses the two neighbors who'd testified about the fights at Stuart's house, as well as some or all four of the officers who'd responded to the domestic disturbance calls. All of these people were already waiting outside the courtroom. As was Debra Dryden, whom Abrams presumably was going to question regarding her five-day idyll with Stuart up in the mountains.

But evidently Bethany's unambiguous testimony that it was Stuart's car at the murder scene, and Gina's inability to shake that, had convinced Abrams to quit while he was ahead. Certainly, Bethany's eyewitness identification of Stuart's car seemed to put him at the house at the time of death. Since he denied being there, the only reasonable explanation was that he had killed his wife. That having been established, Abrams clearly decided that he wanted to save the remaining witnesses for trial, so he'd have something to show Stuart's defense team next time around that it hadn't already seen and analyzed.

So, much to Gina's surprise, when Bethany had left the courtroom, Abrams rested the People's case. Judge Toynbee asked Gina if she would be ready to begin calling her witnesses after lunch. She told him she would, and he brought down his gavel and called the recess.

THIRTY-FIVE

WHEN GINA FINALLY GOT HOME THAT evening, it was at a little after seven o'clock. She walked into her bedroom and changed out of her court clothes. Normally, she coped with enervation and mental fatigue by putting some miles on her running shoes, and she reached almost automatically for her sweats, but then stopped herself. There was very little that was normal about the bone-weariness she was experiencing now.

At last, feeling guilty about the lazy slug she had become, nevertheless she changed instead into some baggy chinos and a black tank top.

Catching sight of herself in the mirror on the closet door, she brushed a wisp of hair off her forehead and tried to smooth away the darkness under her eyes. Sighing, she went barefoot out to the kitchen and ran hot water over a washcloth, which she applied to her face, then made it a few more steps onto the living room rug before she all but collapsed, folding upon herself down to the floor.

Now, pole-axed from the rigors of the day, she lay flat on her back, awake but nearly unconscious, her chest slowly rising and falling, the tepid washcloth folded over her eyes.

The afternoon session had been grueling and frustrating, which she would have gladly endured had it been effective as well. But it had not been; it had been a disaster.

She'd known that she had to try to get PII somehow into the record, and she'd called Fred Furth, thinking to have him elucidate Caryn's connection with the company, her concerns over the clinical trials data, her professional relationship not only with Furth himself, but with Bill Blair and Kelley Rusnak. Abrams, his objections perhaps numbering close to fifty, had been a bulldog. In the end, having never established a rhythm or even the tiniest objective relevancy to whatever had happened to Caryn, she'd had to excuse Furth without her theory gaining much traction.

So her assault on Robert McAfee, trying to establish him as another legitimate suspect, had begun with her on the defensive. The court had just formally warned her not to waste its time. And as she began her direct, she couldn't completely escape the conclusion that this was exactly what she was doing. True, McAfee appeared to have had a strong motive to have killed Caryn. True, they'd been lovers once and might have been again. Yes, he stood to gain financially and professionally from her death. Finally, his alibi for the night of the event had just gone south.

But the plain fact remained that there was no hint of McAfee's involvement on any level with PII, or with Kelley Rusnak. And without that, Gina knew in her heart that in her exhaustive attempt to implicate the doctor, she was really just whistling Dixie. The theory was probably arguable, but at best it was no less a sham than Abrams' attempt to portray Stuart's drive down the Peninsula as a flight from justice that screamed consciousness of guilt. The underlying cynicism of it had worn her down as she went on, until at last she couldn't even take pleasure in shattering McAfee's alibi, which didn't stop her from doing it.

So she'd spent almost the entire afternoon smearing the name and reputation of a probably pretty decent guy, whose only mistake had been forgetting that he'd gone out one night after a day with his kids to buy some Ovaltine so he could get some sleep. Gina no longer thought it was reasonable that Bob McAfee had killed Caryn. She didn't even believe that implicating him would do any good for her client. Not as far as Toynbee was concerned. The fact that there might be another plausible suspect in no way removed Stuart from suspicion; Gina wasn't proposing that McAfee had been driving Stuart's car, was she? But she'd gone ahead anyway. Building nothing, but hammering nails all day just the same.

The thought of it, of the damage she'd done to the doctor's good name, made her sick.

She put her hands up to the washcloth and pressed the now-cool cloth down on her eyes.

"I thought we were going to stop meeting like this," Gina said.

Wyatt Hunt stood in her doorway. "I know," he said. "We were. It just got too hard." The rain had stopped. He stepped out of the wet cloud that hovered at street level into Gina's apartment again. "Miracles do happen," he said, "I don't care what they say."

"What's the miracle?"

"I figured I'd get it over with, so I called Devin after work and mentioned your idea that he could still do some good around this case. He wasn't exactly enthusiastic, but luckily I happened to mention that he could even become an actual hero if he wasn't careful. I happen to know," Hunt said modestly with a self-deprecating smile, "that the guy's got a bit of a hero complex and that this was the magic word. Anyway, he had me make a call to Kymberly's number and since there was a subpoena out on her anyway, there wasn't even a conflict with him using his magic GPS positioning and calling out some troops to run her down."

"Where was she?"

"Down by the Maritime Museum, living out of some van with her boyfriend."

"You talked to her." Not a question.

He nodded. "Just came from there. Although, again, I know this is starting to sound familiar and I apologize in advance, but you might not be happy with what I found out."

"Tell me."

"Yosemite."

"What about it?"

"That's where they went when the weather turned last week. Last Thursday. They stayed through Sunday." He spread his hands, empty. "Which means she didn't give any pills to Kelley Rusnak on Friday night. And, if you need more . . ."

"Sure, kick a girl when she's down."

"Her dad might have mentioned Kelley's name to her, but I don't think it stuck. When I mentioned her as her mom's lab partner, she was all like, 'Who?' She could have been faking it, I suppose, but if she was, she's way, way better than I'd give her credit for."

Gina found herself sagging against the wall.

"Hey, are you okay?"

She tried a brave smile. "Just tired." She looked up at him. "I can't believe my man is going down around this. It's just so wrong."

"You'll get another chance."

Her eyes found a faint flash. "I don't want another chance. I want to get him off this time around while I still can. There's something we're missing. I know there is. It's right here and I can't put my damn finger on it."

"Well, I hope it goes without saying, but if whatever it is comes to you, I'm here twenty-four seven."

A genuine smile now. "You're a good guy, Wyatt. And you do good work. I'll keep you in mind."

"Anytime," he said. "And Gina?"

"Yeah."

"Don't kill yourself over this. He's going to need you for the trial."

"You're right," she said. "You're right." She straightened up. "You have a good night, Wyatt."

"You too."

But she wasn't having a good night.

Now it was 8:43. Someone had twisted a heavy wire braid around her head and tightened it down as though it were a tourniquet. That same someone had thrown fine-grained sand into her eyes. She'd long ago emptied and spread out on the coffee table the entire contents of her litigator's briefcase. She'd already gone through almost every page of it—certainly anything that had meaning—at least twice.

Now she decided that even the marginally related stuff rated intense perusal, and she was going through it all yet again. In her desperation, she studied the ARCO receipt for what seemed an eternity, hoping to find something in it that could help her case. Maybe she should call the station and ask the clerk to check and see if perhaps the clock in their printer was off by an hour or so. She hadn't ever gone out and personally verified the timing—that could have been the detail she'd missed.

But even as she made a note to have Wyatt Hunt check this out, she knew it wasn't.

Here again was the transcription of Stuart's first interview with Juhle. All the foolish admissions that delineated his motives, the evident lack of grief, the objection to the autopsy, his suggestion about the Vicodin and the alcohol and the hot tub temperature. All of it understandable, all of it ill-advised. She finished those pages and randomly picked up the next item in the pile, the picture of Stuart and Jedd Conley and their other buddy on their fishing trip to the Bitterroots. Turned it over, studied the writing on the back, the date.

Nothing.

Who was that third guy anyway? Another detail she didn't know. Another fact she'd neglected, another note for Hunt. And what had happened to Thou Shalt Not Kill in the time Stuart had been in jail?

He might have tried to contact Stuart again on his computer back at his home. He might even have confessed to killing Caryn, and no one would know. Certainly she didn't know, because she hadn't thought to look.

Sick with herself and her incompetence, she sat back on her couch and looked first to her bar—an Oban or four would be nice right now—then to her telephone. She felt she desperately needed to talk to somebody. She checked the time. It wasn't too late. She could perhaps call Hardy or Farrell and just vent, or talk strategy. They were both guys who had been in similar situations to hers before. One of them could help talk her through the despair.

Or maybe—the rogue thought sprung upon her full-blown— maybe she could call Jedd, for a different kind of release. She had his business card from the day she'd met Stuart. His private number. And they'd both be discreet. No one would ever have to know.

God, what was she thinking? She wasn't that weak, that needy. She was not going to go to bed with a married man, and that was the end of that subject.

Shaking herself from the temptation, she came forward again, al- most angrily grabbed the next sheaf of papers, and forced herself to start again on Wyatt's reports and transcripts on the Parnassus staff from the other day. Delgado, Pinkert. Thirty pages of overkill about the schedule and speech topics of a state assemblyman.

Exciting stuff. Not.

She'd never even glanced at these pages before—and why should she have? Now, mindlessly, automatically, she turned the pages one by one, barely noting the individual names and places except for the immense variety of them on every page. Jedd's life was evidently a never-ending circus of appearances and events: the Bayshore Rotary Club, Girl Scout Troop 17, the Young Presidents Association, the Restaurant Workers Union, the Haight Street Rape Crisis Center (whose executive director, Gina knew, in the small-world depart- ment, was Wes Farrell's live-in girlfriend, Sam Duncan), La Raza, the

Old Wops, AYSO San Francisco . . . the list went on and on, none of it with any possible bearing on her case—until finally Gina simply had to stop, the pages in her hand dropping back onto the table.

She looked at the time again. Barely 9:00. She should go to bed. Tomorrow would be another day, and it might turn out to be worse than this one.

Out of the corner of her eye, she noticed the camping picture again, and her hand reached for it as though of its own accord. There was Jedd, still and again. Smiling out at the camera. Rugged and handsome. In his element, really. A very attractive guy who'd known what he was doing around the bedroom twenty-some years ago and probably had learned a few tricks since.

Stop it!

But she couldn't take her eyes off the picture.

The picture.

The picture.

"Jedd," she said into the telephone, "it's Gina. I've been thinking about when you were here the other night, and how maybe I shouldn't have been so . . . difficult. And cold. I know it's a little late, but I thought if you were on your way home from somewhere, if you were in the mood, you might want to stop by."

Thirty-six

———

Gina's hands were shaking slightly as she applied a light touch of coral-shaded lipstick with greater than average care. She wanted to look not just good, but terrific. The rope-belted chinos and tank top she already had on, she knew, would be good for seduction—almost pajamalike, revealing her curves, accentuating the muscle tone, her flat abs. Not that Jedd was likely to get all the way over here and change his mind because of how she looked, but she wanted to make herself irresistible. Hence the subtle eye shadow to camouflage the more obvious signs of fatigue, the blush to highlight her cheekbones, the glossy lipstick she hadn't used since her time with David.

She wasn't going to think about David. Not now.

Checking herself one final time in the mirror, satisfied, she said, "Not bad for an old broad," and left the bathroom, turning out the lights behind her. In the living room, she put on the old classic Tony Bennett/Bill Evans album, the volume so low as to be nearly inaudible. She'd already long since packed away her case materials and her briefcase, and now she crossed over to her bar area and poured two solid Obans into her good crystal glasses.

Dimming the lights to an intimate level, she took a last look around. Everything was perfect; she was ready. And still the soft knock on her door nearly made her jump. Crossing over to the window, she looked out and recognized Jedd's car again parked on the sidewalk across the street. She let out a long breath of relief.

Okay, he was here. She could stop thinking about what could go wrong and just be in the moment now. It would be all right.

She went to open the door.

"Why, Gina Roake, the scotch in your glass is shaking. I do believe you're nervous."

"Why would I be nervous?"

"I don't know why. You really shouldn't be." Conley was sitting back, smiling, his hand with the drink in it resting on the couch's arm, one ankle crossed onto the opposite knee. "We're pretty much the way we were, a couple of old friends, just doing what comes naturally . . ."

"After a gap of over twenty years, Jedd. I'm not exactly the same as I was back then. In fact, I'm not even close."

"Well," he said, "anybody tells you that you're still not beautiful, they need their eyes examined. I hope you're not telling me that you've spent any time alone that you didn't want to be. That would be criminal."

Gina sighed with a bit of theater. "It may be a little harder than you think it is out there. Of course, you, with all your power and charisma . . ."

"And a wife whose daddy controls the purse strings, and I mean all of them. My darling Lexi gets any idea that this kind of harmless fun is any part of my life, I can kiss the so-called power and my promising career good-bye. And I'm not kidding." He took a good pull at his drink. "By the way, the other night when I told you I'd be discreet? I know you already realize it, but just to be upfront about things, that's got to be part of the rules."

Gina put on a little artificial pout, a twinkle of humor in her eye. "Rules already? And here I thought we were wild spirits, running free."

"That too. But I find it's better to get the ground rules settled up front. It avoids a whole lot of unpleasantness down the line."

"Actually," Gina said, "I'm with you on that." At the other end of the couch from him, she lifted her glass. "Here's to that dying breed, the consenting adult."

"Hear, hear." Conley clinked his glass against hers, had another sip.

Gina did likewise, then said, "Okay, I'm officially not nervous anymore."

"Good. Me, neither."

"But you weren't to begin with."

"I was, a little. After the last time, I thought I'd get here and you might change your mind."

"Well, Jedd, I don't think that's happening, not tonight." She hesitated for a calculated time. "But I do have kind of an idea, if you don't mind. Though it may be a little kinky."

"Kinky's not the worst thing in the world." He flashed a look across at her. "What is it?"

"No, never mind."

"Gina. Come on. What?"

She sighed dramatically. "The main thing is I don't want to scare you off. I mean, what I said earlier is true. I've grown up a little bit since . . . since we were together. I'm not exactly the same in what . . . what works, I guess is the best way to say it."

"Well, we want things to work."

"Yes, we do."

Jedd nodded and continued to stare at Gina with open approval— surprised, perhaps delighted, and certainly no less interested. He tipped up his drink. Then, putting the empty glass down, he spoke deliberately and confidently, a smile starting to form at the corners of this mouth. "I very much doubt if anything you suggest is going to be so kinky it scares me off. What do you have in mind?"

"I'll just tell you, and if you don't want, it won't matter. We can just stay here."

"Okay. As opposed to where?"

"Well, that's my idea. Stuart's house."

For the briefest of seconds, he couldn't keep the shock from showing in his face. But he recovered quickly, back in the game. "Stuart Gorman's house?"

She came forward, brought her knee up onto the couch under her, clearly excited. "Nobody's there, Jedd. And I've got the key. So we sneak in and go up to Stuart and Caryn's old bedroom and do it on their bed. I don't think the place is even a mile from here."

"Well, sure, I know where it is. It's just—"

"No. It's okay. Never mind. You're right. Dumb idea."

"I didn't say that."

"No, really, it's okay. We can just stay here." But in the guise of an explanation, she kept up the pitch. "I've just kind of got this . . . tradition, you might say. Do you know about the Mile High Club?"

Jedd grinned. "Sure. I'm a member, as a matter of fact."

"Why am I not surprised?" She put on another fetching pout. "Not me. Not yet at least. Anyway, my own private little club is kind of like that. When my clients are in jail, if the opportunity's there, I go to their houses."

"You have got to be kidding me." Conley stared at her in pure admiration. "You're a fucking dangerous woman, Roake."

She nodded. "I like to think so."

"How many times so far?"

"How many times what?"

"Have you done this?"

"This would make lucky thirteen. If you go, that is. I've been waiting for number thirteen. It had to be special."

Getting into the idea, Conley asked, "Who were the other guys? I've got to know some of them, don't I?"

"I'm sure you do."

"So?"

She wagged a finger at him. "Uh-uh-uh, discretion. Remember? Nobody knows, nobody tells." She threw in another chip. "And it doesn't have to be on the bed, if you don't want."

"And you've got Stuart's keys?"

"Yep."

"Where are they now?"

"My purse, in the bedroom."

He couldn't seem to take his eyes off her, and finally, he nodded. "Maybe you're going to want to go get them."

As he drove, Jedd put a hand on her thigh and gave it an affectionate squeeze. She put her own hand over his and held it where it was.

"If I guess the right guy," he was saying, "you could just nod. That way you wouldn't actually be telling me."

"No," she said.

"Anybody more than once?"

She squeezed to hold his hand in position. "Two. Twice," she said, riffing effortlessly. "But that's all I'm going to say."

"Any sports figures or movie stars?"

"Oh, that's right. Yes, several of those. Each. And one potentate of a small Arab country." She looked across at him. Inane though the conversation was, she was thankful that they were talking, apparently relaxed. "I'm just a poor country lawyer girl, Jedd. I'm afraid I don't hang out much with celebrities and potentates."

"No celebrities at all? All right, how about this? Potentates aside, let's go for rank. Nationally known politicians?"

A laughed escaped her. "No."

"Any other legislators?"

"*Other* legislators?"

"I mean, besides me."

"Well, technically you're not quite on the list yet. And I don't know any other legislators."

"Okay, then, we can rule them out. See? I'm narrowing it down. How about judges?"

"Jedd."

"Higher up than judges? Federal judges?"

"I can't say. You wouldn't want me to tell anybody else about you, would you?"

"I don't know. As long as you kept it from Lexi and her dad, it might be cool if it got out in the right crowd." He hesitated. "I'm guessing all men, though, right? No women."

She took the opportunity to remove his hand entirely. "I would think that would have been obvious to you by now."

"You'd be surprised," he said. "And don't get mad. You can't really tell. But I'm sorry. No offense meant."

The hand went back to her thigh. She put hers over it again. "None taken. But maybe it would be better if you'd just drive."

"Here we are."

"Pretty dark," Gina said. "Except look up there."

"Where?"

"That top front window. Bethany Robley. The eyewitness. Her light's still on, which means she's up and doing homework. Damn. I forgot all about her. What if she sees us?"

"You're Stuart's lawyer and I'm his old friend. No problem. Hey"—Jedd squeezed her thigh—"we've come this far. You can't chicken out now. Well, you could, but it wouldn't be fair. Besides, no guts, no glory."

She hesitated one last time, let out a heavy breath. "You're right." She squeezed his hand. "Are you ready?"

"I am so ready," Jedd said.

Gina nodded. Gave him a last smile. "Me too. Let's go do this bad thing."

Jedd opened his door, slid out, and closed it quietly behind him.

Gina, her heart sledgehammering within her, her pulse an audible sound in her ears, immediately pushed the button to lock all the car's doors and reached across to Jedd's visor, where he had attached his garage door opener. She pushed on the bar of it, her eyes on the Gormans' garage door off to her right, but nothing happened.

God, she thought, what if he hadn't parked close enough? Sometimes she had to get right to the front of her own automatic entrance at her condo before the gate would swing open. The signal on these things tended not to be too strong. She should have had him park in the driveway. But, stupid her, she hadn't figured out a way to ask without giving herself away.

Jedd was directly behind the car now, coming around.

There was no light in the car, but when Conley had opened his door, Gina had seen the three buttons up by the rearview mirror. Now she reached up, found and pressed the first one, on her far left. "Okay," she said. "Open up." Her eyes were glued to the garage door.

But it didn't move.

The second button. She pushed and held it for a long three-count. "Please please please."

Nothing.

No longer aware of where Jedd had gotten to, she pressed the third button. "Come on," she whispered urgently, "*come on.*"

But nothing happened.

Oh God! Don't let me be wrong. I can't be wrong.

And then, right at her ear, a knock at her window. Jedd standing there, leaning over, looking in, a mild questioning look on his features. Gina whirled back to face him, made an elaborate shrugging motion, as if she didn't understand exactly what was happening. The car's door had locked somehow and she couldn't get them open. She shrugged again. He tried the outside handle.

He was reaching into his pocket for his keys. He'd open the door in seconds.

She turned back toward the front, hitting his garage door opener's bar and all three buttons again in quick succession, and got the same result. Nothing.

And then suddenly, at her window, another sound, this time much louder than the polite knock on the glass. A slam. Conley's flat palm up against her window. She looked out and up and saw his face, understanding now what she must be doing, and in a desperate fury. His palm slammed on the window again.

But still maintaining some kind of control. "Gina! Gina, open up! What are you doing?"

His keys were out now. He was trying to fit them into the lock below the door's handle. Gina reached to her side and covered the pop-up locking button with her hand. As Conley turned the key outside, she pushed the button back down on the door. He tried again, and again she kept the door locked, but she could not keep this up for too much longer.

Jedd wasn't about to fight that battle either. He backed up a step and pushed at his key and Gina heard the distinctive "clunk" as all of the car's locks, except the useless one she was trying to hold down, popped up.

He was opening the passenger side back door, right behind her. "Gina, goddammit!"

The glove compartment!

Reaching down, praying that Jedd wasn't one of the few paranoid souls who lived with his glove box perennially locked, she found the handle and gave it a pull just as from behind her Conley's hands found the back of her shoulders, tried to get purchase around her throat.

She tried to scream, but the sound, to her horror, was already choked off.

Then he was coming over the center island between the seats, enough of him to get his power into what he was doing now. Gasping with the exertion, trying anything to save herself from his brute strength and determination, she reached out and scratched at his face, then threw an elbow that seemed to hit him in the throat.

And for an instant, his grip lessened.

It was her last and only chance. She fumbled blindly in the glove box as Jedd's left fist connected with the side of her head, slamming it against the window. She had her hand around something plastic and rectangular—another garage door opener—and as the second blow sent pinwheels of light through her field of vision, she managed to press the bar. And hold it.

Until another blow to the side of her head reduced her world to a sharp, searing pain, and then to darkness.

THIRTY-SEVEN

AT JUHLE'S INSTRUCTIONS, THE TWO UNIFORMED officers who'd helped him with the sting had delivered Jedd Conley up here to the tiny interrogation room on the fourth floor of the Hall of Justice. Now the state assemblyman from San Francisco had been in the room, handcuffed to the table, and alone, for most of the past hour and a half. Dealing with the ambulance and other issues, Juhle had remained at the crime scene out on Greenwich Street for the better part of the first hour, then had come back here to his desk in the homicide detail and caught up with most of another hour's worth of paperwork.

Checking the clock on the wall, seeing it was now 12:45 a.m., Juhle knew that he had delayed long enough. He had to start his interrogation of Jedd Conley before too long. But he had some serious problems.

Critically, the provenance of the all-important garage door opener was unproveable. Trying to get Stuart off on his murder charge, Gina could have bought the damn thing at Home Depot and easily, with her access to Stuart's house, have set it to the frequency that would open the garage door. She could have carried it with her over there tonight in her purse.

Now, with Conley's brutal assault on Gina, Juhle had grounds for much more than a simple and general discussion with the assemblyman. But time was running out, and with all of Conley's powerful connections, Juhle felt great trepidation that if he let him walk out of here tonight without confessing to Caryn Dryden's murder, and maybe even Kelley Rusnak's, he'd never get his hands on him again.

He couldn't let that happen.

At last, he went to the control room to make sure that both the audio and video feeds were running, then knocked on the door and opened it up, talking as he entered. "Sorry to have kept you," he said breezily. "Lots of stuff to take care of back at the scene. I got a little hung up. How you doin'?"

"How am I doing? What is that, some kind of a joke?" His suspect, his face scratched from fingernails and now swollen at his jawline and around his eyes, held up the handcuffs. "I'm exhausted. I'm hurt. I'm ready to go home. It's intolerable that I should be kept in here like this for all this time. I won't have it."

"Well," Juhle said. "I'm afraid some of that's out of my control. At least I can take off your handcuffs. The patrolmen tell me that you got picked up in the act of assaulting a woman. I find that hard to believe. Did the officers Mirandize you on the way down here?"

"What for? This whole thing is ridiculous. Look at my face. She was trying to kill me. It was self-defense."

Juhle remained calm. "I figured it must be something like that. But in the meanwhile, you're a lawyer, aren't you? You know the drill. I've got to tell you you're under arrest and read you your rights. You have the right to remain silent. Anything you do say can and will be used against you in a court of law. Do you understand this right?"

"Of course. You don't have to—"

But Juhle held up a hand, stopping Conley's objection. "You have the right to an attorney. If you can't afford an attorney, the court will appoint one for you. Do you understand this right?"

"Jesus. Yes."

Juhle continued. The end of this litany could end with the words, "Having these rights in mind, do you wish to talk to me now?" But the courts had ruled that *Miranda* would be deemed served without them, so Juhle skipped them, and simply started in. "There's a laundry list of formal questions we've got to fill out, and the sooner we're done, the sooner it's over, okay? Okay. For the record, your name?"

"Jedd Conley." And with those simple two words, the assemblyman waived his right to demand an attorney for this interrogation. Juhle walked him through a few perfunctory questions—his address, age, occupation—just to get him to keep talking. Then Juhle said, "So tell me what was happening out there tonight."

"All right. It started when Gina—the woman, Gina Roake . . ."

"Yeah, I know who she is."

"Well, she called me around nine and asked me to come over to her house."

"And why would she do that?"

"You know this, Inspector. I know who you are. She's defending Stuart Gorman. Maybe you don't know he's an old friend of mine. I don't practice law actively anymore, so when Stuart got in trouble and came to me, I told him he ought to get together with Gina. Big mistake."

"Why's that?"

"Because she just wasn't any good. If anything, she just got him dug in deeper. Now her hearing's going in the toilet, and she wanted to ask my advice about what she should do."

"At her house?"

"The truth? I would have preferred her office." He shrugged. "My position, I can't afford even the appearance of impropriety. This thing tonight's going to be a bitch to spin. I don't know what I'm going to do. But beyond that, my wife's got serious issues with infidelity. Frankly, so do I. Plus, so you know—and I'm laying it all out for you here as honest as I can—Gina and I had a spent a few nights together before I was married. I didn't know she was still carrying a torch." He shrugged, a victim of Gina's feminine wiles. "But I knew she needed help with Stuart's defense, and he's my bud, and that's where she was, at home. So I went."

"But when you got picked up, you weren't at her home?"

He shrugged. "Because right after I walked in the door, I knew I had to get out of there."

"Why was that?"

"Why do you think? She'd poured us both a couple of stiff shots of scotch. She had on a pretty provocative top. It didn't look to me like her plan was to parse the law. She said she had the key to Stuart's, and said maybe we ought to go by there, give the house another look. Maybe we'd find something you guys—the police—had missed."

"And how'd you react to that?"

"It seemed weird to me. But she was trying to get all over me by then, and I thought it would be a good idea to get out of the house. I didn't know what was going on, but I didn't want to offend her. Okay? So we drove over to his place and I don't know if her drink had hit her or what, or if maybe she'd had more alcohol before I got to her place, but she was getting pretty worked up before I even pulled over. She still loved me from before, that kind of thing. I never should have stopped seeing her. She was letting herself get pretty hysterical."

"And then what?"

A deep sigh. "She tried to come over and kiss me, but I wasn't going there."

"What did you do?"

"I told her it wasn't going to work. If she wanted, we could see if we could find anything that might have been missed at Stuart's. Otherwise, I was going to drop her back at her place and go home. I just got out of the car, hoping she'd calm down. But she didn't."

Juhle, all in all impressed with the story Conley had concocted in the lengthy time he'd been stewing in the interrogation room, was moderately curious to find out how Conley was going to explain the fact that he'd been coming out of the back passenger door when the officers had apprehended him—maybe the love-crazed Gina Roake pretended that she couldn't get her seat belt off, intending to ravage him sexually as he reached across her to unfasten the lock, but Jedd guessed what she was planning, so he came in the back door to undo the seat belt from there. And that's when she'd finally attacked him for rejecting her. Over the seat.

Juhle didn't think so.

And besides, he'd heard enough. "But as the officers pulled up, they distinctly saw you pounding on the door, trying to get into the car."

Conley licked his lips. "Well, yes," he said. She had accidentally locked him out, and he'd become frustrated with the situation, but the cops were wrong if they thought they'd seen him attack her, and he had no idea where the garage door opener had come from. Roake must have brought it—got it from Stuart, perhaps.

"Well, no, sir," Juhle said. "I'm afraid that won't work either. In fact, the officers didn't just happen by. They were watching the house. And so was I."

"The house is a murder scene. I assumed it must have been under some kind of surveillance."

"Actually, no, though. That wasn't it. In fact, Gina Roake had her investigator call me up earlier in the night. He asked me to come on down to Stuart Gorman's place and wait for you and Gina to drive up in your car and stand by." Juhle's statement seemed to shake something loose in Conley, who hesitated slightly, his mouth open to refute a charge that Juhle hadn't quite made. "The idea was that she could open Gorman's garage door from your car."

Another small but obvious hit. Quick as a bird, Conley looked away, blinked, looked back. "Why would she want to do . . . ? How was she going to do that?"

"She thought you'd programmed your car so you could get in and out of the Gormans' garage without leaving your car on the street. And also, of course, so you wouldn't be seen coming and going. Or else so that people, at a glance, would assume it was Stuart, as Bethany Robley did."

"Who's she?"

"The neighbor across the street. She saw your car open the garage on the night Caryn Dryden was killed."

"Well, no. That wasn't me. It couldn't have been me. I wasn't anywhere near the house that night. I was at an event for Greenpeace, I remember. She must have planted that garage door opener."

"You remember that specific night, do you? Among all those events you go to?"

"I happen to remember that one, yes. I mean, after hearing about Caryn, the night stuck in my memory."

"So you were never at Caryn's house on that Sunday?"

"No. Of course not."

"But you know, as it turns out," Juhle said almost apologetically, "and you might not have noticed with all the excitement, but Gina did open their garage tonight from inside your car. That was our signal to come running. And she had a tape recorder in her purse, so we know whose idea it was to go to the house." The inspector's blood was starting to run high, but it would not do to show anything. Helpful, courteous to a fault, he went on. "You're certain you weren't there on that Sunday?"

"I told you that. No, of course not."

"But you'd been there recently, at least?"

"Not even that. Lexi and I didn't see them socially. I haven't been to their house in several years."

Sadly, Juhle shook his head. "I'm afraid that's not going to do, sir. Even if it isn't your fingerprint on the one large shard of broken wineglass we found—and I think it is—some of your fingerprints are going to be somewhere in the house, don't you think? Probably in the bedroom. The problem was, we didn't have your fingerprints in the criminal database the last time we looked. And now, of course, that won't be a problem. Same thing with the blood we found in the garage. With your DNA sample, we're going to get a match, aren't we? God," Juhle said, "this is thirsty-making work. Can I get you a Coke or a water or something? I'll be right back."

Juhle walked out the door and crossed the homicide room to get a couple of paper cups full of water. On the way back, he looked in to check the video screen again. The camera was camouflaged into the wall and Conley, though he probably suspected that he was being filmed and/or recorded, couldn't know for sure, and that uncertainty would help to keep him off-balance. His head was whipping from side to side, up to down, as though searching the room for a place to hide or escape. Juhle watched until that stopped and Conley rested his head down upon his open palm.

Coming back into the interrogation room, Juhle pushed the water across at his suspect. "I don't know if you realize it, sir, but at the hearing, Gina Roake made a damn good case for the fact that Caryn might not have been killed at all. Somebody being there at her house on Sunday doesn't necessarily mean that they killed her. It might very well have been an accident. I can understand why you wouldn't want it to come out that you were there. Maybe you really weren't having an affair. Maybe it was just a harmless business meeting, but you were afraid of how it would look. This is really important now. I can't imagine that you would have killed her, but you have to tell me what happened."

The lifeline thrown, Conley stared at it for a long moment, then made a reach for it—the only move he had left. "All right. But it was early in the day. She was a wreck about her invention. You know about that, don't you? The Dryden Socket. She wanted my advice about what she should do."

Same as with Gina, Juhle noticed—a woman needed his advice. Maybe Conley's creativity was drying up under the stress. "So in fact you did go by on that Sunday?"

He nodded. "I think it was sometime around noon. She was very much alive when I was with her, of course." Changing the tone, working the story to try to fit the new facts, he went on, "I couldn't very well admit I'd been over there that day. You understand that. I mean, the day she was killed. But it was all business."

"You weren't anywhere near the hot tub with her?"

"No. We never left the kitchen and living room. Look, Inspector, I know what you're thinking. I even know what it looks like. But we weren't having a physical relationship. The plain fact is that Stuart was jealous of me, and I had to try to keep him from ever seeing us together. She had a key to the back door of my office. I only came by her place when he wasn't home. But I had a great deal of business and even some personal issues with Caryn—okay, I'll admit that—but nothing more. Nothing inappropriate."

Juhle slowly took his paper cup of water and lifted it to his lips. Putting it down, he sighed, hoping to convey his reluctance to vocalize what had to come next. "Mr. Conley," he said, "that shard of wineglass with the fingerprint on it that I mentioned? It was under the hot tub. And your car pulled into the garage at eleven thirty that night."

Juhle knew that Bethany Robley had identified the car as Stuart's during the hearing. But he'd also been at the untaped portion of her interview with Gerry Abrams when the assistant DA had reminded her that Stuart's license plate said GHOTI, and if it had been Stuart driving his car, that's what she must have seen.

Conley sat with Juhle's damning words for a long time. Juhle could almost see him conjuring with the various escape possibilities as each new set of facts tightened the noose. Now Conley nodded, settled on his next course. "Okay. All right. We . . . we were . . . shit. *Intimate.* All right. It wasn't anything I planned. It just happened."

Juhle said nothing.

"I don't know what happened to her that day," Conley went on. "It must have been some kind of accident after I left. She fell against something. I know she'd been drinking, she'd taken some pills. That combination, with the hot tub, it can be dangerous by itself. But I swear to God, she was alive when I left."

"She stayed in the hot tub?"

"She must have. Yes."

Juhle had his hands linked on the table in front of him. The clock on the wall told him they'd been at this for over an hour. On the one hand, it seemed to him as though it had been five minutes, but on the other, half a night. And now, he knew, it was coming to an end. "Mr. Conley. Sir," he said, "the neighbor across the street saw you leave the house at twelve forty-five. Caryn was already dead at twelve forty-five. Which means if you do the math, and I have, that you either killed her or were someplace else in the house and she died. Maybe you fell asleep, came downstairs to find her dead, and panicked?"

Conley's stare was blank, his bank of ready lies about played out. Juhle decided he had to hit him with one last good question from another direction, put him down for good with a hint he'd gotten from Wyatt Hunt earlier while they'd been waiting for Conley's car to pull up to Stuart's house. "If we look, sir, and we're going to, we're going to find that you've got a standing order prescription for amytriptilene, aren't we?"

A long, faraway look, a thousand-yard stare, in the dead silent room.

Jedd Conley was done.

Juhle watched the second hand on the wall clock move from two to five. Then to six. Seven. When Conley finally spoke, it began in a whisper. "I had these incredible migraines for a year," he said. "The doctor said it was probably stress." A bitter little chortle escaped. "Yeah, doc, what was your first clue? You try being married to Lexi, to the whole fucking Horace Tremont family. You'll find out about stress soon enough. Christ." Conley hung his head. "You know what's funny?"

"What's that?"

"You know why I recommended Roake to Stuart? Why I hand-picked her?"

"Why's that?"

"Because she never beat me in court. Never, not once. I think we did like fifteen trials against each other, and I killed her every time. Can you believe that?"

"First time for everything."

Jedd squeezed his temples, rubbed his fingertips over the expanse of his forehead. Finally, he looked across at Juhle. "I don't know what got into her."

"Who?"

"Caryn. All of a sudden, she wanted us to get married. But that had never been in the plan—not for me, not for her. We had a deal. Both of us with our unhappy marriages. But hell, that was the price I'd bought in for. I knew what it would take, this career. It would take Lexi and her goddamn father and his goddamn money. But that would get me what I needed, what I had to have. And Caryn knew that too. At least she always had before. That was our deal."

"But she changed her mind?"

"Friday she told me she had to see me. She was divorcing Stuart. We needed to talk."

"So you set up the date, Sunday?"

"It started out okay. But she'd had half the bottle by the time I got there, and then the more she talked, the more wound up she got. She knew I loved her more than I loved Lexi. She couldn't live any-more the way she'd been doing." He looked pleadingly across at Juhle. "She was going to tell Lexi. She told me that up front. Plus, I saw it in her eyes. She was going to do it. Then I'd be free and we could be together."

"So you hit her?"

"I told her no. She flew into a rage, came at me with the bottle. It was self-defense, I swear. She fell and hit her head, then she got in the hot tub. I left. I never thought she'd drown. That was an accident. Really. I didn't hurt her at all."

Juhle didn't move, let him go on.

"I just didn't want to be with her, not that way." Conley shook his head miserably, looking in vain for some sign of understanding or forgiveness from across the table. "Goddammit," he said. "Not that way."

Gina opened her eyes to poor focus in an unfamiliar room. High-ceilinged, brightly lit above, though here where she lay the light somehow felt muted. She closed her eyes again; it was better with them closed. Acoustic guitar music was playing somewhere, barely in the range of her hearing. Gradually she became aware that something felt funny about her face and her scalp, but for a long moment she couldn't seem to place what it might be. When it came back to her, all in a rush, she moved her hands up to the bandages, then in a small panic, tried to sit up far too quickly.

Involuntarily she moaned, sinking back into the bed.

Footsteps approaching, and then she dared open her eyes again. "Wyatt?" Her voice was cracked and dry. Her mouth tasted like blood.

"She moves."

"No, she doesn't." In fact, she lay flat and immobile. "Where am I?" Then suddenly, she jerked up again. "Oh my God, the hearing! Oh!" Hands back to her head, she gently lowered herself down onto the pillow.

Wyatt sat down on the side of the bed. "The hearing's been taken care of. It's over."

"What do you mean?"

"I mean Jedd Conley confessed."

"Jedd confessed? Then the garage door opened?"

"You don't remember?"

"I never saw it. I remember pushing the button, then lights out. He really confessed?"

"Enough. He said so many stupid things last night, they'll probably get him on Kelley too. Devin sweated him and he broke."

"There you go. I knew the guy was good for something."

"Hey. Be nice."

"I thought I was being nice, giving him all those extra chances to finally get it right." Closing her eyes again, she took a few conscious breaths against the pain. "So how bad am I?"

"Not too, all things considered. You'll probably live." Then, more seriously. "You really don't remember?"

"The whole night's kind of in and out." A pause. "So how bad am I?"

"The diagnosis? Best guess is you've got a concussion. Plus a few really attractive stitches by your left eye. You'll be glad to know that the thread color they used coordinates nicely with the black eyes."

"Color coordination. The secret to adult happiness."

"Well, you've got it. Oh, and you're supposed to take it easy the next few days."

"That won't be too hard." Her eyes scanned the room. "So where am I?"

"My place. You didn't want to stay in the hospital."

"That's because I hate hospitals."

"That became kind of clear."

"Was I difficult?"

"Only a little. But they really wanted to make sure there'd be somebody to keep an eye on you in case you started dying or something. So I volunteered."

"It's starting to come back." She labored through a few more breaths. "What about Stuart? Somebody's got to tell him."

"Already done. Devin was going to be on it."

"Is he out of jail?"

"By now, he should be."

"Could you check, please? That's got to happen." She started to raise herself from the bed. "If Abrams tries to keep ahold of him . . ."

Wyatt put a hand on her shoulder, gently pushing her back down. "Easy, easy. I'll find out. If he's not out by lunchtime, I'll put Diz on it. It'll happen. Promise."

With a last token show of reluctance, she settled into the pillow again. "Okay. God, my head hurts."

"I'm not surprised. You took a few pretty good hits." He took a beat. "Gina?"

"Wyatt?"

"How did you get so sure? It couldn't just have been their cars being the same."

"No. That really wasn't much of it, actually. It just turned the key. Then, once I got past my ego, I started to put the pieces together."

"What did your ego have to do with it?"

The corners of Gina's mouth went up a fraction of an inch, but she wasn't smiling. "Everything, Wyatt. Everything." After a pause, she continued. "This isn't easy to talk about."

"Well, then, let it go. It's all right."

"No. It's not. I can't just let it go. It's smack in the middle of how I got it." She drew a long, slow breath. "Hard as it was to deal with, I had to accept the fact that in the real world Jedd would never have called me in to handle a high-profile murder. He knows every great lawyer in town, and every one of 'em would be happy to do him a favor. And I think I always knew that even when we were together, he never really respected me as a lawyer."

"I didn't realize you two had been together at all."

"Never seriously, and a long time ago, but that's a different story probably not worth telling. The point is, once I could accept that Jedd didn't pick me to win the case, the ugly truth finally dawned on me—that he'd picked me to lose it. The bastard. Anyway, once I realized *that*, a few other things came back as significant. I remembered your list of Jedd's appointments, for example, one of them at the Haight Street Rape Crisis Center." At Hunt's vacant look, she prodded him. "Sam Duncan's center?"

"Wes's Sam?"

"Right. So I called her." And found out, she told Wyatt, that Conley's talk at the Rape Crisis Center had been about the date-rape drug, Rohypnol. Conley told the story during his visit there that although this drug was of course illegal, to prove how easily laws against it could be circumvented, he had some male members of his Sacramento staff pose as college students at one of the local campuses and return to his office the very next day with several doses. He'd then, of course, turned over his information and the drugs to the police. "Except," Gina concluded, "it looks like he kept some of it. But Jedd even being around Rohypnol was pretty damn compelling to me. I just needed a connection to Kelley to be sure."

"So what'd you do?"

"I called Stuart at the jail."

"And what did he know?"

"He knew that Jedd had come to see him in jail last week and that they'd talked at length about Kelley Rusnak." As it turned out, she told Wyatt, Stuart knew that Jedd himself owned a good chunk of PII stock—Caryn had talked him into buying it. So he wasn't merely helping Caryn in her negotiations with the company out of altruism. Beyond that, evidently Jedd had convinced his father-in-law and some of his megarich friends that the stock was a can't-miss investment, and many of them had invested heavily themselves. Gina didn't yet have a specific motive for Jedd to have killed Kelley— maybe as Caryn's lab partner, she'd known about her and Jedd's affair, maybe it was to nip her whistle-blowing in the bud—but the previously unknown PII connection was all the symmetry Gina had needed. "It was Jedd, no doubt in my mind. So it followed that he had to have a way to open the garage."

"And what were you going to do if the garage didn't open?"

She shrugged. "I knew you and Juhle and some other cops would be there, Wyatt. I underestimated the danger, okay, but only because I didn't plan on Jedd getting so physical so fast. But everything else was conjecture, something I knew but couldn't prove. Without a way to open that garage door, Jedd walks. So what I did was the only thing I could have done. I had to take the risk."

"I hate it when it gets to that."

"Me too."

"So," Wyatt asked, "you think you could eat something?"

"Maybe later. For now, maybe I'll just close my eyes a little longer. Would that be okay?"

"It would be fine."

Mostly now, he went by the name of Walden.

Stuart Gorman's release from jail had been big news right through the weekend, and Walden wanted to give the story time to cool down before he took his action. It wouldn't be wise to have hordes of journalists or even simply the curious lounging around in the street in front of Stuart's house, keeping tabs on the celebrity. But Walden didn't want it to be too long afterward, either, so that people might have already forgotten Stuart, who he was exactly, what he stood for.

There would be one perfect window of opportunity and now, two weeks to the day after the Friday that Stuart returned to his home, Walden considered the timing to be ideal. As far as targets went, Stuart had gone from adequate, back when he was merely a moderately popular outdoor writer, to superb—a high-visibility media presence. If you were ever really going to get your message out there, to make a long-term difference, you needed a vehicle like Stuart Gorman. Now, although probably for not too much longer, Stuart was as close to a household name as he was ever going to get.

Stuart, Walden had discovered in the past week, was pretty much a creature of habit. Every morning he seemed to wake up at or near the same time; every morning he came outside and picked up his morning newspaper off his steps. Last night, the lights had gone off when they usually did, around ten thirty. So he was probably on his regular schedule. If he was slightly off, Walden could always just come by tomorrow, or the day after that. It was a limited window of opportunity, true, but a day or so one way or the other wouldn't make any difference.

Now, just short of seven o'clock in the morning, Walden sat at the curb, peering through the fog at the front door of Stuart Gorman's house. His shotgun lay halfway across the passenger seat, its muzzle down on the floor of the stolen Honda Accord. Walden had already rolled the passenger window down. There was very little traffic on the street, and no pedestrians.

Suddenly, the light came on over the front door, and Walden turned the ignition key, then grabbed for the shotgun. At the house, the door opened and Stuart, with a coffee mug in his hand, started down the steps. One. Two. Three.

The newspaper was on the sixth step down. Walden had had a little trouble seeing it, making sure it was already there when he'd driven up. He'd even brought another paper to throw onto the steps, just in case. But no, it had been there.

Four. Five.

Walden raised the barrel of the gun.

Six.

He pulled the trigger.

THIRTY-EIGHT

———

CityTalk

By Jeffrey Elliott

The police shootout and killing yesterday at the Sausalito home of San Rafael High School biology instructor Enos Crittenden added yet another bizarre chapter to the ongoing story that began last September with the hot tub drowning of Dr. Caryn Dryden. The drama connected to this series of events continued through the assassination attempt on Dr. Dryden's husband, the outdoor writer Stuart Gorman, later in the fall by a shadowy figure only tentatively identified at the time variously as "Walden" or as an e-mail presence who signed off with the words "Thou Shalt Not Kill."

Also connected to this extraordinary chain of events has been the decertification by the FDA of the Dryden (Hip Replacement) Socket, several dozen subsequent lawsuits against its manufacturer, Polymer Innovations, Inc. (PII), the bankruptcy filing of PII and the suicide in February of that company's chief executive officer, William Blair. With the trial of former California Assemblyman Jedd Conley for the murders of Dr. Dryden and Kelley Rusnak, her lab assistant at PII, scheduled to begin next week, the story's eventual ramifications may endure for years to come.

Yesterday's developments began about a week ago when one of Crittenden's students hacked into a private e-mail site linked to his regular teacher's website. Discovering threatening letters written to several prominent public figures, as well as links to other websites dedicated to environmental terrorism, the student informed first his parents, and then the police. When authorities appeared at San Rafael High to question Crittenden, he fled, leading police on a chase back to his home, where he opened fire on them. He held the SWAT team at bay for nearly an hour before a sniper bullet to his chest ended the standoff.

Crittenden, 34, had a lengthy history of activism on animal rights and other "green" issues, although no criminal record. In his basement, police discovered a large cache of weapons and ammunition as well as several boxes of literature on various environmental issues. Much more threateningly, they discovered over 500 pounds of the fertilizer ammonium nitrate and several gallons of the fuel oil nitromethane, ingredients that had been used in the bombing of the Alfred P. Murrah Federal Building in Oklahoma City in 1995. According to Homeland Security spokesman Marshall Brice, plans on Crittenden's website indicated that he was planning to bomb a "large target" in San Francisco to protest the sale of meat and meat products. (Sources close to the investigation, speaking under condition of anonymity, have told this reporter that the intended target was the Ferry Building.)

It also appears certain from books, newspaper clippings, e-mails, and other material discovered in Crittenden's basement, that it was he, identifying himself as Walden, who had shotgunned and critically wounded Stuart Gorman in the days following the outdoor writer's release from jail after charges that he had drowned his wife had been dropped in favor of Assemblyman Conley.

In a chilling bit of irony, Mr. Gorman, who professes himself completely recovered from the assassination attempt (although he still walks with a pronounced limp), will be signing copies of new paperback editions of his three books, *Reflections on a Lake*, *The Mysterious Stream*, and *Healed by Water*, at 7:00 this Friday night at Book Passage in the Ferry Building.

Gina waited back among the shelves until the other customers had gone. There had been close to a hundred of them. Stuart remained seated alone at the small writing table, pulling copies of his books over from the pile on his left and signing them one by one, methodically, moving them to a growing pile on the right as he finished. Finally, she came up to him. "Hey."

He broke a smile. "Hey, yourself. I'd get up and give you a hug, except I'm still having a little trouble with the hip. How are you, Gina?"

"I'm good, Stuart. How about you?"

"Getting by. It's been a bit of a year, in case you haven't noticed."

"Yeah. I read about the wedding, too. It's kind of what made me decide to come down and say hi. That and Jeff's article reminding me."

"I'm glad you did." He shrugged. "It's weird. I can't seem to avoid making the news anymore. Beware of what you wish for."

"I never thought you wanted fame."

"No. I never wanted money. Fame was all right. Fame opens doors. It's okay."

"And how's Debra?"

"She's good." He shrugged, perhaps with some embarrassment. "We're good. I never thought I'd marry my wife's sister, but there you go. I never thought I'd get tried for murder, either."

"You never did," Gina said.

He shrugged. "Close enough. Anyway, the whole Debra thing. She's been good with Kymberly. I never thought I'd say that, either. I'm starting to think there might be hope for her. Maybe even me getting shot wasn't all a bad thing. It made her realize she could lose me too, and she finally didn't want that. She's even back at school."

"That's good. I'm glad to hear that."

"It is good," he said. For a moment, a silence built. "And you'll be glad to hear I've finished the new book."

"So you said."

"You were here all along? Tonight, I mean?"

"Hiding out in the back. I didn't want to get in the way of your talk. It's a little bit of a different title for you, isn't it? *The Imposter Syndrome.*"

"Yeah. Breaking out of fishing psychology and into true self-help. It's a bit of a leap, but my publisher thinks it's a winner. It's the idea that came to me in the courtroom that day, you know. You remember?"

"I remember you getting it. Not what it was, though."

"Well, you'll have to read the book, but it's all about figuring out why I felt like I had to keep protecting Kym, instead of confronting her and trying to help her deal with her problems. It was because I couldn't really do anything else except write, and writing's one of those things—sometimes you lose the sense that it has any real intrinsic value. So if I can't do anything else, and what I can do doesn't have any real quantitative worth, what became important was the illusion that I was at least a good father. Raising a successful child is something you can point at that you've done."

"But you are a successful writer, and it sounds like you're on the way to having raised a successful child."

"Well, let's hope," he said. "Maybe. Anyway, the book takes off from there and goes off on my usual tangents. I got something out of writing it, and that's what's important. That and keeping things together with the family." Suddenly remembering, he squinted up at her. "And how's your writing going? Still at it?"

"Actually," Gina couldn't keep some pride out of her voice, "I just finished mine, too. It's probably no good, but I least I got to the end."

"That's the hardest part. Now you just go back and fix everything you don't like."

Gina laughed. "That's all, huh?"

"Pretty much. But I'll bet you won't need to do too much. Not if you did trial scenes like you did at my hearing."

"Well . . . that's nice of you to say, but we'll see. Anyway, I just had to come down and make sure you were okay and say hi. I'm so happy for you. You deserve a little peace."

"And the only reason I've got any is because of you. Don't think I don't realize that."

Gina looked down at her former client. She reached out and touched his shoulder. "Take care of yourself, Stuart. Stay out of trouble."

"Don't worry," he said. "That's my new motto."

Gina had started on the vigorous circle hike around the lake at a little after noon, and now, coming into sight of her camp, the sun was just about to go down behind the mountains. Her critic was still sitting where she'd left him three hours ago, the stack of pages next to him telling her practiced eye that he was probably getting pretty close to the end.

No way was she going to interrupt him now, so she cut off the trail and walked down to the lake. She stood still for several minutes on the shoreline, drinking in the beauty around her, never tiring of its ability to refresh and nourish her. Then, sitting on a boulder, she undid her shoelaces and pulled off her hiking boots and socks. Hot and sweaty, she unbuttoned her shirt and dropped it and her shorts to the ground, then got rid of her underwear.

The first few steps into the cold water were shocking, as they always were, but she walked through the shallows, grinning like an idiot, until it was deep enough to let her dive. She stayed underwater, eyes open, for as long as she could, pushing the water behind her with strong and broad strokes, skimming over the seaweed, hoping to catch sight of a trout.

When she came back up, she treaded water for a second, and gloried in another eyeful of wilderness. But with the water temperature under fifty degrees, she couldn't stay in it too long, so she went under again and pulled for shore. When she got to where she knew she could stand, she stopped and surfaced.

He was standing on the shore, holding her pages.

"It's great," he said.

"You really think so?" She was coming toward him. "I want the real truth."

"I just gave you the real truth. It's fantastic. I couldn't put it down. It's really good, Gina. I mean it."

She was out of the water now, standing right in front of him. "You're not just saying it because you're hoping I'm going to let you kiss me, are you?"

"Would that work?"

"No. I'd be able to tell you were lying."

"But I'm not lying."

"All right, then, Wyatt Hunt," she said. "Then you can kiss me."

ACKNOWLEDGMENTS

———

Writing and publishing a book is not so solitary an endeavor. It takes a whole lot of friends, advisors, helpers, editorial and marketing folks. I'm very fortunate that the whole gang working and interacting in various ways on my books takes such a proprietary and committed role in the finished product.

This time out, I had some early, critical story help I'd like to specially acknowledge from Bob Zaro, who gave me the initial idea that hit the starter button. Also, right at the beginning, Michael W. Chapman, MD, gave me some great medical insights as well as an insider's perspective on some of California's alpine lakes. For other medical and business issues that turn up in the book, I'd like to thank John Chuck, Oliver Stanton and his partner Peter Kolbeck; Mark Detzer, PhD (and his bride, Kathryn Lescroart Detzer) and of course my continuing guru for medical overview and martini mixing, Peter S. Dietrich, MD, MPH. Even with all this help, errors sometimes have their way of creeping into the text, and if they do, they are all entirely the fault and responsibility of the author.

Closer to home, my children, Justine and Jack, continue to inform every part of my creative process. Anita Boone, assistant extraordinaire, does everything and more, perfectly every time. Rick Montgomery helps keep the passion going for writing, music, food and most of the other good things in life. Frank and Gina Seidl keep the party going. Don Matheson, perennial best man, livens up many and many a day. My great friend the brilliant writer Max Byrd is a constant source of inspiration, wisdom and advice. Karen Hlavacek once again did her proofreading magic with the galleys. Tom Hedtke and Vicki Lorini make sure I don't forget that it's okay, even good, to be a working writer in a competitive world.

Tom Steinstra, fishing buddy, television star and, not so incidentally, outdoor author and writer for the *San Francisco Chronicle* ("Men love him, fish fear him") was a huge inspiration for this particular book. Obviously, Stuart Gorman and Tom are nowhere near the same person, but I can honestly say that if I didn't know Tom, there would have been no Stuart. So thanks, Tom—your very existence helped me get it all off the ground.

As always, Al Giannini is my main collaborator. I'm not a lawyer, and these books wouldn't be technically accurate if it weren't for Al's devotion, insight, brains and just plain hard work. Additionally, he's there for those pesky everyday questions without which the book simply couldn't progress. My books wouldn't be the same without Al's input, and I remain intensely grateful for his involvement in them and in my life.

At Dutton, my deepest thanks go to Mitch Hoffman—a superb editor and great guy. It's a tricky business working with someone whose job is to make you better, and Mitch pulls it off with a cheerful élan and intelligence that is a joy to work with. The rest of the Dutton/Signet team is also a pretty spectacular group of people— Brian Tart, Lisa Johnson, Kara Welsh, Rick Pascocello, Susan Schwartz, Erika Kahn, Robert Kempe, and Rich Hasselberger.

As has been my habit for the last few books, I've named some characters in this one to support the generous contributions of individuals to various charities. In this regard, thanks to Kelley Gray Rusnak (Court Appointed Special Advocates, or CASA); to Trish Schooley, for the character Trevor Stratton (California State University at Fullerton); and to Peggy Furth (Imagine 2006 Charity Wine Auction) for the character Frederick Furth.

Finally, my agent and friend, Barney Karpfinger, is just the best in every way. I wouldn't have a career, or half as much fun, without him.

ABOUT THE AUTHOR

John Lescroart is the author of seventeen previous novels, including *The Hunt Club*, *The Motive*, *The Second Chair*, *The First Law*, *The Oath*, *The Hearing*, and *Nothing But the Truth*. He lives with his wife and two children in Northern California.